Tales of the Magatama

Dragon Sword and Wind Child

Tales of the Magatama

Dragon Sword and Wind Child

Noriko Ogiwara

Illustrations by Miho Satake

Translated by Cathy Hirano

HAIKASORU

SAN FRANCISCO

SORAIRO MAGATAMA
Copyright © 1988, 1996, 2005 by Noriko OGIWARA
Original edition published in Japan in 1996 under the title "SORAIRO
MAGATAMA" by Tokuma Shoten Publishing Co., Ltd.
Published in arrangement with Tokuma Shoten Publishing Co., Ltd.
through Japan Uni Agency, Inc.

Illustrations copyright © 2005 by Miho Satake
Cover design by Yukiko Whitley

HAIKASORU
Published by
VIZ Media, LLC
295 Bay Street
San Francisco, CA 94133

www.haikasoru.com

Library of Congress Cataloging-in-Publication Data

Ogiwara, Noriko, 1959-
   [Sorairo magatama. English]
   Dragon sword and wind child / Noriko Origawa ; translated by Cathy
Hirano ; [illustrations by Miho Satake].
      p. cm. -- (Tales of Magatama ; [1])
   Summary: Raised in the ancient Japanese village of Hashiba, fifteen-
year-old Saya discovers that she is the reincarnation of the Water Maiden,
princess of the underworld, who must try to reconcile the powers of heaven
and earth.
   ISBN 978-1-4215-3763-4
[1. Princesses--Fiction. 2. Good and evil--Fiction. 3. Fate and fatalism--
Fiction. 4. War--Fiction. 5. Japan--History--To 645--Fiction.] I. Satake,
Miho, ill. II. Hirano, Cathy. III. Title. PZ7.O344Dr 2010
   [Fic]--dc22
            2010037475

The rights of the author of the work in this publication to be so identified
have been asserted in accordance with the Copyright, Designs and Patents
Act 1988. A CIP catalogue record for this book is available from the British
Library.

Printed in the U.S.A.
First paperback printing, November 2010

Dragon Sword and Wind Child

chapter
one

THE WATER
MAIDEN

Like the swift flowing waters
Parted by a rock in midstream,
We shall be reunited.

—The retired emperor Sutoku

The Water Maiden

IN HER DREAM, Saya was always six years old. Long fingers of flame rose up against the darkness, lighting the sky above. Fire blazed spiteful and triumphant above what she had once thought most secure—her home, that safe, warm refuge that she was so sure would always be there. The glowing hearth; the single room in which her family lived permeated with the smells of cooking and familiar people; her own wooden bowl; her mother's soft, plump lap covered in rough-woven cloth—all were consumed by the flames. The child Saya had somehow managed to find her way to the marsh at the edge of the village, but with no one there to lead her by the hand, she could go no farther. Crouched in a clump of dying reeds, she trembled with terror, choking down the hard lump of fear in her throat, unable even to cry.

The oppressive air of the swamp overwhelmed her with its thick, cloying stench of mud and decay. Water from the sodden ground had begun to well up between her toes, and her bottom was soaked. She was miserably uncomfortable, yet she could not move, for on the other side of the swamp, demons prowled in search of her. Peering through the reeds, she could just make out their shapes by the faint bluish light of their torches. There were five of them, widely disparate in size. Although she remained undetected, at any moment one of them might push aside the reeds, calling out, "I've found her!" The

9

thought filled her with such despair that she almost wished they would find her then and there, just to end the agony of the suspense. They seemed to stay forever, peering back and forth, while the blue light from their torches skated across the inky black waters like a lonely water insect.

The scene changed abruptly. Saya was inside a large building. Great, evenly spaced columns of cypress supported the stately roof, and a polished wood-floored corridor led off into the distance. Torches in iron brackets blazed comfortingly, dispelling the darkness. Somehow she had managed to slip through the demons' grasp and escape into a large shrine, yet one eerily devoid of any sign of life. She gazed up at the ceiling, then down at her bare feet. Gathering her courage, she began to move deeper into the sanctuary, gazing fixedly ahead.

The only sounds that accompanied her as she walked past the innumerable columns were the echoes of her own footsteps and the hiss of the torches. The only sign of movement was her own shadow, which leapt ahead as she passed each torch. She came at last to the end of the corridor and saw a room from which shone a brilliant light. A solitary figure clothed in the white robes of a shrine maiden knelt before a wooden altar adorned with offerings of a wand decorated with dazzling white paper streamers and a forest of dark green sakaki branches. Although Saya could not see her face, she knew the maiden must be beautiful. The white skirts of her robes spread out around her, and her slender form seemed to be bathed in light. Her long, glossy black hair gleamed on her head and shoulders, cascading to the floor like a waterfall.

But there was something wrong. Uneasy, Saya hesitated and glanced back the way she had come. Catching sight of her own shadow stretching behind her, she knew what was wrong. The shrine maiden had no shadow.

Saya was caught like a snared rabbit. Fleeing the fox, she had plunged straight into a trap. She opened her mouth to scream, but no sound came forth. Fear washed through her.

Don't turn around! Please! she pleaded silently.

She must not look at her face. If she did, something terrible would happen and she would be powerless to stop it. She must not look. Yet she could neither shut nor avert her eyes.

Please, don't turn around! The demons will eat me!

The maiden, who had remained as immobile as a statue, began to turn slowly toward the desperate Saya. Her hair swayed gently about her face. Saya glimpsed her pale cheeks and then her eyes, as her cool gaze fell upon her.

The demons will eat me!

SAYA WOKE WITH A START, bathed in sweat, and felt fresh air caressing her face. She must have had the covers pulled over her head. It was dark and a few stars could still be seen in the sky framed by the small west window. Her mother, who lay beside her, turned in her sleep and asked drowsily if she was all right. Her father continued to snore peacefully.

"I'm fine," Saya whispered. "I was just dreaming." Relieved that she had not cried out in her sleep, she drew the covers around her and rested her cheek once more on her pillow.

"Same old dream?"

"No," she answered hastily. When she was younger, Saya had often woken with a scream to find herself crying hysterically. Just the other day she had reassured her mother that she had outgrown that nightmare, but she had lied. In fact, the older she grew, the more vivid and detailed the dream became, exercising an increasingly relentless hold over her.

This was Saya's only trouble in an otherwise peaceful life. It was a constant reminder that she was not a native of Hashiba, that the elderly couple she lived with were not her real parents, despite the fact that she did not remember any other home, let alone one beside a marsh, and had long forgotten the faces of her real mother and father. Irritably brushing a stray lock of hair from her face, she bit her lip and fiercely told herself not to cry. It was anger that made her want to cry: anger at herself for continuing to have the same nightmare.

I turned fifteen this year. I've lived most of my life in this village. I can't even remember any other home, she thought impatiently. *Who is that foolish girl still wandering about in that swamp? Well, it isn't me! It certainly isn't me. I escaped all by myself and found another father and mother.*

In fact, she had no memory of her escape. She had learned much later that some villagers had chanced upon her, wandering in the mountains, almost dead from starvation. It was as if a great and merciful hand had wiped away all memory of her suffering while she lay stricken with a high fever. Although she knew that she must have been fleeing from the war in the east, the thought meant very little to her. The indigenous people in the east refused to worship the God of Light and continued to resist the army led by his immortal children, Princess Teruhi and Prince Tsukishiro. But this did not matter much to her either. Three generations ago, the head chieftain of Hashiba had accepted the dominion of the God of Light. A shrine had been built in the forest and in it was placed a burnished copper mirror as an emblem of the god. Since that time, the area had been blessed with peace and plenty, and its people were content.

Surely the demons can't enter a place like this that's protected by the sacred mirror. Why doesn't that girl come here? thought Saya.

The terror that the demons in her dream had evoked was vividly revived and she shivered under her covers, thankful that she was now awake. This was the real Saya: the girl who slept in this bed, in this house, in the land of Hashiba. It was here that she would reach womanhood, marry, and care for her parents. She was already fifteen. It would not be long now.

Deep down, however, Saya knew that as long as the girl in her dream continued to flee from the demons, she would also continue to flee. But what could she do? Would it be better to let the demons destroy her? And what did it mean anyway? She could find no answers to these questions.

THE MORNING MIST rising from the river cleared to reveal blue sky. Sunbeams played upon ripples of water, creating shimmering patterns of silver and gold. The sun's rays warmed the stones in the riverbed, glancing off quartz crystals with sudden and dazzling brilliance. The village women, gathering at the river to wash clothes, exchanged greetings and remarked on the warm weather. Although they still wore their winter clothing of indigo and ocher, the cliff top on the opposite bank was already robed in the fresh green of budding leaves and the vivid red of wild azaleas. Summer was fast approaching and soon it would be the Day of Changing, when winter garments were put away in favor of summer clothes of white linen.

"Morning." Climbing down the bank to the water's edge, Saya found most of her friends already there.

"Morning, Saya. What's the matter? Don't keep your sorrows to yourself."

Saya blinked in surprise. In the dazzling light reflected from the water, the village girls seemed like sprightly young minnows darting after bait with which to fuel their banter.

"What do you mean?" she asked.

"Come on now. You know you can't hide anything from us. You were walking like a dreamer. Out with it! Tell us the name of the man who's troubling you."

Saya was at a loss for words, in itself enough to make all her friends laugh. "You've got it all wrong. It was just a bad dream," she protested.

"A dream? Here, let me exorcise you. *Togano no shika mo yume no mani mani.* Don't think about it anymore. Thinking about bad things can make them happen, you know."

"What did you dream? I'll tell you what it means."

"Oh no you won't!" Saya hastily emptied her basket and began rinsing the clothes in the water. The dream was something she could not share, even with her friends.

"Saya keeps her own counsel," remarked the girl who lived next door. "She's the only one who hasn't told us who she wants as her partner at the Kagai."

"That's right. And we've all vowed to find out."

The Kagai was to be celebrated at the next full moon, and, with the event so close at hand, it was the focus of the village girls' conversation. On the day of the celebration, people in all the villages of

Hashiba would put on brand-new summer garments, and everyone but the children and the elderly would climb Mount Itsuki, the highest peak in the area. A bonfire would be lit in the center of a glade partway up, around which they would dance and sing until morning. The men would take a gift—a comb, a jewel, or a small box—to present to the woman who responded to his song with one of her own. It was a time-honored ritual that everyone looked forward to with eager excitement. But for the young men and women, it had a more important meaning: the exchange of songs at the festival was the first step toward betrothal.

"You don't know who I want for a partner? How slow you are!" Saya exclaimed. "Can't you guess?"

The girls' faces lit up with anticipation as they tossed the names of at least ten possible candidates in her direction.

"Too bad." Saya laughed, restored to her normal self. The lively exchange with her friends had chased away her gloom. Cupping her hands around her mouth, she whispered confidentially, "Prince Tsukishiro."

This remark earned her a flurry of good-natured shoves and blows.

"That's not fair!"

"Saya! You'll pay for that!"

"Besides, he won't even be at the Kagai!"

"Don't be so sure of that," replied Saya, restraining a hand tugging at her hair. "They say that the God of Light witnesses our vows at the Kagai. If so, then why shouldn't his son attend it?"

"Even if he had a thousand bodies, he couldn't possibly attend all the Kagai in Toyoashihara."

"And besides, he's at the battlefront right now, leading his troops."

"Wearing his silver armor," added Saya with a look of rapture. "Oh, how I would love to see him just once for myself. He must be more splendid than the full moon. Isn't it amazing that the Children of the God actually walk the earth?"

"You sound just like the shrine maiden. Are you going to remain chaste for the God of Light and live the rest of your life alone?"

"No ordinary village girl like us would ever be chosen for such an honor anyway."

"You're right," said Saya, laughing. "I'll have to find a husband. After all, I'm an only child."

"That's more like it. Dreams are just dreams."

Yet, although she knew she must face reality, Saya could not take the idea of finding a husband seriously. There were many eligible young men in the village, but not one of them appealed to her in that way. She suddenly felt ashamed of misleading her friends, for none of them suspected her true dilemma. "Well, if I can't find a husband, maybe the shrine maiden will take me on as a servant."

This remark resulted in further teasing. "What's the matter with you this morning? Has someone broken your heart? I knew it!"

Their speculations were interrupted by a voice from downstream, where the older women gathered. One of them called loudly, "Don't just stand there talking all day. Get to work. Look! You're so careless you've let something float away." She pointed at the water. The girls, turning to look, saw a light green belt in the shallows slithering downstream like a luminous water snake.

Saya leapt to her feet. "Oh no! My belt!"

Without a moment's hesitation she gathered her skirt up to her thighs and, ignoring the shocked expressions on the faces of her elders, set off after the belt, striding through the stream, her white legs flashing. Gazing after her determined figure, her friends burst out laughing.

"She'll never be a shrine maiden, that's for sure!"

SAYA WAS MISTAKEN in thinking that she would soon catch up with her belt. To her surprise, it slipped through the water without once catching on a rock or weed, leaving her far behind. A colored belt was one of the few luxuries that the village girls owned, and she was not about to lose hers. Although the water was shallow, never reaching above her knees, the stones in the riverbed were loose and one false step could cause a fall. But Saya was quick and agile and she strode fearlessly, never faltering. Her nimble feet danced through the water, sending up a silver spray as she forged her way down the sparkling stream. Something about her suggested a wild creature, unfettered and free. Her waist-length hair tied at the nape of her neck danced upon her back like a lively tail. She was slim for her age, but her slender arms and legs were strong and tireless. Her small oval face with its expressive eyes drew people to her, yet there was something unsettled and impetuous about her. A keen observer would see that beneath this lay an intelligent circumspection, a wisdom born of her early childhood experience. She consciously strove to be polite and modest before her elders, doing her best to escape attention. In fact, some adults believed her to be a modest and thoughtful young girl. But the village boys still talked about her reputation as a leader of mischief. While both represented part of her character, behind these lay another Saya, an insecure and lonely girl always in search of home—a girl known only to Saya herself.

The river gurgled as it flowed along, winding around a craggy outcrop in the bank, where it turned and fed into a channel thickly lined with reeds. Saya stopped abruptly as she rounded the bend, surprised by the scene before her. Concentrating on her belt, she had come much farther downstream than she had realized, reaching the stepping-stones of the ford. In the middle of the ford a figure was kneeling on one of the stones, busily fishing her belt from the water. He was small, a boy two or three years younger than herself, but he looked so different from the people of her land that she hesitated to call out to him. He wore faded black clothes, almost too short for him, with fur leg guards, leather sandals, and a hat of braided sedge. Around his neck hung a handsome necklace of red stones that belied the condition of his clothes. Saya had never seen anyone like him.

Holding the dripping belt in one hand, he stood up and looked straight at her. His face under a thatch of unkempt hair, which looked like it had never been combed, resembled that of a saucy, stubborn puppy. He stared boldly at Saya where she stood in the middle of the river, her skirt still bunched in her hand, as at a rare and interesting sight. Then, with what Saya thought extreme impudence, he laughed and said, "Is this your belt? If you want it, come and get it." With the belt still in his hand, he sprang across the stepping-stones and clambered up the right-hand bank. Furious, Saya strode through the water, stepped onto the bank, and ran after him.

"Give it back! What do you think you're doing?" Saya reached out to grab him by the shoulder, but the boy in black was faster, whirling out of reach to face her. He was not in the least disturbed by her anger and even seemed to think it was funny. Having dealt with many unruly boys in the past, she recognized in him a formidable opponent.

At that moment, however, three men, obviously the boy's companions, came into view. Saya faltered and drew back. They might be thieves or kidnappers. She fought back a scream as various frightening possibilities raced through her mind. There was something about them that was completely alien to the world she knew. But the men made no move to accost her. The three of them, wearing the same black clothes and fur leg guards as the boy, merely stood silently staring at her. To her frightened eyes there appeared to be not three but five or ten of them. Their large stature and cool composure certainly suggested the assurance of greater numbers. She could have fled back to her friends but, to her own surprise, she turned once more to the boy and held out her hand. "Give it back, please," she said. "That belt is mine."

The boy gazed coolly into her face for a moment. Then a high-pitched fragile voice came from behind him. "Give it back, Torihiko."

Startled, Saya looked up. It was not one of his three companions feigning a woman's voice. Rather, among them stood a small, white-haired old woman leaning on a staff. She was so tiny that Saya had not seen her at first. The boy called Torihiko smiled with unexpected meekness and offered the belt to Saya.

What an odd group of people, she thought.

She could not help but stare at them as she took her belt. Although all three men seemed huge, on closer inspection only the one standing in the middle was truly gigantic. His companions were not that much bigger than the village men. It was their air of power that made them stand out. They wore their hair bound in loops by their ears, in accordance with common custom. But their beards were thick, their skin, deeply tanned, and their eyes shone with an unearthly light. One wore a black leather patch over one eye, and this, coupled with the bright gleam in the other, made him appear particularly forbidding. The second was younger and slimmer, but his eyes, too, gleamed dangerously. The man in the middle surpassed ordinary men in girth and height and had arms as thick as young tree trunks, but, of the three, he looked the kindest.

The old woman, in contrast, was about the height of a five-year-old, giving her the appearance of a wizened child. Her staff was at least twice her height, and her head and eyes seemed too large for her spare frame. A halo of white hair like thistledown made her head appear even bigger than it was. In this company, the boy seemed almost normal. But why were they just standing there staring at her, as if they had been waiting for her all this time?

The old woman suddenly blinked, froglike, and spoke. "Excuse me, but is it much farther to Chief Azusahiko's house?"

"No, it's just over there," Saya answered quickly. "Follow the river and bear right when you come to the pine forest. You can't miss it."

"Could you perhaps guide us there? We've been invited to the Kagai and wish to pay him our respects."

"Oh, I see." Saya relaxed. "Are you the musicians for the festival?"

"Yes."

Suddenly their dusty sandals and leg guards, their sedge hats and the old woman's staff did not seem so strange. It was quite common for traveling musicians and performers to wander from village to village at festival time. Until now Saya had seen musicians only during festivals, playing the koto or the flute, but no doubt they had all come from far away. It was the custom for musicians to be entertained at the home of the head chieftain for several days before and after the festival before they resumed their wandering.

"I'd be happy to take you there if you would just wait a moment while I go and get my washing," Saya said.

As she was turning to leave, however, the boy casually remarked, "You have a small birthmark on your right palm, don't you?"

Saya turned back in surprise. She had a pale pink oval mark like a flower petal in the hollow of her palm. Normally, she never thought of it, but it bothered her to think that this sharp-eyed boy had been staring at it.

"I was born with it. What about it?" she answered somewhat brusquely. She was used to remarks about red birthmarks being caused by seeing a fire.

"You weren't born in this village either, were you?" he asked with a mischievous look.

Saya frowned. Although deeply shaken, she kept her poise. "What makes you say that? Does having a birthmark automatically mean that that person wasn't born in this village?"

Just then, she caught snatches of something the man with the eye patch murmured to his neighbor. "The same as . . . You can tell because . . . She has the face of the Water Maiden."

The Water Maiden? Who's that? She stiffened. Although she had never heard the name before, it filled her with a sense of foreboding that she could not shake. Her heart pounded and the blood drained from her face as though she had been touched by an icy finger. Aware that the old woman was watching her, Saya asked hoarsely, "Where do you come from?"

She waited expectantly, thinking that they must come from the east. Perhaps they knew something about her true origins. But instead the old woman answered casually, "From the west. And some of us from the south. There are many small but prosperous villages hereabouts." The old woman's inner thoughts could not be read in her wrinkled face. All her energy seemed to be concentrated in her gleaming eyes, but these, too, betrayed no flicker of emotion. Slightly disappointed, Saya remained silent, when suddenly the old woman asked, "Have you ever heard of Princess Sayura?"

"Princess Sayura? No."

"Mmm, I thought not. I thought not." The old woman nodded to herself. "It's been a long time since she passed away, although her death in the palace of the Prince of Light seems like yesterday to me."

"Was she a relative?" Saya asked, puzzled. The old woman spoke of the Princess as if she were her own daughter, yet the palace in the capital city was the home of Prince Tsukishiro and Princess Teruhi. No one was even allowed through the palace gates unless they were of very high rank.

The old woman did not reply, and the boy smothered a laugh. Saya suddenly felt ashamed and a little angry, as if she was the only one who had missed something obvious.

In the next moment she was hailed by cheerful voices from the grassy riverbank. Several friends had followed her out of curiosity. "Hey! Saya! Are you all right? Did you get your belt?"

The girls, who had raced to the top of the bank, stopped in their tracks, eyes wide with surprise as they caught sight of the strange group of people. Grateful to her friends for rescuing her from an awkward situation, Saya hastily explained, "These people found it for me. They're the musicians for the festival. I'm taking them to the head chieftain. Won't you come with me?"

The girls' faces brightened. Anything out of the ordinary was a welcome diversion. Laughing excitedly, they rushed back to collect their washing.

"What odd people!"

"They remind me of Ground Spiders."

"Stop exaggerating. That's not a very nice thing to say."

"But just look at them. You know what they say. Ground Spiders are either long of leg and arm or really short. They sleep in nests in the trees in summer, and in winter they live in caves. That description fits them perfectly, doesn't it?"

Everyone laughed. None of them had ever met a Ground Spider. They knew that it was a derogatory name given to the frontier people who refused to worship the God of Light, but, not knowing any better, they used it for anyone who looked odd or different. As such, it aptly expressed the musicians' strangeness, and Saya laughed, too. But her smile froze as she recalled her friend's words: "long of leg and arm or very short." At last the reason for her anxiety crystallized. She glanced quickly behind her at the sober black figures on the grassy riverbank. The disparity in their sizes was almost comical. And there were five of them. Five.

Suppressing the sudden racing of her heart, Saya told herself fiercely, *Impossible! It's just a coincidence. My dream couldn't possibly have come back to haunt me, not on such a sunny day as this. Not in broad daylight. It can't be.*

2

"PROMISE?"

"Yes. I promise," Saya said solemnly. "I swear before the God of Light that I will not accept gifts from, or reply to, the songs of Akihiko, Muraji, Toyo, Ohiro, and—um—Mahito."

"All right, then. That's settled." Although they spoke lightly, the girls were serious. Beneath their excitement and anticipation lurked an insecurity they could not totally suppress. The surrounding hills were robed in a breathtaking display of fresh, new leaves that seemed to tinge even the white cloth of their garments green. Intoxicated with their own youthful beauty, they wavered between shyness and pride, aware that the pure white of their clothes, the alpine roses in their hair, and the azalea adorning their sashes became them now more than they would at any other time.

"It looks as if I've lost out," Saya remarked to the girl beside her.

"Well, it's your own fault. You're the one who didn't choose some-body."

"Don't worry about Saya. She won't have any trouble finding a partner!" interjected a girl who wore a bright yellow sash.

"Why do you say that?"

"Why, she asks! Saya, you're unbelievable!" exclaimed a girl crowned with a wreath of green leaves. "Don't you know how attractive you are? Just the other day someone was saying you don't look like any ordinary village maid."

"What do I look like then?" Saya retorted.

"Cheer up. They meant that you're beautiful."

"Beautiful. Just like a princess. Princess Saya."

"Oh, stop it!" Saya exclaimed irritably. She was in no mood for joking about herself after what she had overheard the one-eyed musician saying. "She has the face of . . ." Whose face? Was she really that different from everyone else?

The girl beside her gave her shoulder a friendly pat and laughed. "Don't worry! No one who knows your true character could ever mistake you for a princess."

Meanwhile, on the southern slope of Mount Itsuki, in a glade marked by a large camellia tree and surrounded by a forest of oak, horse chestnut, and chinquapin, young men were busy laying wood for an enormous bonfire. Each village had its own spot in the glade where the older women were busy preparing food for the Kagai and dishing it out onto oak leaves. A rope of woven straw encircled the glade with folded paper decorations hung along it at regular intervals. Beneath each of these was placed a barrel of sake. The men were already flushed with its effects. Although the camellia flowers had fallen, a little farther into the wood alpine rose bushes with silver-backed leaves bore large red blooms, and golden kerria and white brier roses bloomed like stars along the mountain stream. The village girls, whose job it was to distribute flowers, were busy choosing the best for themselves.

"AFTER ALL, we're the bearers of spring," said a girl with a madder-red cord around the middle of her sash. "It's only natural that we should wear the prettiest flowers."

"That's right. We're supposed to entice the god down off the mountain peak and back to the land. At least, that's how it was in the past."

"In the past?" Saya asked.

"Before the shrine was built honoring the God of Light. That's why the shrine maiden doesn't approve of the Kagai. But I don't blame her. Just think. She has to stay up all night long with no one for company!"

"Who was the god that came down from the mountain?"

"I don't know. The Kagai is just a custom now. But it's a good one. I'd hate to see it disappear."

Another girl, who was adding sprigs of yellow kerria to the posy in her sash, remarked flippantly, "But the old gods are dead. The radiance of the God of Light was too much for them. The only ones who worship them now are the Ground Spiders."

"Oh, how horrible! I certainly don't want to entice any god of theirs!" said another girl.

"Of course not. There's only one person you're interested in enticing," Saya remarked dryly, causing several of the girls to laugh.

As she picked the golden kerria that resembled miniature sake cups, Saya felt herself drawn to the idea of a god descending from the mountain. It seemed sad that they should be preparing themselves in this way when there was no longer any god to greet.

THE SUN SANK SLOWLY behind a distant mountain peak and the sky deepened from blue to red, from red to purple, and then rapidly to indigo. The moon, like a disk of beaten copper, rose in the eastern sky, and at its appearance the bonfire was lit. A great cheer arose from the crowd. The flames leapt higher and higher, rising to a pillar of fire that lent the glade a midday brightness. Saya blinked and stared at the smiling faces illumined by the firelight, merging with the shadows crouching at their feet. The festival had begun. Chief Azusahiko made his way to the front and delivered a speech, encouraging them to enjoy the evening. Already white-haired, he was a man of integrity, untainted by ambition, well respected by his people. The only complaint ever raised against him was that he was a little dull. As soon as his speech ended, the music began. With a shiver of apprehension, Saya stole a glance at the makeshift musicians' platform. All five were there.

She had not seen them since the day they had met on the riverbank. No longer garbed in dusty black, they wore robes of the finest hemp cloth—perhaps a gift from the head chieftain. Their hair was adorned with sprigs of leaves, and they bore themselves with dignity. In fact, they looked much better than before—almost normal. The largest beat the big drum, the two other men played the hand drum and reed pipes, while the boy played the flute and the old woman the koto, leaning over so far that she almost straddled the instrument.

Besides, no matter how suspicious they might have appeared, no one could have complained about their music, which rang clear and bright over the glade, slipping effortlessly into the hearts of the people and raising their spirits high.

"Those musicians are great!" someone remarked, impressed.

"Saya! Don't just stand there. Come and join the dance. If you stay there daydreaming, the girls from other villages will beat you to it!" Saya started from her reverie to find that the girl beside her was tugging at her sleeve. Nodding her thanks, she set off at a run.

The people circled the fire several rings deep, their bodies swaying and their feet stamping out a simple rhythm as they danced around it. The heat of the flames fused with that of the dancers, reaching fever pitch. Although, at first, some laughed loudly or played the fool, the drumming of their feet gradually became a single rhythm as if some irresistible force drew them together until their footsteps beat in perfect unison, shaking the very mountains and echoing from the treetops. By the time the moon had reached its zenith and its silver face gazed down upon the glade, the spellbound dancers were drunk with excitement and the clearing pulsated in time with the fire. It was a perfect festival evening: the full moon shone hazily through a mist of downy deutzia flowers, scattering crystals of pale light in the night air.

When the dancing had reached its peak, the rhythm of their drumming feet faltered. The dancers no longer had ears for the music, searching instead for that one special person who would return their gaze—man for woman, woman for man. For this one night, even married men and women were single again. Here and there songs were already being sung, songs of enduring love for a husband or wife. Those who had found a partner drew close and slipped away from the ring of dancers into the shadows of the trees to exchange their gifts.

As for Saya, she was finally regretting the vow she had made. It had never occurred to her that the boys whom she had sworn to reject would, one after the other, seek her out as a partner. She had played and fought with them as children, but after their initiation into the ranks of the village youth, there had been few opportunities to meet. And even if they had met, they had only greeted one another from afar. She had not realized that these same boys had grown into broad-shouldered young men who regarded her as a woman. She was only now beginning to realize how her friends had tied her hands.

They don't even deserve to be called friends, she thought. Yet she knew that it proved just how sincere their feelings were, for they truly loved the ones they had named. She had no one to blame for her predicament but herself. *What am I doing here?* she thought. She, too, yearned to find someone: to face one man and, with her hands in his, to pledge her heart. But when she turned to face her next suitor, she was so filled with disappointment that she could have wept. Before her stood Mahito, the last of the five youths named by her friends.

"Not you, too?"

Mahito, the former village bully, was three years older than Saya and had once been a troublemaker in the neighborhood. In the short space of time since she had last seen him, however, he had become a handsome young man, the stubbornness receding from his oval face. Even his pug nose had somehow become attractive. When his tall figure drew near, she felt as though she had been touched by invisible fireworks.

"You were always so mean to me," she remarked. Mahito laughed, but his eyes were serious.

"That's because I knew that this day would come, Saya. That when you came of age I would have to kneel before you and beg you to answer my song at the Kagai."

Dazed, she could only stare at him in bewilderment. "But you just ignored me last year and the year before that."

"Last year was last year. This year, Saya, you're the most beauti-ful girl in the land. I can't bear to stand by and see you claimed by someone from another village. Sing me your song. Make it the one I want to hear."

The alpine rose perched above her ear tilted as she bowed her head. She had already exhausted her repertoire of refusals. Along with many love songs, all the young women memorized several songs that would gently put off unwanted suitors. These were traditional songs that she should have known by heart, yet now she could not remember any. What was she to do? Should she refuse him with a hastily improvised song? Or should she . . .

As she hesitated, unable to decide, a third voice rose in song nearby:

> *I have come upon you in a crowd,*
> *You whom I long to meet in a quiet place.*

Saya and Mahito gasped in shock and spun around. For a third person to interrupt before a girl had replied was a direct challenge to the first suitor and could only cause trouble. People with any common sense stuck to the rules of etiquette. Mahito was understandably furious, and an angry flush suffused his face.

"Just who do you think you are? You're asking for trouble!"

"Wait!" Seeing his nostrils flare, Saya recalled his former career as the village bully and hurriedly intervened. The interloper was a slender young boy. When she peered closely at his face, her mouth dropped open in amazement. It was none other than the impertinent little rascal who was supposed to be playing the flute. "You! What are you doing!"

"Get home to bed, brat. You don't belong here!" Mahito snarled threateningly, his breathing ragged.

Torihiko smiled up at them. If he had not been so young, his expression could have been described as bold and fearless. "What about the song, Saya?" he urged. "If you answer one of us, there will be no need to fight."

Flustered, Saya looked from one to the other. Then in despair she sang:

> *If you truly love me, then come.*
> *For surely you will find me waiting,*
> *Alone, in the quiet wood.*

"Saya!" Mahito cried in disbelief. "Why? Why did you answer *him?*"

She felt miserable. "I'm sorry. I just can't reply to your song. Go look for the girl who has eyes only for you. I know you'll find her." She turned and left, almost running away, feeling deeply disappointed.

Why do I have to be so nice?

A SIGH escaped her lips. She was fed up with the Kagai, with this game of courtship and love, to which she had once looked forward so eagerly. The interplay of flame and shadow made her dizzy, and she turned toward the shadows of the trees, hoping to calm her mind in the concealing dark. Not until she had passed the boundary of the glade marked by the straw rope and paper ornaments did she realize that the boy had followed her. She glared at him.

"Just in case you're wondering, I have no intention of accepting any gift from you. Mahito was right. You're just a child! Why did you leave the musicians' platform?"

The boy rolled his eyes in exasperation. His eyes gleamed in the faint light of the moon that filtered through the branches.

"And I thought you might even thank me! After all, I came to your rescue when you were in trouble."

He's such a strange boy, she thought. How had he known that she was in trouble? Had he been watching her the whole time?

"Your name's Torihiko, isn't it?" she said slowly.

"Yes."

"How did you know I wasn't born in this village?"

"I just knew," he said, clasping his hands behind his head and looking insufferably smug. "After all, we came here to find you."

Struggling to keep her voice calm, Saya replied, "If you continue to make fun of me, I'm going to lose my patience. I'm not in a particularly good mood, as you may have noticed."

"Oh my, you frighten me," he responded. Adopting a slightly less irreverent attitude, he continued, "But it's the truth, you see. We came looking for a girl who disappeared from a village burned to the ground at Princess Teruhi's command nine years ago. The girl was six years old and had a red birthmark on her right palm. That mark was proof that she was born clasping an amulet, a magatama that made her the rightful successor, the rebirth of Princess Sayura."

"Stop," Saya whispered.

"Princess Sayura is one of the highborn among those who serve the Goddess of Darkness; it is she who guards the Dragon Sword—"

"I said stop!" Saya shouted, cutting him off in mid-sentence. She shook her head violently, sending a flower flying from her hair. "I don't want to hear any more! Go away! I said go!"

Torihiko winced at this outburst, and said reproachfully, "You could, at least, refrain from yelling at me as though I were some unwanted cur. I may not look it, but I'm quite a bit older than you."

Saya turned on her heel and tried to run back to the Kagai, back to the familiar faces of the people she knew, people who understood laughter and tears. But no matter how far she ran, she seemed to move deeper and deeper into the dark forest. The glade with its bright fire should be just a few steps away, just past that tree, but still it did not come into view. Changing direction made no difference. No matter which way she ran, only the silence of the mountain forest rose up to greet her. Finally she came to a halt and clung to the trunk of a tree. She steadied her breathing, trying to control her panic.

Calm down, she thought. *It's useless to fight it.*

"There is nothing to fear." It was the tiny old woman. "You have the power to believe. You can accept what Torihiko has told you."

There. You see, Saya told herself.

She pressed her back against the tree, bracing herself for whatever might come. There before her in the darkness stood the five musicians, wrapped in a pale phosphorescent glow. She knew then that she was finally facing what had filled her with terror for so many years. Having no other choice, she drew a deep breath and exhaled slowly. She was no longer afraid. Perhaps her calm arose from sheer desperation, or perhaps she was just numb. No, she was far from numb. Rather, she was consumed with a smoldering rage. Staring evenly at the five figures, she said coldly, "So you are demons, after all."

The old woman, who stood in front, regarded Saya steadily with no change in expression. "No, we're not demons," she answered calmly. "We are at least as close to you as the people gathered for the Kagai."

"And our feelings can be hurt, too," added Torihiko, who stood directly behind the old woman.

The one-eyed man began to speak. "This is Lady Iwa," he said. "And I am Lord Akitsu." Gesturing toward the largest of them, he continued, "This is Lord Ibuki, and those two are Lord Shinado and Torihiko. We are all servants of the Goddess of Darkness."

They're Ground Spiders! Saya thought.

The possibility that she, too, might be a Ground Spider made her wish that the earth would open up and swallow her. *No!* her heart rebelled. *No, no! It can't be. I love the light. I love the flowers, the sky, the clouds, everything that lives beneath the sun!*

"Saya, listen," said Lady Iwa. "Do you know the legend of how earth and heaven were formed? The story of the God and Goddess who gave birth to the world? Together, they created the land of Toyoashihara, and hundreds of thousands of gods to populate it. These gods lived in the mountains, the rivers, the rocks, the springs, the wind, and the ocean, and shook the earth with their laughter. But the last child born to the Goddess was the fire god, and she was so horribly burned that she fled and concealed herself in the underworld. In his grief and anger, the God of Light killed the fire god and went to the Land of the Dead to bring her back. But, horrified at how changed she had become, he fled back to the world above, sealing the entrance with a huge stone and severing his ties with her forever. From that time onward they have lived separately in heaven and the underworld, despising one another."

"They divided into the forces of Light and Darkness," Saya said sullenly. "Anyone born in Toyoashihara knows that. The Goddess cursed the land and vowed she would kill one thousand people each day. The God responded that he would build one thousand five hundred birthing huts a day. He is the Great God of Light, who bathes this world in light, nurturing life. And his sacred children are Princess Teruhi and Prince Tsukishiro."

"Does he really nurture life?" the old woman countered in a strangely gentle voice. "Surely it is the earth that nurtures life. And it is water that revives the earth. Water falls from above, quenching all the land, and, in the end, flows into the underworld. That is the road to the Goddess, the road that all living things on the earth will one day tread. Our land of Toyoashihara is dependent upon the eternal flow of water. If this cycle is disrupted, it will stagnate, and evil and corruption will be left unchecked."

Touched by a sudden sadness, Saya looked up, but Lady Iwa's eyes were lowered. Saya was surprised to find herself sympathizing with this old woman who resembled some kind of apparition. It was her vulnerability rather than her ugliness that stood out. She looked like a clumsy fledgling not yet able to fly, waiting patiently to be rescued.

Lady Iwa continued. "In his hatred and anger, however, the God of Light sealed off the road to the underworld. And through his immortal children, Princess Teruhi and Prince Tsukishiro, he rules the earth, hunting down and destroying the gods of the mountains and rivers that he conceived with the Goddess. He intends to destroy all the gods and rule the earth alone, to claim Toyoashihara through slaughter and plunder."

"No! You're wrong!" Saya protested hotly. "That's not true. There's nothing wrong with trying to shed light over all the world and unite it under one ruler. The war is caused by stubborn people who refuse to recognize how precious his light is. It's because some people don't want peace—"

She was interrupted by a voice of steel. It was the first time that she had heard Lord Shinado speak. Although he was the youngest of the three men, there was something in his bearing and in his eyes reminiscent of a keen-edged sword.

"How can you be so heartless? This God of Light that you worship murdered your own father and mother. Flames and horses' hooves trampled your village into the ground. By the time we reached it, there was not one soul left alive. His two immortal children feel nothing, not even as much remorse as a dewdrop evaporating in the morning sun. Yet you would still worship them? Will you choose comfort and ease over revenge against the enemies of your own parents?"

Saya shuddered. Perhaps it was this that she had most feared. But there was something within her that would not yield, that could not back down. She realized that she was stronger than she had thought.

"I don't want to hate," she replied in a small voice. If she was afraid, it was only of Lord Shinado himself, for she was certain of what she said. "I have a new mother and father. They found me and raised me like their own child. I am not heartless. It's just that I prefer to love rather than to hate."

"Hmmm. She reminds me of Princess Sayura," muttered the huge Lord Ibuki. Although he was talking to himself, his voice rumbled like thunder.

Lady Iwa nodded in agreement. "Yes, she said the same thing. We're not saying that you shouldn't be drawn to the Light, Saya. But we must fight. We must prevent the God of Light from destroying all the gods of the land. He has no regard for or understanding of human feelings. He strives to purify the entire earth and to descend upon it. But he neither knows nor cares whether there will be any people left alive when all the gods of river and mountain have disappeared from the land. He cannot understand what this would mean to us."

Lord Akitsu raised his jet-black brows and gazed at Saya. "Water Maiden, come and help us fight. Though you may be weak, you are closest to our mother, the Goddess. You are even capable of grasping the Dragon Sword."

All five of them watched her intently from the darkness, awaiting her reply. Her heart was in turmoil, but she knew it would be useless to try to deceive them. At last she said what was in her heart. "I hate war. I can't do it."

Their disappointment struck her keenly, and somehow she felt a need to defend herself a little. "Why didn't you come sooner? I've lived here, in a village of the God of Light, for nine years. Every day I have worshiped Princess Teruhi and Prince Tsukishiro. It's impossible for me to change now, so suddenly."

After a short pause, Lady Iwa replied, "In their youth, no one realizes that the trees that stretch toward the sky are, at the same time, sending their roots deeper and deeper into the earth. Because we're granted a new life, we, the reborn, must each time experience the ignorance of youth. For this reason we can't tell others of their mission until they are ready. It has been the custom to gather together when the time comes and seek them out. In your case, however, you're right. You disappeared without a trace, and it took much longer than we expected to find you. But despite the danger, we have come into the domain of the God of Light to find you. Still, we can't blame you for that."

She felt for something inside her robe and then stretched her tiny hand out toward Saya. "We must leave you now. Our pursuers will have found our trail by now. But this is yours. Whether in the end you use it or not, it belongs to you."

Without a word, Saya held out both hands to receive a small stone, a magatama no larger than the tip of her finger, still glowing faintly with the phosphorescence from the old woman's palm. It was not round like a ball but slightly flat and curved like the outer rim of an ear. The larger end was pierced by a hole through which ran a thin cord. The stone was a smooth, milky blue, the pale, gentle color of a spring sky.

Without warning, the murmur of voices and leaves rustling gently in the wind returned, and Saya realized that she had been in a space without sound. As if waking from a dream, she looked about her and glimpsed firelight from the glade between the black silhouettes of the trees. The musicians were gone. No doubt she would never see them again. The demons had materialized only to vanish just as suddenly as they had appeared, without trying to do anything. Clutching the magatama in her hand, she thought distractedly, "I must go. I have to get back to the Kagai."

But she had only taken a few steps when she realized that there was nowhere for her to go. Her parents were at home, and her friends had split up and were lost in conversation with their partners. The night was far advanced, and the sound of high-pitched laughter drifted across the glade from the banquet areas of each village. No one else was alone.

A yawning gulf suddenly separated Saya from everyone else. Somewhere in her heart, she had always known that she did not belong, but, unwilling to accept it, she had managed to ignore it. Now, however, she could no longer deny the truth. The demons had been gentle, but only because they had indelibly impressed their mark upon her. Turning away from the brightly lit glade, she headed deeper into the forest. And as she walked, the tears she had held back for so long began to fall.

IT SEEMED that her tears would never run dry. She wept as she walked and walked as she wept, oblivious of her direction. Saya, who rarely cried, did not know how to stop. Finally, exhausted, she sat down on a fallen log to rest when suddenly the tree beside her spoke.

"Why do you weep?" it asked.

The voice was pleasant, like a breeze sighing through the treetops, and it sounded so natural that she replied without thinking, "Because I am all alone."

"You could find no lover?"

"More alone than that."

At that moment she heard another voice whisper tensely from the far side of the thick grove of trees. She craned her neck in surprise and peered into the darkness.

"It's just one of the village maidens crying. There's no cause for concern," the first voice answered quietly.

The shadows beneath the cedars were so thick that it was impossible to tell if anyone was there. Saya sniffed loudly, an action she regretted immediately, and asked suspiciously, "Who are you?"

At last she saw something move and a figure stepped out from the trees into the moonlight. He was tall and graceful, like a young cypress tree. Beneath the white light of the full moon, it was clear that he was more than just an ordinary man—far more. Saya caught her breath and froze. She had thought that nothing more could surprise her after the events of that evening, but now she doubted her own eyes, sure that she must be dreaming. On his head he wore the same silver helmet that she had so often imagined, shining with the radiance of a hundred moons.

Before her stood Prince Tsukishiro himself.

3

THE PRINCE stood bathed in moonlight—a silver statue in a trough of darkness amid the rustling leaves. Though he appeared phantomlike, his presence was palpable. His feet were just as firmly rooted to the ground as the surrounding mountains. Yet he was far too beautiful to be human. Saya felt the hair rise along the nape of her neck and realized for the first time that this sensation could be caused by something other than fear.

The Prince was armed for battle, wearing chain mail, helmet, and gauntlets, with a quiver slung across his back and a long sword resting at his hip. The clothes beneath his armor were white, his shirtsleeves bound by cords ornamented with small beads. His face under the shining helmet was fine-featured, with an aquiline nose and exquisitely gentle eyes. He exuded an air of refinement and grace, while at the same time radiating an awe-inspiring strength, an overwhelming power such that, just by standing there, he caused the night to change its shape and the forest its fragrance.

Saya was so lost in admiration that she completely forgot he could see her face clearly, too. By the time she came to her senses and covered her face with her sleeve, Prince Tsukishiro had already had plenty of time to inspect her.

"Why do you hide your face?" he chided gently.

"I was crying." She was so embarrassed. She blushed behind her sleeve to think how awful she must look.

"I know. You cried a long time." His voice held the hint of a smile. It had a beautiful timbre.

"Lift up your face." Although his tone was gentle, his words commanded. Saya obeyed him automatically, before she had even had time to think.

As she gazed up at him, he said, "Are you not the Water Maiden?"

Saya recoiled as if she had been slapped in the face. Her eyes grew to twice their size. "How . . . how do you know that name?"

His eyes were hidden now in the shadow of his visor. But his voice remained gentle. "I know a maid with a face like yours. No, I knew her . . . a long time ago. It was just a short while, but she lived in my palace at Mahoroba."

Who am I? thought Saya in despair. *Am I just the shade of Princess Sayura?* She clasped her hands together tightly to keep them from trembling and replied in a small voice. "Some demons came to me tonight and called me by that name. They told me that I belong to the people who serve the Goddess of Darkness. But until today such a thing had never occurred to me. I was raised in Hashiba and have always worshipped at the shrine of the mirror. In spring before the planting, I prayed to the moon, and in fall before the harvest, I prayed to the sun. I don't know what to do. I long to be blessed by the light, even now. But can this still be possible for me? I have always—"

Despite her efforts, her voice broke. She was amazed that she still had tears left to weep. *Go on, Saya,* she told herself fiercely. *Say it now, or never.* Summoning all her courage, she continued, "I have always loved you, Lord . . ."

For a moment, Prince Tsukishiro gazed down at her silently. The armed soldiers of his party slowly appeared and formed a guard behind him. Saya felt her courage seep away as she watched.

But then the Prince undid his chinstrap and removed his silver helmet. He shook his head with pleasure, and the beads woven into the long, looped braids on either side of his head made a pure, clear sound. *He's so young!* He looked so much younger than she had imagined.

"WHAT'S YOUR NAME?"

"Saya," she replied, her eyes fixed upon his face, begrudging every blink.

"We came here following the thick spoor of darkness. Although we did not find our enemy, we gained instead something infinitely precious," he said gaily. Then he asked, "Tonight they should be celebrating the Kagai in Hashiba. Is it near here?"

Saya nodded distractedly, still overwhelmed.

"Take me there. It has been so long since I have seen the Kagai. For months on end I have traveled over mountains and rivers, only for the sake of war. No, we won't go on foot." The Prince turned and called out, "Bring me my steed."

The people of Hashiba, including Chief Azusahiko, were dumbstruck. Legend had come to life. A god had descended to earth to visit the Kagai. The only horses in the village were sleepy plow horses. No one but the head chieftain owned a saddle horse, and even his mount looked like a different species from the majestic gray stallion with star-dappled flanks that seemed to float suddenly into the circle of firelight. And the one who rode him, one whom even the shrine maiden had only glimpsed distantly in the shrine mirror, far exceeded the people's imagination.

The milling crowd, held back by the stern-faced warriors who guarded the Prince, gazed in open-mouthed astonishment. But what astounded them most was the sight of the slender girl, a maiden from their very own land, perched sidesaddle on the gray stallion in front of the Prince.

Prince Tsukishiro's retinue advanced slowly, parting the wall of people, and came to a halt before the platform where the head chieftain sat. By this time the chieftain had scrambled from his seat and prostrated himself on the ground, his face almost scraping the dirt. The shrine maiden, keeper of the mirror, had done likewise. Seeing this, the villagers came to their senses and followed suit, hurriedly throwing themselves upon the ground.

Prince Tsukishiro looked over the backs of the crowd of silent worshippers who filled the glade. The crackling and popping of the bonfire echoed strangely and sparks danced in the night sky. "On with the festival!" he said. "You need not fear. I have come to watch the Kagai. Dance and sing, drink and be merry. Find yourselves good wives. I will celebrate your vows. Strike up the music."

Thus commanded, Chief Azusahiko raised his face a fraction and spoke in a trembling, muffled voice. "It is an unexpected honor that the Prince of Light should deign to attend our humble festival. We desire to obey, but unfortunately the musicians have disappeared . . ."

"No musicians?" Prince Tsukishiro said in a puzzled tone and looked at Saya questioningly. Unable to reply, she shrank in embarrassment. In fact, she was longing to get down from his horse, where it stood amid her people who knelt with their foreheads pressed to the ground.

"How can you celebrate without music? Never mind. I will play for you," the Prince said casually. He slipped easily to the ground, lifting Saya down after him; then, drawing out a flute, he leaped lightly onto the musicians' platform. Crossing his legs and brushing the hair back from his face, he took a deep breath and began to play a clear, ringing melody.

No one could believe it: the festival would continue to music played by the Prince of Light himself. It was inconceivable that they should celebrate the Kagai in the presence of the hallowed Prince whom they worshipped. But before they knew it, they were dancing, and the festival continued even more merrily than before. The sound of the flute melted their hearts like magic and filled their hands and feet with joy. They wept and laughed and clapped in time, drunk with excitement.

Saya, watching from where she stood behind the platform, suddenly noticed that no one could look Prince Tsukishiro in the face. They glanced up at him only to turn their heads away immediately as if his countenance were too bright to behold. But their smiling faces glowed as if a torch had been lit in their hearts. Passionate vows were exchanged in the clearing.

Am I the only one who can see him? wondered Saya. It was a strange thought, but her feet were itching to move. She, too, wanted to dance with abandon around the fire. Just as she was about to stand up, she felt a hand on her shoulder. She turned in surprise to find Chief Azusahiko. He looked at her intently and said, "You're Otohiko's daughter, aren't you? How on earth did you manage to bring the

Prince of Light to our festival? But never mind that. Don't leave his side tonight. You must stay and serve him. Offer him sake and fish. You understand?"

And so it was that Saya bore the tray of offerings to the Prince when he rested from his music-making. He sat back, relaxing with one knee raised as he watched the festival, and his handsome features softened into a smile when he saw Saya standing shyly before him.

"Come," he said. Saya knelt before him and offered him a sake cup. As she poured, Prince Tsukishiro asked, "Did you receive a gift tonight?"

For a moment she thought of the magatama, but immediately dismissed it. He was asking about the Kagai and it certainly was not a betrothal gift. "No."

"In that case, will you accept mine?"

Saya raised her head in surprise. The Prince's gaze was deep and unfathomable. But she supposed that when they were feeling relaxed, the Children of Light must jest, too.

"As the Prince of Light wishes," she replied noncommittally, and he smiled faintly.

"Your heart is pure. It has not yet been tainted by the Darkness. How fortunate that I found you so soon. I would protect that purity. Come and be a handmaiden at my palace. Won't you come with me to Mahoroba, Saya?"

The handmaidens served the immortal Children of Light in their palace in the capital of Mahoroba. This was the highest honor a shrine maiden could attain and was reserved for the daughters of select families in the most powerful clans. Saya was taken aback. "But that's impossible. I have no training. And my family—"

"There is no need to concern yourself with your origins," the Prince said lightly. "It is a peculiarity of the people of Toyoashihara to be so concerned about lineage. It doesn't concern our celestial father, ruler of the heavens. And I have heard that the Goddess of Darkness doesn't choose people by their lineage when it comes to rebirth. Isn't that so?"

Saya could only stammer, nonplussed.

A smile touched the corners of his mouth, but there was little joy in it. "The people of Darkness are reborn. The Children of Light are ageless immortals. In neither case is the God or Goddess concerned with kinship or lineage."

He drained his cup, revealing his shapely white throat. Saya, sensing some derision in his words, wondered whom he was mocking.

Setting down his cup, the Prince commanded, "Look at me."

She obeyed, but could not read his expression, for his noble features surpassed the splendor of the moon in the sky above.

"That is what qualifies you as my handmaiden. Don't you understand?" the Prince said softly. "The people of Toyoashihara never look me in the face. They can't. It would be unthinkable."

He turned his face toward the people of Hashiba, who were enjoying the festival. Couples, friends, everyone was laughing merrily.

"I know." And this time, she did understand. She also sensed, though vaguely, that some sorrow enveloped him.

"Come to Mahoroba, Saya. Whatever happens, I want you by my side," he said more forcefully perhaps than he had intended.

Before she answered, scenes from her nine years in Hashiba flashed through her mind: the peach tree behind her house, her playmates, rice flowers, frogs on the embankment, frosty mornings, midsummer afternoons, her mother and father pounding straw, light through the window. Sorrow and joy were so intermingled that she felt emotionless. She heard her own voice as if from a great distance.

"As the Prince of Light wishes."

For a brief moment the Prince's face was brightened by a joyful look that suited his youth. "How fortunate that I found you. How fortunate that it was I and not my sister," he said with a curious intensity.

As soon as she had agreed to go with him, Saya felt a weight lift from her heart, and she was filled with relief. It was as if, after wandering for so long, she had at last found something to hold on to.

I will follow him, she thought. *I am lost no longer.*

4

THAT NIGHT would surely be talked about for generations to come. The tale of the Kagai at Hashiba spread far and wide. The extraordinary rumor that Prince Tsukishiro had left the battlefield just to grace the festival and had chosen a mere village girl to become his hand-maiden, an unprecedented appointment, was spoken of with hushed astonishment. Hashiba became famous overnight, and Chief Azusa-hiko, who suddenly found himself a successful and prominent figure, could not stop smiling. The Prince had provided priceless fabrics and gold to outfit Saya as a court handmaiden, so that Hashiba had prospered in fact as well as name. Saya was amazed at the turn of events that found her cosseted and protected by the head chieftain, but otherwise felt numb and empty.

She stared in disbelief at the fine silks and wondrously dyed woven cloth, which had arrived in numerous wicker boxes and now filled the tiny house with a rainbow of color that seemed totally out of place. "Are these all to be made into clothes for me?" she asked.

"Yes! And we're going to have to ask the village women for help. I can't possibly sew them all before you leave!" her mother said, half laughing, half crying, as she caressed the shimmering fabrics with her gnarled fingers. "I never thought to cut such valuable cloth in all my life."

"Let's leave some of it here, then," said Saya. "Surely it's not neces-sary to make it all into clothes at once."

Yatame shook her head. "No, it's not as simple as that. I won't have you made miserable among the great princesses."

"Mother!" Saya laughed dryly. "I can't possibly hope to rival any princess! I'm just a village maid, nothing more or less, and that will have to do."

"No. You're different," Yatame insisted. She paused for a moment before continuing. "Somehow I always knew that you wouldn't ex-change ordinary vows with an ordinary man at the Kagai and come back to me. Of course, maybe I did hope a little that my dream would be fulfilled, that your children would be born in this house, that we would make a happy, noisy family. But the sky didn't fall when they told me the news."

Saya looked at her mother. She was old, her face creased with wrinkles and her back bent by hard work in the fields. For Yatame, who had lost her son in an accident and had adopted Saya in her old age, the birth of her grandchildren was the only thing she had to look forward to.

"I'll come home soon," Saya said quickly. "Maybe they'll send me back."

At this Yatame snorted, bristling with pride. "What a foolish thing to say! If you come back, what will the rest of the village think? I won't even let you in the door. Now let's get to work on these clothes. Just because you're going to become a handmaiden doesn't mean I'll let you be lazy."

It was unusual for Otohiko to drink, but when he came home that night and watched Saya hold up a half-sewn kimono for him to see, he asked for some sake. Through the head chieftain, the Prince had bestowed such riches on his house that the old couple could never use them all. It was so sudden that they could barely believe it.

"Chief Azusahiko told me that there's no greater joy than a dutiful daughter." Otohiko laughed as he raised his sake cup. "He's probably regretting the day he foisted that little monkey of a girl he found in the mountains on me, and wishing he had taken her himself. You weren't a very pretty sight then, you know. Black from head to foot, just skin and bones wrapped in a few rags, two big eyes staring out from a thicket of bamboo grass."

Saya laughed wryly. "Just like a spawn of the Ground Spiders. Why did you take me in?"

Otohiko looked at her from under his bushy gray brows. "Who wouldn't reach out to help a little child wandering lost and alone, no matter whose child she was? It would be inhuman not to. Saya, I know you and your friends call those people 'Ground Spiders,' but they belong to Toyoashihara just like us, even though we were separated after the God of Light appeared."

"I know," Saya replied in a small voice. She felt her chest constrict. She wanted to thank them both, to apologize for leaving without properly returning their kindness. But she could not find the right words.

"Father . . ."

As if he had guessed her thoughts, he smiled, the wrinkles crinkling at the corners of his eyes. "You're our child. You're a child of Hashiba. I'm proud of you. So you should be proud, too, wherever you go, to Mahoroba or anywhere else."

SAYA walked along the river for one last look. Tomorrow she would leave. It was a clear, early summer evening before the start of the long rainy season. The willows with their leaves unfurled swayed in the wind and frogs croaked. The breeze already smelled of summer, heavy with the fragrance of deep green leaves and the scent of grass from the warm fields. The last rays of the sun rested on the tips of the mountains, and downstream the water gleamed red where it reflected the sky. Standing on the stones at the edge of the water with not a soul in sight, Saya strained to see the river's end.

How often she had played here; how often she had dreamed of places unknown, people unknown, gods unknown. On little leaf boats she had set her dreams sailing, never once thinking that she would leave this village. Mahoroba was said to lie far to the west of the end of the river. She had never before thought of its location in relation to her village. She had only imagined a misty palace somewhere far away in the direction she would now journey.

She gave a small sigh and removed the magatama on its cord from around her neck. The sky-blue stone, warmed by her skin, seemed to breathe. She laid it in her right hand, as she had done so often, against the birthmark on her palm. She found it difficult to believe a baby could be born with this squeezed in its tiny fist. But she could not deny its beauty. How proud she would have been if only it had been a betrothal gift.

"I'll throw it away."

She had already made up her mind. That was why she had come

to the river. She would return the Water Maiden's stone to the water. She did not need it. She could not carry this shadow with her if she was to become a handmaiden at Mahoroba. She must bury all connections to the people of Darkness here.

Grasping the magatama in her right hand, she raised her arm. *Like this, as far as I can!* she thought.

But she could not throw it. It was almost as if someone was holding back her hand. She faltered in stunned surprise, and then glanced furtively around as if she had done something wrong.

Dusk was beginning to creep along the river. Her sharp eyes detected a figure coming down the path from the bank farther upstream. She hurriedly concealed the magatama in her sleeve. She would have been ashamed to have someone discover her trying to throw it away. The figure seemed to be approaching her. *Who can it be at this time of day?* she wondered, peering intently. It was not difficult to guess. Although the person's face was hidden in the twilight, the outline was unmistakable: the hair piled high; the long skirt reaching to the ankles, which no ordinary villagers wore; the thick short figure, shoulders rounded by middle age. It was the shrine maiden, keeper of the mirror. Saya bowed hastily.

"Good evening," she said, puzzled. She had never seen the shrine maiden walking alone. If that was true of the daytime, how much stranger was it to see her walking like this at dusk.

The shrine maiden halted and looked down at Saya haughtily. She was always like that, even looking scornfully upon the head chieftain at times, but now her gaze was particularly frigid. And the words she spoke took Saya by surprise. "I am no longer the shrine maiden. I have returned the mirror." An icy fury filled her voice. Saya shuddered and stared at her in astonishment.

"So suddenly? But why? You're the only shrine maiden in the village."

Standing stiffly erect as if the hair piled on the top of her head would fall should she bend, the woman replied, "Because you, Saya, received Prince Tsukishiro. It was you who made obeisance before him, you who offered the sake, you who received his ritual words of greeting, and you who were chosen as handmaiden. And I? When the Prince of Light came to our village, I, the keeper of the mirror, was unable even to attain his presence, and received not one word of acknowledgment. How could I remain meekly guarding the mirror after that?" Without thinking, Saya took a step backward. The shrine maiden continued. "I'm leaving this land. But before you go to Mahoroba, there is something I want to tell you." She took a deep breath and suddenly her expression changed drastically. Her eyes dilated and her mouth split grotesquely wide. Unaware that the woman's face was now filled with murder, Saya stared fixated with horror, thinking that she was undergoing some strange transformation.

The shrine maiden shrieked as one possessed, "You are evil! You are of the Darkness! Did you think I did not know? How cleverly you have tried to deceive Prince Tsukishiro. Do you think that I will surrender you to him? Do you think that I will let you go?"

With surprising speed, she drew a dagger from inside her robe. The fading light glowed dull red along the short blade.

"I'll send you back to the Darkness here and now!"

Saya dodged instinctively, but was too dazed to comprehend that she was confronted with death. It was only when she saw her sleeve hanging in tatters, slashed where the knife had caught it, that she was jolted to her senses and felt terror sweep through her like a wave of nausea.

"Stop! Please! I serve the Light!"

The shrine maiden shrieked in a voice like grinding metal, "Silence! How dare you make such a claim?"

"But it's true! I serve the Light with all my heart," Saya cried as she dodged the approaching blade once again. Then, turning, she began to run. The older woman's feet were slow and Saya should have outdistanced her with ease, but she tripped on a rock and fell hard on the sharp gravel. She had no time, however, to feel any pain. The woman was already upon her. The black silhouette of her demonic form towered above Saya as she brought the blade down with a triumphant cry.

She'll kill me! thought Saya. Just as she closed her eyes, a piercing scream rent the air. Realizing that the voice was not her own, she opened her eyes in surprise to see the shrine maiden cowering in fear, shielding her face with her arms. Two black shapes swooped down upon her, attacking repeatedly. Blood spurted from her arm, and once again the woman screamed. Her cry mingled with the sound of beating wings. Birds. She was being attacked by two crows.

The woman swung her dagger, but struck only empty air. The crows were swift and cruel. Saya saw blood dripping from one eye in her contorted face. Her screams and gasps grew fainter, gradually dwindling into sobs. Finally, exhausted, she sank to the ground and lay still, clutching her head in her hands. Only her shoulders moved, rising and falling with each ragged breath.

Through all of this, Saya had not moved from where she had fallen. The blood on the stones lost its color in the twilight, looking like a black stain. She felt sick. Her ears rang, and she thought she would faint if she tried to stand. The crows, which had stopped attacking as soon as the shrine maiden quit struggling, settled on a large round rock a slight distance from Saya, where they began preening themselves as if nothing had happened.

They stole surreptitious glances at her from their crafty, gleaming eyes while she stared back at them. Satisfied with their appearance, they flapped their wings and sharpened their beaks on the rock. Then one of them calmly croaked, "Sa-ya . . ."

"Stu-pid . . ." the other added.

Saya's mouth dropped open in amazement. Just then, another voice came from behind her.

"Are you still too scared to move?"

There, small and slight, stood Torihiko. He seemed to have materialized out of thin air. He wore the same old black clothes, and his uncombed hair was tied in a careless knot.

"Are you all right?" He peered into her face, his hands behind his back. He wore an expression of feigned innocence and did not look in the least concerned.

Saya said hoarsely, "What are those?"

Torihiko eyed the crows. "Ah, you mean my birds. This is Big Black and that one is Little Black."

Then, leaping from stone to stone, he went over to the cringing woman and gazed down at her. "Why don't you hurry home, lady, and take care of those wounds? I'm so sorry that I cannot escort you. But you tried to kill Saya, you see?"

"Ohhh!" The shrine maiden groaned loudly and staggered to her feet, one hand pressed tightly to her eye. Her hair had long since fallen into complete disarray.

"So! Spawn of evil. You have shown your true self," she hissed, gasping for breath. "Just wait. Princess Teruhi will . . ."

"You sent the mirror back, didn't you? So how will you report this?" Torihiko said calmly.

"Just—just remember. You can't fool Princess Teruhi. She knows who the new handmaiden is. I already sent her a full report. She'll—"

"Do you intend to keep on talking?" Torihiko interrupted impatiently. "I would think it would be rather inconvenient to lose your other eye as well."

There was something in his offhand manner that sent shivers up Saya's spine. The woman closed her mouth sharply and, hurrying off, was swallowed by the twilight.

Saya finally brushed the hair from her face. "She'll be blind in one eye for the rest of her life," she said accusingly.

"What difference does it make if you're about to die anyway," Torihiko said, unconcerned. "She obviously came to the river with the intention of killing herself. But, judging by the amount of energy she had just now, she may be so angry that she'll change her mind."

He spoke as casually as if talking about the weather. Gazing at him, Saya wondered if this was a characteristic of the people of Darkness or just a quirk of his personality.

She sighed. "I thought you had already gone. What about the others?"

"They left. Only I stayed. Because I was a little worried, you know."

He grasped a wooden box that dangled on a cord from his belt. The crows immediately flew to him, landing on his shoulders and cocking their heads in anticipation. Opening the lid he took out some finely cut shreds of dried meat and fed the crows by turns.

"And I was right, wasn't I? I hear you're going to Mahoroba?"

"That's right," Saya murmured, feeling somewhat uncomfortable.

"Why do you never learn? You always drive yourself into a corner. You're going to tag along after Prince Tsukishiro just for the sake of his pretty face."

"Leave me alone! It's none of your business!" Saya spoke sharply, blushing deeply. "That–that isn't it at all. I love the Light. I want to live under the sun. That's why I accepted the chance to be his handmaiden. But someone like you would never understand!"

Torihiko folded his arms across his chest, the two solemn-faced crows perched one on either shoulder. "Now, take Princess Teruhi; she's got that same pretty face. But she's dreaded by everyone. She'll be more than you can handle. She may look young, but she's older than your great-great-grandmother. And that's not all. There are bound to be at least fifty thousand or so ladies like the woman who was just here. Are you sure you still want to go? Saya, you're throwing yourself into the midst of your enemies, where there'll be no one to help you, no one to comfort you."

Without replying, Saya stood up and brushed the dirt from her clothes. Blood was oozing from a scrape on her knee. Her mother would surely scold her. Well, no matter. It would not show. From tomorrow, she would be wearing a long skirt.

"I can't turn back now," she said simply. "No matter what happens, I have to find out who I am. I couldn't stay here in the village any longer without knowing the answer. I'll go to Mahoroba and see what happens. If I suffer for it, it will have been my own choice. You can do whatever you like; I won't interfere. So let me do as I please."

"Stu-pid . . ."

"Sa-ya . . ." The crows croaked as if mocking her.

She looked at them indignantly. "Get rid of those birds, will you."

"But they're clever," Torihiko said, laughter in his voice. "They're trying to remember your name."

After a slight pause, Saya said, "Thank you for rescuing me. From here on, I'll take care of myself."

"Stubborn old mule," Torihiko murmured and shrugged his shoulders.

"What did you say?"

"Nothing." He looked up at her affectionately, but he spoke like an adult. "I see that I can't change your mind, so there's no point in saying anything more. Just remember: it was your own choice. Because you're sure to start doubting once you reach Mahoroba."

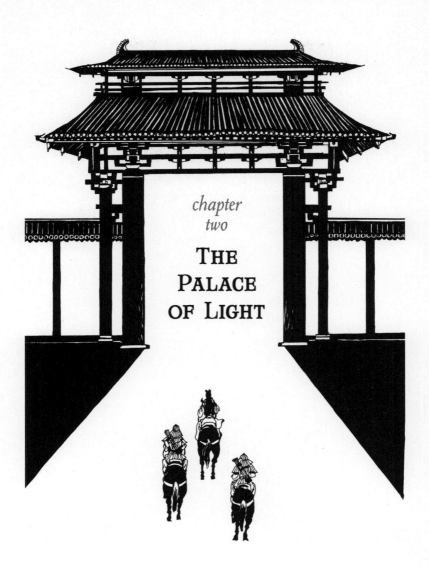

chapter two

THE
PALACE
OF LIGHT

At eventide, I gaze beyond the clouds,
lost in thought,
Dreaming of my beloved so far away.

— Anonymous

The Palace of Light

M AHOROBA DERIVED ITS NAME from its location at the center
of the lands of Toyoashihara. From here a road had once led to
heaven. According to legend, the long valley, running north to south,
was formed by the foot of the God of Light when he returned to his
celestial home, and it did indeed resemble a huge footprint, as though
someone had stepped in the middle of the mountains. Within this
imprint nestled the extensive buildings of the Palace of Light and a
multitude of lesser manors that housed the palace subjects, together
comprising the capital.

The journey had lasted many days, during which time Saya had
become accustomed to horse and saddle. She had even ridden on a
ferry with the horses. What surprised her most as she crossed the
mountain wall was the orderliness of the mountains hemming the
capital; that and the way their vivid green slopes crowded in on every side, cutting off the sky. Comparing Mahoroba to her childhood
home in the east, and to the countless mountains and rivers they had
crossed in between, was like comparing a smooth bowl produced
upon a potter's wheel to a rough-hewn wood carving. Here one would
find no reedy marshes that took half a day to cross, no precipitous
cliffs of red rock rising sudden and sheer in one's path. Everything
was delicate and orderly, as if cradled tenderly within the palm of a
giant hand. *The vengeful gods of the earth do not reside in this land.*

That's what makes it Mahoroba, Saya thought.

Nature wielded no power here; rather, power was vested in human hands. The roads, the cultivated fields, the buildings of men, which usually appeared insignificant before the creations of wind and water, had reached their zenith in Mahoroba. They rode past irrigated rice paddies, the water levels of which were carefully regulated. The pale green of the young rice seedlings and the dark purple of the irises along the embankments seemed to melt into the humid haze. A fine silken rain fell continuously, though it did not hinder their progress. Despite the heavy clouds hanging overhead, the sky was bright and glowed like dull nickel. The capital, which Saya saw for the first time in her life, was clad mysteriously in a light robe of early summer rain. Several times they passed local people wearing straw rain cloaks who, as soon as they caught sight of the procession, scrambled off the road and knelt in the mud, not daring to raise their heads until the horses' hooves had passed.

Finally a huge gate set in a tall stockade came into view through the misty white haze. The gate was roofed, sufficiently large to house many people, and heavily guarded. Saya, expecting to see the main hall once she passed through the gate, was surprised to enter a large square from which the road stretched still farther before them. Countless lofty buildings, each enclosed behind its own walls, lined the road.

"Well," she muttered to herself, "how many layers will it take to satisfy them? Mahoroba is just like a set of nested boxes."

They passed through two or three more gates. All she could see were earthen walls, pillars painted cinnabar red, and guards; the place seemed unnaturally still. It was so imposing that Saya, who was nervous anyway, was overwhelmed. When they passed through the last gate, however, the surroundings suddenly brightened. Despite the fact that it was midday, wood burned in metal brackets. The enormous plaza in which they stood was the courtyard of the palace's main hall, an immense structure with two stately wings extending to either side and behind which soared a high wooden tower. People thronged the main steps and crowded along both wings, waiting to welcome them.

Saya's eyes were drawn to a resplendent figure standing at the top of the main steps. Her hair was fastened in many loops through which were thrust long golden hairpins, and the delicate ornaments dangling from them swayed gently, framing her face. She wore robes of layered crimson and purple, beaded with white pearls and covered in a silver shawl of gossamer silk. Her ears were adorned with charming earrings of jade. More dazzling than all of these, however, was the beauty that radiated from the Princess herself.

Prince Tsukishiro urged his dapple-gray stallion forward to where his heralds, who had preceded him, stood waiting respectfully. The horses of his aides halted next, and Saya and the others fell in behind them. When they had dismounted and stood at attention, Prince Tsukishiro uttered a formal greeting in clear, ringing tones.

"Long have we been parted, O sister. I have returned from the war in the remote lands of the barbarians to the east."

"Let us rejoice at your safe and swift return," replied Princess Teruhi, her scarlet lips brighter than the building's pillars. Her gaze and the clear ringing tone of her voice, unusual in a woman, were identical to her brother's. "And how handsome is your figure garbed in armor, my brother, even in the rain."

A wry smile briefly touched Prince Tsukishiro's face. "And you, my sister: the beauty of your figure in such robes surpasses that of your golden armor shining in the midday sun. Even more so when to behold you thus is as rare as a rainbow at dawn."

Princess Teruhi responded with a slight scowl. "Let us leave such banter for later. You had best remove your armor, dry yourself, and rest after your tiring journey. And your companions, too."

Having been dismissed, the Prince and his retinue began leading their horses to the stables. Princess Teruhi paused as she was going through the doors and looked back as though remembering something. "Tsukishiro," she called out. "When you're finished, we will meet in your hall. And have your so-called new handmaiden attend us."

WHAT FOLLOWED for Saya was unpleasant. She was placed in the hands of an elderly lady-in-waiting and led off in the opposite direction from the Prince's hall. Although she realized it was outrageous to hope that she might always be near the Prince, she still felt forsaken. Prince Tsukishiro was her sole support, and without him she found everything around her intimidating. She was taken through countless stately buildings connected by passageways to a room which she was told was hers, but it was so far removed that she was sure she would never find her way back to the gate. Feeling like a prisoner, she could find no joy in the room's rich furnishings, its silk screen and thick straw-stuffed mats. And worse, even in Mahoroba, old people were old. Saya's lady-in-waiting gave the impression of having once been beautiful, but sharp wrinkles were etched in her face, and she had a rigid arrogance, assuming that what was right for her was right for everyone.

She looked Saya over from head to toe with scornful eyes and, allowing no protest, dragged her back into the passageway. This time she led her to the bath. Saya, who had always washed in the river, and was therefore totally ignorant of baths, found herself in a room with black wooden walls, a large tub, and a bucket from which steam was rising. Two young servant girls waiting in the room approached the astonished Saya, removed her clothes, and drove her into the tub, which they had filled with steaming water. Next they took a rough cloth and began to rub vigorously. The lady-in-waiting stood watching, commanding the girls to scrub harder, despite the fact that Saya already felt herself to be subjected to punishing abuse. Unable to endure it any longer, she shook herself free, scooped up hot water in both hands, and threw it over the girls. Shocked, the lady-in-waiting shrieked, "What do you think you're doing? This is no place for such unladylike behavior!"

"There's no need to skin me alive."

"But you're covered in grime."

"I am not!" Saya retorted.

Perhaps realizing that Saya was not one to give in easily, the two girls relaxed their efforts somewhat. Even so, she was sure that her skin had been rubbed raw, but when the heat of the bath had cooled she found that it was not as sore as she had expected. Next they brushed her hair endlessly, clothed her, and tied her sash unnecessarily tight. By the time they had finished and she had returned to her room, it was already dark.

"Well, you look a little better," the elderly woman commented. "Would you like some color for your lips? You're a bit pale."

"No thank you," Saya replied, still fuming. "I'd rather have some food. I haven't eaten for ages."

She was acutely aware that the supper hour had long since passed. Delicious smells had come from the kitchens near the bath. Having ridden all day without a meal since morning, she was so hungry that it was no wonder she was pale.

"There's no time for that. It's the hour at which I was commanded to bring you to His Highness," the lady-in-waiting replied imperiously. Sensing an undercurrent of spite in her words, Saya said, "It's of no consequence. I will just ask Prince Tsukishiro himself."

The lady-in-waiting drew herself up haughtily. "Surely you would not dare to sully His Highness's ears with such vulgar concerns."

"Oh no. I will simply tell him that I haven't had a bite to eat since we reached the palace."

"Well!" The lady-in-waiting broke off abruptly and, leaving the room, ordered a servant to bring a tray of food immediately. Returning, she continued, "How childish! You're not in the least attractive. I can't imagine how you managed to catch the Prince's eye."

She was silenced, however, when Saya retorted, "And I suppose your attractiveness has caught his eye?" She sat with her back turned, uttering not another word. Besides a bowl of fluffy white rice, the tray brought by the servant held a variety of dishes, of which some, such as the fish, mushrooms, and greens, were familiar, and others, such as the dried abalone and sea cucumber, were not. Although Saya left the less appealing dishes untouched, she found the rice delicious.

Urged by the lady-in-waiting, she rose and was led hastily through numerous corridors and connecting passageways toward the Prince's hall. Built of unvarnished wood, it was large enough to host a gathering of Saya's entire village beneath its roof. Entering through double doors studded with gleaming rivets, they passed along a floor of polished white cedar, smooth enough to skate on. In the innermost chamber, a canopy hung with floor-length curtains of fine silk and five-colored cords surrounded the low platform where the Prince sat. On the floor in front of this were placed bearskins and armrests for guests. Some fruit had been placed upon a small lacquered table. In each corner of the room, a candle stand had been placed in front of a silk screen, brightly illuminating the pictures. Four strange animals unlike any creatures in this world were depicted there.

Prince Tsukishiro rose and stepped through the curtains. He was wearing a long, pale yellow robe, and, with his hair hanging loose, he looked totally at ease. The lady-in-waiting knelt before him and bowed low.

"I have brought the maiden."

"You're late," said the Prince with some displeasure.

"I beg your forgiveness, Your Highness. The preparations took time."

The Prince looked at Saya and inclined his head to one side, thinking.

"Servant," he said abruptly. "Remove that sash. Pale blue is better. This color is something my sister would wear."

Saya, who was wearing a crimson sash, blushed.

"To hear is to obey. I will bring another immediately." The old woman responded in such a way that only Saya could detect the rebuke in her voice and quickly left the room. It was too late now to do anything about her deliberate unkindness. Saya raised a miserable face and looked questioningly at the Prince. Surely by now he must be tired of this ignorant country girl, but he smiled at her and said, "You prefer light shades, don't you?"

Sitting down on one of the bearskins, he added, "A pale blue sash will suit you. You should wear one. After all, Sayura always wore that color."

Saya's relief had lasted but a brief moment. His last words robbed her of strength. She felt even more miserable than before, but it was useless to complain or give up now. She did indeed feel better wearing the light blue sash the lady-in-waiting brought, and she decided to concentrate on that thought alone.

Shortly after, a young woman announced the arrival of Princess Teruhi. Noticing Saya's anxiety, Prince Tsukishiro said, "If you're nervous, wait behind that screen."

Who wouldn't be nervous if the sun and the moon were to appear before their very eyes? Saya thought as she concealed herself gratefully. She could not stop trembling, but, although terrified, she did not want to miss the opportunity to see such a marvel. Soon she heard brisk, masculine footsteps and Princess Teruhi appeared. It was no wonder that she walked like a man. She had discarded all but the pale peach inner layer of her sumptuous robes. Pleated trousers with garters at the knees replaced the fine skirts she had worn before. All her hair ornaments were gone and, except for two small loops above her ears, her hair hung loose. It was so long that it fell down her back to the floor.

Looking up at her, Prince Tsukishiro said, "Well, well. So you've changed already."

"Of course. I can hardly move in such garments. And I certainly can't sit properly in them," Princess Teruhi replied as she crossed her legs firmly on a bearskin.

There was not a speck of difference between the two faces confronting each other. Yet Saya had never dreamed that they could give such opposite impressions. Like day to night, the spirit of Princess Teruhi was in striking contrast to that of Prince Tsukishiro. She radiated passion; the Prince, sorrow.

Saya could readily understand that people instinctively feared the Princess more. Her beauty was her intensity, a shaft that pierced the heart. The faint musky perfume of her aggressive spirit quickly filled the room.

Smiling like a military commander, she demanded, "Is there no sake? Bring the sake! Let us celebrate your safe return, dear brother."

Other than in her slender form, she gave no sign of being a woman: not in her gestures as she lounged against the armrest, nor in her speech. Yet her behavior was so natural that it was fascinating to watch.

"I'm well aware of your wishes, sister," Prince Tsukishiro replied, and before he had finished speaking, a young woman had glided into the room bearing a tray with a slender-necked glass flask and sake cups. Saya had thought that there was little difference between the work of a village maiden and that of a court handmaiden, except that the latter would be charmingly dressed. This girl, however, was more beautiful and elegant than anyone Saya had ever seen, almost trembling with pride as she served them, a pride that shone in her face.

Staring at her keenly, Princess Teruhi said, "This is not the girl that you brought back with you from the east. I told you to have her attend us."

"You can tell?"

"You underestimate me."

Prince Tsukishiro said teasingly, "It appears that you have come only to see my new handmaiden, dear sister, not to celebrate my return."

Princess Teruhi stuck out her shapely chin. "And it's obvious that you returned despite the lack of progress in the war because of that girl."

Her eyes swiftly swept the room, so that Saya, although she hurriedly ducked behind the screen from which she had been peeking, was too late to escape notice.

"What are you doing there?" Princess Teruhi said sharply, her voice severe. "This is no time for playing hide-and-seek. If you're coming out, then come!"

Saya, her face on fire, reluctantly emerged from behind the screen. Prince Tsukishiro ordered the maiden serving them to leave the room. In Saya's defense, he said, "She was late, actually. I had no time to tell her what to do."

Saya knelt and, placing her hands on the floor before her, bowed low, saying faintly, "I am honored to meet you. I am Saya, from Hashiba."

"Hashiba?" Princess Teruhi repeated dubiously.

"She was reportedly adopted by an old couple when she was a child," Prince Tsukishiro explained.

The Princess's penetrating gaze never wavered, and Saya could feel her eyes boring through her. *What am I doing here?* she wondered. When she thought of her parents and how they had been killed, she knew that she should see this woman as a demon, a deadly viper. Yet she could not hate her. Although she trembled with fear, at the same time, she could not help being drawn to her beauty.

After a brief pause, Princess Teruhi turned to Prince Tsukishiro and said, "I despair of you, brother. Again and again you find and you lose. And now once more the same thing. Are you not weary of it? Why do you harbor an attraction to such an aberration?"

Prince Tsukishiro answered softly, "Is it not extreme to call the Water Maiden who yearns for the Light an aberration? Look at her. Don't you want to scoop her up like water in your hands? She is youth itself, newborn."

With a slight frown, Princess Teruhi brought the sake cup to her lips. "I certainly feel no such desire. Why should I? No matter what you may say, she belongs to the people of Darkness—to our enemy. They die, and then return to life, again and again. Which is why they can never escape from eternally repeating the same stupid mistakes."

"Perhaps you're right," Prince Tsukishiro said in a low voice. "But might that not be a strength in this world? The reborn know defeat, and yet they know it not. They're naïve, and yet they hope that they can move a mountain."

Princess Teruhi glared at her brother. "Where on earth did you acquire such weakness?"

"Victory in the east is certain. Surely there's no harm in viewing things with a more open and generous mind," he replied rather hotly. When his eyes flashed with anger, the resemblance between him and his sister was even stronger. "Considering that we have the Dragon

Sword, they are stubborn in their resistance, of which you, fighting on the western front, sister, must also be well aware."

The Dragon Sword. The name caught Saya's attention, for she had heard it before. Torihiko had mentioned it. And Lord Akitsu, too.

Princess Teruhi glanced sharply at Saya. Resting her elbow on the armrest and cupping her chin in her hand, she remarked in an amused tone, "Look at the little one—her ears pricked up at that. Listen carefully, and you'll make a good little spy."

"I–I came . . ." Saya stammered, then continued, forcing herself to speak clearly, "I came to the palace to cut any ties with such people."

"I'm sure that you speak with all sincerity, but I doubt that's possible," the Princess replied coldly. "I know there's nothing you can do to disrupt the Palace of Light, but I find the very presence of one of the people of Darkness here offensive. If you weren't one of Tsukishiro's handmaidens, I would have slain you at first sight." She looked over her sake cup at the Prince and smiled. "Isn't that so?"

Although she spoke lightly, her tone was serious. Saya could not help trembling, but she mustered the courage to speak, knowing that to show her fear would only increase the Princess's enjoyment. "I have come here solely to serve Prince Tsukishiro."

Princess Teruhi looked taken aback, and the Prince laughed aloud.

"You see, sister. She's an interesting girl."

"An infant will reach out its hand even to grasp hot iron," the Princess said with a snort. "It realizes its mistake only once it has been burned. Whether this child will still appeal to you then is another question."

"I have no intention of letting her get burned," Prince Tsukishiro replied. "I will keep her just as she is."

"Well said," Princess Teruhi sneered. With a scornful smile upon her face, she resembled a sleek and elegant feline. "And I shall see with my own eyes whether or not such a thing is possible. Why do you concern yourself with this child of Darkness? I can't decide whether you are brave or foolish to boldly invite a mortal enemy to your side. Of one thing I'm certain, though." The Princess leaned forward and looked coolly at Prince Tsukishiro. "Whenever you tire of the war, you find the Water Maiden and bring her home."

"Teruhi!" He scowled.

Her eyes gleamed with satisfaction as if to say, *You see*. "I don't understand you, brother. How can you tire of the war that prepares the earth for our father's coming? I have never desired to rest from this task, anxious only for its speedy accomplishment. If it weren't decreed that we should govern Mahoroba alternately, I would never leave the battlefront. Yet you persist in this perversity, suddenly deserting the battlefield in your attraction to the people of Darkness."

Prince Tsukishiro looked grim. Although he did not show his feelings as much as his sister, his smile was cold.

"There's no need to hurry, sister. Neither god nor demon can divert the will of the illustrious God of Light. What is the will of our divine father is the destiny of this world. His advent will surely come."

"You are hard-hearted, brother. It's difficult to believe that we're children of the same father," said Princess Teruhi, disgruntled.

"No, I am his child. Even what you call my perversity is part of him," Prince Tsukishiro replied quietly.

"Our celestial father does not desire you to sully your eyes with Darkness!" Princess Teruhi shouted, slamming her sake cup down on the floor. Her anger flared like a sudden blaze of flame. Unconsciously, Saya recoiled and gradually began edging away.

"What business does the God of the Pure Light have with them? Only by sweeping the Darkness from the face of the earth will a new and radiant world be created. That's the reason our divine father intends to descend to this earth."

"I wasn't proposing anything to the contrary," the Prince responded, evading outright argument. "What you say is always true."

Having lost a target for her anger, Princess Teruhi folded her arms and scowled at him. "Why is it that you always go round in circles? I have despaired of the youngest member of our family, who is a total failure, but you never do what I want you to either. What's wrong with you?"

Prince Tsukishiro regarded his sister with an unfathomable expression. Finally he said, "We get along best when we don't spend much time together. When you're at Mahoroba, I'm at the battlefield. And when I'm at Mahoroba, you're at the battlefield. So it has been since ages past. Yet originally you were our divine father's left eye, and I, his right. Both of us should be looking at the same thing."

Princess Teruhi rose indignantly. Her long hair swept the floor. "Nay, brother, you and I look at all things with our backs turned to each other," she said bitterly, looking down at him. "As you have said, now that you've returned to Mahoroba, I should leave as soon as possible for battle in the west. However, I didn't foresee such a sudden return, and therefore there is still much to do. We will have to endure each other's presence a little longer until I have completed the work at hand."

With those words, she stalked out of the room. It was as if a sudden storm had passed. Only her sweet perfume lingered behind. Saya remained staring after her blankly.

After a time Prince Tsukishiro sighed quietly. "It's always the same. We rejoice at our reunion and the very same day we begin to quarrel." Although there was sadness in his words, he smiled when he looked at Saya. "It would seem that the people of Darkness are not the only ones who excel at repeating the same mistake."

REPEAT, *repeat. I wonder what they're talking about,* Saya thought absently. A spool for winding thread came to mind. And the girl who held the spool in her hand as she wound was someone with a face unknown: Princess Sayura.

Everywhere I go, they tell me it's not the first time; it's a repetition, a rebirth. It's not fair. It's not fair at all, when for me everything is new and I'm still struggling to find my way. She was upset at being talked about as if she were some kind of puppet. Besides, it did not make sense. *After all, I thought very carefully before I chose what seemed right to me . . .*

"Do you intend to sleep all day? It's time to get up." Saya started when she heard the lady-in-waiting snap at her. "Everyone has gathered in the morning room. The sun rose long ago."

Saya blinked. She did not feel that she had slept at all, yet the morning sun poured through the latticed window and spilled across the wooden floorboards. She could hear sparrows chirping.

"The morning room?" she asked, rubbing her eyes.

"We gather together to pay obeisance to the immortal Prince of Light, and then break our fast. If you do not wish to eat, there's no need to rise."

"I'm coming." She was starving.

After dressing hurriedly, she followed the lady-in-waiting along the passageway, but suddenly a horrible suspicion entered her mind.

"Will you be serving me from now on?" she asked.

"So I have been commanded," the lady-in-waiting replied with obvious displeasure. "Most of those honored to become handmaidens employ both a manservant and a child servant, but as you have none, the extra tasks fall upon my shoulders."

Oh dear, Saya sighed to herself.

The morning room was long and narrow and ran along an outside corridor. Trays on short stands were arranged in two rows, facing each other, and young women with their long black hair neatly tied at the nape of the neck knelt on the floor before them. The morning ceremony had already begun and the room was hushed. There was a dais at the front with an ornately decorated seat, but the Prince was not present. It seemed that he did not necessarily attend. Saya slid into the last empty place. There were about forty people. A dazzling light poured in from the corridor, and the girls sitting in two neat lines appeared as fresh and elegant as lotus flowers blooming in the early morning. The diverse colors of their garments—white, pale blue, soft mauve, grass-green—reflected the season, refreshing the eyes. Most of them were maidens in the first blush of youth, but as far as Saya could tell, she was the youngest.

The ceremony ended, and Saya, mimicking the actions of the others without really understanding, began to eat, but the food stuck in her throat. Although they whispered among themselves, none of the handmaidens spoke to her. Not only that, but they rose one by one and left after barely picking at their food, as if they wished to get away from her as quickly as possible. Saya soon found herself sitting on her own. While she was wondering whether or not she should lay down her own chopsticks, she sensed someone approaching. Looking up, she saw the two older women who had been sitting closest to the dais looking down at her. Although both were past their prime, they preserved a well-polished beauty. The woman robed in purple appeared to be the older of the two.

"You're the novice who arrived yesterday. His Highness informed us. I am the senior handmaiden and this is my assistant."

"My name is Saya," Saya said hastily, placing her palms formally upon her knees.

The assistant, who was wearing indigo and white, raised her sleeve to her mouth to hide a smile. "It would seem cheap to call you by such a name, don't you think? As if you were a mere servant . . ." There were hidden thorns in her voice. "Let's see. As light blue suits you so well, how would it be if we call you Lady Blue? Would that be acceptable?"

"Yes." Saya nodded uncertainly.

The senior handmaiden continued, "We've heard that you received no training for your new position. Our instructions are to train you in etiquette, comportment, prayer, and oracles every day from the end of the morning meal until the evening chores. You must be able to perform your duties as a handmaiden by the time of the purification ceremony, which will take place at the end of the sixth month of the lunar calendar. You'll be very busy, but I'm sure you're prepared for that, aren't you?"

Feeling their gaze upon her, Saya started and answered hurriedly, "Uh, yes. Of course. Thank you."

She was taken to a drab-looking building, which she later learned was where handmaidens of lower rank worked, and there she remained without setting foot outside until dusk. She practiced walking for the entire day. She walked from one corner of the room to the other hundreds of times, and by the end she was so exhausted that she could barely stand. Her instructors, however, paid no attention.

"Tomorrow we'll begin practicing how to carry a tray. Come here promptly after your morning meal," and with those words they left. Their departure, like that of the women in the morning room, was incredibly swift. No doubt she would soon undergo training in how to leave the room, Saya thought in exasperation.

As the lady-in-waiting did not seem likely to come and get her, she tried to find her own way through the intricate passages of the enormous complex. At one point she almost collided with some servants who were hurrying along with trays, but otherwise she managed to find her way back to the familiar roof of her quarters without incident. An unexpectedly large number of people passed to and fro along the corridors and passageways. The majority of them were servants: serving girls and child servants wearing ankle-length pleated skirts. The handmaidens ministered to the personal needs of the immortals, preparing their meals, sewing their clothes, purifying the royal throne. In return, however, they were not required to lift a finger for themselves. All their needs were taken care of by other servants. Beneath these servants were more servants, and beneath them again more servants, so that Saya wondered how many people the palace supported as their numbers multiplied. She could not begin to guess.

Walking along the passage after finally locating her room, she suddenly became aware of voices coming from behind the reed screen of another room. Several of the handmaidens were gathered there.

"Even some of the servant girls are of better birth than she is."

"They say that she didn't even bring a manservant with her. She just sneaked into the palace without a proper ceremony."

"His Highness is occasionally subject to strange whims, you know."

"Anyone with a grain of sense would have restrained themselves and declined his offer. She has some nerve!"

Saya stopped walking. She could have cleared her throat to let them know that someone was there, but practicing how to walk all day had dampened her sprits. The voice continued.

"Did you hear that she actually ate that evening?"

"What! With Her Highness here? Even though the Prince is always so bad-tempered when the Princess is in the palace?"

"An oddity only attracts while the novelty lasts—like girls of lowly birth."

"We mustn't let it go to her head. It's ridiculous that she should be considered one of us."

Deciding that she had heard enough, Saya walked quietly away. *I never expected them to welcome me with open arms,* she told herself. *And it's fine with me if they complain about my lowly birth. It's far better than if they knew I was one of the people of Darkness. If they knew that, they'd stop at nothing.*

She recalled the face of the shrine maiden from her village as she had raised the dagger above her head. Would these beautiful, elegant girls become like that? The thought was too depressing, and she shook her head to chase it away. But that night, memories of her home in Hashiba flooded her mind and she could not sleep.

2

DISMAL DAYS of drizzling rain continued.

Saya practiced constantly, but was puzzled to find that the more she learned, the more distant she felt from the Prince of Light. On the day she had first innocently looked into his face, she had imagined that she could at least partially understand his feelings, whereas now, in Mahoroba, although he was but a stone's throw away, he was fast becoming distant and unattainable. He closeted himself within his hall, so that she rarely saw him, and even when she glimpsed him from afar, he never noticed her.

Saya sat on the edge of the damp porch gazing out through the curtain of rain falling from the eaves. Clouds hung low in the sky, water dripped from the trees, and the surface of the ancient pond surrounded by moss-covered rocks in the inner garden was clouded. Though it rained, she never got wet. Any outside business was taken care of by servants responsible for the outer area. How miserable to be imprisoned by damp floorboards and wooden posts, watching the rain like an indifferent bystander! If she could just get her feet wet, just step in a puddle, she would feel how the earth and the plants rejoiced in this weather.

She could not understand why people living in the palace made such a fuss about getting their hair or feet wet. Without touching the rain, how could they know its diversity, or the delight it could bring? Of course, depending on the type of cloud, rain could be hard, cold, or bitter. But summer rain was usually sweet and gentle. Each time it fell, it bore a different fragrance from the distant heavens.

On this particular day, the senior handmaiden had suddenly canceled the lesson, and Saya had nothing to do. She was so bored that she felt mold would sprout inside her. Watching a snail crawl along the top of the wet railing, her thoughts returned to the question that nagged her.

What am I doing here?

The other handmaidens continued to exclude her and did not forgo even the most trivial excuse to make things unpleasant, but Saya viewed this optimistically as an endurance test. This was not the first time she had experienced such rejection. When she had first arrived in Hashiba, all the neighborhood children had ostracized her. No matter how friendly or how meek and obedient she might be it had no effect on them. In the end, time had solved the problem. As long as she did not complain or exaggerate her suffering, she knew that someday the door would open to her. And she had no intention of brooding over it. No, the cause of her depression was the unattainable Prince Tsukishiro.

Although she tried not to let the rumors that she had followed the Prince out of vanity bother her, she had known that it was partly true. Her aching heart, however, gradually informed her that it was much more than just partly true. The night of the Kagai when they had exchanged look for look seemed like a dream of long ago. She had believed that she alone could touch his heart, and that likewise his was the only gaze that would ever reach hers. She had left her home in response to his kind words, only to find that this belief had been nothing but the conceit of an ignorant girl. It hurt to know that not even she could grasp the moon, which illuminated the world from on high.

How could I have fallen so in love with him? Saya asked herself. *I turned away those who had come so far to find me just to follow him here*. Deep in her heart, she knew the answer: she had fallen for his face. She thought back to the night of the Kagai, remembering his gentle smile, his handsome profile as he gazed into the bonfire.

I followed him because he seemed so lonely. Forgetting everything else, blindly. But I should have known that it was impossible for me, a lowly village girl, to ease his pain, when his grief is not that of mortal men.

She pulled out the azure stone, a habit she had fallen into whenever she became depressed. Unable to throw it away, and fearful that someone like the lady-in-waiting might find it, she always carried it with her, and strangely enough, looking at its color and curved shape always comforted her. It was a warm pastel blue, gentle yet at the same time imbued with hidden strength. Gazing at it, she thought, *I wonder why the magatama of the Water Maiden who drifts in darkness is such a bright blue, the color of the sky. It seems odd.*

THAT DAY she could not finish her supper. Considering that she felt a pain in the pit of her stomach whenever she saw the senior handmaiden and her assistant, it seemed strange that she could not eat today when there was no lesson. But the lessons, in which sparks often flew, were still preferable to boredom. Anger at least gave her energy. Leaving her food virtually untouched, an unusual thing for her to do, she rose and, for the first time, realized that this was as much as the other handmaidens ever ate.

Perhaps everyone here is suffering from melancholy, she thought.

All the handmaidens were as slender as willow branches swaying in the breeze. Saya had always tended to be thin, and although she had filled out somewhat since her childhood, her friends in the village still teased her about her small chest, her narrow waist. Here, however, she seemed to compare favorably with the rest.

Returning to her room, she found the lady-in-waiting already there. Saya braced herself when she saw her kneeling respectfully. The woman had not come for some time, and whenever she did appear, it was usually to complain.

"What is it?"

"I'm here to accompany you. Please follow me," she said with some reluctance, and rose. Saya was startled. The lady-in-waiting had spoken to her this way only once before. After hurriedly smoothing her hair, Saya traveled along the dark passages, following the light of the oil lamp held by the lady-in-waiting. As she had expected, she was led deep into the palace to the Prince's chamber.

Although a full month had passed, the Prince and his surroundings remained unchanged. It was as if only a day had passed since she had first come. The only difference was that this time the Prince wore white. He looked at her as though he had met her just recently. She felt that she alone had aged.

"Just as I thought, that sash is much better," the Prince said with satisfaction, leaning on the armrest, his long hair flowing over his white robe. "And you are better dressed, much better than last time."

"A month has passed, O Prince of Light." While she felt it was useless to remind him, she could not help herself, although a month must seem no more than the blink of an eye to one who lived forever.

"You have grown even more beautiful in that short time," said the Prince, making her glad that she had said it after all.

"Come." He invited her to sit in front of him. A simple meal had been prepared.

"Would you care for some sake?" the Prince asked. Saya, surprised, accepted the jade-colored sake cup he offered and took a tiny sip. The sake had a slightly bitter taste.

Although both the immortals drank sake, they rarely touched their food. The place set for the Prince in the morning and evening rooms was merely a formality, for he never came. The Children of Light had no need of sustenance from the earth. This thought made Saya a little sad. They were different: they had no connection with the land.

"Why do you cast down your eyes?" Prince Tsukishiro asked curiously.

She was surprised that he needed to ask. "I am being instructed in matters of etiquette, Your Highness," she replied. Unintentionally, a note of reproof had crept into her voice, as if she felt her efforts deserved praise. "I have learned many things."

"Etiquette can be very tedious at times," Prince Tsukishiro said. "Customs are formed, and the descendants of men are trapped therein. The generations pass without a chance to weed out the foolish from the essential—a regrettable situation."

Reaching out his hand, he touched Saya's chin and raised her face. She felt as if the sky would fall in her shock that the Prince of Light had touched her.

"And you, Water Maiden, aren't you here having transcended those very conventions?"

Unable to speak, Saya could only stare at his fresh, handsome face. To her surprise, her chest constricted and she felt tears well in her eyes. Yet she could not look away, for she had no idea when she would see him again. In a husky voice, she managed with great effort to put her thoughts into words. "All I have is now. I cannot transcend anything. I know nothing of the past. I am simply Saya, Your Highness."

"That is your strength. You're able to start afresh," said the Prince almost enviously. "On the night of the Kagai you consented to accept a gift from me, didn't you?"

"Yes," she replied in a small voice. "And I have come to Mahoroba. But"—her voice grew even fainter so that it was difficult to catch her words—"I now realize my conceit."

Prince Tsukishiro looked somewhat taken aback. "Did you think that I would break my promise?"

"No, of course not." Saya shook her head, wiping away the tears that fell. "I don't know how to say it. But . . . I didn't realize what it meant to become your handmaiden."

"Little Water Maiden," Prince Tsukishiro said softly, "it seems you really do not understand. That is my fault for not knowing how to hurry."

He ran his hand through his hair, and then leaned forward, looking at Saya with a merry gleam of mischief in his eyes. "I meant that I wanted to give you a betrothal gift. You can't imagine that I brought you to faraway Mahoroba just to clean and dust." He took her hand in his and laid his other hand upon it. "I thought you knew that a man and woman who join hands like this on the night of the Kagai exchange more than just a jewel or comb."

Certainly Saya should have known this. Her mother had spoken of it obliquely, and her friends had whispered about it. The gift was a symbol of permission to exchange love, and it was love that was most important. It was sacred and mystical, and looking into each other's eyes, lovers would know how to express it. But his words took her completely by surprise, and her mind, in its confusion, went totally blank. She was at such a loss that she felt like an owl that had fallen out of its nest in midday.

"I—" Gripped by an instinctive fear, she tried to pull away.

But Prince Tsukishiro would not release her hand, and her fear, whose cause she did not know, increased. Although he appeared slender and elegant, his grip was like iron.

"There is nothing to fear. You are the one who said you loved me. Am I wrong?" Prince Tsukishiro spoke quietly, but there was something suppressed in his voice. Saya could sense it, too, in his dark eyes, in his sigh. Flustered, she looked frantically around the room for help, but found only the screens with their overwhelming images of outlandish creatures. Feeling faint, she closed her eyes and was pulled closer to him. She caught the fragrance of anise from his stiffly starched clothes.

At that moment a voice echoed unexpectedly in the room. "Really! You said you would keep the girl just as she is. But no sooner have the words left your lips than you behave like this!"

Feeling Prince Tsukishiro's grip relax, Saya gathered her courage and sprang away. For an instant she was grateful to the speaker, but her savior, Princess Teruhi, stood with folded arms, looking upon them coldly.

Prince Tsukishiro, however, did not seem surprised.

"I thought you would come, sister."

"Of course. For I told you that I would see with my own eyes whether you kept your word," said Princess Teruhi, advancing. As usual, she was dressed in trousers, and tiny gold bells attached to the garters below her knees jingled faintly as she walked. Her sharp, sweet scent wafted toward them. "Unlike you, I keep my word."

"Have you made some progress with your work?" asked Prince Tsukishiro.

She glared at him angrily. "I'm sure that you would love to be rid of me as soon as possible, but the priests wish me to perform the purification ceremony. I will proceed to the campaign in the west when that's finished."

"You are certainly more suited to perform the purification than I, sister."

"Is that sarcasm?" she snapped. Sweeping her hair out of the way, she sat down. Although her gestures closely resembled her brother's, she radiated such energy that even his brightness faded beside hers.

She turned to Saya, who, having brought her fear somewhat under control, sat huddled in the corner unable to leave. She smiled. "At times like this, the Water Maiden usually flees without a backward glance. This one seems to have the nerves of a chicken who forgets the heat once the scalding broth has passed its throat. It appears that when you and I are together, her curiosity gets the better of her and she just can't leave."

Prince Tsukishiro defended her. "That's because she has done nothing of which she need be ashamed."

"She's just a child!" Princess Teruhi said derisively. She gave the Prince a searching look. "Do you really intend to make such a little innocent your bride?"

He raised his eyebrows. "She will not remain naïve forever. She is not like us, someone who never changes."

"I see. So she will grow old and feeble, then wither and die before your very eyes," she said in a mocking tone, but her eyes blazed. Only the Prince could withstand the intensity of that gaze, so fierce it would have made the hairs rise even on an innocent bystander. "That will never be, brother," she said in a low voice. "The Water Maiden will never live long enough to grow old. Soon she will take her own life and slip like water through your fingers. Do you understand,

Tsukishiro? I will not tolerate a repetition of this useless behavior. I was not made to live on this earth in order to watch such folly. I will not allow you to make that girl your wife. I will destroy your foolish obsession with my own hands."

Prince Tsukishiro raised his head abruptly. His expression was grimmer than Saya had ever seen it. "What can you do? You excel at destruction above all else, but you can't see where my passion lies. How then, sister, will you destroy something you cannot see?"

Princess Teruhi's cheeks were tinged with red. She looked breath-takingly beautiful, and dangerous. "And how can you possibly see something that I cannot?"

"Your eyes, my sister, are so fixed on our celestial father's brightness that they see nothing else."

"Are you saying that you do not love our father, the God of Light?" she cried in a thunderous voice.

"Of course I love him," Prince Tsukishiro replied, his voice as stern as his sister's. "I, too, look for the day when the land of Toyoashihara will be transformed into a land of pure light befitting the coming of our celestial father. That is why we are here, you and I, the demigods bequeathed to the earth."

"And one other, though that one be a failure," Princess Teruhi murmured.

Prince Tsukishiro paused for a moment and then continued. "Even for us, however, a long time has passed since we first stood upon this earth. I never imagined that the purification of Toyoashihara would take this long. And recently I have begun to wonder what our celestial father truly desires . . ."

Princess Teruhi shook her head. "And I can't help thinking that if you didn't repeatedly fall into the snare of the people of Darkness as they strive to make you their ally, they would have been exterminated long ago." She rose, her hands on her hips. "You asked me what I can do. Don't forget that it was I who seized the Dragon Sword. If we can but use it to slay the Goddess of Darkness, her people will be destroyed along with her. It can't be long now. As for that girl, she is the last of the Water Maidens."

PRINCE TSUKISHIRO looked at his sister, his face an emotionless mask. "As I said, what you cannot see is the direction in which my passion lies."

His voice was very quiet. Princess Teruhi returned his gaze with a baffled expression, then turned her back on him abruptly. "Of all things, I like least the frivolous words of men," she said and left without a backward glance.

With a start, Saya hastily pressed the palms of both hands to the floor and bowed low. "Pardon me, but I beg your leave to depart," she mumbled hastily and dashed out of the room. Peering through the darkness, she ran along the wood floor of the passageway, brushing the entangling train of her skirt roughly aside. Perhaps the noise of her steps reached the Princess's ears, for she turned at the corner and looked back, allowing Saya to catch up.

"P–please!" Saya leaned against a pillar and gasped for breath, thankful for the darkness. Without it, she could not have spoken like this to someone who inspired such fear in her. "Please! Tell me. How did Princess Sayura die?"

A faint glow like starlight seemed to float from Princess Teruhi's clothes as she stood in the darkness. But Saya could see only her slender silhouette, and not the expression on her face.

"Please!"

"Well, well. You're brave, or perhaps 'foolish' would be more apt," said Princess Teruhi, scrutinizing her.

"Is it true that Princess Sayura took her own life?"

"Quite true," Princess Teruhi replied bluntly. "Your people considerately die one after the other. As soon as the odds look bad, you kill yourselves. Of course, you're reborn, but I will never recognize that as a strength. To die is to escape. It is weakness. Try standing in the shoes of we who may never hope to, nay, are not permitted to run away from our mistakes. Do you understand? Because the next time you throw yourself into the pond, I will wrap a rake in your hair and drag you out. Be prepared."

And with those words, she walked away, leaving Saya in pitch darkness. She slumped down onto the cold floor. Her head ached in confusion. But one thing she had clearly understood.

Prince Tsukishiro's gaze is not directed at me. Not now, not ever. He doesn't see me.

At first she had thought he was seeing Princess Sayura rather than herself. But she had been wrong. Perhaps Princess Sayura had grown weary of life because she realized that his heart was not hers. While drawn to the Water Maiden, in reality he was gazing far into the distance, and even the Prince himself did not really understand. But Saya did, and most likely Princess Sayura had, too: the object of his gaze was Teruhi's reflection glimpsed in the water's surface.

Intuition, like the sixth sense of a small animal, gave her this insight. That the immortal twins quarreled every time they met was not simply because they did not get along. It was because they revolved around each other like orbiting stars. Just let an outsider try to intrude upon such an unfathomable love-hate relationship, to break the intense bond in which the violence of their feelings caused them to repel each other!

No mortal can possibly ease the Prince's pain, the rift created by the gods, when heaven and earth were sundered. No one can but the two immortals themselves, the sun and the moon who each represent one half of the other.

Saya knew that she had at last discovered the truth, but it did not help her. She could only meditate on the emptiness of her two open hands.

"PERHAPS we should call for a physician. For Lady Blue," the senior handmaiden said to her assistant after Saya had left. The assistant, who was putting away the writing desk, turned and smoothed her hair.

"But she has become much more pliable. With the ceremony soon to take place, a great weight has been lifted from my shoulders."

"Ah, but it makes me nervous when she is so well behaved day after day. There was a time when she ate a shameful amount, yet recently she hardly touches her food. I wonder if she is ill."

"I see what you mean. Perhaps you're right." The assistant pondered the problem.

"It would be bad for our reputation if people thought that she had become ill because we harassed her. We'll have to do something," the senior handmaiden said.

It did not take long for her quick-witted assistant to come up with a plan. "A physician might be overdoing it. But what if we gave her a child servant? Having no servant of her own, she has had to do everything for herself. Perhaps this would ease her burden."

The other woman nodded in agreement. "An excellent idea. And perhaps if she had her own servant, the other girls would be less inclined to treat her as a serving girl."

"Well, as to that, who knows," said the assistant with a faint sneer.

EVERYTHING SEEMED like too much trouble. It was partly the change in climate: the rainy season had been followed by intense summer heat and relentless sunshine. But more than anything else, Saya, who had never before lost her appetite from heartbreak, was defeated by herself. Her confidence in every area had evaporated, and she no longer even hoped to continue as a handmaiden.

Maybe if I fall ill and die, Princess Teruhi won't revile me, she thought. But it would be too galling to be confined to her bed and treated as a nuisance by the coldhearted people of the palace. She longed for her home in the east. There, when the heat became intense, they had swum freely in the river and brought out benches at night to sleep under the stars. But neither the cool breeze nor the fresh morning dew reached the deep recesses of the palace. There was only the sun glaring down on the hard dry earth. Summer in the palace hung heavy and stagnant.

One sleepless night, Saya thought she really would die. Although she did not really understand what it meant to die, it seemed as if her soul was flailing wildly trying to escape her physical frame and all its troubles. It no longer mattered to her whether it would be she who discarded her body or she who would be left behind. She only knew that if she could just get away, she could find relief and flee into the bracing freedom of emptiness. Like a bird, something within her beat its wings, poised for the moment of flight.

If I'm going to die anyway, I don't want to leave my body lying here, she thought suddenly. *I'd rather die in a purer place—yes, in cool, peaceful water . . .*

She imagined her hair spreading out like a fan on the water, swaying gently like waterweeds. That would not be so bad. It would look beautiful.

She sat up abruptly. All was quiet and it seemed that the night watch was far away. Stealthily she slid open the double doors. The half moon hung in the midnight sky, casting a clear light. Its reflection floated serenely on the still surface of the ancient pond surrounded by a thick grove of trees. Drawn by the deep stillness of the water's surface, Saya stepped forward only to stop dead in her tracks. A small black shadow, like that of a little urchin, crouched at the top of the steps, blocking her path.

"Who's there?" she whispered hoarsely. "What do you think you're doing in front of my room?"

"I have been sent as your new servant," the shadow replied. "I have come to serve you."

"I don't recall summoning you. Get out of my way."

"I have some skill as a physician. I was told that you weren't feeling well."

"I have no need of a physician either," Saya replied firmly.

"Really?" The child's tone suddenly changed.

Saya caught her breath in amazement. She had heard that voice before. "Torihiko! Is that really you?" Kneeling down, she could make out his large mouth opened in a grin, and his sparkling acorn eyes. Still she could hardly believe it. This boy always appeared at the most extraordinary times.

"Officially I am your servant, Lady Blue," Torihiko said gaily. "The senior handmaiden told her footman, the footman told the guard, the guard told a servant, and the servant grabbed an appropriate-looking person from outside the gate. It seems that even the notorious palace guard has a few holes in its armor."

"But this is insane!" Her voice rose and she hastily lowered it. "I don't like it. The two of us together—think what would happen if your identity were known. Even if we tell them we are not plotting, no one would believe us. Why did you come? You know how dangerous it is!"

"I came because I am plotting, of course," Torihiko said coolly. "Why are you always so slow? You heard about the Dragon Sword. That sword will determine our fate, so naturally, I want to get it back."

"Well, it has nothing to do with me," Saya said. Then she suddenly stood up, drawing in a sharp breath. "You . . ." she said in a low voice, clenching her fists. "Surely you didn't plan this all along, that I should come unsuspecting to the palace, just so you could get your foot in the door?"

"I thought I told you to remember that this was your own choice," said Torihiko, laughing. Not knowing how to reply to that, she crouched down and looked at him crossly.

"It's all right, Saya. You don't have to do a thing. It's even all right if you love Prince Tsukishiro. You still won't give me away, right?"

She turned away primly. "Don't be so sure. I'm a member of the palace now. Who knows what I will do . . ."

"Are you really happy here, as a handmaiden?" Torihiko asked, his voice suddenly filled with unexpected concern. Once again Saya was unable to reply. Before she could stop them, tears began to flow and she cursed herself, wishing she could do something about this new habit.

Torihiko watched her silently while she struggled to control her weeping, and then said calmly, "Let me speak as a physician, Lady Blue: the primary cause of your melancholy is that for far too long you have lacked contact with the earth, with water, with green and growing plants. You're not the kind of person who can live apart from these things. Like a wild bird in a cage, you will lose the will to live. You have to get outside."

"Yes." She nodded like a little child. "You're right. I've been longing to do all the things they've said I mustn't do. Just now I couldn't control my urge to dive into that pond."

"Then don't try to control it. Go for a swim," Torihiko suggested simply. "It's sticky and humid tonight. A swim would be perfect. I need one, too. I stink of sweat."

Saya's eyes grew round. "But it's the palace pond. You wouldn't dare do such an outrageous thing," she started to protest when suddenly her sense of mischief overcame her. It was the first time in a long while. "But then it's so out of the way that the guards probably wouldn't see us. Maybe no one will ever find out."

"Of course they won't find out. No one here would ever dream of doing such a thing."

At Torihiko's lighthearted urging, Saya jumped to the ground in her bare feet. The familiar sensation of earth against the soles of her feet, the pungent fragrance of grass and trees in the dead of night, and, best of all, the summer darkness wrapped her in a close embrace. There could be no sweeter pleasure than to do what was forbidden. Like a nocturnal creature, she stole through the shadows, suppressing her excitement, until she came to the grove of ancient trees in the depths of the garden. Here, blinded by the darkness, the trees dreamed the dream of a deep mountain forest. Enticed by a gentle breeze, the grove was enveloped in the ancient song of the pine, the long-ago tale of the cedar. The moss on the bank of the pond was warm and damp; it felt as if she were standing on the back of a furry creature. Looking at the moon floating on the water's surface, she laughed aloud.

Torihiko was undressed first. He slid into the pond and parted the water with easy graceful strokes.

"You swim like a frog," Saya commented as she slipped into the water.

The water in the pond was softer than river water and the sensation filled her with exhilaration. She had never swum at night before, but there was no undercurrent and nothing frightening lurked in the water, which seemed to have been cleansed by the moonlight. She swam like a fish, gliding this way and that, forgetting all her cares. She could now laugh at the troubles that she had previously thought would cause her to waste away. Torihiko's appearance seemed another rich joke. Whatever would be would be.

"Wouldn't it be wonderful just to turn into one of the fish in this pond?" she said as she floated on her back. As if in response, a huge carp leaped right beside her. For an instant his scales and fins flashed like silverwork in the moonlight. Saya laughed aloud.

"Did you see that, Torihiko? It was the king of the pond."

"Why don't you give him our greetings? Tell him we apologize for swimming in his pond without asking his leave," Torihiko responded from the far bank. Pretending to obey his command, Saya dived neatly underwater. Naturally, it was dark, but, surprisingly, she could see—or rather, she could see the carp. His body seemed to glow with a faint light. He was magnificent—longer than her arm and fit to be called a king. His whiskers were long, too, and his face seemed very ancient.

She could see all this clearly because he had swum up close to her, apparently curious. He seemed to know no fear. Then, waving his fins in front of her nose, he spoke.

"So I'm not the only one who wishes to become a fish on a summer's night. But if that is your wish, why not turn into a carp? Your body is much too awkward to enjoy swimming properly."

Saya thought it was Torihiko teasing her. In her surprise, she exhaled and had to swim quickly to the surface. When she turned her head, Torihiko was standing on the bank squeezing water from his hair.

"Torihiko!" she screamed without thinking. A sharp stab of fear went through her as she was suddenly pulled under, swallowing a great mouthful of water. If Torihiko had not realized that something was wrong and pulled her out, she would have drowned. When she finally lay clinging to a rock, racked by coughs, a light appeared between the trees. Torihiko started and blinked his eyes in surprise. Two forms stood at the top of the bank: Princess Teruhi, with a torch in her hand, and a manservant carrying a rake.

"I thought I warned you that I would wind a rake in your hair and drag you out," Princess Teruhi said, her voice charged with anger. "Do you wish to drown yourself so badly that you would risk such humiliation?"

"I was just swimming," Saya gasped, still coughing. In her close brush with death, she had mislaid all courtesy. "Get out of my way and let me out please. There's an evil spirit in this pond. Let me out of here."

"Oh-ho! An evil spirit, she says." Princess Teruhi feigned an exaggerated interest, as if baiting her. "You certainly have some nerve to claim that there is an evil spirit in the Mirror Pond, in the very midst of the Palace of Light."

Saya, her coughing finally under control, was slipping on her clothes, her hair streaming with water, but she said defensively, "It's true. A carp came and talked to me. He looked straight at me and asked why I didn't become a fish like him. He said, 'So I'm not the only one who wants to become a fish on a summer's night.'"

The manservant had his back turned to Saya out of propriety, but his shoulders suddenly began to shake. He seemed to be having difficulty suppressing his mirth.

Princess Teruhi, however, did not laugh. Her eyes narrowed for an instant; then, she said casually, "You never cease to entertain us. If you're going to walk around half-asleep, you could at least do it more quietly."

"It wasn't a dream. I would never dream such a crazy thing," Saya said hotly, and then quickly held her tongue as Princess Teruhi's gaze suddenly grew fierce.

"It was a dream. Don't mention it again," the Princess snapped, her voice shaking with anger.

"WHAT ON EARTH could it have been?"

The next morning, Saya still puzzled over it. Her grief and her desire to kill herself seemed unreal now; the evening had ended in farce. Yet, while the longing to die had certainly vanished like a dream, the carp's voice still echoed in her ear. Torihiko, of course, assured her that it had not been he.

"A long time ago, even the trees and the plants could talk, or so they say. But now when there are so few gods left, that's not possible. And I can't imagine that one of the gods could still be alive in the middle of the Palace of Light. This is the last place a god would be."

Torihiko shrugged. "It must have been your imagination, no doubt caused by an empty stomach."

"Even you don't believe me?" Saya said indignantly. But when she thought about it, she was starving. Her appetite seemed to have returned. Once again her normal self, she hurriedly headed for the morning room.

If I hear that voice again, I'll recognize it, she thought.

She continued thinking about it while she ate. It was not an evil voice. Rather, it was a young voice: distinctive, guileless, and, considering that she had heard it for the first time, somehow familiar. *Princess Teruhi behaved strangely. She must have some idea whose voice it was. She knows something. There must be something there.*

chapter three

CHIHAYA

I long to fetch water from the mountain brook,
bedecked with Japanese rose,
but alas for me that I know not
the way which I must go.

— Prince Takechi

Chihaya

"The sacred ritual of purification is essential for the elimination of the evil and defilement that unavoidably cling to those who live upon this impure earth, and for the attainment of heavenly purity. In particular, the great purification ceremony, held twice a year, is essential to cleanse the entire Palace of Light and preserve its honor." The senior handmaiden was instructing a group of five or six younger novices, including Saya.

"On that day the Prince and the Princess, followed by all those in important positions, will assemble beside the Nakase River at the West Gate and wash all defilement into the river. Therefore you must on no account fail in your task. The handmaidens of Princess Teruhi's hall will also be performing the ceremony at the river, so be careful that you do not disgrace us." She placed particular emphasis on the final words. There was considerable rivalry between the attendants of the Prince and the Princess. Although Saya sat respectfully, listening with one ear to the lecture, her mind was wandering.

Princess Teruhi will leave for the battlefield in the west after the end of the month, she thought. *Prince Tsukishiro will be alone. I wonder if his feelings will change once she is far away. Will he be able to turn to me with his whole heart?*

She knew it was useless to hope. But unrequited love means just that: the inability to live without hoping even though one knows it is futile. She realized that she was waiting in anxious anticipation. *I wish the ceremony would come sooner . . .*

Having carefully explained the role that the girls must perform in the ceremony, the senior handmaiden changed her tone of voice. "Do you understand what purity really means? Or what defilement is? As handmaidens, you of all people must grasp the meaning of the bounty bestowed upon us by the illustrious God of Light."

She called on one of the girls to answer. With shining eyes and flushed cheeks, the novice responded readily. "The bounty bestowed by the illustrious God of Light is the transformation of Darkness into Light. Darkness refers to those things which die and decay. The God of Light will descend to purify this earth, which is defiled by Darkness, and to confer eternal life and beauty."

That's the shrine maidens' creed. Even I could have said that, Saya thought. *I've heard it so often this last month that I'm sick of it.*

"Exactly," the senior handmaiden said with a satisfied nod. "The Palace of Light is the only place in all the lands of Toyoashihara that mirrors the purity of heaven. You should not be content merely with having the good fortune to be chosen as handmaidens. If you work even harder at your duties and constantly strive to purify yourselves, someday you may even approach the perfection of the Immortal Children of Light." She placed a hand proudly on her bosom. "Through the blessed bounty of the God of Light, this is my sixty-fourth year of service as a handmaiden."

At this the girls, who had been sitting with eyes cast down, hoping for the lecture to end, raised their heads simultaneously in astonishment, doubting their ears. Saya was no exception. Although she had heard rumors that the senior handmaiden was older than she looked, she could not believe she was that old. Even if she had entered service at the age of fifteen, she should long since have been stooped with age.

The senior handmaiden looked at the girls' amazed expressions with satisfaction and smiled. "You must offer yourselves, both body and soul, in service to the God of Light. Through this the road will be opened to you. First you must strive to purify yourselves from all defilement."

She gave no indication of being past her prime as she swept her train elegantly aside and glided from the room. Cold and rigid as she was, her beauty was unrivaled. The girls gazed after her, dumbfounded. But once she had gone they were released from the spell and immediately gathered together to gossip.

"Is it true? Can we really keep our youth through purification?"

"From what I've heard, it's true. They say there's no rite as terrible as the great purification."

"Terrible?"

"Because of the human sacrifice."

"No!"

"Shhh!" One of the girls put her finger to her lips. "We aren't supposed to talk about it. But they say that the Nakase River is also called the River of Bones. Because ashes and bones are washed away in the river."

"Oh! How horrible!"

"In other words . . ."

The girls who were huddled in a corner of the passageway suddenly fell silent. They had remembered that Saya was there.

"Let's go," one of them said loudly, and, turning cold glances in her direction, they quickly left. Saya was disappointed. She wanted to know the rest of the details. It bothered her that someone was to be sacrificed in the ceremony.

I guess I shouldn't have expected the purification to be a mere ritual like the ceremony at our village festivals. After all, this is the Palace of Light.

While she stood thinking, she heard indignant voices beyond the corner of the passageway. It was the girls who had just left.

"My! Did you see that? The serving boy who just went by?"

"He didn't even bow."

"Whose servant is he? Imagine! He was walking across the bare ground!"

As Saya expected, Torihiko came running into view. His forelock was neatly trimmed and he was dressed in cool blue linen, but the propriety of his outward appearance was marred by the fact that he was cutting across the garden without using the walkway.

"Stop walking across the ground," Saya said with a frown. "Thanks to you, my reputation will be even worse."

Laughing indifferently, Torihiko perched on the railing and perfunctorily slapped the dirt from the soles of his feet. "That would be silly, when there's a good shortcut. It's only fifty-three steps from your room to here. Do you know how I got here?"

How he remembered she could not tell, but within the space of a few days, Torihiko had mastered the entire layout of the enormous palace and flitted about wherever he pleased.

"Let's go back to my room. Along the walkway," Saya said cuttingly. "I have something to say to you."

AFTER CHECKING to see that no one was near, Saya lowered the reed screen over the door and said, "You know about the purification ceremony, don't you?"

"Sure. Just another five days to go." Torihiko sat down on the floor and drew his knees up under his chin.

"Because I'm a handmaiden I'll help perform the ceremony. Purification means to cleanse away the Darkness, you know."

"Yeah."

"Will everything be all right? The entire palace is to be purified."

"There's nothing for you to worry about, Saya. Just do what you would normally do. You have Prince Tsukishiro, and besides, you've never been tainted by the Darkness."

Exasperated, Saya snapped, "It's you I'm talking about, Torihiko. Will you be all right even if you undergo purification? Won't you be found out?"

Torihiko tilted his head and rolled his eyes upward. "Well, now—hmmm. I suppose I wouldn't come out safely. I expect I would be singled out just like a bird who doesn't belong is pecked out of the flock."

"It's no joke. How can you talk about it so lightly!"

He grinned broadly. "I knew I couldn't stay very long in the palace. I'm too conspicuous. Darkness sticks out here like a sore thumb. For the moment, people are merely offended by me, but that won't last long. That's why I have to make my move as soon as possible and finish my business here."

"Your business?"

Torihiko lowered his voice and said, "To retrieve the Dragon Sword."

It isn't just an act. He really is a daredevil, Saya thought. He intended to seize the Sword from the palace all on his own.

"I have a pretty good idea of where it's kept. The palace complex is built with the high tower in the center; Teruhi's hall and Tsukishiro's hall on either side are mirror images. Even the servants' wings are in exactly the same locations. But there is one difference. There's a narrow path leading off from Teruhi's hall. It disappears into a dense grove. I couldn't see where it leads, but according to some people there's a shrine for the God of Light at the end which only the Princess and certain select handmaidens are permitted to enter. That shrine strikes me as suspicious."

"Do you intend to sneak inside?" asked Saya, drawn despite herself into his plan. He raised a thoughtful face.

"Someone must be stilling the Sword. But I haven't yet figured out who it could be. It wouldn't be safe to just leave the Sword lying around. It needs a special priestess to still it. There can't be many who could do it. In fact, I can't believe that there could be one here at all. After all, the Dragon Sword belonged to the people of Darkness for countless generations, and the Priestess of the Sword was always the Water Maiden."

"The Water Maiden?" Saya raised her voice in surprise.

"That's right." Torihiko nodded. "I suppose you wouldn't know, but it's the same sword that the God of Light used to slay the last-born son of our mother, the Goddess. Fury, malice, and damnation were seared into it when it was stained with the blood of the fire god. It's the most fearsome power existing in the world today. The Dragon

Sword owes allegiance to neither the Darkness nor the Light." His eyes glowed with excitement. "In other words, it's the one weapon that could destroy even the God of Light himself."

"But that's extraordinary," Saya whispered. "Who could possibly slay the God of Light?"

Torihiko suddenly shook his head. "You're right. Nobody can touch the Dragon Sword except the Water Maiden. She's the only one who can still the fire god's curse. Even Princess Teruhi had to abduct Princess Sayura, the most recent Water Maiden, along with the Sword in order to take it. That's how Princess Sayura came to Mahoroba."

"Ah, I see," Saya sighed. "So that's how it happened."

"Our people tried to rescue her. But it was no use. Some say that she didn't want to be rescued."

Saya remained silent. She could imagine what the Princess must have felt, yet at the same time she did not want to.

Torihiko scratched his head. "I heard all this from Lady Iwa. She's the only one who remembers everything. For you and me, it all took place in a former life."

"And I . . ." Saya spoke hesitantly. "Do I also have the power to still this terrible Sword?"

"Probably." Torihiko threw her a quick glance. "Are you willing to help me get it back now?"

"Not in the least," Saya retorted. "I would gladly give it away."

"I see. Too bad," he said without a trace of regret. "If that's the case, I'll just have to do what Princess Teruhi did and steal the priestess along with the Sword."

"That's outrageous!" Shivers ran up Saya's spine. He reminded her of the boys in the village who liked to show off by going exploring in the mountains, boasting that they could do the impossible. But in this case, Torihiko's life was at stake.

"Don't underestimate the Palace of Light," she warned him. "For one thing, Princess Teruhi is way out of your league. Give up this foolish idea and get out of here as quickly as you can. If you leave now, you'll make it in time."

"Are you kidding?" Torihiko said teasingly. "I'm doing what I want. Just like you, remember? You're the one who said 'just leave me alone.'"

"But you'll be killed!" Saya found herself shouting.

What he was thinking she could not tell, but his eyes were full of compassion. "Why would someone who belongs to the people of Darkness fear death? Don't worry. I don't intend to throw my life away needlessly."

DON'T WORRY, *he said. How could I not worry?* Saya changed the position of her pillow. No matter how she tried, she could not sleep. The night wore on and a cool breeze blew through the half-open latticed shutters. Shell wind chimes hanging from the eaves made a dry sound as they swayed, faintly disturbing the still darkness. She lay awake anxiously, her eyes wide open, staring up at the darkness where it nestled against the ceiling. She thought she could see the faintly colored, shapeless forms of the dreams of those sleeping in the palace flitting across it. While she followed their aimless paths, she had a sudden shock of realization, as if she had stumbled across a large gaping hole. *Torihiko was lying when he said he wasn't afraid of dying. Not even the people of Darkness could really wish for death.*

The more she thought about it, the stronger her conviction grew. *He came here knowing that the purification ceremony would soon take place. For me, to help me. It was Torihiko who saved me from the shrine maiden's blade. Twice he has pulled me back from death. How foolish of me to forget.*

She chewed her fingernails, stung by remorse.

No matter what he says, I'll make him leave. If I don't, it'll be like standing by and letting him be killed. He may be cheeky, but he's still younger than I. He can't be so eager to die. He can't be indifferent to death.

"LOOK AT THAT. What are they?"

"I don't like it. What could they be up to?"

Once again, Saya heard shocked voices outside her door. Thinking from their disgusted tone that it must have something to do with

Torihiko, she rose and went outside. But the boy was nowhere in sight. Instead, two handmaidens were looking up at a tree in the garden.

"Is something wrong?" Saya asked.

One of them pointed to a red pine. "They've been sitting there like that for over an hour. They were there the last time we passed by, too. They give me the creeps."

"Perhaps it's an omen."

Saya looked up and saw two large crows, black eyes gleaming, perched saucily upon a branch high in the gnarled pine tree. Then, as if they could understand what the frowning handmaidens were saying, they suddenly began to screech. Their voices were hoarse and menacing and the two girls jumped in fright and fled. Saya remained staring at the crows. Although she could not have told one crow from another, they just might be . . .

"Sa-ya," they croaked.

Looking about quickly in consternation, she ordered them to hush. "You're Little Black and Big Black, aren't you? You can't stay here."

But the two crows ignored her and flew happily to the boxwood tree in front of the eaves. Saya stepped back. Up close, they looked huge and their sharp beaks were frightening.

"Food," they cried somewhat plaintively.

"Get some from Torihiko. Go on now," Saya said severely.

But they bobbed their heads up and down as if trying desperately to shake out the words. Finally, one of them croaked, "No food."

"He won't give you any? Did you do something bad?"

"No food."

"None."

They shook their wings, disgruntled. Saya tried to think of something handy to feed them, but just then, she heard voices behind her. It sounded like the two handmaidens had brought a guard.

"Over there. Shoot them. Quickly."

Saya waved her hands frantically at the crows. "Shoo! Go on now! Hurry!"

Beating their wings, Big Black and Little Black took to the air.

By the time the guard with his bow and arrow turned the corner, the two birds had flown over the roof.

That's strange, thought Saya. *Come to think of it, I haven't seen Torihiko since yesterday* . . .

For the rest of the day, she waited for him to come, but it was no use. When the sun began to set, she made up her mind to go to the senior handmaiden.

"My servant hasn't appeared since last night. Has something happened to him?"

The senior handmaiden was untying a scroll by the light of a lamp and she did not bother to look at Saya. "What are you babbling about?"

"I can't find my servant," Saya persisted.

The older woman rested the scroll on her knees and looked over her shoulder coldly. "Is that so?" she said in an expressionless tone. "Then let us summon another as soon as possible."

"Has something happened to Torihiko?" Without realizing it, her tone of voice had become harsh.

The senior handmaiden fixed Saya with a haughty stare and replied, "Such shameful behavior. What are we to do if someone who claims to be a handmaiden makes such a fuss about a servant or two? It seems that you didn't listen carefully enough to my instructions. I thought I told you exactly how the sacrifice must be made for the purification ceremony."

"I did listen carefully," Saya replied. "The purification rite transfers all defilement to the sacrificial offering, which is then placed within a metal cage, and after cleansing by fire, it is washed away in the river. I know the procedure. But what I want to know is—"

"Exactly. That is the answer to your question," the senior handmaiden interjected. "He has been chosen as the sacrificial offering by Her Highness, Princess Teruhi."

Saya stood with her mouth agape, unable to utter a word. As the meaning gradually penetrated her mind, the blood drained from her face. "But that–that's—"

"It is not permissible to speak of it," the senior handmaiden admonished her sternly. "You have no right whatsoever to complain. All servants of the palace dedicate themselves body and soul to Their Royal Highnesses. You must realize that those who are chosen, despite their lowly birth, are gloriously honored." She picked up the scroll once more. "You may leave. And do not trouble me any further."

ALTHOUGH THE WOMAN had turned away, Saya could not leave. Struggling to calm her turmoil, she asked, "Where is he? The one chosen for the sacrifice?"

The senior handmaiden turned her head to reveal a look of undisguised contempt. The deep cleft between her brows marred her face with the startling ugliness of age. "Are you deaf?"

Saya could do nothing but retreat under that threatening glare. With her head reeling, she staggered out into the outer passageway. She grasped the railing and fought down her horror.

What a terrible place I have come to. The palace is a dreadful place— a dreadful place.

While listening to the procedures for the sacrifice, she had thought that the purification ritual was perfectly normal. Even the references to a human sacrifice had not concerned her much until Torihiko had been selected as the victim. But now she understood: the true role of the handmaiden was to transfer defilement to another human being, to burn that person alive, and to wash their remains into the river! This was how the purity of the palace had been maintained twice a year for countless generations.

I'll be killing Torihiko with my own hands.

At this thought she groaned in despair. Prince Tsukishiro's hall, shielded by a fence, towered in front of her, its ornamental crossbeams soaring against the red evening sky. The senior handmaiden's room was the closest of the attendants' quarters to the Prince's hall. Staring across at it, Saya felt that the tall, black fence that rose between her and the Prince had never been so high.

"I have to find out where Torihiko is. I just have to."

It was time for the evening meal. She decided to make her way to the kitchens around the back. The servants gathered in the courtyard to the north of this building to take their supper. Thick clouds of steam and heat billowed from the earthen-floored kitchens where the sweat-drenched cooks labored beneath soot-blackened beams. Saya was astonished at the size of the ovens and pots used to feed the palace. Many servants were gathered around an enormous pot ladling out rice stewed with vegetables and various other things into large bowls. The child servants were eating the same fare, and they cradled their bowls carefully as they escaped into the cool back garden. Table manners were unknown and no one scolded them. Filled with the friendly clamor of people enjoying their meal, the place was in a lively uproar. To Saya, the food looked much more appetizing than what the handmaidens ate. It was like what she had eaten at home in Hashiba.

Catching sight of a group of boys sitting on some rocks shoveling food into their mouths, she walked toward them. She was sure they must know Torihiko.

"Have you seen Torihiko?"

One of the boys raised his face to look at her and almost spilled the contents of his bowl at the sight of a long-robed handmaiden standing before him. "Nah. I dunno—I mean, he has not yet arrived, ma'am."

"Stupid. He won't never come," the boy beside him muttered.

"Oh, right. I forgot."

"He's probably being made to clean the shrine in punishment."

Saya, feigning ignorance, asked, "Why won't he come?"

"Someone from Princess Teruhi's hall took him away. I think there was some complaint. He was always wandering around that place even when he had no business there."

Across from Saya, one boy whispered to another, "He boasted that he would sneak into the shrine. If Her Highness knew that, he'd get a hundred lashes."

The boys knew nothing of the sacrifice. Saya felt a pang of sorrow.

Who would ever tell them? If they knew that one of their friends was to be burned alive, they would not continue to serve here.

Leaving the kitchens behind, she felt a faint spark of anger kindle in her breast. This was not a childish anger, flaring and fading with her changing moods, such as she had known before. It was the first true anger that she had ever felt.

THE LADY-IN-WAITING appeared in her room and knelt before her, saying, "I have come to accompany you."

Saya was startled but immediately bit her lip and said, "I am ready."

The lady-in-waiting drew in her chin, faintly surprised by Saya's tone. "Is something wrong?"

"No. Nothing," Saya replied flatly, and saw a vexed expression cross the other's face. Tonight Saya had the advantage. She was not to be trifled with by the likes of this woman. The two passed wordlessly along the corridors.

"I have brought Lady Blue," the lady-in-waiting announced through the door and then withdrew.

Saya stepped forward, knelt down, and, placing both hands on the floor before her, bowed low.

Laughter broke the silence. Saya raised her face and saw Princess Teruhi at Prince Tsukishiro's side, leaning languidly toward him.

"I was curious to see what face you would wear tonight," she said with a mocking laugh. "You have spirit at least, and that's something. I hate whimpering."

Saya cast her eyes down demurely but felt a sudden hostility within her. After all, didn't Princess Teruhi always come between her brother and Saya? Every time Saya had been summoned to his hall it was so.

"Your Highness," she said, turning to Prince Tsukishiro. Unlike his sister, the Prince did not mock her but, rather, seemed sympathetic.

"Come," he commanded, and Saya approached him, deliberately choosing the side opposite to Princess Teruhi. "I have heard that your servant has been chosen as the sacrifice. However, you must surely know the reason for this choice."

Saya's fingertips, placed decorously before her on the floor, trembled. But she said in a brave voice, "I intended to dismiss him this very day. I won't allow him to come near the palace again. So please, grant him your pardon."

"Do you really believe such a thing is possible?"

Saya looked squarely at Prince Tsukishiro. "Yes, I do. Like the shadow of an insect straying within these walls, he is unworthy of your notice. It is possible for you to overlook him, just as you allowed me to enter this palace."

Prince Tsukishiro laughed wryly. "That you can say such a thing so innocently is very fetching. But it is not possible to free the sacrifice. You must be purified."

He checked her as she was about to speak. "This is your test. As long as you remain attached to that servant, you cannot be cleansed of Darkness. By completing the purification ceremony in public, you will become a true handmaiden and attain your rightful station."

Throughout, his voice remained gentle. "I intend to make you my bride. This is permitted to a handmaiden. Once the end of the month has passed, we will have a formal ceremony. Your station will exceed even that of the senior handmaiden."

Saya was speechless with astonishment. "I—you mean me?"

"Is it not to your liking?"

"But I am not qualified."

Prince Tsukishiro gave her a captivating smile. "Once again you protest. Yet you are the unrivaled princess and priestess of your own people."

She could not tell him that she protested because she did not believe he loved her enough to become his wife. It was no ordinary man but the Prince of Light who was asking her to be his bride. And, she thought gloomily, what sacrifice might she have disregarded had his gaze been only for her?

"She will surely reject your offer," Princess Teruhi said, gazing around the Prince's shoulder at Saya. "The people of Darkness are always more concerned for their comrades than for themselves. If her friend is killed, she will never open her heart to you again."

Prince Tsukishiro said without looking at her, "Teruhi, Saya and Sayura are different. Saya is a child of Hashiba. She is not kin to Darkness."

"Don't be ridiculous."

"I am a child of Hashiba," Saya said, contemplating the words. "My father told me to take pride in that. And I intend to do so."

Prince Tsukishiro nodded. "That is best. Be purified. As a child of Hashiba, as one of the people of Light. And your undefiled youth will last longer than that of any other."

Princess Teruhi looked at Saya like a cat teasing a mouse. "Tonight the moon rises late. It's a fleeting summer's night," she said brightly. "I shall stay here till daybreak and talk the night away. Handmaiden, you may leave us. I summoned you merely to see if you wore a tearstained face. You had best strive to cleanse yourself of defilement. If you understand, then go. Inform my servants that I won't be returning to my hall tonight."

Saya bowed, her face as rigid as stone. "I beg leave to depart."

When she had fled from the room, Prince Tsukishiro looked reproachfully at Princess Teruhi. "Was that spite? You are unkind."

"To take one such as her for your bride dishonors the name of the Palace of Light," Princess Teruhi retorted angrily.

Prince Tsukishiro laughed and shook his head, then took the glass flask and poured some sake into his sister's cup.

"Sister, do you not see that this is one way to destroy an enemy? Think what a blow it will be to the forces of Darkness if I make the Water Maiden mine. You wish to kill her, but if you do, she will only return to the Darkness and be reborn again. Instead, I would protect and nurture her innate attraction to the Light."

"Well, after all, I'm just a woman whose sole talent is destruction," Princess Teruhi replied sarcastically, turning away. "Anyway, the trap is set. If she shows her true colors as one of the people of Darkness, I will brook no argument from you. I'll throw her into the iron cage along with the sacrifice and burn them both alive. That way I will feel much easier about leaving for the campaign in the west."

"Well, it doesn't matter." Prince Tsukishiro raised his cup slightly. "I can't argue with you. Not if you really intend to spend the night here."

"Of course. Do you think I would fight with you?" Princess Teruhi replied and, gazing at the Prince, suddenly gave a carefree laugh. "We should be able to pass the night without quarreling. For the end of the month draws near."

"Yes, the end of the month draws near," Prince Tsukishiro repeated. "The moonless, sunless night, the night that comes but once a month to our shining palace."

Hearing the concealed hope in his voice, Princess Teruhi grinned rakishly. For a brief moment his concern conveyed to her the fragrance of falling blossoms. Stretching out a graceful arm, she caressed his cheek with her hand, and placed her lips, which carried her sweet breath, upon his.

2

SAYA was so furious that she felt like kicking something as she walked along the passageways. Princess Teruhi toyed with her heart as with a bauble. *"Inform my servants," she says. Does she think she can use me as she pleases? I'm not her servant. I'll go back to my room and sleep.*

But as she walked, her initial anger cooled and changed to an aching pain that snaked its way through her. Strangely enough, it was not the malicious words of Princess Teruhi that had wounded her, but rather Prince Tsukishiro's proposal to make her his bride. It had been her greatest wish, although she had scarcely dared to dream of it. If only it could have been achieved by any other means.

Yet she still believed in the righteousness of the immortal Children of Light, and could not stop worshipping them. Their splendor remained unclouded, and even their brutality, their complete disregard for other lives, was pure. For them, human sacrifice was as simple an act as wiping the dust from one's chair before sitting down, and they probably viewed the total extermination of the people of Darkness in the same way. They felt neither rancor nor prejudice. But for the same reason they could never feel any love for the creatures of the earth. Never.

Or for me either. Even if his intention to make me his bride is sincere.

Although it was painful to acknowledge, she could no longer deny it. Now when she imagined herself as Prince Tsukishiro's wife she felt chilled to the bottom of her soul.

Is that really what it means to be purified?

Despondent, she entered her room. The light was out and it was pitch-dark. She fumbled about for the lamp and took the flints out of the box beside it. But as she was about to strike them together, she stopped. In the darkness, Torihiko's face came vividly to mind, as did his mocking laugh, his affectionate gaze, the nimble movements of his childlike limbs. She remembered his face the time he had snatched her green belt from the river, his easy stroke when swimming in the moonlit pond. Even if the supreme God of Heaven had commanded that these things should be erased from the face of the earth, how could she not oppose it? Torihiko was someone she knew, someone whose blood pulsed in his veins, who lived, who raised his voice in laughter.

If to be like the immortal Children of Light means to forget Torihiko, to be indifferent to these things, then I can't do it. If I do, the Saya that I know will die, too. I can't be purified. I belong—to the people of Darkness.

Without realizing it, her hands, which gripped the flints, had fallen to her sides. Her knees buckled, and she sank to the floor. She was stunned and asked her heart once more to be sure. But the answer was clear, intensified by its release from long restraint.

I belong to the people of Darkness.

She could not help but feel sorry for herself, a fledgling who had seared its wings trying to soar to the moon, but the knowledge that there was something she must do brought her strength. Quietly replacing the flints in their box, she thought carefully. *If I don't light the lamp, everyone will think that I'm still at the hall. If I'm to do anything, it must be now. Tomorrow the three days of purification will begin and the guard about the palace will become even tighter.*

Torihiko must be held in the shrine he had told her about. She could not think of any other place he might be. Fortunately, Princess Teruhi was far away in the Prince's hall . . .

Saya felt a twinge of doubt. Had Princess Teruhi purposely emphasized the point that she would stay there? Was it a trap?

I can only try it and see.

Once roused, she could not imagine being able to sleep. She took out a long dark purple cloak from the chest of drawers in the corner and, wrapping it about her, stole carefully out of the room.

THE RUSTLING OF THE CLOAK against her skirt, which she usually never noticed, made her nervous. Although she regretted wearing it, it was too late now. Once past the high wooden tower, she was in unknown territory. The palace grounds were strictly divided into Princess Teruhi's in the east and Prince Tsukishiro's in the west. Although the handmaidens lorded it over others within their own area, one step outside and they would be regarded with glances colder than those given the servants. She knew the layout of the two halls was identical, but lacking Torihiko's sense of direction, she frequently had to stop and think. She also had to take care that she did not cross the path of the palace guards who patrolled the gardens.

Still, she felt little fear of danger. This was partly due to her excitement, and partly to her realization that the dark was her ally. In fact, she should have understood this the night she swam in the pond. Despite the darkness, her sight had remained keen, and even the blackness into which shadows seemed to melt had not frightened her. When she was a child, her parents had warned her not to go out at night because an unknown demon lived in the dark, and she had been afraid. But now, knowing that only she herself was concealed by the darkness, the black curtain of night was a friendly robe that protected and enveloped her—a robe as light as wings. As she became accustomed to the dark, she also became extremely sensitive to light, always noticing the guards with their torches before they saw her. With each encounter, her confidence increased.

Torihiko used to sneak about just like this. Now she could understand why. Although she felt slightly uneasy, she could not deny that she also felt a thrill of pleasure.

She made her way undetected to Princess Teruhi's hall. Skirting the familiar handmaidens' quarters, she climbed over a hedge and came out behind the hall. There she soon ran into a wooden fence more than twice as tall as she. It was solid, built without a single crack between the boards, and surrounded a large area. She was sure that the shrine must be inside. She walked alongside it until she came to the rear of the enclosure, but her heart sank when she saw the entrance. A bright watch fire burned near the gate, which was bolted with a heavy bar, and two guards bearing spears stood motionless before it as though rooted to the spot.

She hid in the nearby bushes and stared at the gate for a while, but finally turned away, realizing that even if she stayed here all night, there was nothing she could do. It would be impossible to sneak in without some sort of plan. Cursing herself for her lack of foresight, Saya had retraced her steps to the hedge in the garden near the handmaidens' quarters when she suddenly froze in her tracks. Someone else was moving about without a light in the middle of the night. And there was more than one.

Have they seen me? she wondered.

For the first time that night she felt the cold sweat of fear, and she concealed herself under the hedge, pulling her cloak about her. The figures in the darkness continued on, however, showing no sign of looking for someone. Soon they stopped and gathered together to perform some task. It was not hard for Saya to guess what they were doing. The dry scraping sound of a bucket and the muffled sound of water deep underground echoed in the stillness of the night. A well. They were gathered around a well and were drawing water with awkward, jerky movements. To judge from their laborious efforts and their shapes, they were quite old. Curious, Saya drew a little closer, following along the hedge. As she had suspected, they were three old, hunchbacked women.

They poured the water into an earthenware jar until one of them whispered hoarsely, "That's enough. It's overflowing."

"Oh, already?" another exclaimed in surprise, dropping the bucket to the bottom of the well with a loud clatter.

"The water of the star well must not be carelessly wasted."

"It was just a little."

Yet another of the women gave a deep sigh. "Hasn't Her Highness returned?"

"Not yet. Tonight we must carry the water."

"Won't she come back?" the woman lamented. "It seems to me that we are not equal to the task at our age. It's difficult for these old bones to climb those steps."

"I wonder if the one within will struggle tonight."

"Those bonds cannot possibly be broken. Her Highness has tied them with great care."

"But still . . ."

"The poor thing. Our blindness is a blessing."

One of the women picked up the water jar. "Well, the water is drawn. It's time to go to the shrine."

Saya's heart began to pound violently. These old women must be the handmaidens who were permitted to enter the shrine with Princess Teruhi. Although she was amazed to see anyone so aged and decrepit within the palace, she was even more surprised that all three of them were blind. The very existence of such women came as a shock, for she had grown used to the fact that all the inhabitants of the palace down to the lowest servant were perfect in face and form. Whether the old women had lost their sight in order to be allowed to enter the shrine or had been specially selected because of their blindness, she did not know, but it was obvious that the shrine was extraordinarily sacrosanct.

Staring after them as they returned to their quarters tapping their canes along the ground, Saya racked her brains.

How can I get in?

A SHORT WHILE LATER the old women reappeared. This time all three were wrapped in long white shroudlike garments. The cloth covered their heads, and a fold at the front concealed even their faces. Only their canes protruded from the front of their garments. They looked like white pillars of cloth feeling their way along. Darkness made no difference to them. From the confidence in their steps, Saya suspected that they had walked this path for countless decades. When she saw that the procession was heading for the wooden gate out of the garden, she crept under the bottom of the hedge and waited beside it. One woman and then another passed directly in front of her. The last, weighed down by the water jar, was slightly slower than the others. Saya reach out her hand and deftly hooked the hem of her garment with her finger. The woman, who held the water jar in one hand and her cane in the other, was unable to restrain a cry of dismay when she felt her wrap slipping.

"What's wrong?" The two women in front halted.

"Nothing, nothing. Don't trouble yourselves. I just caught my hem on a branch sticking out of the hedge. It seems that the gardener hasn't been doing his job," the last priestess said in some embarrassment. "You go on ahead and have them open the gate of the shrine. I'll soon catch up."

The two continued on while the remaining handmaiden set down her water jar and stooped to gather her wrap. There was no time to hesitate. Biting her lip, Saya raised her arm high and brought her fist down upon the nape of the woman's withered neck. It was a trick that she had learned in the days when she had played with the village boys, guaranteed to make an opponent's head swim without inflicting any real injury. As she had never had a chance to use it in a real fight, she had no idea that it would be so effective. The old woman sank to the ground without a murmur. It was almost shamefully easy.

I'm sorry. Saya apologized silently. She swiftly dragged the woman through the wooden gate and, laying her in the shadows as comfortably as possible, covered her with her cloak. She then wrapped herself in the handmaiden's shroud, picked up the cane and the water jar, and hurried to the shrine enclosure.

The first two women were already waiting there. The gate was open. Saya approached them in a cold sweat, taking great pains to mimic the gait of an old woman, but it seemed that her efforts were unnecessary. As soon as they saw her cane the guards at the gate bowed respectfully and let her inside without question. To her relief, they did not attempt to touch her. She crossed the threshold and stepped within the shrine enclosure.

Inside, the grounds were paved with round white pebbles, uniform in size. They glowed faintly in the starlight, making the area appear even larger than it actually was. Amazed at her own boldness, Saya stole surreptitious glances at the sacred precincts from the shadow of her wrap, her eyes full of wonder. The shrine stood at the far end, its side facing her, with several small storehouses nearby. Behind it rose a dark grove of cedars, their sharply pointed tips thrusting up into the night sky. A cool breeze carried their tangy fragrance along with the wild perfume of honeysuckle. Saya thought that the shrine must be located near the foot of the mountains. The sanctity of this spot was intense, even within the Palace of Light. It was as if the Milky Way had descended into the depths of the night to create the white emptiness of the garden upon which the shrine stood. The sound of the handmaidens' regular footsteps on the smooth pebbles dissolved into the rising stillness. Saya shuddered, filled with uneasiness, a feeling that she would never be able to return again to where she had come from. The water jar was heavy in her arms, and the water slopped up and down, setting her nerves on edge.

The procession finally reached the shrine. The building appeared small to one used to the large buildings of Mahoroba. But it was tall for its size and the floor was raised high off the ground like a granary. A grown man could easily have walked between the round columns under the floor. The space beneath the building was as spotless as the garden, and the central column was encircled by a rope of braided straw and surrounded by sakaki branches set in the ground. Double doors were set into one end of the shrine and a single, treacherous-looking ladder led up to them. The ladder was just a narrow log not even the width of her foot, and shallow notches provided the only footholds. And of course there was no handrail. The women stood side by side at the bottom of the ladder and prayed soundlessly. Casting a sideways glance in their direction, Saya mimicked them. After standing this way for some time, one of them said, "You must not be afraid. As Her Highness is not here, it is you who must take the water inside."

"Do not fail in your duty," the other added.

At last Saya realized that she alone was expected to perform the acrobatic feat of walking up the log. She stepped forward, wondering how on earth a blind old woman carrying a swaying water jar could possibly do it. One slip of her foot and she would fall. She swallowed hard as she looked up its length, then, summoning her courage, she pulled up the hem of her shroud and placed her foot upon the log. All she had to do was make it to the top without falling. It was a question of doing it before she lost her nerve.

She did not fall. She lurched and swayed, but somehow she made it. The doors were made of unvarnished wood studded with rivets, like the palace doors. She pushed against them with the force of her ascent and they opened without a sound, as if beckoning her within.

The bright light of torches struck her eyes. Torches in iron brackets, burning with an intensity too great for mere illumination, were ranged in two rows stretching to the far end of the shrine. Raising her eyes, she saw high ceiling beams blackened with soot, while the floor beneath her feet was so smoothly polished that she could see her reflection. She frowned, struck by a strange uneasiness. She felt that somehow this had all happened before.

But that can't be.

She closed the door and began walking cautiously. The farther she went, the more her uncertainty about herself and her surroundings increased. She felt as though she were walking on a cloud. Her shadow, summoned by the light of the torches, fled before and after her, whispering, and she was afraid that if she stopped to listen, she would lose her mind.

Get a grip on yourself. What did you come here for? Wasn't it to rescue Torihiko? she remonstrated with herself. But at that very moment she saw before her a brilliantly shining altar . . . a forest of sakaki branches placed as offerings . . . snow-white paper streamers . . . and a white cedar altar gleaming as bright as day. Saya caught her breath and stood riveted to the spot, memory flooding back.

It's the altar from my dream. This is where I meet the shrine maiden.

A quiet terror crept up through the soles of her feet, and she began to shake as if with fever. It was a fear the very quietness of which seemed to push her to the brink of insanity. Her reason, no longer to be governed, fled, and Saya was suddenly a girl of six again. Her rigid body refused to move. And there before her very eyes, like a dream come to life, was her worst nightmare, her greatest fear: a white-robed, black-haired shrine maiden kneeling before the altar with her back to Saya. This time, surely, it was a dream from which she would never wake again . . .

3

FOR AN INSTANT Saya must have lost consciousness. The clay jar slipped from her arms and shattered as it hit the floor, drenching her from the knees down. The cold shock of the water jolted her back to her senses. She was suddenly aware that this was no dream and remembered what she was doing. Hastily stepping out of the puddle, she raised her eyes and met the gaze of the shrine maiden, who had turned around to look at her.

You see, Saya told herself calmly. *She has a shadow. She's human. Now, what were you so afraid of?*

There was certainly nothing threatening about the girl who stared up at her. She looked to be about Saya's age, and although she was clothed in pure white, and had long, glossy black hair like the maiden in Saya's dream, her face held nothing but innocent surprise. Nor did she seem in the least suspicious of this intruder. She was, however, just as beautiful as the dream had suggested. Taller than Saya, she was endowed with a refined elegance, and her slender face was exceptionally comely. Her clear, dark eyes seemed tinged with sadness. A thick hemp rope bound her hands and feet. Incredulously, Saya's eyes followed the rope to where the girl's feet were tethered to a pillar. She was a prisoner. The old women had not been talking about Torihiko after all.

The white-robed maiden did not seem to be troubled by her plight. Instead, she stared guilelessly at Saya. Finally she spoke. "These days I find it difficult to distinguish between dream and reality. I feel I've met you somewhere before, but where could it have been?"

Saya uttered a cry. "I know that voice. So it was you!" It was one she would never forget—the voice of the carp that had talked to her in the pond that night. "You're the one who pretended to be a fish and talked to me, aren't you? Thanks to you, I almost drowned!"

"Oh, yes!" The girl's face lit up in a smile of recognition. "I met you in the Mirror Pond, the night I dreamed I was a carp. You were swimming there, too."

Overcome with curiosity, Saya went right up to her, knelt down and peered into her face.

"Who on earth are you?" she demanded.

"I am Chihaya," the girl replied. "The third-born child of the God of Light. The last of the immortals."

Saya blinked in surprise. No one knew of any immortal children besides Princess Teruhi and Prince Tsukishiro, although, thinking back, she remembered that Princess Teruhi had mentioned something about another sibling. Still, it was incredible. Deep within the palace grounds lived an immortal whom no one had ever heard about. And this one was bound!

"Why are you tied up like that?"

"You mean these?" Chihaya replied, completely unperturbed. "My sister tied these knots for me. Because I dream. While I dream, my body must be kept here."

"Dream? You mean the carp dream?"

"Yes, a carp or whatever. I can become anything—a bird, an insect, a furred creature. My sister never lets me outside because I'm a disgrace to my family. So instead I learned to pass the time this way." There was no resentment or discontent in her voice, only a hint of resigned loneliness.

Now I see, Saya thought as she listened. *Her voice sounds like Prince Tsukishiro's. That's why I thought I recognized it the first time I heard it.*

This also explained her exquisite beauty. Yet she lacked the powerful, commanding presence that characterized her brother and sister. Instead she appeared very young and forlorn.

"But my sister doesn't like my dreaming, either," Chihaya continued. "Although I suppose that's to be expected, because it seems to cause so much trouble. I don't know what happens when I dream, but when I see how the handmaidens fear me, I assume that I must look like I've gone crazy." She tilted her head and said thoughtfully, "Or perhaps I'm insane to start with. I'm not really sure."

She spoke with such indifference and lack of self-pity that Saya was drawn to her.

"You look perfectly sane to me," she said sympathetically. "If you took off those ropes and went outside, you would look even saner."

Chihaya's eyes grew wide with surprise. "What a funny thing to say. And who are you, who says such things?"

"I'm Saya, one of your brother's handmaidens," she replied with a hint of irony directed at herself.

"Saya," Chihaya repeated, as if testing the sound. "Saya, you remind me of my sister."

Saya looked at her in astonishment. "What makes you say that?"

"You aren't an old woman," she answered innocently.

Saya's expression relaxed. "I see. You don't know very much, do you?"

"Maybe not. Although when it comes to things experienced outside this body, I know more."

Saya could not decide whether to confide in her or not. Despite the fact that she was an immortal Child of Light and seemed to lack common sense, Chihaya did not seem to be an enemy. No matter what Saya did, it would make little difference—she would still be in danger. Mustering her courage, she began. "Actually . . . I came here looking for my servant. He was taken away as a sacrifice for the purification ceremony. I'm sure he's in here somewhere. You don't happen to know where, do you? He's my friend, the boy who was swimming with me in the pond. Won't you tell me where he is?"

"The sacrifice isn't kept here; it's kept at the West Gate," Chihaya replied readily. "There's a small iron cage called the Hut of Abomination beside the river just in front of the West Gate. I saw it clearly when I flew over the river as a bird this morning. That's where your servant is."

"The West Gate!" Saya exclaimed and then quickly lowered her voice. She wanted to protest, to tell her she must be wrong. But she realized that no one had told her Torihiko was in the shrine. She had simply assumed that for a variety of reasons. Thinking about it objectively, it was obvious that a sacrifice would be too defiled to enter a shrine and would be kept where the ceremony was to take place. She cursed her stupidity. But it was too late to gnash her teeth or weep. The West Gate was at the opposite end of the palace from the shrine that she had so painstakingly entered.

So I did all this for nothing. How could I be so stupid!

Dismayed, she buried her head in her hands. Chihaya looked at her curiously. "Why would you want to see your servant this late at night?"

"I belong to the people of Darkness," Saya replied, reckless in her despair. "So does that boy, Torihiko. I can't let him be killed. I have to save him, but I'm such an idiot, I've come to the wrong place."

"You mean the people who serve Mitsuha, the Goddess of Darkness?" Chihaya asked without any hesitation. Saya stared at her in amazement. Even in Hashiba, it was taboo to refer to the Goddess by name. She would never have dreamed that the Goddess's honorific title would be mentioned in such a sacred place as this.

"Well, you've just added one more thing to the list of what needs to be cleansed in this palace," Saya said. This made Chihaya laugh.

"Me? Be purified? My sister would faint from shock."

Saya snorted. "Princess Teruhi faint? Now, that I'd like to see, if only it were possible."

She stood up. Time was swiftly passing while she sat here. Even if the effort were wasted, she could not bear to spend the rest of the night doing nothing.

"I'm going to the West Gate to see," she said. "Although there's little hope, I must do what I can. One of the people of Darkness called me heartless. Now I know that he was right."

"I'm sorry I can't help you," Chihaya said placidly yet sincerely. "All I have is the knowledge of my dreams. Now if you were a mouse, I could tell you the fastest way to the West Gate."

Saya smiled. "Thank you. I wish I were a mouse and could speed under the floors and scurry up the walls. Then I could rescue Torihiko without anyone ever knowing."

Chihaya's reply surprised her. "Have you ever tried to become one?"

"No."

"You might be able to if you tried."

Saya, who had already turned to leave, looked back at her. "I'm not like you. It's not something I can do just by willing it."

"Are you sure?" Chihaya asked. Saya was nonplussed. "That night in the pond, you were already half fish. That's why I was curious and spoke to you. You could even hear my voice, despite the fact that I was a fish. The other handmaidens can't do that."

"But," Saya murmured, blushing as she remembered, "but it's impossible. I don't know how."

"Maybe I can teach you."

She looked hard at Chihaya's tranquil face. And as she looked, she began to feel that they were not so different after all. If anything, Chihaya's idea was no crazier than the one of leaving the shrine and making her way across the entire palace. Inspired, she sat down. "Then teach me. I'll try anything."

SAYA STARED at a young gray mouse that Chihaya had summoned. It seemed bewildered to find itself sitting there on the bright floor for no apparent reason.

"Engrave the image of this mouse in your mind so that you don't lose the way back to your soul," Chihaya said. "Then close your eyes and leave. Your body will stay here while you catch the mouse. Returning is much easier than leaving so you don't have to worry about the rest. I'll take care of your body while you're gone. Now, you must be decisive. You can't leave your body if you haven't made up your mind to do it."

Saya closed her eyes and imagined herself standing before a notched log like the one she had climbed to enter the shrine. She felt herself traversing the narrow beam without the aid of a handrail. Someone, however, was kindly supporting her, urging her along—probably Chihaya.

Oh, I know. I know how to do it.

She had to find the place where her soul waited, longing for release, and open the door to set it free. Exhilarated, she leaped into space. And with a little help from Chihaya, she slipped inside the mouse.

At first it was so strange that she thought she wouldn't be able to stand it. She could not see any of the things that she should be able to see. But that was only natural, because from a mouse's perspective, Chihaya's face was far in the distance. On the other hand, her sense of smell was exceptionally keen, informing her that there were two creatures looming like small hills nearby. She had to run about a bit to calm down.

From somewhere far above her, she heard Chihaya exclaim with delight, "So you did it! I thought you would." This helped her bring herself under control. Recalling that time was running out, she ran through a hole in the wall, slipped under the floor, and sped to the West Gate along the path that Chihaya had carefully described to her.

Several times she ran into other mice along the way, but whenever they saw her they shrank back and made room for her to pass, as if afraid. Despite the borrowed body, she was still Saya, and apparently other mice could tell the difference. Perhaps she looked like one possessed by some evil spirit. But, racing as she was against time, this was fortunate. She ran as fast as her little mouse legs could carry her, stopping only to sniff out the proper direction.

At last, the air began to smell damp. She sensed a large amount of water flowing beyond the palisade: a river—the Nakase River, winding alongside the West Gate and then snaking south. The mouse's sensitive nose could detect even the river's width and the speed at which it flowed. It was almost as if she were seeing it. She was nearly at the gate. Grateful that the mouse still had energy to spare, Saya ran under the palisade and scurried into the brush on the riverbank. At the bottom of the bindweed-covered slope was the wide riverbank where the ceremony would be held. It was cordoned off with braided rope, and numerous watch fires burned around it. The place was thick with guards.

To her frustration, she could not get a clear view due to the mouse's nearsighted vision, but she sensed that the Hut of Abomination was in the center of a circle of lights. She boldly approached it. The shadows of the stones along the riverbank concealed her gray fur. Although she passed by the feet of one of the guards, he did not even notice her.

So this is the Hut of Abomination.

She raised her head and wiggled her long whiskers. It was a small structure covered with tightly woven bark and straw, and from the outside appeared somewhat similar to the birthing huts in the villages of Hashiba made for women in labor. But a pungent metallic stench told of the cold iron beneath the straw. A thin string hung with tiny gold bells, like the ones Teruhi wore on her trouser garters, was strung round the hut, tied to sticks driven into the ground. It resembled a bird rattle set out in the rice fields in fall to chase away sparrows. Ignoring it, Saya passed underneath but, without her even touching it, the bells began vibrating, making a faint but clear sound. Immediately, someone shouted, "On your guard, men! Some evil has entered here."

Saya's heart skipped a beat and she jumped in panic, scurrying to hide within the nearest shadow. Only then did she realize that she had run under a long robe worn by a priest who sat perched on a folding stool. She could smell his bony, old ankle right beside her.

"But, sir, we saw no one."

"I know what I'm talking about," the man sheltering Saya replied.

"Search the entire vicinity. Someone must be hiding nearby. In the name of Her Highness, search every shadow. Nothing must stop the purification ceremony."

Saya calmed her racing heart. *Thank goodness,* she thought. The old priest ordered the others about while he himself remained seated and showed no sign of budging. It never occurred to him that the intruder might be concealed under his hem. While he glared dourly under lowered brows toward the gate, she slipped out behind him and scrambled up the wall of the hut.

As she parted the straw and squirmed her way through, her feet touched iron bars. It was indeed a merciless cage. The sacrifice would remain trapped within while he was burned alive. Just the thought of it made her hair stand on end. It was pitch-black inside, but she could still make out a huddled human form.

"Torihiko! Torihiko!" she shouted loudly, except that she did not seem to use the creature's mouth, but rather called him from some other place. He responded immediately. Raising his face from the ground, he peered around in search of her.

"Saya?" he whispered faintly. "Where are you?"

"Here. Are you all right?" Her voice trembled with concern. Her nose told her that Torihiko was badly hurt.

"They broke my legs so that I couldn't escape."

"How cruel!" Saya's tiny body shook with indignation.

"How did you get here? And through all those guards? I would never have guessed you could do that."

"It doesn't matter," Saya replied, not wishing to go into detail. "We've got to find you a way out of here. We can't let them burn you alive without putting up a fight."

Torihiko remained silent for so long that she was afraid even his sharp wits had been defeated. Finally he spoke.

"I don't understand girls. It would have been so much easier to help me get the Sword in the first place than to come all the way here now."

"So that's your way of welcoming me, is it?"

Why was he always so cheeky?

"But it's true. This place will be guarded continuously until the purification ceremony is over. The Prince, the Princess, everyone in the palace is watching this spot. To try to escape would mean taking on the entire palace army. It's impossible. I can't even move," he said as if merely stating the facts. "Saya, take the Sword and escape. Do for me what I couldn't do."

Saya struggled to keep her voice calm. "Look, that Sword won't die if I leave it behind. But you most certainly will."

"I'm not going to die," Torihiko replied cheerfully. "I'll just return to the Goddess of Darkness. I'll be born again somewhere and come find you."

"And just when will that be? Don't be ridiculous!" Saya was so angry she could have cried. "Do you think we'll ever meet again? Even if we did, it wouldn't be me anymore. I'll have forgotten all about you. I won't live forever, you know."

Torihiko seemed surprised. "Saya, you're strange. You'll never be able to fight if you think that way."

"Look, I'm not Sayura. You've never met her, and neither have I. She isn't me. Can't you see that?"

"The Water Maiden sure is different, a real oddball."

"You're the oddball," Saya retorted.

"That's why you're always attracted to the Light, because you think like that."

She was about to snap at him but recollected herself. "This is no time to argue. But just you remember what I said, because it's true."

Torihiko reached out his hand and groped in the direction from which her voice came. But of course he did not find her; instead his hand came up against the iron bars. "Saya, where are you really?" he asked uncertainly. Suddenly he looked like the wounded boy he was, and she regretted not having her own body so that she could grasp his hand in hers.

"I'm right here. But I'm using the body of a mouse."

"A mouse?" He stretched out a finger, and for the briefest of moments she allowed him to stroke her fur.

"You see?"

"How did you do it?"

"The girl who was the carp in the Mirror Pond taught me. She was in the shrine. Her name's Chihaya, and she's the youngest of the Children of Light. She's a little odd, and is kept tied up."

"In the shrine? One of the Children of Light?" Torihiko gasped, at a loss for words. "You mean you went into the shrine?"

"Yes. That's where my body is."

"Then you've got to go back now! Immediately!" he said, his voice strained. "That girl must be the priestess. She's the one who stills the Dragon Sword. I wondered how she could do it, but she's one of them. Saya, if you just reach out your hand, you can take the Sword. I can't believe it."

"But rescuing you comes first."

"Listen, if anything can beat the combined forces of the entire palace, it's the Dragon Sword," Torihiko said in a subdued tone. Once he had said it, he seemed afraid. "If you use the Dragon Sword—although just the thought is terrifying—this iron cage won't stop you. In fact, I don't think even the Children of Light would be able to withstand it."

She could feel his fear, the first she had ever seen him show, and she wondered what kind of sword it could possibly be. "All right. I understand. If taking the Sword is the only way, then—"

"Saya," he interrupted, deadly serious. "You've unwittingly placed yourself in grave danger. I don't know who Chihaya is, but it's dangerous to trust her. She's your rival. There can't be two priestesses for the same sword."

"She seemed very nice. And she doesn't know that I'm the Water Maiden," Saya said a little anxiously.

"In that case, grab the Sword before Princess Teruhi discovers you. You should be able to take it without wakening it."

"I'll try. Wait for me."

"Beware of Chihaya. Don't let her fool you."

With his warning following after her, Saya raced off. And as she ran she began to think that maybe she was naïve to have accepted Chihaya's words at face value. Chihaya was a Princess of Light. Saya had even told her that she belonged to the Darkness. Yet, despite this, she had left her defenseless body with Chihaya in the perilous shrine.

Perhaps it is I who lack common sense.

Although the guards were still searching everywhere, they were not looking for anyone as small as a mouse, and Saya slipped past them. She crawled within the safety of a roof and ran along the beams. As she passed Princess Teruhi's hall, she noticed that the Princess's chamber was empty. Was she still with Prince Tsukishiro? Or had she gone somewhere else? The two old women were still offering prayers before the shrine. She would have to think about them also. Had the third priestess in the shadow of the wooden gate regained consciousness yet? At last, she raced up a column beneath the floor and crawled through the hole in the wainscoting, returning to her starting point.

There's my body!

Just as Chihaya had said, it was much simpler to return. Her body seemed to summon her impatiently, sucking her inside with such speed that her head swam. She opened her eyes and felt sensation returning to her limbs. And was scared to death at her predicament. She was lying flat on her back, her arms and legs flailing wildly as she struggled desperately to escape the menace bending over her. And holding her down, restraining her, was Chihaya, her beautiful hair in complete disarray. Saya's blood ran cold, but at last she maneuvered herself into a position from which she could push the girl away.

"What do you think you're doing?" she exclaimed in a quivering voice.

Chihaya looked relieved. She relaxed and sank to the floor, saying, "Oh, good. You're back." She raised her arm and wiped the sweat from her forehead. "The mouse panicked and tried to run outside—without understanding anything."

"You're lying!"

"No, I'm not."

"You are, too! You're lying!" Saya cried furiously. She was so flustered that for a moment she had trouble controlling herself. The blood rushed to her face and she felt as if her cheeks were burning. She backed away. "You're a liar. You–you—!" In a strangled voice, she finally managed to gasp, "You're a boy!"

Chihaya looked perfectly calm. He did not even pay attention to his wildly disheveled hair. "I don't recall ever claiming to be a girl," he replied seriously.

"But you're dressed like one. Look at you!"

Chihaya looked down at his white sleeves and long flowing robe. "This is what my sister makes me wear to fulfill my duties as the Priestess of the Sword."

"Torihiko was right. I shouldn't have trusted you!" Saya snapped, staring him in the face. It was infuriating to think that such beauty belonged to a boy. Her cheeks grew even redder. "What were you doing to me?"

"Nothing."

"But you had your hands on me."

"You were kicking and struggling. I was just trying to hold you still."

He did not seem to be hiding anything. Rather, he seemed perplexed at her anger. Judging from his blank look, he really could not relate to her feelings. "Now I know what they're talking about when they say I struggle during my dreams. Once the soul has left, the body doesn't listen."

Saya, recollecting that Chihaya's hands and feet were tied, relaxed a little. "Well, once was enough for me," she grumbled. "I'm never going to become another creature again. It makes me shudder to think that something that wasn't me was moving around inside my body."

She looked at Chihaya and wondered if he simply did not care about himself. What could he be thinking of, to allow his sister to dress him in women's clothing, to give up his freedom, to leave his body behind while he dreamed? She might have understood it if he appeared grotesque but he could have rivaled even Prince Tsukishiro if he wanted to.

"It seems that you're the black sheep of your family. Well, I'm the same for the people of Darkness," she said candidly, and then shrugged her shoulders, laughing at herself. Now that she had herself under control, she could be more objective. The fact that he was bound was fortunate, for it meant the odds were in her favor.

"The Dragon Sword is here, isn't it," she said, confirming the fact rather than asking a question.

"Yes."

"Would you show me?"

"So you really did come to take the Sword. My sister warned me that the people of Darkness would try to get it." There was a hint of disappointment in his voice.

"Yes, I did. I need it to rescue Torihiko."

"I've heard that no one can touch it."

"I'm supposed to able to," Saya said somewhat dubiously. "Because I'm the Water Maiden."

"The Water Maiden?" Chihaya, who until now had appeared rather absentminded and slow, became animated for the first time. His eyes widened in surprise. "You mean you're the real Priestess of the Sword?"

"According to some people," Saya replied humbly.

"Now that you mention it, didn't you spill the water of pacification earlier? Yet, despite that, the Sword didn't roar."

"Roar?"

"Yes, it roars, and it howls, too. Because it longs to be reborn."

Saya's mouth dropped open. "Just what kind of sword is it?"

"Well, I don't know what the Dragon Sword's original form was," Chihaya said seriously. "But if you want to see what it looks like when it's sleeping, it's over there." He raised his bound hands to indicate the altar. "You seem to have the right. It's kept inside the coffer on the altar."

Saya looked up at the shining altar and approached it. When she had climbed to the third step, she saw before her a rectangular receptacle of stone, black as ebony. Despite its flawlessly polished surface, it was so black that it reflected nothing. She peered fearfully over the edge to find the box lidless and filled with clear water. And in the bottom lay a naked blade. The bright light of the torches reached into the water's depths, and the Sword gleamed faintly where it rested on its jet-black bed. The metal was blue-black and the blade was longer than any Saya had ever seen. The pommel was round and dark, and crimson stones were set in the hilt.

It reminded her of something lurking in wet grass against which one must always be on guard. *Like a serpent. A poisonous serpent,* she thought. Although it had an unearthly beauty, she felt no affinity for it. She looked back at Chihaya.

"If I take the Sword, what will happen to you?" she asked almost teasingly.

"My sister will certainly despair of me," he answered after some thought.

"Then will you try to stop me?"

"I suppose, if it were possible," he muttered without conviction. "Although I've never fought anyone before."

"Really? Never?" Saya said, descending the stairs and staring at him. "Wasn't it decreed that the Children of Light would fight continually from the day they came down to this earth? And if you are truly a child of the God of Light, then you must have lived much longer than I."

"My sister is ashamed that I'm his son. She often says that she wishes it weren't so. She says that although I'm his child, I'm a misfit, obsessed with death. My dreaming is proof of that."

"Well." Saya drew in her breath. Then she asked timidly, "Do you wish to die?"

"I don't know." Chihaya shook his head. It seemed that he lacked conviction about everything. "But when I'm alone, I think of how my father followed the Goddess to the underworld. If he wanted so badly to have her by his side, how did they come to hate each other? And when I think of that, I begin to wander away from the palace. That's why my sister won't let me go outside." He sighed softly. "I'm a failure as a Child of Light. That much I do know."

"Why?" Saya looked into his eyes. "Why do you call yourself a failure? Why don't you try and realize your desire? You're as securely trapped as Torihiko. But you have folded your wings of your own accord."

Confused, he lowered his head. "Because my sister always speaks the truth. She says that if I leave this place, a great evil will occur."

"Well, if you're talking about evil, I've been cursed as evil, too. But that's not the point. What do *you* wish, not Princess Teruhi? You try to escape through dreaming, but wouldn't you rather walk upon the earth with your own two feet? Don't you long to see with your own eyes the marks the Goddess left in Toyoashihara long ago?"

Chihaya could only blink under this barrage of questions. Stray wisps of hair hung about his face, accentuating his bemused appearance. Saya smiled. It was the kind of smile she had shared with her friends when they had played together in the mountains around Hashiba. She said in a warm voice, "I feel I can understand you. We're opposites, and yet we're very similar. We're both drawn to something beyond the confines of our own people. I longed to be one of the people of Light, and your brother brought me to this palace. So why shouldn't you, if you wish, go to the Land of the Dead? Even if, as for me, it doesn't work out in the end."

She pointed to the altar. "Give me the accursed Sword. I will take it and destroy the iron cage where Torihiko is held. And at the same time I will destroy my own cage, the foolish cage of my illusions. Then I will return to the people of Darkness."

Marveling at the strength running like a clear stream through her voice, Chihaya whispered, "You are the Water Maiden." He had nothing with which he could dam that flow. The vigor of surging water was in her face, in her gaze. She laid her hand upon his arm and said, "Let's take the Sword and go together. I would break the cage and sever the cords that bind you with the same blade."

4

"THE MOON has risen over the mountain," Princess Teruhi said abruptly. "Our dalliance is over. Release me."

She rose brusquely when Prince Tsukishiro pulled himself wordlessly away, and parting the curtain, she stood beside a column on the balcony. High above them a thin sliver of moon, like a crescent of fingernail, had emerged at the edge of the night sky. Although the glow it cast was almost too ephemeral to be called light, the Princess standing with her back turned to the Prince seemed bathed in a sudden coldness. "I'm worried about security at the West Gate. Surely they wouldn't let our prize slip through their fingers."

Prince Tsukishiro said with a sigh, "I know that as long as there is light in this world you live only to serve our divine father, but is everything else just dallying to you?"

"What's wrong with that?" Princess Teruhi asked, turning to face him.

"Then what," he asked, "will you do when our father comes once again to rule this land?"

Princess Teruhi was caught off guard, but she replied without hesitation. "I'll do as I've always done. I'll worship and obey him. My greatest desire is to behold once more his illustrious face, from which I have been parted for so long."

Prince Tsukishiro lay stretched out elegantly on the floor, but at this he raised himself on one elbow and looked at her. "What blind affection. Sister, you're just like the handmaidens of the sacred shrine."

"I've had enough of your constant grumbling."

"Sometimes I almost feel sorry for our younger brother."

Glaring at him as he ran his fingers through his hair, Princess Teruhi snapped, "Don't bring Chihaya into this just to please your whim. Are you saying that you understand his degenerate mind?"

"No, I don't," Prince Tsukishiro said flatly. "Although I would feel easier if I could. Chihaya's eyes are fixed on something else; the path he follows differs from ours. Why do you think our divine father made him so different?"

"Surely it was an accident," she replied sullenly. "I can't believe that he would intentionally produce such a good-for-nothing."

Prince Tsukishiro folded his fingers together and said thoughtfully, "I used to think so, too—that he was not what our father intended. But recently I have begun to think that the opposite might be true— that Chihaya might in fact represent our father's true purpose, one which he has kept hidden."

"What do you mean?" Princess Teruhi watched him intently.

"You and I were born to act as our celestial father's two eyes. We have been placed upon this earth to watch over it for him. But Chihaya was born from our father's nose, through which his breath flows. Born from a sigh that expressed our father's true feelings, he is closer to our father's heart."

Princess Teruhi gave a short laugh. "That boy? Even though he'll never grow up and his only talent is dreaming? What part of our miserable brother do you claim expresses our father's feelings?"

Hesitating, Prince Tsukishiro paused and then said, "That boy loves the Goddess. He's constantly seeking the entrance to the place where we immortals can never go."

Princess Teruhi jumped like a startled deer and bore down upon the Prince with a menacing glare. "I will not permit such a thing to be suggested again, even by you, brother." Shaking with rage, she shouted, "You speak as though our divine father, the God of Light himself, still wishes to meet the Goddess of Darkness."

Prince Tsukishiro regarded her calmly. "If . . . just if this were so, what would become of us?"

"That's impossible! Don't be ridiculous," Princess Teruhi berated him, waving her hand impatiently as though driving the thought away. "Chihaya's attraction to the Darkness is necessary only to give him the power to still the Dragon Sword. Because that's the only thing he's good for. It's proof of our father's wise decision to render the loathsome Sword as useless as Chihaya. Nothing could possibly cloud the illustrious will of the God of Light. The fact that Chihaya loses himself in dreams is merely a compensation for stilling the Sword along with himself. All we need to do is let him dream as much as he wants. He protects the Sword and we protect him because the Sword is powerful and needs a guardian. Isn't that enough? What are you worrying about? Why do you waste your time with these delusions?"

"You're right. It's just a delusion," Prince Tsukishiro whispered. "In any case, it doesn't change the fact that Chihaya's power has been sealed inside him."

Princess Teruhi knelt and placed her hands on Prince Tsukishiro's shoulders. She frowned, looking into his face. "You're behaving very strangely. Within but a short space of time, victory will be ours."

Recollecting himself, Prince Tsukishiro smiled faintly. "I shall return to the present. It's just one of those whims that you, my dear sister, so dislike."

The expression of concern vanished from her face and she turned away. "This happens because you insist on bringing that Water Maiden into the palace," she said angrily. "The air becomes impure and you begin to doubt. There's no need to waste your efforts trying to purify her. The only solution is to destroy her."

Striking her knee with her fist, she rose and picked up her sword, fastening it at her waist. "I'm going to see what's happening at the West Gate."

"Saya won't be there."

"Can you be so sure?"

"I'll go with you, then." He stood up swiftly.

At that moment a roar shook the silence of the sleeping palace. Like a giant bubble, it rose from the depths of the night and burst. It was like the growl of an enormous creature or the rumble of thunder from the edge of the earth. When it reached their ears, the trees, the grass, even the columns of the palace quivered momentarily. The earth itself trembled with terror at the low-pitched sound, and the air swelled with fear.

The twins started and recoiled, glancing at each other.

"The Dragon cries," Princess Teruhi whispered. "Did the old women neglect to bring the water of pacification?"

"What can Chihaya be doing?" Prince Tsukishiro asked. "The Sword hasn't made such a clamor since he began to watch over it."

The expression that suddenly crossed Princess Teruhi's face was one she had never worn before. "It can't be! That girl!"

SAYA gripped the Sword gingerly in both hands, staring at it blankly. It had begun to shriek when she yelled at the guards accosting them to keep away. The sound shook the air with a disturbing resonance, pulsing in a way that set her nerves on edge. Needless to say, the guards paled and fled.

"Why is it doing this?" Saya asked, bewildered as she struggled to suppress her desire to fling it away.

"Saya, calm down," Chihaya said anxiously from beside her. "The Sword will overpower you if you get upset."

How could he possibly expect her to calm down, she wondered. The place was in an uproar, and she could hear the angry voices of the guards calling for reinforcements. It was clear that within moments the entire palace guard would be ranged against them. To sneak quietly away, taking Chihaya with her, was now utterly impossible.

"Let's go to the West Gate. There's no point in trying to hide any longer," she said in desperation. She urged Chihaya on and they broke into a run. An intricate network of fences and buildings hemmed the narrow streets, obstructing their view so that soldiers responding to the alarm repeatedly ran into them head on. Without exception, however, the soldiers blanched and fell back, unable to stop the fleeing pair. The Sword continued to shriek, making the palace rumble, and it also began to glow. The stones in the hilt blazed like murky red lidless eyes, glaring at those who crossed their path, and blue-white sparks fell from its tip. A bluish light radiated along its entire length, illuminating Saya from the chest up and making her look like a madwoman. Even the bravest men trembled at the sight.

Saya and Chihaya ran without stopping while behind them a clamor rose in the streets and lights came on in every wakening mansion. *Just a little farther,* Saya pleaded silently.

They had almost reached the West Gate. But only a few paces behind them came the people of the palace. To a night bird hovering above them as they raced from one side of the palace to the other, they would have appeared to be drawing the people toward the gate in order to sweep them from the city.

The brightly lit West Gate came into view. Saya and Chihaya halted, gasping for breath. Between the gate's two pillars stood the Prince and Princess, arms folded. And surrounding them were the very best soldiers with bowstrings drawn.

"Saya," Prince Tsukishiro called in a thunderous voice. The rebuke in it struck her forcefully. "Control yourself. Such behavior does not become you."

The Sword's howling ceased abruptly. Stillness spread through the night, as if a curtain had been drawn back. Saya stood immobile in shock. The Sword weighed heavily in her hands and she gradually lowered it. The blade was so long that the tip almost touched the ground. The light that glowed within began to fade as the wild agitation in her heart slowly subsided.

"Well, you couldn't have chosen a more spectacular way to get here, little one," Princess Teruhi said, her hands on her hips. Although her voice was steady, Saya could feel the anger seething beneath. "Were you trying to disturb the palace? Where did you learn such behavior?"

"Let Torihiko go. That's all I want," Saya said hoarsely. "I don't intend to harm anyone. Just let us go."

"Go? Where do you plan to go?" Prince Tsukishiro said in disbelief. "Do you think you can turn your back on me and return home? If you think the people of Hashiba will welcome you back with open arms, you're gravely mistaken. And surely you don't intend to go to the people of Darkness. For of all things, you loathed most your tainted birth among those who worship the Goddess."

"I know," Saya whispered, "yet that is where I belong."

"Look at me," the Prince commanded sternly. Biting her lip, Saya raised her head. His face was rigid and hard but, more than anything else, sad. And as he stood there, his commanding presence still embodied all that she loved.

"I thought that I had given you all that it was in my power to give. I thought that you had vowed to cherish it. What could have been lacking that you should turn from me in this way? You always leave me. What do you seek that I can't see?"

Saya was on the verge of tears. His sincerity was heartrending. "I'm not turning my back on you. I love you—and I'm sure that I always will. But . . ." Shaking her head, she fixed him with a sad and hopeless gaze. "That which I seek and which you can't see is my soul, the source of life. It's something that the people of Darkness can never forget. So please, forgive me. I can't stay here."

The Sword began to hum faintly.

"Let me pass."

Princess Teruhi spoke. "If you wish to go, then go. But I will permit neither Chihaya nor the Sword to pass through this gate."

Chihaya fell back a step under his sister's gaze.

"Why have you done what is strictly forbidden?" she demanded in a tone that would have caused even stone to tremble. "Why, when I strove so hard to keep you from the eyes of men, have you left the shrine?"

Certainly the people of Mahoroba milling at a distance all had their eyes fixed on Chihaya. It was obvious that he was no ordinary person. With his white robes, he looked like a bird that had alighted from above, and his long black hair flowed like a river of night. Looking bemused and uncertain, he seemed more like a celestial angel newly descended from heaven than a youth.

"Sister," he whispered hoarsely.

"I command you to take the Sword from that girl and return to the shrine immediately," Princess Teruhi said imperiously. "I don't know how she managed to lure you out, but you can't live anywhere else. Without us to protect you, you won't even be able to dream."

"Don't listen to her. You're walking out of here on your own two feet," Saya said sharply. The Dragon Sword began to glow again. Sparks sprang soundlessly from the blade, and the red stones awoke and glared threateningly.

Chihaya remained silent for a while; then, looking Princess Teruhi squarely in the eye, he held up his hands. "Sister, I have cut the bonds that held me. Once I desired to cut them, it was easy. And I realized that until now I had never even wished to be free."

"And that is how it should be," Princess Teruhi retorted, lashing out at him. "You've never realized the peril you represent. Even if you knew, there was nothing you could have done but curse yourself and suffer needlessly. I didn't wish to expose my own brother to such a fate. To remain in the shrine is your sole hope for happiness."

"Liar!" It was Saya, not Chihaya, who screamed. Shaking with indignation, she said, "I know the truth. It doesn't matter whether someone is your own kin or not, you're only capable of using them."

To her astonishment, light suddenly gushed from the Sword and shot up into the sky, tracing a thick line. Within seconds, a swirling cloud had formed, a cloud that responded to the Sword. The sky split in two above the stunned crowd, and from the cleft a flash of orange light spilled forth. With an appalling roar it struck the ground, generating a warm moist wind, and, before their very eyes, the main hall burst into a pillar of flame. With a cry of terror, the crowd crested like a wave and broke, scattering like baby spiders spilling from the nest. "Water! Water!" someone shouted.

Saya, shocked beyond fear, stood rooted to the spot, staring at the dancing flames. She found that she could hold the Sword no longer. She had reached the limits of her courage.

"Chihaya," she whispered. "Take it, please. I can't still the Sword. I'm too weak."

He looked at her in surprise. "But that can't be . . ."

"Please," she begged him. Although she did not want to admit it, everything was growing dark and stars were dancing at the edge of her vision. "I think I'm going to faint. Please, before I fall."

Chihaya hastily put his arm around her and gripped the hilt of the Sword next to her hand. Princess Teruhi, turning her eyes from the fire and seeing them thus, gave a triumphant smile.

"That's it. Now take the girl and go back to the shrine. When the fire is out, we can take our time deciding what to do with her."

Chihaya looked at the exhausted Saya and the Dragon Sword. When he gripped the hilt a little more firmly, Saya's hand fell limply away. He alone now held the Sword, and though it still glowed faintly, its humming subsided. But from the quivering in the palm of his hand he could feel its impatience to move again.

"Sister." Chihaya raised his voice above the noise of the fire.

"What?"

"I wish to return this girl to the people of Darkness."

A slightly puzzled expression crossed Princess Teruhi's face, gradually changing into one of astonishment. "You what?! Do you intend to take her yourself?"

"Yes."

"Of your own free will?"

"Yes."

"No! I won't allow it!" Princess Teruhi screamed, her voice shaking. "You're insane! Don't you know that if you do this, you can never return? We'll have to fight against one another, to despise each other. If you take but one step outside this gate, your fate will seize you. It's clearly written in the stars."

"I have no desire to fight you or my brother. But no matter what the consequences, I can't stay." Chihaya spoke calmly, but the Sword in his hand grew steadily brighter. "The Water Maiden has broken the dam and released what was contained behind it. I wish to go and seek the Goddess, as my father intended."

"Tsukishiro, come!" the Princess cried desperately. "Stop him, stop Chihaya! The Dragon Sword will be reborn."

Prince Tsukishiro was directing the soldiers' efforts to extinguish the fire, but he turned, paling, at her words. And saw Chihaya grasping the Sword in one hand and supporting Saya with the other as he attempted to pass through the gate. Realizing that it was too late to run after him, he set an arrow to his bow as swiftly as a hawk. Aiming for his brother's heart, he pulled the bowstring taut. But at that moment the ground bucked beneath him. With a great rumbling and a blinding light, the earth shook with quake after quake, so that not a soul was left standing. The main hall, still burning, collapsed under the shock, and an anguished cry arose from the people who were assailed by showers of sparks. The entire vault of heaven glowed dull purple, as if the world were turning upside down.

Prince Tsukishiro crawled to Princess Teruhi's side and shielded her from the scraps of burning wood that fell from the sky. For a long time the two remained there on the ground, but when the earthquake had finally abated they raised their faces and looked up at the sky. Above their heads a dragon danced—an enormous blue-white dragon dancing wildly in pain, or in exultation.

Reckless, blind, it sped from cloud to blue-black cloud with chilling lack of purpose. Below, all the roofs of the main hall had crumbled, belching forth flames, and the deafening roar of dry wood burning drowned out the cries of the people scattering in terror. Smoke as black as soot spouted into the air, swirled and spread across the sky, which flickered with lightning.

"The fire's curse has been unsealed," Princess Teruhi whispered. "That which brings evil to both the Darkness and the Light."

She turned and gazed blankly at the West Gate beside her, which was now burning furiously, and then at the Hut of Abomination, which was likewise engulfed in flames.

Prince Tsukishiro tightened his grip on her shoulder. "Let's go to the river. We're in danger here."

5

SAYA COULD HEAR the sound of water: the low murmur of a great river. Opening one eye and then the other, she saw that it was dawn. A faint white light touched the horizon. She was lying on the soft grass of the riverbank. She sat up, feeling as though she were waking from some bad dream that she could not remember. She was not afraid but rather filled with a forlorn helplessness, like a lost child. Where was she? Seeing Chihaya sitting beside her, she smiled with relief. The air was clear and still and she could hear the sweet chirping of an early bird.

"Ah. So you're all right."

"Yes. And you," Chihaya replied. His soot-smeared clothes were scorched and riddled with holes. There was a black smudge on the bridge of his nose, but he seemed not to notice. He no longer looked like a heavenly maiden, and she was dismayed to see that his beautiful hair had been singed into frizzy brown tufts. Then she noticed that her own clothes were also scorched and burned along the edges.

"What happened?" Saya asked. "Where's the Sword?"

"The main hall was burned to the ground. Smoke is still rising in the northern sky, so I suppose that it's still burning. As for the Dragon Sword, it's here. It sleeps after its rampage." Chihaya pointed to the Sword lying upon the grass, its darkened blade grim in the pale morning light.

"It seems so far," Saya said in surprise, looking up at the sky to the north. "We've come a long way from the palace, then. How did you do it?" She tilted her head, perplexed. "And what about Torihiko?"

Uncertainty crossed his face and he seemed unwilling to reply. Saya frowned anxiously but at that moment sensed someone approaching. Startled, she turned to see a tiny old woman with a large head appearing from the shadow of the bank. White hair haloed her head like thistledown.

"Lady Iwa!" Saya exclaimed in surprise.

"They came and helped us. We used their raft to float down the river until we reached this spot," Chihaya explained.

Unable to wait for the old woman's short legs to carry her to them, Saya jumped up and ran to greet her. She knelt in front of her and looked into her face, demanding impatiently, "Lady Iwa, where's Torihiko? What happened to him?"

The old woman's eyes filled with compassion and she stroked Saya's cheek. "The brave boy was courageous to the end. He said to tell you not to cry but to wait for him."

"You mean—" Saya whispered. "There—in that cage . . . like that?"

"We did our best, we and that young man over there. But there's not much anyone can do when the Dragon Sword is dancing. Now, now, there's no need to grieve. He's just resting awhile with the Goddess."

"How can you tell me not to grieve?" Saya wailed, venting her anguish. "Why do you think I took the Sword in the first place? Why do you think I turned my back on Prince Tsukishiro? It was all for Torihiko—just to see him alive and well again."

She burst into tears and threw herself upon the grass. Even stamping the earth with her feet could not have assuaged her feelings. Torihiko had been burned alive in the iron cage, leaving only this show of courage behind. If she had just been a little stronger—if she had just tried a little harder, he could have been saved. But he had died alone because she was such a hopeless failure.

The sky lightened and the sun shone down, evaporating the morning dew, yet Saya's face was still wet with tears. Chihaya approached softly to see how she was. He seemed perplexed by her weeping.

"Are you—hurt somewhere?" he asked hesitantly.

"You can't understand because you've got nothing to lose," Saya said between sobs. "I've lost Torihiko. I'll never see him again. He's not here anymore."

Chihaya felt a shadow cross the sky and looked up. Black wings stood out like a stain on the blue sky.

"Crows. Two crows. They've been circling us for a while."

"That must be Big Black and Little Black." Saya looked up and felt fresh tears start to her eyes. "I bet they're still looking for Torihiko."

"Sa–ya," one of the crows called familiarly, and, folding its wings, it dove down out of the sky and landed on the grass with such force that it had to flap its wings and flutter about. It hopped right up to her and tilted its glossy black head. "Man, I'm tired! I searched all over for you. I never dreamed that you'd come this far."

Stunned at the bird's eloquent speech, Saya stopped crying and stared.

"It's me," the crow said, hopping onto her knee. "Didn't you get my message? I told you not to cry, and to wait for me."

"Torihiko!" Saya shrieked, but could not say another word. She stared at the crow, which resembled a little demon with shining black eyes, too astounded to even consider whether she was happy or sad.

"I had to think about it—whether to go to the Goddess or not. But I figured that the Goddess wouldn't cry if she didn't see me, whereas you would. So I gave up the idea of going. I decided to stay with you even if it means being a crow. It wasn't very nice for Big Black, but I think he'd understand."

Saya looked at Chihaya, at a loss as to how to respond. "You?"

Chihaya nodded. "But he'll never be able to return to his original form. Because his body was burned."

"It doesn't matter," Torihiko cried in a cheerful crow voice. "Did you know that crows live as long as human beings?"

*chapter
four*

REVOLT

Corpses fill the sea
and the mountain grasses deep.
I shall die by my emperor's side;
a peaceful death I will not seek.

—Shoku Nihongi

Revolt

SOON AFTER THEY HAD successfully rescued Saya, Chihaya, and Torihiko, the infiltrators consisting of Lady Iwa, Lord Shinado, and two attendants discarded their raft and headed into the mountains. They followed the ridges, spending the night on one of the peaks, and continued walking the next day. In the afternoon, as they descended a mountain slope, they glimpsed the scenery far below them. The dense forest of pine and chinquapin ended abruptly at the mountain's foot, and beyond it shone a bright band of water, bluer than the sky that met it at the horizon.

"Is that the sea?" Saya asked Torihiko, who was perched on her shoulder. Even without having seen it before, she could guess what it was.

"That's right. We'll take a boat from that inlet," Torihiko replied.

Once they reentered the shadow of the forest, they lost sight of the sea, but the head wind, which grew gradually stronger, carried the booming sound of water crashing on the rocks. The angry moaning of the sea set Saya's nerves on edge. Perhaps it resembled the voice of the Dragon Sword in some way. But the roar of the waves summoned rain rather than fire. In the late afternoon the clouds began to thicken, and by dusk raindrops had already begun to fall. The wind buffeted the travelers, and a driving rain lashed their faces, showing no sign of abating.

"I'm afraid we won't be able to put to sea while this lasts," Lord Shinado said to Lady Iwa. "We'll have to wait out the storm on shore."

"That's all right. We don't seem to have been followed, which was my main worry. We can seek shelter in the village down in that cove."

"Wouldn't it be better to avoid being seen? What if this storm continues for several days . . . ?"

"Don't worry. This is nothing, no more than a baby crow's temper tantrum. It'll be over by tomorrow," she replied confidently. "We got here in a night and a day. It can't hurt to sleep in a little more comfort tonight."

Saya inwardly greeted Lady Iwa's decision with wholehearted relief. They had traveled in such haste that she had had no chance to recover from the shock of what had happened in the palace. Her head was filled with a thick fog and everything seemed unreal. The dull pain in her aching feet and the weight of her drenched clothing seemed like keynotes in an endless nightmare, and she desperately needed time and rest in order to wake up and return to the real world.

It was quite dark by the time the travelers reached the shore. They trudged along the bay, unable to light their way with a torch due to the howling wind, until they finally stumbled upon a row of houses. The yellow light of an oil lamp glimpsed through the cracks in one of the doors seemed the warmest, most welcoming sight in the world. One of the attendants negotiated with the head of the household and, when it was finally settled that the men would sleep in the shed and the women in the house, Saya could have cried in relief. The house was a low-roofed fisherman's hut built over a sunken pit of sandy earth, and a pungent, fishy odor assailed them when they entered. The fisherman had brought in a net with scraps of seaweed clinging to it and appeared to be in the middle of mending it. Gutted fish had been strung together and hung around the smoke hole to dry. Perhaps because of the salt air, the round wooden pillars were badly decayed and the house creaked and shuddered with every gust of wind, but it did not come tumbling down. Despite their frugal lifestyle, the family with its many red-faced children was cheerful, and willingly served the guests bowls of hot soup with strips of dried fish. Saya's clothes were barely dry, however, before her eyelids began to droop, and she could hardly taste the soup that passed her lips. She soon left the circle of laughing conversation and laid down in a corner, listening to the raging wind howl outside the thin wooden wall. It drowned out the voices within and bellowed, as if demanding something in a great loud voice of its own.

Who? Where? Why? When? How?

Who could it be talking to? she wondered vaguely, but as she listened to the endless questioning she drifted into a deep sleep.

WHEN SHE OPENED HER EYES the next morning, the fisherman and his family had already finished breakfast and gone outside. They had been up since before dawn. Bereft of even the smallest child, the house appeared large and empty. Lady Iwa sat alone beside the hearth, her small hands moving busily as she worked on something. Saya crawled from her sleeping place and looked out the open door. The storm had passed as though it had never been, and the sky was clear. The fisherman's family stood side by side and greeted the sun as it rose above the rocky crags in the distance. Saya's heart ached as she watched their still figures from behind.

Lady Iwa called to her. "There's some rice porridge in the pot for you. You should eat it while it's still hot."

Saya turned away from the door as if shaking herself free and removed the lid from a large cauldron hanging on the hearth hook. This was the sort of breakfast she used to eat at home. Sitting down with a bowl in her hand, she looked at what Lady Iwa was doing. The old woman had patiently hollowed out two pieces of wood and was now binding them together with wisteria vines.

When Saya asked what the old woman was making, she casually replied, "A sheath. For the Sword. You can't carry that blade un-sheathed forever."

"Hmm," Saya murmured noncommittally and glanced at the Sword, which lay nearby, thickly wrapped in cloth. The thought of it depressed her. Everyone feared it, even Lady Iwa and Lord Shinado. She, too, dreaded it as much as everyone else, yet they forced her to carry it, insisting that it must be guarded by the priestess. Having no alternative, she had wrapped it in cloth and carried it on her shoulder, but it was a cumbersome burden, constantly catching on thickets as they traveled along the mountain paths.

Why was I chosen as Priestess of the Sword? Will I have to carry this thing with me for the rest of my life? What on earth is going to happen?

She longed to ask Lady Iwa but kept losing her nerve. As she was rolling the questions about on the tip of her tongue, she sensed someone standing in the doorway. Looking over her shoulder, she saw an unknown youth and stared up at him suspiciously until she was able to discern his features against the backlight. Then she cried out in astonishment.

"Chihaya? I didn't recognize you!"

Lord Shinado must have arranged it. Chihaya was dressed in a faded indigo jacket and knee-length trousers like those the fisherman and his children wore. His singed hair had been evenly trimmed and fastened in loops on either side of his head. Although he was perhaps a little too pale, to the casual observer he could pass for an ordinary boy. Saya was so pleased that she laughed aloud. It made her glad to think that Lord Shinado had noticed Chihaya's ragged appearance. Since their first meeting, she had stood in awe of Lord Shinado. There was something in his dark face, rugged features, and piercing gaze that suggested he would be a hard judge of others, and despite the fact that he had come to her aid, she was afraid he would never forgive her for following the Light without a thought for her own people. This was one reason she had not yet told anyone how or why she had left the palace with Chihaya. And apparently it never even occurred to Chihaya to explain himself. Saya wondered at his reception by the people of Darkness. They did not reject him as he tagged along, but neither did they welcome him or ask him any questions. Rather, they ignored him, behaving as if he was not there. This had nagged at her mind, although she had had no energy left to spare for others. Chihaya's new outfit, however, indicated that Lord

Shinado and the others had accepted him as part of their group. "Not bad," she teased him. "It suits you."

But Chihaya did not seem to hear. His appearance was of little interest to him. Instead, he began talking excitedly on a totally different subject.

"The children ran off, saying that there's a sea monster."

Saya blinked in surprise. "A sea monster? What's that?"

"I don't know. They said it was washed ashore by the storm." Chihaya's innocent excitement was catching, and Saya turned to the old woman. "Can we go and see, too?"

"It's just a shark," Lady Iwa said. "You can go, but the sea's still rough. Be careful not to get swept away by the waves." Saya practically flew out the door.

The narrow spit of sand below the shallow terrace curved gently out to the headland, and waves pounded against it defiantly. The waves were a somber brownish green where they swelled and broke in a rush of noise, scattering white foam, but out to sea they were a sparkling blue. Their sharp-peaked crests rose steeply and raced toward land. For the first time in her life, Saya stood at the edge of the sea. Unlike the endless expanse of blue that she had seen from a distance, the ocean at close range seemed like a live and cunning creature on whom it would be unwise to turn one's back. The smell of the wind was unfamiliar and it, too, seemed shrewd and intelligent. And yet she felt that she had known this scent even before she was born. Birds wheeled in the sky above, and she heard their plaintive cries carried on the wind.

The smell of the sea was even sharper as they walked along the beach strewn with debris from the previous night's storm: brilliantly colored seaweed, driftwood, various species of small fish, jellyfish, and starfish. Saya did not recognize half of them. Women and children, baskets in hand, gathered them busily. Saya wanted to stop and pick things up to look at them, but she had no chance because Chihaya kept walking without a second glance.

"Isn't the sea new to you?"

"This is the first time that I've ever seen it with my own eyes, but . . ." he replied.

As she knew only too well what he meant by this, she did not bother to question him further.

Soon they saw a group of boys chattering excitedly. Knee-deep in the surf, they were gathered around a large black object that had run aground on the beach. Coming closer, Saya saw that it was a huge shark twice the length of an average man. It lay on its side with its pectoral fin piercing the sky, looking like a small hill with a flag perched upon it. Its belly was the hideous color of a corpse, and the long teeth protruding from its V-shaped jaws sent shivers up Saya's spine. Bereft of emotion, its eye, which seemed small for its body, stared blankly at the sky. She grimaced at the sight. It was obviously a monster from another world, not something that should be exposed thus to the light of day. She felt nauseated but was not sure if it was from disgust or pity.

Beside her Chihaya whispered in awe, "What a beautiful creature."

Saya looked at him in astonishment. "Beautiful?"

"Beautiful, and strong. Look at the line of his body. Think how fast this fish could swim underneath the waves . . ."

Chihaya pointed at its pectoral fin, and at that very moment it moved. Then the shark's flank undulated and its thick tail thrashed weakly against the sand. The children shrieked and leaped away.

"It's still alive!"

"Let's get the others."

Although she did not scream, Saya clutched Chihaya's arm so hard her nails dug in. "Look out! It's alive! Move back."

Chihaya, however, stood rooted to the spot. He stared wide-eyed, his gaze riveted on the shark. Saya, realizing that something was wrong, tried to shake him, but his body was so rigid it did not budge.

"Chihaya!" she screamed, putting her mouth to his ear. But her voice did not reach him. He was listening to a different voice.

"GREETINGS, O young and solitary god. I am the God of the Sea who abides in the ocean's depths beneath the eternal waves. This creature is the bearer of my message."

"Are you one of the many gods of the earth?" Chihaya asked.

"In some ways, yes; in others, no. For neither the powers of the Darkness nor of the Light can reach me. In that sense, I am most like you."

After pondering this for a moment, Chihaya said, "I think you've mistaken me for someone else. I'm—"

But the God of the Sea ignored him.

"I send this message of encouragement, for I saw you upon my shore. I can do no more. As a mere onlooker, I am powerless to lend a hand concerning your bitter fate. There are but two paths to choose from, and both are cruel. To slay your father, or to be slain by him—a hard choice indeed."

Taken aback, Chihaya wondered what on earth the god meant.

"Although it's no concern of mine, this shore borders on my territory. I'll be watching the road you take. O solitary god, unique in Toyoashihara, I send this message, for I also am alone. Tread carefully, so that you are left with no regrets."

"WAIT!" Chihaya cried. "Please!"

But the ancient voice faded away, and instead he heard Saya's voice calling his name so loudly that it hurt his ear. He blinked and saw her standing right in front of him, her eyes filled with alarm and her face pale with anxiety.

"What?"

"I said move back!" Saya snapped at him.

Chihaya moved back a few paces but said, "If it's because of the shark, it just died."

Saya glanced over her shoulder at the shark's motionless form and then stared suspiciously at Chihaya. "How did you know that? Surely you didn't try to possess that monster? Because if you did, I'll have nothing more to do with you."

Chihaya shook his head. "I couldn't have possessed it. That fish was a messenger from the God of the Sea."

Saya's mouth dropped open in innocent astonishment. "What did you just say?"

Chihaya looked at the fish that had breathed its last, and frowned slightly. "I heard the voice of the Sea God," he said doubtfully. "But I think he must have talked to me by mistake. Surely he was mistaken." Puzzled, he looked at Saya and said in a low voice, "He seemed to think that I was the Dragon."

A chill ran up her spine, but while she stood there speechless, the children came back from the other side of the beach, leading two fishermen. They, too, stared at the huge shark, but when they saw that it was dead, they touched it and said, "This is a servant of the Sea God. We must prepare an altar and suitable offerings."

Saya looked from one weathered face to the other in surprise. "You mean you worship the gods of the earth?"

"Of course. Fishing is our trade. How could we survive if we were cursed by the lord of the sea?"

"But I saw you worshipping the sun this morning," Saya said, and the fishermen laughed, their faces untroubled.

"We wouldn't be forgetting the blessing of the Light, young lady. The key is to live a life full of thanks and praise. Our work is so dangerous that even if we worshipped all the gods in the world, many of us would still die untimely deaths."

"THEY'RE LUCKY," Saya sighed after leaving the fishermen. "Why can't the people of Darkness live like that, without fighting? To tell you the truth, I'm afraid of what's going to happen."

Brushing her windswept hair from her face, she turned to Chihaya with a pensive look.

"I don't want to be swept up in this war against the God of Light. But there's nothing I can do about it . . . Oh, I'm not even sure about whether or not there's nothing I can do. What about you? Have you thought about what you're going to do when we get to the people of Darkness?"

"No," Chihaya replied promptly.

"And you have me worried, too."

Saya sighed again. She was getting used to the fact that Chihaya was hard to understand. But it bothered her not to have the faintest idea what he, a Prince of Light, intended to do among the people of Darkness. She did not know how the latter would receive him either, or even how they would welcome her. Although she was of the same race, she had learned almost nothing about the enemies of the Light.

"I worry you?" Chihaya said in complete surprise. "What about me could worry you?"

"That's what worries me!" Saya said in exasperation.

The sun had risen high in the sky and the tide had reached its lowest ebb when Torihiko came gliding on the wind in search of them. Saya and Chihaya were helping to dig up shellfish on the beach, and the children opened their mouths in astonishment when the huge crow landed purposefully on Saya's shoulder. She quickly walked away and turned her back to them so that they could not be heard talking.

"We leave by boat this afternoon," Torihiko said. "Lady Iwa said not to wander too far from the Sword."

"I know," Saya replied with some annoyance.

"I'll be leaving ahead of you. Flying's faster, so they told me to let Lord Akitsu know when we're arriving."

Saya suddenly felt alone and helpless. She looked at the black crow. "You mean you're not coming with us?"

"Wouldn't you know it! Now that I've got wings they think up even more ways to keep me busy."

"Where on earth are we going anyway? Across the sea?"

"No, it's not that far. We're only going by boat because it's easier to go around the point and enter from the shore. From here on, the mountains are very rugged, so it's impossible to approach by land. Lord Akitsu resides in a hidden valley called Eagle's Manor." Torihiko broke off, and hunching his shoulders, he preened his feathers with his beak. Then he continued smugly. "Of course, it's not much of a fortress if you've got wings. Old Akitsu will sure be surprised to see me."

Saya bit back the words that sprang to her tongue. Torihiko seemed almost to be enjoying his new form. At least he never complained. And if he did, she knew he would never be caught griping about his fate in front of her.

"Take care," was all that she said.

"See you later." Watching him fly exuberantly into the sky, Saya wished that she had even half his talent for making the best of necessity.

2

THEY BOARDED TWO BOATS AT NOON that summer's day and set off into the dazzling sea. The two attendants steered, sculling with practiced hands. Saya, who rode with Lady Iwa, shaded her eyes with her hand and watched the other boat some distance away. She thought idly that the grim figure of Lord Shinado contrasted with the slender, fragile form of Chihaya made him look like a slave dealer taking home a newly purchased prize. Although the little boats rocked back and forth, there was no fear of capsizing, and they forged ahead, trailing a wake behind them. Skirting the sheer cliffs on the cape at a distance, they rounded the promontory. On the other side, the cliffs gradually sank in height and the dense black forest covering the top came into view. Passing several reefs where white waves broke, they approached the shore cautiously until suddenly a hollow appeared within the bluff, revealing a hidden cove. As they passed between the cliffs, gazing up at the rock ledges lined with seabird nests, the water turned smooth and tranquil. Under the blazing sun, shore and forest were wrapped in silence, augmenting the air of secrecy.

Or perhaps this was only Saya's imagination, sparked by her anxiety concerning those who awaited them. It seemed to her that the entire cove held its breath, watching them intently. But there was no sign of anyone waiting in ambush when they landed on the empty beach near the mouth of a river flowing into the cove. They set out on foot, following the river in the sweltering heat. No one spoke, and the only sound to be heard was the chirring of the cicadas. Soon the river entered a steep valley and the path became increasingly rugged and lined with boulders.

Chihaya glanced up suddenly, and Saya, following suit, glimpsed tiny forms at the top of the cliff ahead, where the canopy of leaves was thinner. She thought she saw them wave, and then they disappeared. The idea that she would have to climb so far was almost too much for her. It was a windless afternoon, hot and humid even in the shade—certainly not the season for sweating one's way up a rock cliff. However, she need not have worried. They had gone only a few paces farther when they were met by a group of brawny men.

The bearded leader bowed his head respectfully. "Please forgive our delay. We apologize for not coming sooner, but we had to make sure that you weren't followed." There were at least twenty men with him. They all wore black headbands and protective vests of hard leather over their bare, tanned chests. Although they appeared respectful at that moment, Saya felt that underneath they were rough and dangerous. Lord Shinado accepted their greeting solemnly.

"Thank you for your trouble. Bring the litters here."

Two litters without canopies, each supported on long poles and carried by four men, were immediately brought forward. Saya was gazing at them curiously when Lord Shinado said, "You should get on."

"Me?" she said in surprise. It had never occurred to her that she would ride while Lord Shinado walked. Confused, she looked from left to right and stammered, "I–I can walk. I'm not that tired."

"It's all right," Lady Iwa reassured her, already seated on the other litter. "Go ahead. Remember, you're the princess of our people."

Having no choice, Saya sat down, but in the end she found it much more tiring than walking, for she held herself rigid the whole way lest she should burden the bearers.

Finally they came to a hollow behind which rose a rock wall shaped like a folding screen. Before them lay cool green meadows and cultivated fields. As they came closer, Saya saw houses built in rows along the bottom of the cliff and a crowd of people gathered in front of them, cheering loudly. She recalled the day she had reached the Palace of Light and how the people had waited in the fine rain, lined up in an orderly fashion. This was a much more boisterous crowd, with children and dogs racing about.

"Look! She's come back at last."

"The Princess of the Sword has returned!"

"There's the mistress of the sacred Sword."

These words were on everyone's lips as she passed by. Immensely thankful for the thin silk veil hanging from the brim of the straw hat that someone had lent her to keep off the sun, she hid herself within its shadow. Of any reception she could have received, the worshipful adoration of these people was the most unsettling. Wondering what on earth Torihiko had told them, she struggled as best she could to conceal her discomfort.

LORD AKITSU's hall came into sight at the far end of Eagle's Manor. The space before the entrance formed the largest courtyard in the valley, and the back of the hall was set against a sheer cliff. The floor was raised high off the ground, resembling a wide shelf perched on the cliff face. Saya did not think it was very large. In fact, she had seen much grander structures owned by mere vassals in the capital of Mahoroba. But she later learned that she was mistaken, for the main part of his dwelling was inside the cliff itself.

The one-eyed lord came to greet them at the gate. Although he smiled, his smile was as stern as a rock long weathered by blizzards. In one hand he grasped a gnarled staff, on the top of which perched Torihiko, looking nonchalant, as if he were merely an ornament.

"Well met," Lord Akitsu greeted Saya in a deep resonant voice, the beautiful timbre of which belied his looks. "You're a brave girl. That's even clearer now."

Wondering perversely what they would think if she burst into tears as she wished to do, Saya bowed her head silently as her common sense dictated.

"Lord Ibuki will join us in a few days. Then we'll all be gathered together once more. But first you must rest yourselves in my hall."

He beckoned them inside, as if he noticed nothing unusual, but his one eye missed nothing as it fixed shrewdly upon Chihaya. He waited until Lady Iwa passed him and then spoke in a low voice so that no one would overhear. "That boy, he can't be . . ."

"But he is," Lady Iwa replied, looking up at him.

Lord Akitsu could not hide his surprise, and he stared after Chihaya's receding figure. "Him? But he's so young."

She blinked her heavy, sparsely lashed eyelids. "Yes, he's but a child not yet fully developed," she whispered. "Which is precisely why he may yet become ours."

THE ROOM to which Saya was led was long and narrow, with one wall of stone, and she felt that she had indeed been placed upon a shelf, although it was much cooler and more pleasant than she had expected. Tired, she sat where she had been left, dozing, but she started when she noticed a young woman kneeling respectfully beside her. The girl was round-cheeked and cheerful-looking. Although her hair had been put up in a bun, it looked as if it had been fastened only with much effort, and many obstinate locks had already escaped.

"My name is Natsume. I have been assigned to serve you. Please don't hesitate to tell me what you need," she said in a clear, crisp voice. Not much older than Saya, she nevertheless radiated a calm confidence.

"Really? Oh, I'm so glad!" Saya exclaimed, jumping to her feet. "I'm so glad that you're not an old woman. Will you be my friend?"

Natsume's eyes widened slightly, but then she broke into a smile and said, "Yes. Gladly, if I'm acceptable to you."

"Are you married?" Saya asked, wondering if it was also the custom here for married women to wear their hair up.

"Yes. I was married this spring," she replied, her cheeks turning a charming pink.

"How nice. What's your husband like?"

Still blushing, Natsume began to laugh. "Really, my lady! One of these days, I'll tell you. After all, he, too, serves the lord of this hall."

NATSUME was a hard worker by nature, completing her tasks quickly and efficiently, and she made sure that Saya experienced no inconvenience in this unfamiliar place. She enjoyed her work so much that just watching her was a pleasure. Now that Saya had found someone with whom she could feel totally at ease, she took full advantage of Natsume's attentions and did not leave the hall for the next few days. Chihaya, she heard, also had a servant and lacked for nothing. While it may have been normal for Chihaya, however, it was unlike Saya to remain indoors, ignoring a new people and a new land. Although she herself remained unaware of it, she had not escaped unscathed from the string of events that had led her here, and the scars of that experience had made her timid. She also found the reverent glances cast her way by the people of Eagle's Manor confusing and intimidating.

Still, she was young and quick to recover. Within a few days, her natural curiosity began to reassert itself. She had just reached the point when she could no longer stand being cooped up in her narrow room all day and was trying to think of some excuse to go out when Natsume returned from preparing the evening meal.

"I wonder if he's looking for something," she said.

"Who?"

Natsume blushed. "I don't know his name, but, you know, the handsome one."

"Oh, you mean Chihaya." Puzzled, Saya looked at the flustered Natsume. "What about him?"

"I saw him beside the main building. He seemed to be looking for something, so I spoke to him, but he walked away as though he didn't even hear me."

"That's strange."

She could not think of any reason for him to do that. Yet, the fact that he was walking about alone did not bode well. She rose. "I'll go and see. Would you take me to where you saw him?"

When they reached the courtyard adjoining the kitchen to which Natsume led Saya, they did not see Chihaya anywhere. They walked a little farther until they neared the wooden fence enclosing the hall, and there they found him surrounded by several guards in front of the guardhouse.

I was afraid it might be something like this, Saya thought. The guards, catching sight of the two hurrying toward them, released Chihaya's arms and bowed their heads respectfully to Saya.

"My lady! We didn't expect the honor of your presence in such a shabby place."

Although she had known her appearance would have some effect, she was disconcerted by this sudden deference. Somehow it did not seem right to be treated this way when, such a short time ago, she had been just an ordinary, insignificant girl. At the same time, she could not reprove them for showing respect.

"Has he been causing trouble?" she asked as she went to Chihaya's side.

"He ignored our challenge and began to approach the armory, so we ordered him to stop. He doesn't even attempt to answer our questions," one of the guards replied.

"Well!" Saya looked at the dreamy-eyed Chihaya. "What did you want in the armory?"

His gaze, which had been roving far away, finally focused on her face. "Nothing," he said. "I just wondered if there wasn't some way to get to the top of the cliff."

When they heard this, the guards' expressions once again grew grim. "And what business do you have up on the cliff? Only the sentries are permitted to go there."

Saya hurried to defend him. "I'm sure he had no special reason. He just isn't used to being in a place like this."

"We know that he's a guest, one of your company, my lady, but we can't ignore such suspicious behavior," said a serious-looking man who appeared to be their leader. "If anything should happen . . ."

"What will you do with him, then?"

"Those who behave suspiciously must be imprisoned and interrogated."

Saya gasped in shock. "I give you my word that he can be trusted. I'll talk to Lord Akitsu myself, so please, couldn't you let him go this time?"

The leader of the guards looked uncomfortable, but said, "My lady, it's our duty. If we fail to fulfill it, we'll betray our lord's trust. Please try to understand that."

Saya bit her lip in consternation. But at that moment someone spoke behind them. "It's the Princess of the Sword who begs this favor of you. Why don't you let him go?"

Turning around, she saw Lord Shinado standing there watching them. His lean figure, while not particularly remarkable, conveyed more force than all the guards combined. He, too, was an honored guest at Eagle's Manor, and, having nothing to do, he had apparently just happened along at that moment.

The head of the guards protested. "I beg your pardon, Lord Shinado, but he ignored our challenge as if he didn't even hear us. How can we be expected to preserve order in the fortress if we overlook such behavior?"

"It's not worth worrying about. He simply doesn't have the brains of an ordinary man, that's all. Like the lady, I'll vouch for him, so let him go."

"Oh, I see. Is that how it is?" The guard looked hard at Chihaya, and his expression turned to one of pity. "In that case, we'll overlook it as long as it doesn't happen again."

"Why, of course," Saya said hastily. At her urging, Chihaya came away quietly. As they walked back toward their lodgings, Saya glanced uneasily at Lord Shinado walking beside her. She did not know whether she should thank him or not. While she appreciated the fact that he had come to her aid, she was annoyed by his choice of words.

Lord Shinado, his face stern, also gave Saya a sidelong glance, and then said curtly, "Don't let Chihaya behave in such a way that he betrays his lineage. Most of our people aren't ready to accept a Prince of Light into their midst. I can't guarantee his safety should they find out. If he's going to walk about as he pleases, he just might be better off in prison."

Saya was about to retort, but he left her side abruptly and, turning his back on the hall, walked away. She vented her feelings to Chihaya. "Don't you care what he says of you? He called you a fool."

"Oh, really? I didn't notice." His response was so vacant that there seemed no point in going on, and she held her tongue.

Overcoming her irritation, she asked, "Why did you want to go to the top of the cliff?"

Chihaya's face instantly filled with a lively enthusiasm, making him seem like a different person.

"Something was there early this morning. It was too far away to touch my mind, but I know something came. Something that I've never seen before—like the shark."

The change that came over him made her realize just how little the argument with the guards had registered in his mind. When she stopped to think about it, Chihaya had been extremely taciturn during their journey and since their arrival. In fact, she suddenly realized that she had never seen him talk with anyone other than herself. This made her even more anxious about the future.

Could it be that Chihaya wasn't ignoring the guards but actually didn't hear them?

THAT NIGHT, Saya was summoned by Lord Akitsu and told much the same thing she had been told by Lord Shinado, although he chose much milder words to convey his meaning. He wished to know, however, why Chihaya had suddenly taken it into his head to venture to the top of the cliff.

"I'm not sure, but he said that there was something up there, something that attracted his interest," Saya said thoughtfully. "Although he seems so absentminded most of the time, he's very sensitive in unusual ways, so I believe that there was indeed something there. Chihaya seems to perceive things differently from the rest of us. When we were on the beach the other day, he said he heard the voice of the Sea God."

Lord Akitsu was listening intently. "Is that so?" he remarked. "Yet I don't think any god resides on the top of this mountain. Except for the sentries, there aren't even any human beings up there. Only deer and mountain goats."

"It could be something like that," Saya said hesitantly, "because Chihaya is drawn to beasts rather than to people."

"Hmm." The one-eyed lord nodded as he considered this. Then, as if he had suddenly hit upon a brilliant idea, he said, "In that case, tomorrow I shall climb to the top with him. I have been thinking that it was about time to do something like deer hunting to keep from getting stiff. Has he ever used a bow? No, of course not. Anyway, I'll guide him. You should come, too, if you like."

3

EARLY THE NEXT MORNING, Saya fastened the garters of her trousers and set out in high spirits. When she had said, half in jest, that she would need trousers in order to follow the hunt, Natsume had actually produced a pair. In Hashiba, women were not permitted to wear such things, and in the Palace of Light she would likely have been punished just for mentioning the idea. But Saya had always wanted, at least once, to stride boldly forth like Princess Teruhi, unencumbered by long skirts. Natsume had laid out an outfit of white trousers and a jacket with a light green border and red garters adorned with little bells. Seeing Saya's excitement, she said, "In times of war, all the women of Darkness must don men's clothes and fight as bravely as the menfolk. We all have one such outfit to wear should the need arise."

"Would you fight, too, Natsume?" Saya asked in surprise. Fighting seemed as appropriate to her gentle nature as fangs to a fawn.

"If the enemy attacks us, then I will defend what must be defended," Natsume replied, adding somewhat harshly, "for the army of Light gives no quarter to women and children."

When Saya went outside, Torihiko flew down from a branch and alighted on her shoulder. "Well, well. You're wearing trousers."

"Of course. Don't I look dashing?"

"About as dashing as Chihaya," Torihiko replied. "His arm is at least as thin as yours. His bow is weeping. Look."

She turned and saw Chihaya dressed in hunting attire with a bow and a quiver of arrows, but, at best, he appeared only to be carrying them for someone else. Beside him Lord Akitsu stood smartly equipped, every inch an experienced huntsman, with a falcon perched on his forearm. When Saya approached with Torihiko, he glanced over his shoulder at them and frowned slightly. "Torihiko?

You aren't planning to join us, are you? You'll upset Madarao."

The falcon, a cord fastened to one leg, screeched, opening and closing its wings repeatedly. It seemed poised to fly at the crow at any moment, but in fact was terrified of him. Chihaya was staring intently at the falcon.

"What difference will it make?" Torihiko calmly retorted. "It's obvious you intend to hunt bigger game than falcon bait today considering the number of beaters you sent out this morning."

"You're a hard one to beat. Well, never mind. Just don't get so close that Madarao breaks his jesses and escapes."

"Why would I want to be near you? I'm going to stay with Saya." Bobbing his head up and down, he said to her, "I'll teach you how to shoot a bow and arrow. I used to be a good shot with the short bow."

The hunting party left the gate and, cutting across Eagle's Manor, set off along a mountain path. Torihiko told Saya in a low voice that there was actually a direct path from the rock face behind Lord Akitsu's hall to the top of the cliff.

"But it's a secret. Lord Akitsu's a shrewd man. He thinks of everything, although he doesn't let on," Torihiko told her softly. "Take that falcon, for example. He doesn't need it for the hunt. He brought it along on purpose to attract Chihaya. He's hoping it'll make him open up."

Saya realized that Chihaya had been so engrossed in the falcon that he had followed the lord ahead, leaving them behind. She shrugged. "Well, I hope that at least they can become friends."

The leaves were thick on the trees in the forest, and thickets and creepers grew densely, making visibility poor. It was certainly not the best season for hunting, but the lord and his company did not seem to mind. As the hunters moved rapidly ahead, Saya gave up trying to keep pace with them to the site of the kill, stopping instead at the edge of the forest to practice archery with Torihiko. They stayed there till the sun rose high in the sky while Saya shot at a wooden target mostly for the fun of it. Through the trees, the faint sound of the beaters' whistles and drums could be heard intermittently. The beaters had left before dawn and now were gradually tightening their circle, driving their prey in the direction of the river, where the archers waited. Hearing without really listening, Saya thought not of the excitement of those waiting with bows drawn but rather of the trembling of the living creatures who fled from the sound of approaching death. Run! Run! Run! To those fleet of foot and sharp of hearing shall the reward of life be given.

"Is something wrong?" Torihiko asked, jolting Saya back to her senses.

"No. Nothing."

"Saya, I'm afraid you'll never make a good archer. For one thing, you have no concentration," Torihiko said bluntly. But at that moment there was a slight movement at the edge of Saya's vision. A bright reddish brown form passed swiftly and silently on the other side of the trees.

"Shoot! Shoot!" Torihiko screeched, flapping his wings, beside himself, but it never occurred to Saya to shoot. What she glimpsed through the thicket was a spectacular stag. Stately eight-branched antlers soared on his proud head. The fur at his throat was silver, while his back was dark, proclaiming him to be a long-lived veteran of many hunts. He glanced questioningly at her with glistening black eyes, and then disappeared once more without apparent haste. He bore himself with a spellbinding grace. Saya gazed after him for some time and then said to Torihiko, "He was like a god. If someone told me he was an earth god, I'd believe it." She had no idea what an uproar this stag would soon cause for the hunters.

It grew hot, and the hunt should have been winding up when Torihiko, who had flown off to check on the hunting party's progress, returned in a fluster.

"Saya, Chihaya's run away! Everyone has stopped chasing game to chase him."

"What?" Saya raised her voice in astonishment. "I can't believe it. Why would he do that?"

"Lord Akitsu said to come quickly. Hurry!"

Saya rose and ran after Torihiko.

Lord Akitsu was in the middle of the forest, far above the hunting site along the river's course. When he caught sight of the breathless Saya, he began to speak before she even had a chance to ask. "I don't understand it. He suddenly threw down his bow and quiver and ran off. I've never seen anyone move so fast. We still haven't managed to catch him even with so many people searching."

"When did this happen?" Saya asked. "When did Chihaya leave you? Or should I say leave Madarao?"

"Madarao's with the falconer now, looking for Chihaya. But the falcon no longer seems to interest him. He ran off after he saw the deer. A stag more than eight years old, a rare sight to behold, leapt out in front of the beaters, but before we had a chance to shoot, Chihaya ran off."

"After the stag?"

"No, in the opposite direction."

"Why would he do that?" Saya wondered.

"You mean you don't know either?"

"I don't know that much about Chihaya."

"Well, I can tell you one thing: he's amazingly fast. He didn't seem human," Lord Akitsu growled. "I was totally deceived by the way he looked."

Saya, who was now quite worried, pleaded, "Please don't accuse him of anything until we find out what happened. I'm sure there will be a simple explanation for this. In some ways he's just like a little baby."

Lord Akitsu nodded but continued to frown. "All right. But if he won't come quietly, we may have to catch him with a net like a wild animal. Although I'll do my best to see that he comes to no harm."

In a short while the men who had tried to surround Chihaya reported that he had slipped through their circle and disappeared. It seemed that the manhunt would continue for some time. There was one possibility that worried Saya, but she was so uncertain that she decided to keep quiet until she could see Chihaya for herself. The sun sank steadily lower in the sky. Lord Akitsu finally turned to her and said, "The mountain paths are treacherous at night. My servant will take you back to the hall now before it gets dark. Don't worry. We'll find him and bring him home."

Torihiko remained behind to help for as long as his bird's eyes could be of use. Saya was sorry to leave, but she could not go against the lord's wishes.

If only I had stayed with him, she thought bitterly. She descended the steep mountain path in silence, rebuking herself for her reluctance to rejoin Lord Akitsu's company just because she had found the hunt boring. When Eagle's Manor came into sight, she noticed a crowd of people in the distance.

"What's going on?" she asked her companion, but he did not seem to know either. As they drew near, he exclaimed with relief, "Ah, Lord Ibuki has arrived. I must tell him why Lord Akitsu isn't here to welcome him."

By this time Saya was able to make out the giant of a man who stood conspicuously in the middle of the crowd. Beside him even the tallest men looked like children clustered around their father. They wove their way through the wall of people until they reached Lord Ibuki. He noticed Saya at once. His bearded bearlike face lit up and broke into a broad grin. "Well, well. If it isn't Saya, the Water Maiden! I'm glad to see you looking so well."

But Saya did not bother to return his greeting for her eyes were riveted on the squirming, struggling young man in his arms, who had until then been obstructed from her view by the crowd. Covered in scratches, he flailed desperately, trying to wriggle out of his captor's grip, but Lord Ibuki did not budge, whether kicked or hit. When the captive began to use his teeth, however, he hoisted him onto his shoulder in exasperation. Marveling at this feat, Saya finally found her voice again.

"Chihaya!"

Her companion also blurted out in surprise, "Where did you find him? Lord Akitsu is in the forest searching for him right now."

Lord Ibuki blinked several times and rubbed his face with his free hand. "Well, actually, thinking that I'd like to bring a little present with me, I went into the forest, but instead of game this thing sprang out. I couldn't really leave him there tangled in the brambles. But what a surprise to learn that Lord Akitsu is looking for him." He glanced at Chihaya who was struggling wildly on his shoulder. "Such a handsome lunatic is a pathetic thing indeed."

"Please—just put him down."

When he finally stood before her, Saya took a close look at him. It seemed that he had indeed been caught in a thorn bush for he looked a terrible mess. His hair hung in disarray, his clothes were in tatters, and blood oozed from countless scratches covering his face and limbs. But more than anything else, it was his eyes that shocked her, for in them resided only naked terror, ignorance, and despair.

"Lady, I will return to the mountain and report that Chihaya has been found," the manservant said.

He was turning to leave when Saya shouted, "No! No! This is not Chihaya!"

"What do you—" he began.

But Saya cut him short. "This is not Chihaya. What stands before us is a deer—a stag whose body has been possessed by Chihaya."

Lord Ibuki blinked again, as if he hoped that by blinking he would gain enlightenment. "Hmm. I'm having some difficulty following you."

"What I mean is Chihaya has possessed a stag. Without thinking of the consequences, in the middle of the hunt."

This was the result of borrowing others' bodies. Saya recalled the time when Chihaya had restrained her. Then her body had been occupied by a mouse's spirit, and even now the thought gave her the shivers. She held out her hands, but Chihaya fell back and lowered his head, ready to charge her with nonexistent antlers.

"Don't be afraid. It's me, Saya," she said in a soothing voice. "Don't you remember? I didn't shoot you with my bow and arrow. I promise not to hurt you. I just want to help you. Relax. I'll see that you get back to normal as soon as I can."

She spoke gently and repetitively, and his breathing became slower.

Gradually, he relaxed, looking timidly into her face. When she held out her hand once more, he sniffed it first, like a wild creature, and then came meekly to her.

"There, there, easy now." Saya stroked his twig-tangled hair lovingly. Suddenly recollecting herself, she turned abruptly to the servant and said, "Go quickly and tell Lord Akitsu that I want him to catch the stag with the eight-branched antlers. But he mustn't shoot it, because that's the real Chihaya. Oh, but it would be faster to take his body there."

She was suddenly filled with impatience. At any moment Lord Akitsu or one of his men, ignorant of the truth, might shoot the great stag as he carelessly approached them. It would be just like Chihaya.

"We must hurry! Please, show me the shortcut that leads to the top of the cliff. If we don't go right away, it will be too late."

"But . . ." the manservant protested, looking troubled.

Glancing at the others, Saya realized that no one had yet grasped the situation. But Lord Ibuki said, "Do as she says. It's the Lady of the Sword who speaks. Even if we don't understand, she's bound to have a good reason."

Lord Ibuki's words seemed to carry special weight with the servant, who obeyed immediately. But then it would be difficult not to accord special respect to the words uttered by a man whose barrel chest towered high above him. The servant led Saya and the others toward the side of the lord's hall. There they saw a cave concealed behind the building. It was a natural hollow that had been further shaped by the hands of men, and steps had been carved in the rock at the far end, leading upward. The servant, bearing a torch, beckoned them. "It's this way."

Although Saya herself did not mind, it required great effort to lead the terrified Chihaya along the passageway. She had to stay by his side, soothing and coaxing him so that he would not panic, and they moved ahead only one slow step at a time. Lord Ibuki followed, but he had to fold himself in two to keep his head from scraping the roof. Even so, the sound of his head hitting stone echoed countless times in the narrow cave.

After some time, their patience was rewarded, and they finally felt a breeze and saw the night sky. Stars twinkled. It was already dark. The sentry challenged them but let them pass when the servant uttered the password.

"Did you see a stag? One with huge antlers?" Saya asked, squinting against the glare of the watch fire. But the sentry shook his head. Chihaya, however, appeared calm and turned his face to the wind. "Let's wait a little. If he's not a complete fool, he'll come here in the end." Before she had even finished speaking, she sensed something moving among the trees at the edge of the light cast by the watch fire. Everyone turned to look and saw two black eyes glinting in the firelight and the trembling black silhouette of a pair of high, branched antlers.

"Chihaya!" Though Saya tried to speak calmly, her voice rose to a shriek. "Come back here! Right now!"

The stag leaped suddenly. But its movements were awkward. Saya felt a stab of remorse at the sight of a broken arrow shaft sticking out of its hind leg.

From beside her, Chihaya suddenly spoke. "Phew! I'm tired!"

Startled, she whirled to stare at him, and at that moment the stag bounded into a thicket. "Wait!" she shouted hastily after it. "You're hurt! Let me dress your wound."

But the stag disappeared into the darkness, never to return.

"DO YOU REALIZE how much trouble you caused everyone?" Saya scolded Chihaya furiously after they had returned to the hall. In her relief, she was suddenly filled with anger. "We were all scouring the mountainside for you, including me. Not only that, but everyone in Eagle's Manor is now convinced that you're crazy. And just think of that poor stag!"

Chihaya stared at her as though she were talking about someone else, then finally remarked, "So Saya gets angry, too, just like my sister."

"And who wouldn't be angry!" Saya snapped. "How can you treat your own body so carelessly? No wonder you can't understand what it was like for that poor stag. Doesn't it even bother you that you were cut up so badly when you weren't in your body?"

Chihaya looked at the numerous gashes upon his arms. "Oh. I'll fix them."

"Well, you can't fix the stag. It may even die because of that wound," Saya said, holding back angry tears. She could not forget the trusting gaze of the stag when it had come to her. Chihaya had been twice as attractive then as now, she thought.

"All right, all right, from now on, I'll think carefully before I dream. Or I'll ask you first."

"I don't want you to dream ever again," Saya said. "You're not in the shrine anymore. There's no one to bind you or keep you hidden away, so there's no need to leave your body in the care of a wild creature while you go out to play. You should be ashamed of yourself. You should be more responsible. Surely you realized what a dangerous game you were playing when you were hit by that arrow."

"Mmm," Chihaya nodded, but he did not appear repentant. "That was the first time I've become such a large creature. It's difficult to control something so big and strong. When it's faced with danger, it's impossible to stop it. But when it runs, it's wonderful! Simply wonderful! It springs from a rock and the next instant knows exactly where to land—not by sight but by feel—through its hooves. When it runs at full speed, the whole world changes. The ground seems transitory, the wind thickens, and they both become like water . . ."

Saya was just thinking how unusual it was for Chihaya to speak at such length when, before she knew it, he had lain down on his side, still talking, and fallen fast asleep the instant his head hit the woven rush mat with a soft thud. He was out quicker than a gambler loses a fortune. She was so taken aback by the suddenness of it that she lost the will to be angry and instead sat gazing at his face.

It was the face of a sleeping child—untroubled, eyelashes casting long shadows, lips slightly parted. He looked so innocent.

"My Lady," Natsume said quietly from behind her.

"Will you treat his wounds?" Saya said. She was surprised to find herself speaking in such a gentle tone. "Carefully, though, so as not to wake him."

"I brought herbs and hot water for just that purpose," Natsume
replied. She dipped a cloth in the basin of hot water and began to
wipe the blood and dirt from his wounds. But a moment later she
uttered a stifled cry.

"How could this be?"

Saya looked over, too, and could not believe her eyes. For beneath
the crust of blood that Natsume had washed away, the skin was
smooth and clear. There was not even a pink scar where it had healed.
It might never have been cut.

THE NIGHT was far advanced when an unfamiliar girl came to
Saya's room. She bowed and said, "The lords are meeting in Lady
Iwa's inner chamber. They request the presence of Your Ladyship
and Chihaya."

Realizing that she must be one of Lady Iwa's servants, Saya said,
"Chihaya is already asleep. Must he go, too?"

"Two places have been prepared. They are expecting both of you,"
the girl replied politely but uncompromisingly. So Saya shook Chihaya
awake and led him, yawning nonstop, after the girl.

The inner chamber referred not to a room in the front of the hall
but to one which had been carved into the cliff. There could be
countless such rooms hidden away in this hall. Saya pondered the
strangeness of the building. She did not know whether existing caves
had been expanded or whether the rooms had been dug into the
rock, but in either case, they must have been the product of intense
labor. The walls of the corridor carved in the rock were smooth and
unmarred, and not one of the supporting columns or ceiling beams,
which were set in a complex pattern, could have been easily executed.
The stronghold, lit by the faint yellow glow of tallow candles, was
pleasantly cool. No doubt in winter it would be warm. It was perhaps
more magnificent than an ordinary palace.

At last Saya saw a light glowing through a silk curtain at the end of
a passageway, and they arrived at Lady Iwa's room. Furs and silk wall
hangings draped the quarried rock walls, and the floor was covered
in thick woven fabric. Although the atmosphere was rather solemn,

the room was spacious enough that it did not seem oppressive. It had a faint but pleasant smell. Or it may have been the fragrance of the unusually large candle that stood in the center of the room, casting wavering shadows in four directions. Each person sat on a woven rush cushion on the floor. Lady Iwa was at the far end of the room, with Lord Akitsu and Lord Shinado to her right and Lord Ibuki and Torihiko to her left. The sight of Torihiko in crow's form claiming a seat all to himself was so absurd that Saya relaxed a little. The two nearest seats completing the circle were vacant. Food and sake had been set before each place, but no one except Lord Ibuki appeared to have touched them. When Chihaya and Saya had taken their seats, Lady Iwa spoke in a quiet voice. Even a whisper could be heard clearly, and Saya suddenly realized that no room could be more confidential.

"The Sword and the Priestess of the Sword have both returned to us, completing our strength. Now is the time to rally our forces, which for decades have been outmatched by the enemy. All the omens are in our favor. My lords, you must exert yourselves. The will of the Goddess is with us."

The men all bowed respectfully. Saya was surprised at the amount of authority wielded by an old woman so small that Saya could have picked her up with one hand. Although she spoke in her familiar rasping voice, it almost seemed as if the Goddess herself were speaking.

Lady Iwa paused briefly and then continued. "However, there is something I must tell you. For countless generations the people of Darkness have fought the immortal Children of Light and their followers. Power has swung back and forth like a pendulum between the forces of Light and Darkness, now attacking, now retreating. But now, something different has occurred. We have found the one who was formerly known only in prophecy: he who has the power to wield the Dragon Sword. Whether this means good fortune or not, I don't know. It is unprecedented, and as such transcends fortune-telling. Since ancient times, the Water Maiden has been one of our people, invested with the power to still the Dragon Sword and lull its evil to sleep. At the same time, however, legend tells us that only one being is capable of grasping the Sword and wielding it. That being is called the Wind Child. And having escaped from the Palace of Light, he is here, before our very eyes."

Every face in the room turned to look in astonishment at Chihaya.

4

AS THE LORDS STARED at Chihaya, their bewilderment deepened. Saya was no exception. Nothing could be harder to imagine than Chihaya wielding a sword. He was so sleepy that he appeared even more stunned than usual under their collective gaze, staring blankly off into space oblivious to Lady Iwa's words.

Lord Akitsu said in a choked voice, "Ah, are you absolutely sure, my lady, that—er—he's the Wind Child?"

"Chihaya turned the Sword into the Dragon. And you all know what a bitter blow it dealt the Palace of Light. Is there anyone else who can call forth the Dragon and live?"

"He's an immortal, one of the Children of Light. He cannot die," Lord Shinado said coldly.

"Not in this case. The Dragon has the power to destroy even the Children of Light. Surely you can see that if you think about why Teruhi and Tsukishiro never wielded the Sword themselves."

Lord Ibuki's eyes had never left Chihaya, but it was clear from his expression that he still regarded him as a lunatic.

"To tell Chihaya to wield the Sword would be the same as telling me to," Torihiko said. He spread his wings. "In other words, impossible."

"Even supposing that he really is the Wind Child," Lord Shinado said vehemently to Lady Iwa, "it won't change the fact that he's a Prince of Light, and a Prince of Light serves the God of Light. We would be hatching a snake in our bosom."

"That's not necessarily true," Lady Iwa replied, lowering her wrinkled eyelids and regarding him through half-closed eyes. "Princess Teruhi must have foreseen his potential long ago. She imprisoned him and concealed his existence. It can only have been because some harm would befall them if he awoke. Even after they had seized the Sword, they did not free him or let him wield the Sword; instead they made him play the role of the Water Maiden. Princess Teruhi succeeded not in stilling the Sword but in stilling Chihaya, who had the ability to summon its power."

Lord Akitsu had been lost in thought, a grim expression on his face. He asked abruptly, "But what will happen should Chihaya side with us and wield the Dragon Sword?"

"I have no idea. It will surely bring great peril." Lady Iwa pressed the palms of her thin hands together. "But—and this is just a premonition—I can't help feeling that the appearance of the Wind Child now is a sign that this long struggle is coming to an end. I don't know what the outcome will be, but I believe we should take bold and drastic measures." She sighed disconsolately and looked at Lord Akitsu. "Right?"

The one-eyed lord groaned but did not utter another word.

Lord Ibuki's gruff voice suddenly broke the silence. "If you insist that this little wisp of a boy must wield the Sword, then I'm willing to teach him how. It may not help, but surely we'd be foolish to decide without training him."

After the previous gloomy exchange, his words were so refreshingly positive they sounded totally out of place. The wrinkles on Lady Iwa's face, however, relaxed in a smile. "You're right, Lord Ibuki. While Chihaya has the power to use the Dragon Sword, he's still young and untried. In his lack of training, he's much like the Water Maiden here."

Saya hunched her shoulders at this sudden attention. Lady Iwa gazed straight at her. "Saya, you're the most recent of the Water Maidens who have cared for the Sword. Are you willing to give it to the Wind Child?"

Saya thought of the Sword lying in her room, inlaid with red stones and sheathed in the scabbard that Lady Iwa had made. But no matter how she searched her heart, she could find no feeling of attachment to it appropriate for a priestess. It was a miserable, troublesome, accursed burden, and nothing would give her more relief than to have someone else shoulder it in her stead.

"Yes," she started to reply but then stopped. She remembered the thick black smoke rising over the capital on the day the palace fell, and how she had so easily fainted. Was forcing the Sword onto Chihaya really the answer?

After searching for words, she said, "If Chihaya shows a little more reliability, I'll give it to him."

"That'll do." Lady Iwa nodded emphatically. "That'll do. Chihaya still sleeps. He hasn't yet roused from Princess Teruhi's spell. He needs your help. Having spent too long alone, he doesn't know how to relate to others. Right now you're the only person he can see properly."

Saya muttered, "And I don't think he even sees me properly."

"And likewise you're the only person at this time who can understand him. You should stay with him and support him, make decisions and learn together. For neither of you has as yet developed your full potential."

After shaking the dozing Chihaya awake, Saya excused herself and led him away. While she walked back to her room, she could not escape the feeling that Lady Iwa had talked her into shouldering an even greater burden than before.

ALTHOUGH the days were as hot as ever, the tune of the cicadas was starting to change. And when she raised her face to a stray breeze that coolly caressed the nape of her neck under the blazing sun, Saya occasionally caught sight of red dragonflies darting above. But most of all, it was the dew at dusk and dawn that spoke to the growing things of autumn. Summer was beginning to give way to fall. Saya had become friendly with the sentries and sometimes visited the top of the cliff. Seeing the reddish purple bush clover blooming on the mountaintop made her think of her home lying far beyond the mountain villages at the eastern edge of the sky. The rice in the fields of Hashiba would soon be ripening to gold, heralding the busy season in which the harvest and the coming of the typhoons were the main concerns. The gayest village festival of the year awaited them once the whole family had finished bringing in the harvest.

But here in the land of the people of Darkness, the situation was completely different. Although activity increased as autumn approached, the harvest consisted of stones and wood for arrow shafts. There was a forge near Lord Akitsu's hall, and for the first time in her life Saya saw a foot bellows in action. Black iron ore brought from the bowels of the mountain turned red-hot in the well-stoked furnace, and the heat was intensified by wind from the bellows. The ore, now glowing brightly, began to bend like a snake; then it was hardened, reheated, and beaten. The tremendous heat of the thick enveloping clouds of steam generated when the iron was beaten was enough to intimidate Saya and keep her at a distance. The men beating the iron on the anvils seemed possessed by demons, their shoulder blades, tanned by the summer sun, rising and falling with their mighty efforts, their bodies drenched in sweat. And the results of all this labor were arrowheads and spear points, weapons of destruction; unlike the golden ears of grain that Saya had once harvested as she sang, these products led to death. Yet at the same time they spoke of a rugged heroism that inspired a strange excitement. Even the jarring noise of the pounding hammers seemed to fill those who heard it with eagerness.

The war begins, Saya thought. Despite her lack of experience, that much she understood. The mountain of arms that they were preparing was not for something so insignificant as hunting wildfowl or deer. The soldiers grew animated, joking frequently. Saya enjoyed their banter, but uneasiness squirmed in the bottom of her heart like the premonition of an approaching typhoon.

Almost every night the lords or their advisers gathered in Lady Iwa's room within the stone hall. Day and night, scouts returned to report to Lord Akitsu.

"If we travel north, we can reach the Asakura pastures in two days' time. The pastures supply war-horses directly to the Palace of Light. Let's take those pastures first," Lord Akitsu announced one evening to all those assembled, after various suggestions had been made.

"Us? Take the pastures?"

Surprise spread across the faces of those assembled. The one-eyed lord continued. "We have mastered the art of taking advantage of the terrain to ambush our enemy on foot, but in this war it is crucial to think ahead. We'll need cavalry. The time will come when we must confront the forces of Light face-to-face on the plains."

"Are you saying that we have an even chance in a direct confrontation with the army of Light?" one of the older commanders asked in surprise.

"Exactly. From now on, we must ride the winds of fortune. Isn't that right, Lady Iwa?"

She nodded expressionlessly. "Lady Iwa predicts that this campaign will be a crucial battle leading to a final, decisive confrontation between the forces of Darkness and Light. This is our last and greatest opportunity to reverse our fortune and rescue Toyoashihara from the hands of the immortals."

There was a stunned silence when he finished speaking, followed immediately by a buzz of excited whispering.

"Of course! We have the Dragon Sword. This time we might even have the power to overthrow the immortals themselves."

Lord Ibuki scratched his nose slowly and muttered doubtfully, "The pastures? I wonder if they'll have a horse large enough for me."

Lord Shinado, who was sitting to the right of Lord Akitsu, said confidentially, as if unable to contain himself, "You're surely thinking of Chihaya. He could never keep up with us in battle if we went on foot."

Lord Akitsu smiled faintly as he looked at him. "Actually, I was thinking of Saya. But I suppose it's really the same thing."

"You intend to take the Princess to war?" Lord Shinado demanded, his expression hardening.

"We have no choice," Lord Akitsu replied. "How else can we keep the Wind Child at our side?"

IN A SUNLIT GARDEN bordered by a fence, Lord Ibuki was bellowing in his distinctive gruff voice despite the early morning hour. Brandishing a wooden sword, he moved with an agility that belied his hulking frame. "Come on now! Move! Look! Here's my heart, here's my stomach. You can't even touch me when I'm wide open."

Chihaya lunged at him halfheartedly, but naturally every blow was repulsed. Lord Ibuki's great belly loomed directly before his eyes, but it was not easily reached.

"I've never seen such a clumsy thrust, you numbskull!"

Chihaya narrowly dodged a blow to his head. Although Lord Ibuki had not put his full force behind it, the blow would have resulted in more than a lump if it had connected.

"But this stick is so heavy."

"What are you going to do if even a wooden sword is too heavy? How can you call yourself a man?"

Torihiko, who was perched on Saya's shoulder watching them practice said, "It looks like Chihaya's just fooling around."

"Well, it can't be helped. After all, he doesn't understand why he needs to do this," Saya replied. In fact, Chihaya's progress was so slow she felt that even she could do better. Though he had received blows hard enough to bruise as chastisement, he never once fought back in earnest. Although she did not particularly want him to learn sword fighting, the thought of sending him to war like this worried her. She had begun practicing in private with a wooden sword of her own so that she could help him should the need arise.

"You're working hard, Lord Ibuki," someone called out from the cool shade of a tree. Looking around, Saya saw Lord Shinado leaning his spare frame against the tree trunk. His light blue jacket was open over his bare chest.

"Ho!" said Lord Ibuki, wiping the sweat from his forehead with the back of his hand. "It's you. You're the best sword fighter among the lot of us. Why don't you teach this lazybones some of your secrets?"

Lord Shinado was close enough that Saya could see him clearly as he turned his gaze slowly toward Chihaya. Unaware that he was observed, he let the feelings that he usually kept carefully concealed cross his face for an instant: stabbing hatred and malice.

Chilled, Saya fervently hoped that Lord Ibuki would not give him the wooden sword. But Lord Shinado smiled coldly and shook his head.

"I haven't the skill to teach someone who doesn't know death. For how could he ever understand the meaning of the words 'to fight for one's life'?"

"Ahh—I see." Lord Ibuki looked at Chihaya in surprise. Apparently, it was the first time this thought had ever occurred to him.

Lord Shinado added casually, "Why not try giving him a few mortal injuries? He might just become a little more like us."

He left the shade of the tree and began to walk away. As he passed, he happened to glance in Saya's direction. Incensed by his suggestion, she blurted out, "How can you say such a horrible thing?"

A faint look of surprise crossed his face. Perhaps because she had caught him off guard, he suddenly seemed vulnerable and easily hurt, and she realized that he was not as old as she had first thought. The grave expression he usually wore made him look as old as Lord Akitsu, but he might not even be thirty.

After a brief pause, he said in a low voice, "When I was about your age, Teruhi's troops slaughtered my mother and father before my very eyes. The entire village was massacred, wiped out. Though wounded, I escaped and vowed that someday I would take revenge on the Children of Light. If I could kill them by tearing them limb from limb, I would gladly do it, but they're immortal. So I keep on fighting, hoping that the day will come when I can mete out suitable punishment. No matter how you may insist that the hands of that fool over there are clean, he's one of them. To ask that I stop hating them is to demand the impossible."

Turning his back on her, he added simply, "You should know. You have the same history as I."

Saya winced as she watched him leave. *He's right. We share the same background,* she thought. Perhaps that was why his words always seemed to sting her.

Chihaya continued practicing halfheartedly, showing no sign of improvement. One day, Saya, unable to bear it any longer, turned to Lord Akitsu, who had come to watch, and said, "It's ridiculous to tell Chihaya to fight. It has never occurred to him to attack or wound someone. This whole business is foolish."

"But he's doing quite well." The one-eyed lord smiled and rubbed his chin as he watched the master and his pupil. "Lord Ibuki's patience is paying off."

"What do you mean, 'quite well'?" Saya said acidly.

"You want proof?" The lord strung his bow with the swiftness of a seasoned archer. Then, drawing an arrow from the quiver on his back, he fit it to the bowstring. "Watch. Don't make a sound."

Just as Chihaya sprang away from Lord Ibuki, the arrow flew whining through the air. Saya's breath caught in her throat, but in the same instant Chihaya nimbly dodged the arrow as if it were a bird in flight, and it whizzed past. After a slight pause, he looked toward them in surprise.

"You could have hit him!" Saya screamed. But Lord Akitsu shook his head.

"No. I knew he could dodge it. He must have acquired such instinct through his many experiences in animal form. That's why he can evade even Lord Ibuki's skilled sword arm despite being such a poor fighter. I wish I could have shown you the kind of agility he displayed when he possessed the stag." Lord Akitsu smiled more grimly than before. "That youth conceals a power that neither he nor those around him comprehend. He's like the Dragon Sword."

Saya, however, was so upset that his words did not reach her. She was furious that he had shot so casually at Chihaya.

"If that were your son, would you have shot at him without a second thought? Even if you were certain he could dodge the arrow?"

Lord Akitsu seemed surprised at the rage that shook her voice. "Are you trying to tell me that there was any danger of killing him? But he—"

"Cannot die, right? I know. It's obvious that to you Chihaya is merely a weapon of war that has conveniently fallen into your hands. You're no different from Lord Shinado. Maybe you're even worse."

Unable to stand it any longer, she turned her back on him and ran away. She did not know why she had exploded, but once her anger was spent, she was overcome with a deep sadness.

Torihiko flew after her, flapping his wings. "Everyone's shocked. No one here would dare to criticize Lord Akitsu to his face."

Without responding, Saya picked up her wooden sword from where it was leaning against the fence. She stared at it for a moment and then threw it to the ground with all her might. "I hate this! It would have been better if we had never come here."

Torihiko, who had hastily escaped to the top of the fence, looked down at her in concern. "What a temper! What's the matter, Saya?"

"I don't want to go to war. And because of me, Chihaya will be caught up in it, too."

"But he wanted to come."

"It was my fault."

"No," Torihiko said, his black eyes glittering. "It was the Sword. We are all being made to dance by the Sword."

5

ON THE DAY the army was to march forth, Saya was surprised to see Natsume dressed like a warrior complete with armored breastplate. She no longer wore her hair up but instead had tied it in tight loops above her ears like the men.

"I have no intention of entrusting you to the care of a manservant. After all, it takes a woman to understand another woman's needs."

"For me there's no choice," Saya protested. "I must go to war. But there's no need for you to come, too. That would be crazy. Don't even think of it." She was determined to dissuade her. Knowing that Natsume was with child, she could not bear to think of her involved in battle. "Stay here and defend what must be defended, just like you said you would."

Natsume smiled, but it was the kind of smile that proclaimed she would not budge.

"I'll be fine. Please let me go with you. I'm only in my third month, and I can still move easily. If this baby can't take it, it isn't worthy to be our child."

When Saya continued to protest, Natsume said frankly, "My lady, I wish to go for my own sake also. So that I can be with my husband. He's one of Lord Akitsu's guards."

Questioning her more closely, Saya learned that Natsume's husband, Masaki, was a friendly young guard whom she had met sometimes on top off the cliff.

"We often talk about you, my lady."

"That's not fair. You never told me. It never occurred to me that he was married," Saya said, feigning disappointment. Natsume laughed delightedly.

Having combed her long hair, Saya followed Natsume's example and fastened it in loops, one on either side of her head. She then donned a pair of red trousers and tied each leg below the knee with a cord decked with silver bells. She alone was allowed to wear red, a sign that she was the one and only priestess of her people. Fastening a white headband around her forehead as a symbol of purity, she finished her preparations and, grasping the sheathed Dragon Sword in her hand, went to bid farewell to Lady Iwa, who was staying behind.

Lady Iwa sat motionless upon a mat in the middle of her stone chamber as though lost in meditation. The room seemed rather large and empty. When she noticed Saya, she raised her eyes and gazed at her red and white apparel. "You leave for war," she said quietly, "but a warlike spirit does not become you. Never forget that. Do you have the Quelling Stone?"

"Quelling Stone? Oh, you mean Princess Sayura's magatama." Saya nodded and pulled the sky blue stone from inside her collar, where it hung on a leather thong about her neck. "As you can see, I always wear it."

"It is not Sayura's. That magatama belongs to you," Lady Iwa said somewhat sternly. "You must carry it with you at all times, for it is part of the Water Maiden, part of you. Never having experienced its power, you can't be expected to understand, but you'll need it to quiet unruly spirits. It is the Water Maiden's ability to appease that makes her the Priestess. It is this same ability that gives her the power to still the Dragon Sword. And not only the Sword: she has the power to calm any god and call forth its peaceful spirit."

Saya's eyes widened. "Is that really true?"

"Yes, but only if your own spirit remains unmoved," Lady Iwa replied discouragingly. "War rouses and agitates wild spirits throughout the land. In the midst of battle, it's very hard for just one person to stay calm, something I'm sure you'll experience many times in the days to come."

Saya reflected ruefully that she did not have much confidence in her ability in the first place, and that as for war, she was certainly not going by choice. If she could have stayed behind, she would gladly have crawled into bed and stayed put with the covers drawn over her head. "Lady Iwa," she suddenly blurted out, "why do we have to fight? I still don't understand. Why? And why does Chihaya have to be thrown into battle?" She knew once she had begun that she was treading on dangerous ground, but having started, she could not stop. She continued in a small voice, "I know it's too late to say this. But Chihaya—Chihaya doesn't know how to say no. And so he'll be carried along and try to do what others want him to, to fight. And I—I can't bear that."

Lady Iwa's large eyes gazing up at her were like two dark pools. No matter how hard one might try, one could never glimpse what lay at the bottom. But for a moment Saya thought she saw within them a glimmer of sympathy. The old woman answered slowly, "I belong to the people of Darkness. There's nothing I can do. I would do anything for the sake of my people regardless of the consequences. But . . ." She paused to consider, and then continued, "Someday you'll understand. Right now, we're caught up in the tide of history. If we don't follow the flow, we'll never learn where it leads."

Saya remained silent. She was ready now to accept Lady Iwa's words with an open heart. When she uttered a formal farewell, the old woman nodded. "You're so young to be our one and only priestess. That grieves me, yet I cannot take your place. You must go. Surely there must be some meaning in your very youth."

Saya left the inner chamber and went into the great hall. There she saw Lord Akitsu, clad in black armor, and with him Chihaya, likewise dressed as a warrior. She felt herself recoil at the sight. It was as if she were looking at Prince Tsukishiro on the night she had first met him. When she examined Chihaya more closely, however, she realized that he wore a far from splendid iron helmet and his black-lacquered armor was studded with crude rivets. He looked bored, showing no sign of youthful excitement. Still her first impression continued to plague her, plunging her into an odd mood.

"Saya," Lord Akitsu said solemnly. "Give him the Dragon Sword."

She stepped forward, still puzzled by the sudden awe she felt toward Chihaya. "Your armor looks so heavy," she teased him, trying to conceal her confusion.

"Mmm," he nodded, making no attempt to impress anybody. "But this sword is light," he added as he took it from her hands. "That's a help."

Saya saw the surprise on Lord Akitsu's face as she stood beside him. The Dragon Sword was a long, heavy broadsword. She sighed and thought, *When it comes down to it, I'm the one who drew Chihaya into this war. No matter how much I wish I hadn't, it's my own fault.*

Several hundred soldiers had already gathered and stood in organized ranks before the entrance. Black-helmeted, they carried shields emblazoned with whirlpools in bright and varied colors, and each held a new bow or spear. As Lord Akitsu passed through the gate they gave a great cheer, greeting their general with a twanging of bowstrings and a beating of shields. Applause rose, too, from the crowd of people who were to remain behind from where they had gathered beyond the soldiers. Saya attempted to slip through after Lord Akitsu but was so startled to be greeted with a similar uproar that she almost stopped in her tracks. Whether she liked it or not, she realized that she had no choice but to accept her station. She was the Priestess of her people. Garbed in red, she must live for each one of them on behalf of the Goddess. Just as their general, Lord Akitsu, belonged to them and not to himself. And in return, they would, without exception, throw down their lives for her sake. She was overwhelmed at being thrust so suddenly into this position. Realizing that she was not even a tenth as prepared as she had thought, she feared for the future.

Under Lord Akitsu's command, the company split into groups when the sun had set and rowed out in small boats onto the dark sea. The other lords and commanders parted from them, heading back to their homelands to raise troops. The greatest rising of the people of Darkness had quietly begun.

THREE DAYS LATER, Lord Akitsu and his soldiers were heading toward the pastures, concealing themselves in the shadow of the mountains.

"Saya!" Chihaya exclaimed in wonder just after they had crossed the mountain pass. "There are horses. A whole herd galloping."

Saya could see nothing. Before them lay only an unbroken line of low hills and quiet meadows beneath the darkening sky.

"Yes. A herd of rare and magnificent horses," said Lord Akitsu, despite the fact that he could not see them. "Would you like one?"

"Yes," Chihaya answered simply.

"This place is under the direct jurisdiction of the Palace of Light and usually so well guarded it would be beyond our grasp. Now, however, they're so preoccupied with rebuilding the palace that the guards are thinly spread. We'll split into two groups and attack the barracks, you understand?"

Saya tugged at Chihaya's sleeve. "Listen, don't even think of becoming one of those horses. This is important."

Chihaya nodded. "There were many horses in the palace stables but I never possessed one. It wouldn't do to confuse a trained warhorse."

Lord Akitsu asked Chihaya tensely, "You seem to be able to communicate with animals. Can you call that herd of horses to you?"

"I couldn't call them all at once."

"There must be a leader. If he came, the rest would follow."

"That I could do."

"Good." Lord Akitsu continued without pause, "First we must destroy the shrine mirror. While one group attacks the barracks, throwing our foes into confusion, the other group will skirt the wood and hit the shrine. Then this land will once again be ours. As long as the mirror remains intact, we might as well be face-to-face with the immortal Children of Light."

Next he looked at Saya. "I leave the work of pacification in your hands."

Startled, Saya stammered, "But—but what should I do?"

"Invoke the aid of the Goddess, just as you do to still the Dragon Sword. I've no intention of throwing the two of you into battle. I'll leave some stalwart men to protect you. Move cautiously and don't leave Chihaya's side."

Under his rapid directions, the warriors moved as one, then split up and disappeared into the shadows. Saya caught sight of Masaki among the "stalwart men" and, for the first time, felt somewhat relieved. His amiable young face, even in this place, seemed unchanged. But still she could not suppress her shivering or the goose bumps on her skin. Perhaps because she looked so pitiful, Masaki looked at her and came over to whisper, "Be easy, my lady. Victory is certain. All you have to do is to remain calm."

Battle cries rose as flaming arrows arced through the air, and the barrack's thatched roofs burst into flame. The battle had been joined. The sharp clash of metal on metal and the tumult of voices rose from the ground like a stagnant mist. Saya's group, which was positioned in the rear guard behind those attacking the shrine, immediately began to move forward. Saya could no longer see Lord Akitsu and his men, who had rushed into the barracks brandishing their weapons. She could not take her eyes from Chihaya's sword, but it was impossible to tell if the occasional gleam of red in the hilt stones was a glow from within or merely a reflection of the flames of destruction.

Chihaya suddenly laughed aloud. Saya raised her head in surprise, for not only did he rarely laugh, but their present circumstances were anything but amusing. "What's so funny?"

"I've never seen such a horse! He's fearless."

His face, which glowed faintly in the flickering light of the flames, was animated and filled with eagerness. He turned to the frowning Saya, saying, "He's the leader of the herd. A magnificent horse. I wish I could show him to you, Saya. He's as black as coal. And on his forehead is a single star—like the morning star."

Listening to him, she thought for an instant that she could see a fleet-footed black horse with a star on its forehead, a proud, spirited young stallion roaming across the pastures. But she quickly pushed the image from her mind.

"Well, it's nice to be so carefree when everyone else is fighting for their lives!" she snapped. At that moment she saw fingers of flame rise from behind the trees in front of her, making their pointed black silhouettes stand out in stark relief. The shrine had fallen.

She struggled to fight down a dizziness and something that rose within her like a frightened bird. For Saya, the desecration of the grove, the defilement of the sacred precinct of the mirror, was still almost physically painful. For an instant she felt the awful gaze of Princess Teruhi fixed upon her where she cowered in the shadow of the trees with Chihaya by her side.

Perhaps her anxiety communicated itself directly to the Sword for, as if he had only just become aware of her, Chihaya suddenly asked, "What is it, Saya? The Sword moans."

"The mirror has been broken." The words rushed from her as though she were delirious. "Something—something's coming!"

What it was she had no idea, but it was palpable. She felt it rise from the midst of the darkness, radiating menace. Gradually it took shape—like a swarm of bees forming a cloud, like a lump of fat congealing. They must escape, now, a voice within Saya urged insistently.

"Hurry! Run! We must get away from here!"

The guards looked at her in consternation. "But it's dangerous to move. Stray arrows are still flying. It's all right. Just wait a little longer."

Their soothing words, however, could not quell her panic.

"It's no good. You must flee! Or something terrible will happen!"

But she herself did not have the courage to turn her back on it, and in the end could only stand rooted to the spot, staring. Seeing it with her own eyes would in no way diminish her fear, but she could not bear the thought of being pursued by something unknown. At any moment it would materialize, ripping up the cedar trees in its path. And then, as though it could read her mind, it appeared with an appalling noise, smashing and rending as it came. She heard the men surrounding her gasp.

It had taken the form of a creature the size of a small hill. It had the body of a giant bear on the rampage, and when it stood on its hind legs its face reached the tops of the trees. Its crescent-moon-shaped claws were much longer than any bear's, and a thick, hairless reptilian tail stretched out behind it, the scales gleaming in the starlight. Its face, wreathed in spines, was yet strangely human, a flat apelike visage hideous to look upon. The enormous monster came straight toward them, stamping its heavy feet and raking at the branches.

Gazing up at it, Saya could only gasp in horror. What her eyes beheld was not a thing of this world, and before it any human cry for mercy seemed meaningless.

For a long moment they stood frozen to the spot, and then Masaki, coming to his senses, yelled, "Stand fast! In the name of our lord, stand fast and protect the Princess."

The soldiers, startled by his voice, fitted arrows to their bows or held their spears ready. But Saya knew too well the uselessness of their resistance.

"Run! Run now!"

Whose voice it was she did not know, but the resolute urgency of that cry resounded strangely. She heard it as though unrelated to herself, but then suddenly someone grabbed her arm and hauled her roughly away. As she opened her mouth to protest angrily at this treatment, she almost collided with the glossy flank of a jet-black horse. Right in front of her, snorting and prancing, was a fierce stallion with a streaming mane.

Before she knew it, Chihaya had pulled her up in front of him onto its bare back. Then, feeling the horse's muscles moving rhythmically beneath her, she realized that they were flying across the dark meadow. The wind took her breath away and she buried her face in the horse's mane with the absurd thought that he was more like a shooting star than the morning star.

The monster pursued them. This was the only reason Saya managed to ride bareback on the speeding stallion without tumbling to the ground. Whether it was after her or Chihaya she could not tell, but it had eyes only for them and seemed filled with a malicious desire to harm them. As she clung to the horse's mane, in her mind, she was running on her own two legs. *Flee! Flee! Flee for our lives!*

But the creature was also fast. Its enormous form rushed toward them as though it were swimming through space. Rocks and trees were no more than level ground to its huge crushing feet. It came closer and closer even as she watched, and when the legs of the gasping stallion finally began to falter, it stretched out its long, curved claws almost daintily toward their backs.

The stallion gave a piercing scream and the threesome that had been melded together were scattered in different directions like seeds scattering from a pod. As the horse tumbled head over heels, Saya felt herself thrown through the air and hurled onto a grassy slope; then she rolled for what seemed like ages. But when she finally raised her head, she saw she had not been thrown very far at all. Chihaya was sitting up only a few paces from her. And the creature was but a stone's throw away. Its nightmarish black form seemed about to engulf them.

Draw the Sword! Kill it before it kills us!

It was not a conscious thought, but she knew she must have wished it, for the shining Sword was unsheathed with such speed that she could not believe Chihaya had done it. Then it flew straight as an arrow toward the shadow towering like a mountain above them. Saya gazed up and saw the blade grow longer, twisting and thickening, engraving the image of the Dragon upon her mind. Its eyes gleamed bright crimson against the creature's murky blackness. Then the keenly honed blade moved like flashing light, slashing the monster's head and shoulders to tatters, until suddenly the creature lost its form and melted thickly into darkness. The Sword flashed once again, rising into the air, and raced toward Chihaya as if seeking its next target. Saya shut her eyes.

When she opened them again and looked fearfully about her, however, she saw that the night had once again returned to darkness, and Chihaya stood alone, trying to sheath the Sword with awkward movements. Drenched with sweat as though she had been doused with water and shaking in every limb, Saya was only now aware of how terrified she had been. Unable to stand, she began to crawl toward Chihaya, but he checked her in an unexpectedly low voice.

"You'd better not come too close."

Only then did she notice the bloody wounds that ran from his shoulders down his back. The trail of the creature's merciless claws was apparent even in the starlight, as though Chihaya's flesh had been gouged with a sickle. Looking at Saya's pale, frozen face, he said, "It's nothing to worry about. Renewal will soon begin. The deeper the wound, the faster it begins."

"Renewal? You mean the return to youth?"

"Yes. The wounds will disappear. It's best to leave them alone."

Chihaya spoke as though it were nothing. But Saya, witnessing immortality for the first time, felt as bewildered as if she had come into contact with yet another monster, although one less fearsome. So this was how the Children of Light defied the passage of time and maintained a flawless, youthful form. In this way they rejected the natural flow of life and turned their backs on the road that all others followed to the Goddess.

Masaki and the other guards, who had been frantically searching for them, raced up breathlessly. Asked if she was hurt, Saya shook her head and said, "No. I'm fine. I just got a few bruises . . ." Then, unable to bear it any longer, she broke down and began to sob.

Chihaya was in no condition to walk. He was placed, deathly pale, on a hastily prepared litter, but refused to allow anyone to touch his wounds. Walking quietly alongside the litter, Saya noticed that the black stallion, limping slightly, followed them hesitantly, like a dog worried about its master. But when he saw them enter the camp set up in the shade of the forest, he disappeared like the wind.

"DO YOU FEEL A BIT BETTER?" Lord Akitsu asked, sitting down beside her. Saya nodded. Even with the bright fire burning directly in front of her, she still felt a faint chill in her shoulders, but perhaps because she had been persuaded to drink the medicinal wine that she had at first left untouched, she felt warm inside and slightly light-headed.

"How's Chihaya?" Lord Akitsu asked.

"I think—I think he'll be all right. He's sleeping like the dead right now."

"I had no idea that something like this would happen," Lord Akitsu muttered as if to himself.

"What on earth was it? I've never seen anything so horrible in my life!"

Hearing the terror that still lurked in her voice, Lord Akitsu paused a moment before replying. "I can't say for certain, but I think that what you saw was one of the gods of the earth."

Saya stared at him in shocked surprise. "That monster was an earth god?"

"Our task is to recover those gods that have been lost. The Children of Light captured the earth gods and sealed them in mirrors, then further confined them within the shrines they built. But if the mirror is broken and they are released, a strong god may even return. Many times we have freed the gods of the earth in this way, but never before has one of them borne us any ill will."

He fell silent and the two of them stared at the flickering flames for some time. Finally, Saya spoke. "Are you saying that this happened because Chihaya is one of the Children of Light?"

"I can't think of any other reason," he said bitterly. "And to make matters worse, Chihaya used the Dragon Sword to kill the god we strove so hard to free. He has obliterated it more completely than his brother or sister ever could."

Saya turned to face him. "But we had no choice. Who wouldn't protect themselves if they were attacked by such a creature?"

Ignoring her question, he murmured, "I wonder if Lady Iwa foresaw this. It looks like things aren't going to go as smoothly as she thought. How on earth are we to make the Wind Child our ally if this kind of thing happens?"

chapter five

SHADOW

Should frost chance to fall upon the field
Where the traveler seeks haven,
Shelter him, my son, beneath thy wings,
O cranes that cross the heavens.

—The mother of a member of a Japanese
envoy to China during the Tung dynasty

Shadow

AFTER HE WAS INJURED, Chihaya slept for one full day, but by the next morning he seemed even better than before and, saddling Morning Star, rode off. From the day Lord Akitsu's men had captured the Asakura pastures, the two were as inseparable as lovers. The wild-spirited Morning Star would allow no one but Chihaya to approach him, while Chihaya never even glanced at another horse. The extraordinary pair, so conspicuously different from the rest, showed no interest in anyone else's affairs, creating an exclusive world of their own. At night they slept side by side, and as soon as the sun rose they set off for a morning gallop to drive the sleep from their eyes.

The weather became much cooler. Although the midday sun was warm enough to raise a slight sweat, sundown, which set the sky ablaze with color, brought with it a cool night. The gold-tinged clouds and red sky at sunset seemed to beckon to the trees on the mountains, inviting them to follow suit. And the trees, eager to comply, began to don their autumn colors. When the curtain of night fell, myriad insects set their wings humming in the meadows. Faintly but earnestly they sang of summer followed by winter. It would have been well for all to listen to their song, since in their own fashion they proclaimed that light is followed by darkness, and life, by death.

The army of Darkness remained in Asakura for a while to secure their hold on the pastures. Although this gave the soldiers a brief respite, Natsume flew about as she helped prepare food for the troops. Saya followed along after her, trying to help despite Natsume's protests. She was, in fact, much more comfortable being busy. It felt better to keep her hands occupied so that she would not have time to think.

Wherever she looked, she was confronted by unharvested crops trampled in the fields; by the blackened shells of burned storehouses, their winter stores reduced to ashes overnight; by grieving women laying their husbands to rest or trudging along with faltering steps, carrying their few remaining possessions on their shoulders and leading their children away by the hand. Although Lord Akitsu did his best to deal justly with those who lived within the occupied territory, hundreds of soldiers were now devouring the local food supply.

ONE AFTERNOON, when they had some rare free time, Natsume said, "My lady, be so good as to behave like a lady sometimes instead of following me about like a serving woman."

"Oh, I see. You want to meet with Masaki," Saya replied. "Off you go, then. I'll just wait here by myself until nightfall."

"What am I to do with you!" Natsume laughed, shrugging her shoulders, but then she added, "My lady, I know you truly care about everyone here. But it's all right to take it easy sometimes, too, like the other one. After all, I'm just a servant."

Saya was surprised to be compared to Chihaya. "What? You mean you want me to copy him and be excluded by everyone? No thank you."

Natsume burst out laughing. "I just meant it as an example. You know, the way he keeps aloof, as if he doesn't even see us."

"He's a bit dense, that's all."

"But he's very handsome," Natsume said with admiration. "And recently he's become even more attractive—as if a light shines within him."

Saya cast her an anxious glance. But there was no hidden meaning in her words; she was not implying that Chihaya was a Prince of Light. She could not know. It was true that Chihaya had changed since he was wounded. His face seemed more radiant than before, and Saya caught him smiling more often. However, there was still something strange about him that made him seem unapproachable. Lord Akitsu was not the only one who puzzled over how to treat him.

"I'll have to tell that to Masaki," Saya teased, but Natsume remained unperturbed.

"He wouldn't be jealous, not of someone like that who's in a class by himself."

After Natsume had gone, Saya leaned against the fence at the edge of the pasture and rested her chin in her hands. The gently rolling meadows spread out before her, stirred by the breeze. Far in the distance, wild grasses waved their feathered tips, undulating like silver waves. And there she caught a glimpse of Chihaya, about whom they had just been talking, galloping across the meadow on Morning Star. Man and horse were fused together, racing with extraordinary speed. They seemed to have become one with each other. Although Saya suspected that such a bond could only be the result of horse and man changing places frequently, they had caused no harm, so she let them be.

Suddenly she sighed. *What am I doing here?* she thought. She had never imagined that she would still be asking herself this question once she had returned to her people, to her roots. But finding herself swept up in the war, she was forced to think about it. She had come to the battlefront, borne along by the tide, but she still could not understand why. Surrounded by people who felt a burning sense of mission, people who had staked everything on the struggle, she continued, even now, to wonder what it was all for. She had been so confident when she had faced Prince Tsukishiro at the West Gate of the Palace of Light and insisted that she must return to her own people, but now she found her conviction wavering.

I made him my enemy so that now I must fight against him. What a terrible blow I dealt him by luring Chihaya, his own brother, over to the side of Darkness.

She kept remembering how her mother had lectured her about not thinking ahead. Yatame had scolded her thus for climbing trees, for sliding down steep slopes.

It's true. I never think ahead.

She looked up, startled by the sound of thundering hoofbeats. Morning Star was heading straight for her. Seeing the great stallion bearing down upon her at full speed, his dark flank glistening with sweat, she unconsciously stepped back from the fence, but Chihaya pulled on the reins, easily gentling the prancing horse, and jumped from his back. He looked over the fence at her and said, "The meadow over there is covered with wild roses in full bloom. Do you like flowers, Saya?"

She responded in a small voice, "What goes on in that mind of yours every day?"

But Chihaya continued unperturbed. "Or would you rather see the akebia vines at the top of the hill? They're loaded with ripe fruit. By tomorrow the birds will have eaten it all."

"I like both," Saya replied. "I can like more than one thing, you know."

"Then let's hurry."

Saya frowned at his serious face. "Hurry?"

"Don't you want to come?"

She stared at him in disbelief, then looked at the black stallion by his side and said faintly, "I can't ride Morning Star. I've heard a mountain of stories from people who've been bitten or almost had their necks broken when they tried to ride him."

"But you've already ridden him!" This, she realized, was true. "It's all right. Morning Star likes you. He wouldn't do anything to hurt you."

Still she hesitated, aware that she did not really like this horse and afraid that he would sense it. Surely such a sensitive creature would be able to read her feelings. Contrary to her expectations, however, Morning Star seemed taken with her. When the high-strung stallion flattered her by nuzzling her hand, she finally relented.

The black steed with the white star sped lightly across the fields with the two of them on his back. Unlike the full-speed gallop on the night they had fled desperately from death, it was an easy gait that brought a surge of joy to her heart. They flew along. The wind whipped at her hair until it fell loose and streamed behind her, and she finally laughed aloud. The meadows were bathed in sunlight, giving off a scent of dried grass, and buzzards wheeled lazily in the clear expanse of sky. Together they gathered the dark purple akebia fruit, ripened and splitting, at the edge of the hill and then set off for the field of wild roses. The meadow was a mass of flowers spreading as far as the eye could see, far surpassing her expectations. The hollow was buried in pale purple, and the slender fragile stems swayed in the breeze, creating such beauty that she felt a pang of sorrow. She knew then that she could not pluck even one stem, for such beauty could never be captured in a bouquet.

While she stood speechless in the midst of the flowers, Chihaya waited, silently stroking Morning Star's mane. Many clouds had drifted peacefully across the sky when at last she spoke. "Why can't we be like the trees or the flowers? Flowers bloom for no one in particular when their time comes, and trees bear fruit without ever knowing war. If only we could live like that, too."

As if this was a new discovery, Chihaya asked, "Don't you like war, Saya?"

She looked back at him in surprise. "Do you?"

Chihaya thought for a moment. "Well, I don't know . . ."

Saya was about to scold him when he continued, "But if we hadn't come here, I would never have met Morning Star."

Placing his hand on the horse's shoulder, he gazed at him tenderly. Morning Star lowered his head and began grazing on some thistle flowers, heedless of the prickles.

"And it doesn't matter to you that storehouses were razed and people slain so long as you have Morning Star?" Saya pressed him.

Chihaya paused and finally said, "To gain something, you must lose something first. I think that this is probably true for everyone. Just as I lost my other dreams the night that I found Morning Star."

Saya gazed at him inquiringly. "You mean you can no longer dream?"

Chihaya nodded slightly, his expression hard. It was the first time she had ever seen him look this way, as though contemplating a bitter memory. "I will never dream again. For I can never again forget who I am. I realized that when I couldn't escape from the pain."

Saya felt a stab of remorse. Knowing that Chihaya had the power of renewal, neither she nor Lord Akitsu had given him much thought. It had never occurred to them that an immortal would feel the same pain as a mortal when wounded. Although he had borne an injury that would have killed an ordinary man, he had had to nurse his pain alone with none to comfort him.

Saya asked quietly, "Are you sorry? That you came to join us?"

She thought that she could understand a little what he had lost. It was like the snow-white robe that he had been wearing when she first met him. After she had lured him out into the real world, it had become so soiled that he could never wear it again.

Chihaya, however, looked at her in surprise. "Why should I be sorry? Morning Star is here, and so are you."

Saya was somewhat relieved, although a little annoyed that he put his horse before her.

AS SOON as he was certain that they had secured a sufficient foothold, Lord Akitsu resumed the advance. The army traveled south and captured Kamioyama Pass, a strategic point on the road running east–west. This road was a major thoroughfare, along which passed all tribute from the districts connected to Mahoroba. Moreover, they captured the pass just as tribute for the year's harvest festival was being hurried toward the capital, and all of it fell into their hands. At the same time, they had to destroy every shrine in the neighborhood and shatter the mirrors within them in order to delay the news from reaching the forces of Light. Although Saya felt that the anxiety she experienced each time a mirror was broken took years off her life, no other raging gods appeared, despite Chihaya's presence. It was unclear if this was due to her ability to pacify the gods, but she was content to believe that it was the result of her fervent prayers.

Having at last located the enemy's position, the Palace of Light sent out a punitive force. The area around the pass was engulfed in fighting, so that none dared approach it. Although the battle was prolonged, the army of Darkness clearly had the advantage. They were skilled in swift sorties and surprise attacks that exploited the mountainous terrain in which they were most at home. Materializing unexpectedly, they attacked in small bands and then disappeared again like phantoms.

Relying on the force of numbers, the generals leading the army of Light poured in constant reinforcements, but in the end they were forced to retreat. Saya and Natsume had been removed from the front to Asakura when the fighting became intense, and there they had anxiously wrung their hands. At the news of the victory, however, they rejoined the other troops, laughing with the soldiers and clapping their hands for joy. For the first time Saya understood how people can grow accustomed to war. Intensified by the stark contrast between life and death, fleeting moments of joy such as these could make one almost mad with happiness. United by the bond of life, friends grew closer, much more so than in the ordinary world. To Saya, there was no one as beloved as each and every returning soldier, whether he was dressed in rags, caked in filth, or stained with blood.

One day, the news reached them that Lord Shinado, who had been making for the western border, had thoroughly routed an expeditionary force awaiting the arrival of Princess Teruhi, and that he was now pressing relentlessly eastward. A runner was dispatched immediately, and he returned bearing the message that Lord Shinado's forces would join up with Lord Akitsu's army within a few days.

"What speed! He's well named the 'keen-eyed hawk,'" Lord Akitsu said with a pleased smile. "This must have thrown the palace into a frenzy. But it's too late. By the time the immortals start moving, our army will be large enough to match them."

The soldiers were inspired by Lord Shinado's heroic feat, and morale soared. Saya, who stood apart watching the soldiers as they sang rousing songs with their arms around one another's shoulders, was surprised to see the messenger head her way when he had finished reporting to Lord Akitsu.

"Lord Shinado bade me bring this to you, my lady," he said. He gave her a package attached to a branch thick with dark green leaves. Taking it in her hands, she smelled a sharp, fresh fragrance. Several round yellow fruit nestled among the leaves. Tachibana oranges—she had heard of them, the poet's "ever-fragrant fruit." Opening the package, she found a necklace of bright green beads inside.

"Why this—for me?" she asked without thinking.

"I am not the man of whom you should ask that question, my lady," the messenger answered in some embarrassment. Saya blushed and chided herself for her thoughtlessness. Yet she could not understand it. She had only talked to Lord Shinado a few times, and those conversations had not been particularly pleasant.

The messenger bowed respectfully and said solemnly, "He asked after your Ladyship's health."

Saya, feeling strangely flustered, took the parcel to her quarters and put it away in her wicker trunk. *It's odd,* she thought, *but I can't be glad. Why does that man make me feel so uncomfortable?*

SEVERAL DAYS LATER, Lord Shinado's army joined them as arranged and without incident. Their mobility was impressive, demonstrating Lord Shinado's tactical skill. Although Saya saw him for the first time in a long while, far from alleviating her confusion, the sight of him only served to increase it. She could not bring herself to meet his eyes even though she knew that her behavior must appear unnatural. It was impossible, however, to avoid him forever. Once quarters had been set up for the new soldiers, Lord Akitsu summoned Lord Shinado and Saya privately. When they reached his heavily guarded camp, he made sure that everyone else was cleared from the area before relating to Lord Shinado the details of Chihaya's encounter with the earth god.

"There's no telling what may come of this. It could happen again. Frankly, I don't know how we can hold Chihaya in check. What's your opinion?"

"This type of indecision isn't like you. How can you expect any encounter between a Prince of Light and the gods of the earth to end peacefully?" Lord Shinado said bluntly.

"I know, but we still can't ignore what Lady Iwa said. She called on us to find in Chihaya one who would wield the Dragon Sword on our behalf."

"But if he kills the gods, all our efforts will be in vain. And besides, there's no telling when the wrath of the gods will fall upon us if we harbor someone like him in our midst."

Lord Akitsu stroked his chin. "Yes, I've been worried about that, too. Still, Chihaya hasn't caused us any harm."

"A Prince of Light causing no harm?" Lord Shinado said with a grimace. "He's immortal. That alone is a rejection of everything that lives in Toyoashihara. He deserves to be cursed."

Unable to restrain herself, Saya burst out, "It's not his fault that he can't die, so how can you reproach him for that? Surely our people aren't so narrow-minded as to shun him just because he differs in this one respect."

Lord Shinado said with a cold politeness, "My lady, you appear to be confused. Can't you see that the immortals' powers of renewal threaten our very existence? They seek to create a deathless land in Toyoashihara, removing obstacles like us as though pulling up weeds."

Saya, at a loss for words, was sorry that she had opened her mouth. Lord Akitsu carefully brought the conversation back to the original topic. "For the moment, we must concentrate on stilling the wrath of the gods against Chihaya and pressing forward. As it stands, we can't even get near those gods whose powers we seek to release."

Lord Shinado frowned. "Of course, the most effective way to appease the gods is to offer a sacrifice . . ."

"But we can't sacrifice Chihaya. He can't die. You know that."

"Have you ever thought of trying?" Lord Shinado said flippantly, but then continued seriously. "Even if we don't go that far, Chihaya should at least be imprisoned. Regardless of whether or not he's the Wind Child, he is, in fact, our hostage."

"Hmm," the one-eyed lord grunted, pondering the problem. It was obvious that he had heard such advice before.

Furious, Saya shouted, "No! If you do that, we'll lose Chihaya. Can't you see?"

The two men looked at her in surprise.

"Why do you think Chihaya came here in the first place? Why do you think he stays? Because he was kept imprisoned the whole time he was in the Palace of Light and never given the chance to feel the wind, the earth, the grass. Will we subject him to the same cruel treatment as the people of Light? Taking away his freedom—using him—without even trying to understand him?"

Lord Shinado said in a low voice, "Our first duty is to free the children of the Goddess, the earth gods. Concerning yourself with an immortal when the gods wish otherwise is to invite their wrath."

Saya turned away, sweeping back her hair, and said defiantly, "If you're trying to say that I failed in my task of appeasing the gods, then you're right. It was my fault. Because I couldn't stop the Dragon Sword. But in that case, it doesn't make sense for you to condemn Chihaya. Why don't you take me and offer me as a sacrifice instead?"

Lord Akitsu intervened. "There's no need to get so riled up. Especially you, Saya, as Priestess." Saya looked somewhat ashamed after this mild rebuke and he added, "Still, I can understand why you feel angry. Let's wait a little longer and see what happens before we decide what to do with Chihaya. After all, it only happened that one time. Your power as priestess must be having some effect."

Although the meeting had been short, Saya was exhausted. She was about to hurry back to her quarters when someone called out to her from behind. It was Lord Shinado. He stood, arms folded, beside a slender red pine tree. Saya stopped and turned, feeling uncomfortable. She remembered with embarrassment that she had not yet thanked him for his gift. "The other day, I didn't deserve such a—"

"Never mind that," he interrupted abruptly, yet he did not seem angry. Rather, his tanned face bore the expression of one deep in thought. "How can you defend someone like him?"

Hiding her surprise, she replied, "Because I have no reason to hate him. I feel sorry for him. He seemed unhappy in the palace."

"Unhappy? What we call happiness or unhappiness can only be measured by standards of our own making. And those standards don't apply to what the immortals feel. You spend too much time worrying about them. And your concern is in vain. Take an honest look at Chihaya. He has less compassion or capacity than even the most ordinary of men."

His words struck a little too close to home. "How would you know?" Saya retorted. "I know him better than you do."

"If you think about the meaning of the word 'compassion,' it's obvious," Lord Shinado replied emphatically. "How could someone who doesn't know death know true fear, true separation, true sorrow? How could they possibly understand the bonds that join our hearts together, or sympathy or consideration for others? It's the very knowledge that someday we must die that makes us love one another when close, and long for one another when apart. Isn't that so?"

She could not refute this argument. She felt miserable, as though she had been severely reprimanded, yet she did not want to admit to herself that what he said was true. With downcast eyes, she said in a subdued tone, "But is the fact that he can't return such feelings sufficient reason to reject him so cruelly? I don't think that's what compassion means."

Lord Shinado stirred and unfolded his arms. Changing his tone suddenly, he said, "Why is it that whenever we talk to each other, we end up arguing? Still, what you just said is right."

She raised her face and found him gazing at her steadily. "I know it all too well. For I'm not without compassion myself."

She was disconcerted and, even to her own ears, her voice sounded lifeless. "Forgive my rudeness . . ."

"No, there's no need to apologize." He turned away, and, as he was leaving, he said in a low voice, "You should wear the necklace. The color of jade would suit you."

Saya returned to her quarters in confusion. Although Natsume asked what had happened, she could not bring herself to tell anyone.

2

THE ARMY OF DARKNESS had become such an imposing force that it now proceeded east without any attempt at concealment. And all along the way, people joined its ranks, either won over by conciliation or subdued by military might. Some powerful clans even removed the shrine mirrors themselves once they learned which way the wind was blowing. The storm raised by the passing of the army of Darkness exposed something these people had been too dazzled by the Light to see. During the long years of their infatuation with immortality and eternal youth, which exacted continuous offerings, their lands had become utterly exhausted. Many had groaned under the burden imposed by heavy tributes, and this had been compounded by the annually decreasing harvests.

By now there were none in Toyoashihara who did not know the names of Lord Akitsu, commander in chief, and his resourceful general, Lord Shinado. Their ranks swelled with deserters from the enemy camp. The Prince and the Princess of Light, who remained in Mahoroba, sent general after general to oppose them, but nothing could stop the army of Darkness as it advanced toward the capital like a storm cloud covering the sun. At the same time, reports reached the army of Darkness that Lord Ibuki, who had been inciting small-scale insurrections in the east, had brought his troops together to form a single company and was marching west to meet them.

Upon receiving this news, Lord Akitsu told his commanders, "Once we have joined Lord Ibuki, our forces will be complete, and we'll be able to overthrow Mahoroba. The eastern front is heavily protected and there is as yet no crack in their defenses. The outcome will depend on whether we can break through the wall to unite with Lord Ibuki. If we succeed, our victory is almost assured. Now is the time to give full play to our military might."

Under his orders, an unprecedented and ferocious attack was launched. The army split into five, then eight battalions, and advanced against the army of Light, which was strengthening strategic points. Their maneuvers were so complex that it seemed impossible that they could still be controlled. The battle raged for three days and three nights, and after a brief respite fighting erupted again and continued for another three days. Saya, who naturally remained with the rear guard, was more worried about Chihaya than about herself. He was fighting alongside Lord Akitsu, but when the army split and then split again she lost track of his whereabouts. He had disappeared before in the midst of battle and had always come riding nonchalantly back astride Morning Star; however, they had never yet been separated for this long, and she was uneasy.

The next day a rider brought the glad tidings that the two leaders, Akitsu and Shinado, riding side by side, had breached the last defenses of the army of Light. The anxious faces of the soldiers in the rear guard lit up. At the same time, however, a message from Lord Akitsu reached Saya that filled her heart with foreboding. She was requested to join him secretly at the front line.

Pausing only to gather essentials, she spurred on her mount and left with the messenger. As they cut across the battlefield, where the smoke from smoldering grass still lingered, the heart-wrenching sight of the spears and helmets of fallen soldiers drew her eyes. Troops slowly making their way back as they cared for their wounded looked up in surprise at the sound of pounding hoofbeats. But Saya made no attempt to slow her horse, for if she allowed herself to look at the young soldiers, dead or wounded, she was afraid that she would not be able to go on.

The camp to which the messenger guided her was in a copse at the entrance to a valley. Shields were planted in a circle around it, just as they would have been during a battle. Horses were tethered outside the circle, and Saya was startled to see Morning Star tied to a tree trunk, apart from the herd. "Well, what's happened to your companion?"

Morning Star snorted when he caught sight of her. He looked disconsolate, but when without thinking she approached him, he suddenly bared his long teeth as though to bite her mount and she had to back off.

Lord Akitsu himself came out to meet her and led her into a tent. Saya, too impatient to waste time on greetings, immediately demanded, "What is it? Did something happen to Chihaya?"

The one-eyed lord looked exhausted, and even in the dim twilight his face appeared haggard. In a low, weary voice he replied, "It was two days ago. We were moving to a new position when we were un-expectedly attacked from behind. They shot arrows in our direction and fled—more like the way we used to fight—but Chihaya was hit. An arrow pierced his heart."

Saya paled but remained calm. "And what happened to him? He didn't die, surely?"

"Of course not. Renewal began. Although for some time he appeared to be dead . . ."

He lifted a curtain and allowed Saya to pass under it. It was dark within and she could see nothing until a lamp was lit. Then, as the flickering yellow glow illuminated the surroundings, she saw Chihaya lying half-hidden by piles of armor.

"He looks like he's just sleeping now. It's hard to believe until you actually see it—this turning back of time."

Chihaya slept, a peaceful expression on his face, and his bare chest rose and fell gently. Although there was a faint red bruise on his left side, it could no longer be called a wound.

"Oh, thank goodness. There was nothing to worry about, then," Saya said in a cheerful voice, but she regretted it as soon as she saw Lord Akitsu's face. "Is something wrong?"

With a grim expression, he replied, "Everyone saw it. They saw Chihaya 'die.' If he returns as though nothing happened, they'll demand an explanation. Rumors will spread. Soon the whole army will know that he's an immortal Prince of Light."

Startled, Saya looked at Chihaya. But his sleeping face was like that of an innocent child, and as she gazed at it, she felt reassured.

"It can't be helped. It's the truth. No matter how we try to conceal it, someday everyone will know."

"Yes, that's true. But—but I'm not sure that I can protect him."

His voice was filled with anxiety, and Saya looked closely at him in concern. His face, etched with deep shadows cast by the lamplight, was that of a man who had not slept for many days.

"What is it? What do you fear?"

His voice was almost a whisper. "For the last two nights I have seen disturbing shadows. They circled the camp but did not attack us, probably because so much blood was spilled in the field. Angry gods thirst for the blood of sacrifice, but there has been enough death to satiate any raging god. Now, however, the battle is over. Tonight there is no substitute for the sacrifice."

A chill crawled slowly up Saya's spine. Holding her breath, she whispered, "You mean another angry god has appeared?"

"It's Chihaya's power of renewal that infuriates them. Just as death is defilement to the God of Light, so renewal is defilement to the gods of the earth, and they abhor it. So far, you have succeeded in stilling them, but with the power of renewal flaunted so openly, it's only natural that they would bare their fangs . . ."

Saya glanced at the Dragon Sword lying beside Chihaya. Like him, it slept peacefully. Lord Akitsu continued, "Unable to return to the rear guard with him, I summoned you. I wanted your opinion. We can't fight the gods to protect Chihaya. No matter how strong we are, it would be futile. Only you can stand without fear before the gods. Only you have the power to appease their wrath."

For the first time, Saya realized that Lord Akitsu was afraid; he, a seasoned warrior, was overcome with fear. But she, too, was more than sufficiently terrified.

"Soon it will be dark. We can't stay here any longer. What should we do? Should we leave Chihaya here and retreat? Or can you appease the gods?"

In a hoarse voice, Saya asked, "If we leave Chihaya behind, what will happen to him?"

Lord Akitsu reached out a hand and took her by the shoulder, but before he could reply an anguished scream rose from somewhere near the tent. The sound quivered in the air, sending shivers up their spines.

"What's happening?" Lord Akitsu shouted to the soldiers outside.

"It's the horses!" cried one of his men. "The horses are screaming in fear."

The sound came again, and Saya put her hands over her ears, unable to bear it. She was afraid that she herself would start shrieking.

"Saya, calm down. If you panic, you'll wake the Dragon Sword," Lord Akitsu said sharply.

Saya saw that the stones in the hilt were glowing red. But it was Chihaya, not the sword, who awoke. His eyes opened suddenly and he sat up in a leisurely fashion, stretching as if he had woken on a bright sunny morning. He stopped in mid-stretch, however, when he noticed Saya and Lord Akitsu staring at him wordlessly, and after looking closely at Saya, he said, "You're afraid."

"You're so observant," she replied acidly. "We're in terrible danger!"

But at that moment a soldier rushed into the tent. His face was as pale as wax and beaded in sweat. "A pack of wolves is closing in on us. Several soldiers were attacked and taken by surprise. We must retreat."

"Wolves? At this time of year?" Pushing past him, Lord Akitsu left the tent. His guards stood in formation around the camp, their shields grasped in their hands. In the thick darkness between the trees, shadows squirmed toward them along the forest floor. Countless pairs of eyes glowed red in the torchlight. The menacing growl rattling low in their throats seemed to set the very air vibrating. Advancing to the edge of the forest, the creatures glared at the soldiers, their venomous tongues lolling and their yellow fangs bared and glinting in the firelight. Their eyes blazed with savage intent.

One wolf, which had been inching slowly toward the soldiers, closed the distance between them and sprang. It leaped straight for the throat of its prey, but the soldier's sword swung true. Its belly split open, the wolf howled and rolled across the ground while the snarling of the pack grew louder.

Recognizing the profile of the man who wiped the gore from his blade with a swift, practiced movement, Lord Akitsu called to him in a low voice.

"Masaki, is that you? How many were taken?"

"Three. They had no time to draw their swords."

In a heavy, cheerless voice Lord Akitsu said, "We'll be lucky if we lose only three. Listen. No more wolves must be slain. We'll retreat without further resistance. These wolves are earth gods. Do you understand?"

Masaki looked back at him in surprise. "You plan to leave like this? Just run away?"

"That's right. We'll show them that we bear them no malice and withdraw peacefully. I can't set my men against the gods of the earth."

Lifting the curtain, he spoke quickly to Saya within. "We'll retreat. I leave it to you to decide whether or not you come with us."

Chihaya looked at Saya with a puzzled expression. "What's going on?"

"Get dressed, will you. We have to escape," Saya replied. She would run for her life. There was no question about that. She had no intention of standing alone to meet the wrath and malice of so many gods. But at the same time she could not desert Chihaya who did not even know what was happening. When the two of them tried to leave the tent, however, they froze in their tracks at the sound of a familiar dull rumble. The Dragon Sword was starting to roar, its red stones blazing crimson.

"You mustn't draw the blade!" Saya said hastily. Chihaya's hand had moved instantly to the sword as though controlled by someone else.

"It wants out," Chihaya whispered. "The Dragon's awake. What's outside that can call the Dragon as it pleases?"

"Angry gods. But you mustn't draw the Sword!" Saya said earnestly. "Please! Pray that it will be still."

"If I move, I'm afraid I'll unsheathe it." His face was tense, his voice, barely a whisper. "The Dragon is trying to move me."

"BUT the lady is not here," Masaki said.

"Never mind. We must retreat. We can't stay any longer," Lord Akitsu commanded.

"But—"

"The Lady of the Sword knows what she's doing. She has her own thoughts as Priestess, as the Water Maiden. There's no need to worry," the lord said gravely, but without as much conviction as he had hoped.

IT WAS ALREADY TOO LATE. The malicious gods had surrounded the tent where the two remained and were closing in. The violent rage emanating from countless wolves merged into a single entity as if some giant being were glaring down upon the two of them from midair.

I have no power to calm these gods, Saya thought in despair. Their wrath was directed not only at Chihaya but also at herself. She could feel their anger almost painfully, as if it pierced her skin. They could see into the depths of her soul, and they knew. They knew that she still envied and was still drawn to the Light, to youth, beauty, and immortality; that she still worshipped the Children of Light just as surely as the senior handmaiden who had rejected old age.

Chihaya, who had remained motionless, holding his breath, suddenly raised his head sharply.

"What's wrong?" Saya asked.

"Where's Morning Star?" he demanded in a choked voice. "Where is he? I can't feel him anywhere."

Saya raised her hands to her mouth and stared at Chihaya in fright. Morning Star had been tied to a pine tree, unable to escape, all alone.

"He was tethered to a tree outside the camp," Saya said, her voice rising. Before she could stop him, Chihaya rushed out of the tent. Frantically, she ran after him. "Wait!" she cried.

"Morning Star!" Chihaya shouted toward the dark forest, but there was no answering nicker, only a gnashing of teeth and the snarling and panting of bloodthirsty beasts.

Black shadows leaped one after another like balls thrown from every direction at Chihaya, who had stopped in his tracks. Although he instinctively dodged aside, fangs grazed his knees and shoulders and he heard the sound of ripping cloth. His legs were knocked from under him, and as he staggered, his hand went to the Sword.

Seeing the light gush forth, Saya screamed, "No!" but she, too, was attacked by wolves. By the light of the Sword she watched the foaming jaws and bloody fangs aiming for her throat as she cowered, mesmerized, unable to move.

The instant before the teeth of the leaping wolf met her throat a white arrow flew through the air and pierced its side. She gasped and turned to see Masaki casting aside his bow and drawing his sword as he rushed toward her.

"Are you all right? It doesn't look like they're the type to retreat before the power of your gaze."

"You . . ." Saya said in stunned surprise. "Didn't you hear Lord Akitsu's orders?"

"If she heard that I had deserted you, my wife would disown me."

"But you'll offend the gods."

"Two or three times more, what difference can that make when I've already slain one?" he replied with typical pluck. "Now let's get out of here. Come on!"

Saya, unable to reply, ran with him, but her thoughts were dark and gloomy. *Kind Masaki . . . foolish Masaki . . . you should never have come.*

For she knew that mortal strength was not enough. Her heart broke at the thought of his needless death. These cruel and merciless gods would never forgive him.

Her vision was filled with leaping shadows. Many times she was knocked down, many times she felt fangs graze her skin, but each time she rose again and continued to run. It seemed the only thing she could do for Masaki. Soon, however, she was out of breath and only dimly conscious, her mind like thick porridge, so that she no longer knew where she was running, and even began to forget why. Leaping shadows, shadows, shadows . . . interspersed with flashes of light that she could not place. Leaping shadows, shadows, shadows— then flashing light—and more shadows, shadows, shadows. Only shadows . . .

WHEN she regained consciousness and raised her head, the night was hushed and still. It was the stillness that comes just before the dawn, when the night is coldest and silence reigns. Standing beside her, so close that she almost cried out in surprise, was Chihaya. She could see his figure faintly by the blue-white glow of the naked blade that he held in his hand.

He looked at her and spoke as though he had been talking to her all along. "I've finally figured out how to use this thing. This Sword is a fang. All I have to do is become the owner of the fang. Like the wolves. As for wolves, I have been one myself."

Saya shuddered and found her voice. "What happened to them?"

"They've gone. They disappeared when I destroyed the one controlling them."

"I see," Saya whispered. "So you have slain another earth god." Her words held neither praise nor blame. She had merely said the first thing that came into her mind.

"Saya." Chihaya spoke in a low voice, looking down at the Sword. "Morning Star is dead."

She nodded wordlessly. She could not offer him any easy words of comfort. He remained silent for a long time and then said sadly, "Morning Star was the only one who loved me without any hesitation."

Night began to fade into dawn through the mist on the treetops. Somewhere a deer called, searching for a mate in the autumn season. In the faint light, Saya wandered, dragging her feet, and found Masaki fallen facedown on the grass. His body had long grown cold, and dew clung to the blade still gripped in his hand. When she found him, it did not occur to her to weep. She was too exhausted. Instead, she sank down beside him and took his hand in hers as though to console him. One thought kept running through her mind. *What am I going to say to Natsume? Natsume, how am I to tell her?*

When Lord Akitsu came in search of her, she was still sitting there. She saw him approach and knew from his somber expression that he had guessed all that had transpired. For the first time, tears traced their way down her cheeks.

"Why are they so cruel, these gods we worship? Why? Why must we fight for such gods as these?"

Lord Akitsu replied as though meditating on each word. "Cruelty is one aspect of all gods. But it is not the only one. Originally, the gods were loving and beautiful. These traits were twisted by the Light."

"I don't understand it. I don't believe it." Saya shook her head. "I hate the god who killed Masaki. I'm glad that Chihaya destroyed it."

He looked down at her, his face full of pain. "Do you really think so, Saya? If so, then wait one year. Wait and then come again to this spot. You'll find a totally different scene, a wasteland spreading out before you. Never again will this land bear fruit. Never again will flowers bloom. For the land has lost its spirit. Land that isn't nurtured by the gods of the earth lacks the breath of life."

"Really?" Saya whispered. But she could not comprehend it. All she could think of was Natsume's unborn child.

WHEN she returned to the camp, Saya was stricken with fever and remained bedridden for several days. In her delirium, she was plagued by dreams, but the one that troubled her most was her old childhood nightmare, which, though she had not seen it for some time, had lost none of its terror. Again and again, she saw the white-robed priestess turning . . . It did not help to tell herself that it was Chihaya. Fear rose in her throat and she sank into despair, for what was done could not be undone.

If only I hadn't looked at her face, she thought over and over in her feverish rambling. *If only I hadn't looked.*

Finally one morning she awoke to sunlight. She felt like she was waking for the first time in a very long while, as if a mist in front of her had cleared. It was almost noon, and the honey-colored sunlight poured through a small window high above. A man loomed beside her, as big as a bear, blocking the light. Although he had hunched himself over as far as possible, his bulk still threatened to burst the tiny hut asunder. Looking at him, Saya smiled weakly.

"Lord Ibuki. So you reached us safely, then."

"Yes, many days ago," he replied in a thick rumbling voice, although for him this was an attempt to speak softly and quietly. "It seems your fever has passed. That's good. Very good."

"Surely it's thanks to the herbs that your lordship found for us," Natsume said gratefully. As always, she worked diligently, neither secluding herself nor wearing mourning clothes. Saya would almost have preferred her to weep or rage than to nurse her so devotedly, but Natsume never allowed a single tear to show in front of Saya.

"I'm actually an expert at tracking down medicinal herbs. I find them where no one would expect." Lord Ibuki patted his chest proudly with a large, heavy hand, although a less likely hand for plucking the slender stalks of herbs growing in rock crevices would have been hard to imagine.

"Well, well. Wild pinks," he remarked, noticing the bouquet in Natsume's hand. "You did a good job collecting those."

Natsume smiled meaningfully and glanced down at the pale pink flowers with their notched petals. "I didn't pick them. I don't know who it could be, but someone has sent flowers every day since my lady fell ill."

Lord Ibuki gave her a strange look. "You don't know who it is, when the man who just left is one of Lord Shinado's servants?"

"Oh, really?" Natsume feigned ignorance.

"What's this? What's this?" Lord Ibuki roared in his normal voice. "The devil! Who would have guessed from his looks that he was such a simple-hearted—" Seeing the two girls staring at him, he stopped himself hastily. "Well, now. That's just between him and me."

Saya looked at the bouquet of gentians brought yesterday. The flowers were still a fresh blue. Her thoughts unconsciously returned to the field of wild roses she had once seen.

Even though he saw an entire field covered with flowers, Chihaya never thought to pick them, she thought. *Instead, he took me to see the place where they were blooming.*

"What happened to Chihaya?" Her question was so sudden that Natsume and Lord Ibuki looked at her in surprise.

"Why, nothing. He's fine," Lord Ibuki replied hastily.

"Even without Morning Star?"

Seeing the disconcerted look on his face, Saya realized that Lord Ibuki knew nothing of Chihaya's whereabouts. Natsume seemed to hesitate and then in a strange tone answered Saya's question with one of her own.

"My lady, everyone has been talking about it, but is it true that he's a Prince of Light?"

Saya was caught off guard. So now everyone knew, she thought. "Yes, it's true."

"And that even though he was slain in battle, he came back to life as though nothing had happened . . ." Natsume's words trailed off.

Saya did not know what to say. "Yes, but—"

"Well, I never," Natsume said with forced cheerfulness, but she was unable to keep her composure any longer. The hand in which she had held the bouquet of flowers was trembling. "Excuse me a moment," she whispered and left without a backward glance.

"She's a brave girl," Lord Ibuki said in a low voice. "She never utters a word of complaint."

Saya wondered where she went to vent her grief.

Left on her own when Lord Ibuki departed, Saya went out on shaky legs to search for Chihaya. If Natsume had been there, she would certainly not have allowed her to go, but she had not yet returned. Outside, the light was yellow and blindingly bright, and the wind felt uncomfortably cold against her skin. There were some soldiers training, their loud cries resounding, but Chihaya was nowhere to be seen. Nor was he among those returning with food supplies. Before she realized it, she had cut across the dwelling area and was heading for the spring, drawn by the shady darkness.

Fresh mountain water poured out of a rock, forming a deep, brimming pool from which a narrow stream flowed. Lord Akitsu had chosen this spot as their temporary base partly because of this spring. The rocks that formed its banks were fringed with ferns, and above her head a tall, slender katsura tree raised its branches like a guardian spirit. Exhausted, Saya collapsed upon a rock. She thought half-angrily, *That heartless wretch! Making an invalid walk all this way in search of him, when really he should have come to see me while I was sick.*

Lord Shinado claimed that Chihaya had no compassion. Although she did not want to admit it, she thought gloomily that he might be right.

She gazed at the clear water and suddenly felt thirsty. Leaning over the edge of the rock, she bent to scoop up the water in her hands. There she saw the katsura tree reflected in the pond as in a mirror. She began to laugh. After chuckling to herself for a moment, she looked up. "What on earth are you doing up there?"

On a large branch, Chihaya sat like a nesting bird. He looked down at her, his eyes blinking like an owl's. "How did you know?"

"Because you're reflected perfectly in the water. Come on down."

Although he rose slowly, he slid quickly down the trunk to stand beside her. Looking at her more closely, he said, "You look thinner."

"I wasn't feeling well. But I'm all right now." She broke off abruptly, realizing that he was still dressed in the ragged clothes that had been torn by the fangs of the wolves. "What have you been doing all this time?"

"Sitting in the tree. I was thinking."

"The whole time?"

"The whole time."

Saya stared at him in amazement. "What can you have been thinking about for so long?"

Chihaya watched a leaf that he had shaken from the katsura tree riding like a small boat upon the water's surface. "Mostly I thought about the place where Morning Star has gone. All living things in Toyoashihara go there. Yet I alone return. I always come back," he said sullenly. "I thought about why I'm denied entrance when everyone else can go."

Saya was amused by his childish, petulant tone. "That's like crying for the moon. What a thing to begrudge us!"

"But what am I to do when, in the end, there's nowhere for me to go?" he asked earnestly. "Why was I given this body?"

After some hesitation, Saya replied, "I don't know. I don't even understand my own self. But surely the God of Light and the Goddess of Darkness know."

"My father in the heavens?" Chihaya whispered. He sat down, looking even more discouraged, and hugged his knees to his chest. "Saya, if you want to meet the Goddess of your people you can go, right? But I can't go to my father. Not like my sister or my brother."

"Why not?"

"Because I'm different."

They looked at each other. Chihaya said quietly, "My sister used to say that my very existence would harm our divine father. Now I know what she meant."

Before Saya could speak, he drew the Dragon Sword from its scabbard. "Look at this. Then you'll understand, too."

Saya hastily smothered a scream of surprise. The naked blade did not glow. The polished metal merely reflected the rays of the midday sun, and the stones on the hilt remained dark. Chihaya laid the blade gently on top of the rock.

"Put it away quickly! It's dangerous!" Saya begged him anxiously.

"Would you like to pray for the Dragon to appear?"

"Don't be silly!" she said, her voice rising, but Chihaya shook his head, indicating that he had not spoken in jest.

"Even if you prayed, it would make no difference. The Dragon wouldn't come. It wouldn't even raise its voice in a single roar."

Saya looked at the sword suspiciously. "What do you mean?"

"I mean that the Dragon no longer resides in the sword."

When Saya raised her wide-eyed face to his, Chihaya pointed to his own breast. "The Dragon is here."

"Where?"

"In me."

"Since when?"

"Since that night." He averted his eyes.

"The night the wolves came?"

"Yes. You probably didn't notice, but that night the Dragon never appeared. I was the only one there. By the time I realized it, I had become one with the Dragon."

Saya caught her breath and whispered, "How could that happen?"

"I don't know." Chihaya suddenly sounded uncertain. "But . . . I only know that I wanted to give the god that killed Morning Star a taste of his own medicine."

Saya did not know how to respond. As Priestess of the Sword, what should she say to him? She must choose her words very carefully. This new state of affairs might have grave consequences or it might not. While she could not undo what had already been done, the perspective she chose as Priestess and the way in which she pronounced judgment would change their future. In that sense, she had the power to turn bad luck into good, or good luck into bad. That much she knew. It was ironic, perhaps, but she had learned this at the Palace of Light.

"So that means that the Dragon Sword can never again rage as it wills without your consent?" Saya asked.

"Yes." Chihaya nodded. "The Dragon is still in here. I can feel it constantly, like a nesting insect, a smoldering ember."

"Then you have captured the Dragon. You have sheathed it much more deeply and securely than before. That's good. You've made progress."

Chihaya looked at her in surprise. "It's good? To become the Dragon?"

"If you never let it out again, yes; if you yourself become its scabbard. If you're strong enough, you may even be able to keep it locked away forever," she said with conviction. "You just need to become stronger."

"Do you think I can?" Chihaya regarded her doubtfully. "Don't I frighten you, Saya? You used to shun the Dragon with such dread."

"You're not the Dragon," she assured him brightly. "You have eyes, a mouth, you can think and talk. Become greater than the Dragon, grasp it by the neck and don't let go. I'm sure that you can do it. If you're the one Lady Iwa called the Wind Child."

Chihaya picked up the Sword and sheathed it in its scabbard. "If you say so, Saya," he said, smiling shyly. "Now I don't have to think about it anymore."

She smiled back. "I was looking for you. There's something I wanted to tell you. I, too, have done a lot of thinking since that night."

She broke off and looked at the tranquil scene around them. While she paused, Chihaya remained motionless, waiting for her to speak. Coming to her senses, Saya felt slightly embarrassed and shrugged her shoulders, saying, "It's nothing important. It's just that I've finally figured out what I must do. What I mean is this." She pointed to the katsura tree. "You think that this tree is beautiful, too, right? Soon its leaves will turn a brilliant gold. And, of course, it will look spectacular, but in winter when it has shed its leaves, it will still be beautiful in its majesty. And in spring, its branches will be filled with budding leaves, as sweet as newborn babies. Or take the water in this spring, for example. The reason it's so clear and pure is because fresh water is always pouring into it, giving it no time to stagnate. The beauty of Toyoashihara is found in this process of birth and death, always shifting and changing. No matter how loath we may be to accept the changes, we can't put out a hand to stop them. For if we did, in that instant its beauty and purity would vanish."

Turning to face him, she continued. "You, the immortal Children of Light, have a different beauty—eternal, unchanging. But this beauty belongs in the heavens; it isn't meant for Toyoashihara. I don't want you to destroy Toyoashihara. I want you to understand that this land is beautiful just as it is. This is why my people are fighting. And that's what I must do, too."

She spoke as though talking to herself and then caught and held Chihaya's gaze. "You appreciate the beauty of Toyoashihara. I know, because you showed me the flowers. That's why I want you to lend us your power to protect this land. I want you to come with us, to use the power you have over the Dragon for the sake of Toyoashihara."

Chihaya remained silent, gravely pondering her words. Then he replied simply, "If you say so, Saya."

3

THE FORCES OF DARKNESS advanced inexorably, assembling at last at the mouth of the Nakase River. Across the river, only a stone's throw away, lay Mahoroba, where the God of Light was said to have descended to the earth. So far, fortune had smiled on the army of Darkness, which now surpassed the forces of Light, but they were unable to push across the river because the enemy refused to yield any more ground. Even if they did succeed in breaching the enemy lines, it was going to be extremely difficult to capture the almost impenetrable fortress of Mahoroba. Lord Akitsu, favoring caution, held his eager troops in check and settled down on the opposite bank to study the enemy forces. He knew only too well that the first move they made would launch the final battle that would determine the fate of this land. Despite frequent provocation, the front remained deadlocked and the two opposing forces glared at each other across the river. While they waited, the mountainsides turned red, then yellow, and the first frosts covered the ground. The torches for the night watch were cut longer than before. And with each day they waited, neither advancing nor retreating, the anxiety and impatience of the soldiers grew. It was like waiting for a tautly stretched string to break. The conspicuous absence of both Princess Teruhi and Prince Tsukishiro at such a critical point in the war made them particularly uneasy. As the Princess's golden helmet and the Prince's silver one had always shone at the head of the forces of Light, striking fear into their hearts, their absence seemed ominous, suggesting that some evil plot was brewing.

Then one night a troop bringing up the rear position was taken by surprise. Despite heavy patrols that kept constant watch on the movements of the entire army of Light, no one had seen the attackers cross the river. Reinforcements arrived too late, and the army of Darkness received a crushing blow. They lost many supplies and soldiers, who were either killed or scattered, but the loss in morale among the troops was even more serious than the physical loss of men or materials. Speculation spread like wildfire, and some soldiers openly declared that it was impossible to defeat the army of Light. Lord Shinado, who had hastily returned from the battlefield to report to Lord Akitsu, the commander in chief, entered his quarters with a scowl on his face. They were closeted together for some time, finally summoning the other commanders for a council of war.

Saya was not invited. This in itself was so alarming that she could not sleep, but when she heard the results of the council the next morning, she was incredulous. She rushed to see Lord Akitsu.

"Why are you imprisoning Chihaya? What has he done? Are you saying that he's responsible for this last defeat?"

"Saya." Lord Akitsu made an effort to speak calmly, but his face was dark and gloomy. "We're leading a great army. But it would be just as accurate to call it a motley rabble. Many of them have traveled far from their native lands, placing their trust solely in their leaders. It's impossible to communicate the real purpose of the Light or the Darkness without confusion or misunderstanding to people from so many different homelands and with so many different viewpoints. The only way to inspire them to follow us is to present everything in black and white, to reassure them that good is good and evil, evil."

"And is it therefore just to imprison an innocent man?" Saya demanded fiercely. "I can't believe that you would do this. After all, everyone already knew that he was a Prince of Light."

"If we let this continue, he will be in an even worse position. Some people already accuse him of communicating secretly with the other side. Even if we absolve him from blame this time, they'll point to Chihaya every time something happens in the future. This is what I've been afraid would happen all along—the spark of hatred has been fanned into flame."

"But—" Saya broke off abruptly. "That's so selfish! Chihaya has been fighting just as hard as anyone else."

His expression remained grim, but his voice, which was almost a whisper, was filled with pain. "I know. But can't you see that that's why fear and mistrust have spread so rapidly? The more Chihaya distinguishes himself, the more he flaunts his supremacy as a Prince of Light, his limitless power, his immortality . . ."

His words made her wince as though she had been struck. Confused and on the verge of tears, she asked, "Then what on earth is Chihaya to do?"

"Forgive me." Lord Akitsu sighed. "Perhaps it's I who am afraid."

Saya was appalled, but anything she might say would be futile. Lord Akitsu had already passed judgment.

NEAR THE SPRING OF OGIDANI, where the main body of the army was stationed, there was a cave carved by wind and rain used as a dungeon for prisoners of war. It was here that Chihaya was to be imprisoned. Feeling more wretched than she could ever remember, Saya took the Dragon Sword from his hands. A grid of sturdy oak bars was placed across the entrance and stakes were driven in to hold it securely in place. Chihaya, however, appeared surprisingly calm as he faced her through the wooden bars.

"It's all right. It doesn't bother me as much as you think, Saya. I'll just go back to being on my own for a while. I'm sure they'll come to understand in time."

Saya left, feeling worse for having been comforted by Chihaya. Lord Ibuki came after her. Hunching his burly shoulders in regret, he said, "I'm sorry. I couldn't convince them. The cowards just won't see reason."

"How shameful! Not you, Lord Ibuki, but the rest of us, myself included," Saya said indignantly. "Chihaya promised to use his power for Toyoashihara—to fight with us. And yet we turn around and behave so stupidly, so heartlessly."

"Doubt casts a dark and troublesome shadow, making it hard to see clearly," Lord Ibuki said, frowning. "If we just knew the facts, we might still convince them. Doubt breeds fear. It's impossible to solve this while there's still any doubt that he might have done it."

"So even you think there's a possibility that Chihaya did it!" Saya struck out, venting her frustration.

"Of course not!" Lord Ibuki replied in surprise. "After all, I taught him how to use a sword, remember. I've taught young men swordsmanship for twenty years, yet never have I met such a poor fighter. Honestly, I can hardly believe that he's a Prince of Light. When I cross swords with another man, no matter who he might be, I can see what type of person he is."

Saya calmed down a little and wiped her eyes. "And what did you see?" she asked.

"Well, now. He's like a crane who has come flying from far away. Though he puts his feet and beak in the mud, his heart is still wandering above the clouds where he used to roam. How could someone like that possibly deceive other people?"

SAYA went with Natsume to help the troop that had been attacked, tending the wounded and rounding up the draft animals. As she was working busily, she noticed a commotion in the area where supplies were distributed. She could hear Natsume shouting something. Surprised, she laid aside her work and ran toward the commotion. When she arrived, panting for breath, she found Natsume, surrounded by a ring of soldiers, trying to wash a filthy little girl. The child screamed loudly, thrashing in Natsume's arms as the two scuffled.

"No! No!"

"You're a girl, aren't you? At least wash your face!"

In danger of being kicked in the stomach, Natsume finally released her and the little girl rolled away and began rubbing dirt on her face with both hands, glaring rebelliously.

"What's going on? Who's this?" Saya asked. Natsume, drenched from head to toe with spilled wash water, looked over her shoulder with an exasperated expression.

"The provisions corps found her unconscious and brought her back with them. It seems that they mistook her for a deer and shot at her. Fortunately, she was unharmed, but when she came to her senses, she went wild, as you just saw."

She appeared to be five or six years old. She had an attractive face, but her hair was matted and she was covered in mud from head to toe. She seemed more like a wild creature than a human child the way she watched them suspiciously, reminding Saya of the time that Chihaya had become a deer.

"She was in the forest? Alone?"

"She must have lost her home and family in the war. She won't even tell us her name or those of her parents or brothers and sisters," Natsume said with concern. "What a troublesome find. What shall we do with her?"

Moved by the girl's plight, Saya looked at her closely. The child stared at those around her and continued to rub her cheeks with her blackened hands as though they still bothered her. Saya felt as though she was looking at herself many years ago.

"Can't we take care of her? We can't just leave her here," she said, but Natsume and the soldiers looked troubled.

"I wish we could," Natsume answered in a low voice, "but we barely have enough food for the soldiers with our increased numbers. Even though it may be just a little, we have to draw the line somewhere . . . My lady, she's not the only child who has lost her parents in the war."

"Just this one," Saya pleaded. "Please, couldn't we at least help this one?"

One of the soldiers whispered to his neighbor, "We could give her the immortal's food. He won't die even if he doesn't eat. It's a waste to feed him."

Saya turned her face toward them sharply. "Who dared to say such a thing?

"You may leave this army. I don't wish to share food or quarters with such a mean-spirited person."

Everyone stared at her in surprise. She had never spoken so coldly to a soldier before. Looking at each of them, she continued, "I'll share my own rations with this child. That shouldn't cause trouble for anyone else."

Even Natsume stared at her in astonishment. Sensing a sudden gulf between them, Saya was overcome with a feeling of futility and, not knowing where to turn, looked at the little girl. The girl stared back at her, the whites of her eyes shining in her dirty face, as though Saya were the unusual sight.

"Come with me," Saya said warmly. "If you've lost your name, let me call you Fawn, because you were mistaken for a deer. My name

is Saya. I was given that name when I was taken in myself—because
the rustling of the bamboo grass where I was found sounded like,
'*saya, saya.*' At least, that's what I was told."

Fawn returned to the fortifications with Saya and shared her quarters. Within a few days she settled down and adapted extraordinarily
quickly to her new environment. She played without fear among the
soldiers and flitted about with such innocent curiosity it was as if a
baby sparrow had found its way into the camp. But no matter how
often she was scolded, she never stopped rubbing her face with dirt.
Saya, deciding that she must have some childish reason of her own,
eventually gave up mentioning it.

Dreary days of waiting followed for the people of Darkness. Everything seemed to go wrong, as the war dragged on in a stalemate that
seemed insurmountable. An unseasonably cold and dismal drizzle set
in as if even the weather were despondent. Absolving Chihaya from
the false charges laid against him was not going to be an easy task,
and Saya watched the days pass with a heavy heart. Fawn's innocent
antics were her only solace. And she was not the only one beguiled
by her charms. Despite her dirty face, she was a winsome child, and
the soldiers were happy to have her with them. For many she brought
back memories of their own beloved daughters. The cruel winter
drew near, and the thoughts of the soldiers, tired of fighting, turned
toward the warm hearths of their homes far away.

Looking out of her tent at the cold rain, Saya found her brooding
thoughts returning repeatedly to the damp rocks near the spring
and the cave lashed by the north wind. At that moment, she heard
Fawn, who was playing inside the tent, dragging something toward
her. Glancing casually over her shoulder, Saya was startled to see her
holding the Dragon Sword, which she had stowed away safely. She
wondered how the little girl could have found it.

"What are you doing? Don't touch that! You'll be struck dead by
lightning!"

"No, I won't. Nothing's happened. I like it. I want it."

Saya hastily snatched it away. "Well, you can't have it. It belongs
to someone else. It isn't yours, or mine, either. I'm just taking care of

it until it's time to give it back to its owner. Be a good girl and leave it alone."

"Whose is it?"

Saya said solemnly, "It belongs to the person in the cave."

Fawn's voice rose excitedly. "I know! The one everyone calls the Prince of Light, the one in the cage. That's no fun. I'll go find something else to do." She ran out into the fine rain. Saya was about to stop her but thought better of it. She looked at the Sword in her hand and sighed, thinking that she had better find a different hiding place for it.

After a while Fawn saw some soldiers under a shelter gathered around a fire roasting chestnuts, and she squirmed her way in eagerly. One of the men sat her on his lap, and they continued talking without taking any notice of her.

"That's all very well to say, but how can you execute someone who doesn't die?"

"But it's obvious that he's betraying us to Princess Teruhi. I can't believe that she's just hiding behind the shield of her troops. She must have infiltrated our line somewhere and is communicating with that traitor. If we don't hurry up and put a stop to it, we'll be murdered in our sleep."

"I'd feel much easier myself if he were dead, but even if we stopped giving him food or water he'd still survive . . ."

"It makes my blood boil. He sits in that flooded cell as though nothing bothered him."

"The immortals killed my brother."

"They killed my father, too."

"Why should they be allowed to come back from death?"

Just then Fawn said with childish innocence, "But there is a way to get rid of them for good."

The men stared at her in surprise, for it had never occurred to them that she was listening. Fawn looked back at them with wide eyes.

"You want to make sure he doesn't come back, right? My father told me once that there is a way."

The man holding her on his lap asked gently, "And what would that be, little one? What did your father say?"

Fawn giggled as if it amused her. "You eat him. You chop him up like mincemeat and eat him. Then he won't be immortal anymore and the people who eat him will live forever."

A strange expression crossed the faces of her listeners. They exchanged covert glances, but none of them spoke. Only Fawn seemed unconcerned, concentrating solely on the chestnuts she was poking in the fire.

LORD IBUKI came to Saya. "Have you heard any strange rumors?" he asked her in an unusually gloomy tone of voice. "People are saying things that I can't stand to hear. If I knew who started it, I'd have them hanged."

Saya put down her breakfast bowl and looked at him. "What kind of rumors? I don't understand."

Fawn, sitting beside Saya with her nose in her porridge bowl, raised her face. "What does 'have them hanged' mean?"

"Keep quiet and eat your breakfast," Saya said and then turned back to Lord Ibuki. "What rumors are they to make you so angry?"

"Never mind. You're better off not knowing. I can't even bear to repeat them." He shook his head and left.

THAT AFTERNOON Natsume entered Saya's tent with a troubled expression. Fawn was outside playing, and Saya was alone.

"My lady, it's hard for me to say this, but . . ."

"What is it? This isn't like you."

"Well, actually it's about Fawn. I don't think it's good for her to be with you."

Saya looked at her inquiringly. "Is the food shortage that bad?"

"No, it isn't that." Natsume faltered, then, clasping and unclasping her hands repeatedly, finally said, "There's something about her that disturbs me."

Saya was shocked and disappointed. "So all those who are not our kin will be shunned. First Chihaya, and now Fawn?"

"No. That's not what I mean. I, too, feel that Chihaya has been treated unjustly," Natsume responded earnestly. "I'm ashamed that we have placed the blame on him. Of course, I understand how everyone feels—after all, I despised him, too, for a while wondering why he alone should come back from the dead. But that way of thinking is futile and mistaken. I know now that I can bear my grief without hating, thanks to this unborn child."

Natsume tenderly caressed her belly, which was beginning to swell; to Saya, her gesture seemed to embody the Goddess herself.

"Whether it's a boy or a girl, this child is Masaki. When it's born, it will be the same as Masaki returning to life. Now I can believe that."

"That's true," Saya said with feeling. "Bear the child well, Natsume."

A grateful smile touched Natsume's face, but then her expression suddenly clouded. "That girl, Fawn, no matter how I try, I can't get her to recall her parents. She's more like a little demon than a child born from a mother's womb. Perhaps that's what bothers me about her."

"She certainly has an impudent streak, but she can be sweet, too, you know," Saya said.

But Natsume shook her head. For someone so gentle-natured, she had taken an unusual aversion to the child. "Sometimes Fawn stares at me—with indescribably cold eyes. She has the look of one who brings evil."

"Are you sure you're not exaggerating?"

But Natsume continued. "Even dogs treat a pregnant bitch gently, don't they? Although I'm of little use on the battlefield in this state, everyone treats me with kindness. It's not conscious, but they instinctively honor the life they see inside me. I'm grateful and I don't intend to take advantage of it. It's just that the way she looks at me is so different from everyone else."

Saya felt uneasy, but at the same time she did not feel that this was enough reason to censure a five- or six-year-old child. "She's so little she doesn't understand. Without knowing it, she's probably jealous of the baby."

"Perhaps you're right . . ."

Saya pleaded with her. "Please don't hate Fawn. She's like me when I was a child. When my parents in Hashiba adopted me, I'm sure I was just like her—bereft of loved ones, trusting no one, wild and rough. My parents took me in anyway and cared for me with love. We should be able to do the same for her."

Natsume exhaled quietly and seemed to reconsider. "Yes, my lady, you're right. I'm sorry I troubled you over nothing."

Watching her rise heavily with a drawn look on her face, Saya thought that Natsume had probably become oversensitive, owing to the changes in her body. *It can't be healthy for her to be in such a brutal environment. If even I get depressed here, it can't be good for Natsume.*

Leaving Saya's quarters, Natsume passed behind the tent. Distracted by a stray lock, she stopped to remove a comb from her hair and fix her bun. Patting the stray wisps into place, she happened to look into a nearby grove of trees. Her hand froze with shock. In the crook of a tree, just at eye level, sat Fawn, swinging her legs back and forth. At a casual glance she appeared as cute as a doll, but the eyes that peered out from her grimy face were piercingly cruel.

Speaking in a tone that did not match her childish voice, she said, "You're a little too perceptive—perhaps because you bear two lives instead of one." A faint, lopsided smile twisted her delicate lips. "It won't do to have you meddling when Saya is so trusting. Just a little longer and I'll be able to make the soldiers of Darkness do exactly as I wish."

The color drained from Natsume's face. Backing away, she whispered, "Demon—you're a demon in disguise!"

"Far from it!" Fawn sprang lightly down from the tree. "By demons you mean the dirty little gods of field and mountain. You insult me. With extreme forbearance I have come to this squalid spot. But it's exhausting, a waste of the powers of renewal." Her bright pink tongue, like that of a kitten, flicked across her lips. "But two lives in one—now, that would help wash away this defilement."

Natsume, who had continued to edge away, wheeled around. Her hair, which had come loose again, fell down her back.

"Are you going to run away?" Fawn inquired. "But where will you find help? Who will believe you?"

Without waiting to hear more, Natsume ran for her life. Through the chill air, still damp with the recent rain, she ran as though possessed, trampling and scattering the sodden leaves, until she collided with a group of soldiers. They grabbed her in surprise and asked her what she was doing.

"What's the matter? If you tripped and fell, you could hurt the baby."

"Fawn—" Gasping for breath, Natsume babbled like someone demented. "Please. Help me. Fawn is going to kill me!"

"You're overwrought, Natsume. Though it's no wonder, here in the middle of a war," the soldiers replied with concern. "But you must stay calm, especially in your condition. You should lie down and take it easy. We'll make you some herbal tea."

Despite her protests, they kept trying to soothe her. Their concern was real and, finally, unable to resist any longer, she allowed them to put her to bed in a nearby hut. But as soon as they had left, she fled once more.

Her feet, driven by fear, turned at last toward the spring. Passing the pool made by a simple dam, she began to climb. There, surrounded by the bare rock, was the cold, barred cave.

Chihaya sat gazing out through the bars at the distant river mouth, shrouded in mist. From his windy aerie he could clearly see the sandbar. Lonely waterfowl flew aimlessly beneath the low-lying gray clouds. He was attempting to capture the feelings of a bird when his view was suddenly blocked by a shadow. Surprised, he retuned to himself and saw Natsume on the other side of the bars. She sank to her knees and grasped the bars of his prison as though in entreaty.

"Please! Help me! You must help me and the child I bear!"

Chihaya frowned as he stared at her desperate face.

"Help you? Why?"

"The girl—she's trying to kill me. Nobody believes me. But you—I know you'll understand. Because you're no ordinary man."

Chihaya looked troubled. "You're right. I'm different from you. That's why I'm in this prison."

"You have a right to be angered by the way we treated you. I and all my people are to blame. But this child within me is innocent. It has done you no harm. Please, for the sake of the child, protect me."

"But how . . ."

Natsume picked up a sharp stone and tried to break the wedges that held the bars in place. "Please! Come out. These wooden bars shouldn't stop a Prince of Light like you."

Alarmed, Chihaya said in a hushed voice, "Don't do that. You'll get me in trouble. If they find out that I've left the prison, your people will never trust me again."

Natsume began to weep. The tears streamed down her cheeks and splashed onto the rocks. "Will you desert me, then? When no mortal man can stand against her? When it is you alone who can match her?"

"Don't cry! Please!" Now it was Chihaya's turn to become distressed. He was willing to do anything if she would just stop crying. "Calm down and tell me what you mean. I want to help you, but I don't understand what's going on."

But as she opened her mouth to speak, she suddenly reared back, staring up into space. Her outstretched arms flailed in a swimming motion. Chihaya leaped to his feet, shocked at the sight of fresh blood, and there behind her he saw a little girl gripping the hilt of the Dragon Sword, which was plunged deep into Natsume's back, and bathing herself in the blood.

"Natsume!"

He thrust his arms through the bars to support her, but in vain. She crumpled slowly to the ground. The light in her eyes was swiftly fading and already she looked at Chihaya without seeing. After a convulsive shudder, she turned her sorrowful eyes toward him one last time and whispered beneath her breath, "Masaki." Then she slumped lifeless to the ground.

Chihaya gazed speechlessly over her body at the blood-drenched child. She beamed up at him and then, without a word, turned and ran.

"Wait!"

When he unconsciously applied pressure to the bars where his hands gripped them, they popped out easily. He had not time to wonder whether it was Natsume's doing or his own as he rushed out of the prison in pursuit of the girl.

She leaped lightly from rock to rock before him as though dancing through the air, and in three strides she had descended to the edge of the pool. She stripped off her soiled clothing and dived into the cold water. Chihaya pursued her to the edge of the pool but there he stopped. The girl showed no sign of haste as she stood chest-deep in the water, washing. When she raised her face, her skin shone pure white. Though childish, her countenance was as flawless as a jewel. She looked up at him and once again smiled gaily. Chihaya, taken aback, remained rooted to the spot. Next she began to wash her body. Each time she scooped the water, she grew taller. Her hair grew longer as he watched, and spread out upon the water. Her slender arms grew long and lithesome, her shoulders round and smooth, and her breasts swelled like ripe fruit. By the time she had finished bathing, she had undergone a transformation that would have taken a mortal a decade or more to complete. When she turned to climb out onto the bank, the water lapped just below her navel against the rounded hips and slender waist of a young woman.

She rose shamelessly from the water and stood before Chihaya with her wet body exposed. And indeed there was no need to conceal her perfect form.

"Sister," Chihaya whispered.

"An excellent cleansing. That feels better," Princess Teruhi said as she combed her hair with her fingers. "It's quite a skill to return to childhood. Perhaps because a child is weaker, one tires easily. Not to mention the bother of the lesser gods catching the scent of renewal."

"Why did you kill Natsume?"

"Because two lives in one body are a very effective means for purification."

"Sister!"

"You're angry? You?" she said in surprise and looked hard at Chihaya. "You've changed. Even your appearance. I almost wouldn't recognize you. How can that be when those of our line never change?

But never mind. I've come to get you. Let's leave harsh words for another time."

She smiled a not altogether unkind smile. "It was for your sake that I went to such lengths to penetrate the forces of Darkness. When all is said and done, you are, after all, my brother. If possible, I would rather not fight against you. Come back with me to the palace. Surely you've realized by now the foolishness of these people."

After a pause, Chihaya asked, "Was it you who directed this last attack?"

"Yes. I slipped behind their lines in the guise of a girl and stirred the fools up a little. It was easy to twist them around my finger." Leaning her back against a rock and folding her arms, the Princess continued, "And it was I who made sure that suspicion blew in your direction. And I again who shot you with the arrow. And just as I intended, the followers of Darkness have turned their backs on you. That's the sort of people they are. You won't be able to remain here any longer. For they'll soon come to carve you into little pieces."

Chihaya looked at her in disbelief. "But why?"

Princess Teruhi shrugged her white shoulders. "Because they're base and savage. I only planted the seeds. They're the ones who reaped the harvest."

Bending down, she picked up the Sword, which lay on the bank, and meticulously washed the blood off in the stream. Then, carefully inspecting the blade, she murmured, "It's only a sword, an empty husk. You've broken the seals one after the other. So now do you know yourself?"

"A little," Chihaya replied quietly.

"It would have been better had you never known," the Princess said with a sigh. "Then you must also know why we'll be forced to destroy you. You're our father's child and, at the same time, his gravest threat. That is, if you become our foe . . . But there's still time." She gazed at him partly in entreaty, partly as if to compel him. "Don't make me your enemy. If you return to the palace, I'll protect you once again. I'll protect you from your own self. That's what you need."

Chihaya hesitated for a long time. Seeing that his heart was wavering,

Princess Teruhi waited motionless for his reply. Finally, he spoke.

"I—I've already promised Saya," he said haltingly, "to use my power to aid Toyoashihara. I can't break my word so suddenly."

Rage glittered in Princess Teruhi's eyes. She said coldly, "So you intend to set a vow made between children before a request from your own sister? You're the same fool you always were. Let's see if you still say that when the mob descends upon you."

Returning the Dragon Sword to Chihaya, she turned her back on him in fury. "At least you should protect yourself. I wasn't lying. We can't live if we're cut into little pieces. But even should you escape their clutches, I'll come after you and chop you up myself. Consider yourself no longer my brother. I made my request, once and once only. There will be no second chance."

In the blink of an eye, she vanished. Even Chihaya did not know how she managed it. Confused and dazed, he looked at the Sword she had placed in his hand. At that moment a voice clouded with fury smote him from above.

"Hold! Murderer! How dare you slay a woman!"

Startled, he looked up to see two guards, their faces black with anger, standing with their spears at the ready.

"No. You've made a mistake. It wasn't me."

But his voice was drowned by the guard's whistle as it cut the air, sounding the alarm.

4

LORD SHINADO rushed into Saya's quarters, his usual cool composure utterly disrupted. "Something terrible has happened!"

Saya had been sewing, thinking that it was about time for Fawn to return. When Lord Shinado wrenched aside the tent flap instead, she had looked up at him in startled amazement. Struggling to catch his breath, he said in a low voice, "Chihaya escaped from his cell. He was caught immediately, but he has been surrounded by a frenzied mob and we can't reach him. They're demanding his immediate execution."

The needle and cloth fell from Saya's hands. "Where is he?"

"In the clearing by the spring. Lord Ibuki rushed to the scene and is doing his best to calm everyone down, but they're so enraged that they're liable to strike out even at him. You're the Priestess. Do you have the power to still the wrath of mortal men?"

"I have no idea!"

There was no time for further exchange. The two raced toward the hollow, which was ringed by a wood of alder trees. The area was now packed with angry, shouting men. "Kill the Prince of Light! Carve him into pieces!" they cried. Saya was stunned, wondering what could have caused this drunken delirium. Swept up in the maelstrom, the glassy-eyed mob was no longer capable of listening to reason. They did not even see Saya or Lord Shinado, jostling them roughly as they attempted to push through the crowd. The clamor was fused into a foreign tongue that spoke only of hunger and rage.

They're like an enormous, ravenous beast, Saya thought as she struggled to make her way through the seething throng. *They need something stronger than words to appease their hunger. But it mustn't be blood, or they'll become no better than wolves. Oh, how I wish I could dump a bucket of cold water over each one of them.*

Over her head, she heard the sound of someone being struck.

"Where are your eyes? What do you think you're doing to the Lady of the Sword?"

A burly arm reached out and grasped Saya, plucking her from the midst of the crowd as though pulling a plant from the field. It was Lord Ibuki.

"Are you all right?"

"Yes. But what about . . ."

Saya brushed her disheveled hair from her face and looked around. Chihaya stood beneath a leafless tree surrounded by soldiers. His arms were tied behind him around the trunk of the tree, and he gazed off into the distance, unaware of her presence. His face was gashed and his knees and chest were smeared with grime. The soldiers stood with their spears at the ready, but more to protect Chihaya from the angry mob than anything else. Already several men were arguing with the guards, barely restraining themselves from grabbing them.

"Why do they demand his execution when he's immortal?"

Lord Ibuki answered her in a strained voice, "They say that if he's cut into little pieces and each is buried separately, he won't return to life. Whether it's true or not, I don't know."

Saya caught her breath. "Cut Chihaya . . . ?"

"No matter what he has done, Lord Akitsu as our commander should be the one to judge. Chihaya shouldn't be butchered here in a so-called execution. We must take him to Lord Akitsu. Saya, can you help us calm this crowd?"

Still pondering what to do, she looked around and noticed a body shrouded by a straw mat lying at the feet of some guards who held back the surging crowd with their spears. The lifeless hand of a woman protruded from beneath the mat.

"No! Wait!" Lord Ibuki tried to stop her, but it was too late. Saya flew to the corpse and, wrenching aside the mat, gazed on what lay beneath: the lifeless form of Natsume and, beside her, the Dragon Sword.

Without realizing it, she began to scream. Even when she became aware of what she was doing, she could not stop. Her high, thin wail rose clearly above the tumult of the mob, so that even the shouting men heard and were startled by it.

"Natsume! Why? Why? Why?"

She threw herself on the body, shaking it futilely while she continued to scream. For it was Natsume, who but a short time ago had smiled like the Goddess as she placed her hand upon her belly; Natsume, who had so confidently declared that Masaki would return. Saya could not bear the sight without screaming. She could not accept what her eyes were seeing.

"Why? Who did this?"

"The Prince of Light. He took her as his victim," someone said. "The one who does not die brings nothing but evil."

"Kill him!"

"Let us harbor this evil no longer!"

"Kill him!"

"The immortals aren't human! They don't deserve to be judged with justice. Why should they be treated like us?"

"Tear him to pieces!"

The tumult rose once again like sulfurous water brought to the boil.

"Off with his ears! His fingers! Cut him into pieces and make him die!"

Amid the clamor of voices that assailed her ears, Saya finally raised her face from Natsume and looked at Chihaya. He saw her now. When he caught her gaze, she saw his expression change. At first he showed only surprise, but as he stared at her, the expression on his face gradually changed to one of deep despair. As though he were a mirror, she saw upon his face her own expression reflected back at her. The sight filled her with grief, yet she could do nothing to stop it.

Surrounded by the angry roar that filled their ears, they looked at each other as though at a stranger. True, the noise prevented speech, yet the yawning chasm across which they gazed separated them more surely than the tumult. Saya, stunned by the enormity of her loss, turned her face away. If she looked at Chihaya any longer, she was afraid that next she would see distrust and hatred in his face. She could not bear that. Even if his face was just a mirror, she did not want to see such things in him.

In the next instant, the ring of men broke and disintegrated into a surging mob. Having lost all restraint, the soldiers forgot themselves entirely and, with weapons raised, rushed like an avalanche toward the tree where Chihaya was tied. The guards trying desperately to check the sudden onslaught were struck, stabbed, or thrust aside and overrun. Saya, too, was pushed roughly away and almost trampled underfoot, but Lord Shinado snatched her out of the way just in time. She had almost fainted, but, pulling her wits together, she cried out as soon as she could speak, "Stop them! Hurry!"

"Impossible!" Lord Shinado replied, ignoring the half-crazed Saya as he tried to distance her from the jostling crowd. "It would require more than the strength of one or two men. I'd likely be killed myself in the effort."

"Stop them! If you don't," Saya pleaded, trembling, "it is they who will die."

"What?" Lord Shinado stopped to stare at her. But at that very moment a blinding streak of blue lightning flashed across the sky, transforming the clouds. In the same instant a deafening roar smote the earth, shaking the land of Toyoashihara. Not one man was left standing under the terrific impact. People toppled over each other and lay cowering on the ground. Lifting faces ashen with fear, they saw flames erupting from the walnut tree where Chihaya had stood. Blackened instantly from the tip down to the base of its trunk, which was broad enough to put one's arms around, the tree burned fiercely, crimson flames blossoming along its charred branches, until it came crashing down, a harbinger of death to those below. The pitiful screams of people who had failed to escape rent the air. But this was only the beginning of the onslaught. Lightning struck at them again and again. Before their very eyes, the sky turned a murky black, as if ink had been spilled across it, and a raging storm descended. Violent winds assailed them along with a sudden torrential rain, and this, combined with direct assaults from repeated thunderbolts, compounded the disaster. It was almost as if the lightning was being aimed at the water, felling scores of people with one blow. Within a short time the scene presented was more tragic than any witnessed on the bloodiest battlefield. The dead lay where they fell, buried in mud, the wounded moaned, and both were trampled underfoot by the survivors who fled in panic.

Saya, who was fortunate to have been outside the circle, was able to reach shelter behind a rock, but she was powerless to do anything more within this nightmare of driving rain. She could only cower in terror. A god of appalling fury, one whom thunderclouds followed and lightning obeyed, raged even now above them, totally out of control.

Someone grasped her shoulder suddenly, and she almost jumped out of her skin. Lord Shinado stood beside her, drenched from head to toe, his hair plastered to his scalp. He had been there all along, but in her fear she had forgotten him.

"Is this the truth, then?" he said in low voice. His tone and expression were drained of life. He, too, was afraid. "It is Chihaya who becomes the Dragon? The Sword and Chihaya are one?"

Saya nodded, feeling her throat ache with suppressed sobs. Clouds of spray rose from the rocks in the driving rain, which formed countless silver rivulets. The brook had already burst its dam and had swollen into a turbid brown stream.

"Stop him, Saya, please!" Lord Shinado pleaded. "If this continues, we'll be destroyed before we ever have the chance to face the forces of Light."

Unable to restrain herself, Saya wailed, "How? How shall I stop him? When I know full well what we have done to him."

"But aren't you the Priestess of the Sword?"

"We've lost him. Don't you understand?"

She longed to rebuke him. *Can't you see by looking at me?* she wanted to demand. *Can't you see how afraid, how hopeless, how lost I am?* But she knew that her rage should be directed at herself.

Illuminated by flashes of lightning, a huge man ran splashing through the torrent, covering his head with his arms. It was Lord Ibuki.

"So there you are, Lord Shinado, Saya. Won't you lead those who can walk to higher ground? They're in danger here. If the river overflows its banks, they won't stand a chance."

"But the Dragon's up there. Lightning is still falling."

"Have no fear. I'll deal with him," Lord Ibuki said calmly. Lord Shinado and Saya both stared at him in shock.

"How do you intend to do what even Saya, the Priestess of the Sword, cannot?"

Lord Ibuki glanced at Saya. "That's Chihaya, isn't it? If it is, he's my pupil. It's my duty, as his teacher, to admonish him," he stated, slapping the wide hilt of his sword. As he turned away, Saya clutched at him desperately.

"Wait! A sword is no match for his power. You'll be killed. The Dragon has neither eyes nor heart. He can't see you."

"How can we know that if we don't try?" Lord Ibuki said with a flash of white teeth. His was the face of a bold and seasoned warrior, but he was far more than that. "I will not be slain so easily. I'll tell him that if he wants to bare his fangs against his comrades, he must kill me first."

Still clinging to him, Saya whispered, "Please don't go. If we lose you, too, what are we to do?"

Lord Ibuki only stroked her head with his large hand as though comforting a wayward child. Then, gently loosening her grasp, he climbed the rocks in the torrential rain to face the Dragon dancing amid the black clouds.

"SAYA."

A familiar voice called her name. The storm had abated and the lonesome twilight imbued the land with stillness. The red rays of the setting sun finally pierced the clouds, which were only now beginning to disperse, casting a warmer blush on the tips of the crimson-leafed trees. Saya was sitting in a daze outside a small hut. She turned to stare blankly toward the sound, but saw no one, only the tethered horses of Lord Akitsu and the others nudging each other.

"Hey, Saya!"

A little life came into her face when she finally located the owner of the voice perched on the fence. "Torihiko!"

"I thought you'd forgotten me. And I was only gone a short while," said the crow.

"Where have you been?"

"Here and there. I've mustered many troops. Even Lord Akitsu couldn't match their number. From now on, they'll have to call me Lord Torihiko," he joked, but when she did not respond, he flapped his wings. "Cheer up. The Dragon was stilled, right?"

"But it was Lord Ibuki who did it."

"How is he?"

Saya shook her head wordlessly. Then, unable to suppress her feelings any longer, she groaned. "Torihiko, I've failed."

"No you haven't."

"Yes, I have. I've failed at everything. I'm totally useless. How can I be the Priestess, when I can't do even one thing right when I'm needed?"

Torihiko gazed at her in concern as she sat with her face buried in her hands. "I should never have left you," he said.

After a short while an attendant came out of the hut and addressed Saya in a hushed voice. "His Lordship is conscious. He wishes to speak with you."

She followed him through the doorway. In the dim light of the hut, the army's key commanders, including Lord Akitsu, sat silently, their faces grave. It was clear from their expressions that there was no hope of recovery. Her spirits sinking even further, Saya looked at Lord Ibuki's huge, prostrated form. His hair and beard were singed and burns covered his entire body; beneath the white cloth, she caught glimpses of painfully blistered skin. He had lost both eyes. The healer, unable to do more, had applied a cool damp cloth over them in an attempt to relieve at least some of the pain. As Saya stood beside him, he moved his blackened lips.

"Is that Saya? The footsteps were light."

Hoarse and barely audible, his voice, normally loud and booming, was unrecognizable. Clenching her teeth to hold back the tears, Saya sank to her knees beside him and said, "Yes, it's me, Saya. Are you in pain?"

"No. It's not so bad. Saya, I spoke with Chihaya. In the end, he knew me," he said as cheerfully as he could manage. "I told him that since he was the worst pupil I had ever had, I was relieved to see that he could now beat even his teacher."

"It was all my fault," Saya whispered.

"Saya, don't reject him. I'm begging you. Please. He raged blindly, unable to control his own power. He didn't even know what had happened to us. He isn't evil. Far from it. For we hurt him badly."

"Yes. I know." Saya nodded. Her tears overflowed and would not stop. When she thought of losing this man, who was large not only in body but also in soul, and all for nothing, she wanted to rant and rave and pummel the earth. But she could only weep quietly. Lord Ibuki had already set his feet toward the Goddess and was only glancing back at her as he went on his way.

"If you reject Chihaya, he'll reject himself. And that would be a terrible thing, for he will become true evil. He'll become the Dragon. Forgive him. Though the death of Natsume hurt you, Chihaya has also been hurt. Forgiveness is your strength."

"Yes," Saya replied through her tears.

"That's what makes you the Water Maiden." Lord Ibuki let out a long sigh as if suddenly tired. "I go before you to seek rest with the Goddess, but I won't forget you. Tell Chihaya that I hope we meet again in some other guise."

He fell into a deep sleep. And then, as they watched, he quietly breathed his last.

WHEN NIGHT FELL, the sky cleared into a starlit vault. The quarter moon cast a fresh, clean light, etching shadows in the autumn thickets. A wake was held for Lord Ibuki; after placing his coffin within a newly built enclosure, his companions kept watch. There was none who did not mourn his passing, none who did not lament this appalling blow to their military strength. Saya sat a long while in a corner of the small hut, which was thronged with people, but unable to endure it any longer, she finally slipped out alone into the night.

White chrysanthemums floated forlornly in the light of the moon. The smell of frost was in the air. By dawn the ground would be covered in white. To Saya, the cold bite of the air on her skin seemed appropriate. She walked over to a cherry tree that cast a dappled shadow in the moonlight through its sparsely leafed branches and rested her throbbing head against its trunk, whispering softly, "What's done is done and can't be undone." These words kept ringing in her head. No matter what she thought about, in the end, her thoughts always came back to them.

I've lost Chihaya. I'm no longer the Priestess of the Sword. What a fool I was. Natsume, Lord Ibuki—they've both left me behind. Now what shall I live for? How am I to carry on?

Suddenly, she sensed someone walking silently toward her through the darkness. She stepped away from the tree in surprise.

"Who's there?"

A small figure, about the same height as Fawn, walked toward her, silhouetted against the moonlight. But in the pale light her hair shone whiter than frost.

"Lady Iwa," Saya exclaimed, her voice rising in surprise. "Did the news reach you so quickly?"

"I'm always with you. It's just that no one notices," Lady Iwa replied enigmatically. Then, coming right up to her, she asked abruptly, "Daughter, why did you fear, when you knew long ago that Chihaya and the Dragon were one?"

The old woman had cut straight to the heart of the matter. Saya could not answer her at first. But as she gazed into the fathomless depths of her eyes, she realized that Lady Iwa already knew everything. Then it was not words but tears that most adequately expressed her feelings. She burst out crying, like a heartbroken child breaking down before her mother. "I didn't believe it. I don't know what came over me. I saw Natsume and just lost control . . . To think that even for a moment I could believe such a thing of Chihaya, when he placed the Sword in my hands the day he was imprisoned. When the only person who could have taken the Sword from my tent was Fawn."

"Yes, and the child you took under your wing was Princess Teruhi herself. It's just the sort of thing that woman would do."

"Natsume distrusted Fawn. But . . ." Saya murmured.

"The immortals are adept at exploiting human frailties. Playing on your compassion, she infiltrated our lines to carry out her scheme."

"Then if I had just been stronger, Natsume and Lord Ibuki need not have died, right?"

Lady Iwa's large eyes blinked slowly. "It does no good to talk of what might have been."

"But I can't be silent. I've been such a fool that I hate myself," Saya said, unable to stop. "I can never, ever forget the expression on Chihaya's face. I abandoned him when he needed me most. How could I have looked at him like that? I know Lord Ibuki meant what he said to me, but it's too late. Chihaya is gone. I can't take it back."

Lady Iwa waited until Saya's sobs had quieted, and then said gently, "You mustn't despair. That's the worst way to admit a mistake. It's true that some mistakes can never be amended no matter what you do, but that doesn't mean it's all right to give up before you even try."

Saya finally wiped the tears from her eyes. "If I had even the slightest hope that I could make amends I would do anything—no matter how slim the chances."

"Daughter," Lady Iwa said earnestly, "I don't believe that Chihaya has returned to the Palace of Light. Where he has gone I don't know, yet I feel he must be wandering somewhere not so far away."

"Do you really think so?" Saya gazed at her with wide, tear-drenched eyes. "Despite what we did to him, do you really think it's possible that he might not hate us?"

"Yes, I do, because he now knows himself. He's no longer a child who will do as his sister bids him. He can think for himself and will make a move only after he has come to a decision. Of course, he'll never come back to the camp of Darkness of his own accord—"

"But if I were to look for him, I might speak with him," Saya completed her sentence eagerly. "If there's any hope of that, I'll go. I will find Chihaya."

"Yes. It's possible that you may be able to take his hand once again. This time, however, you must choose your words with the utmost care, for Chihaya will never again simply do what you tell him."

Saya took a deep breath and stood up straight. She no longer felt she had lost everything. "It will be enough to say that I'm sorry, as long as we won't be alienated by misunderstanding anymore. I will find Chihaya. That's what I must do."

Hearing the conviction in her voice, Lady Iwa closed her eyes as if lost in thought. Slowly and deliberately she said, "Saya, more than three hundred years have passed since the forces of Light began to rule this land. During that time, we struggled to resist them. Generation after generation, the Water Maiden was born, and each time she was drawn to the Light and destroyed herself. It seemed that this must be the curse of the maid who kept the Sword. Yet you found Chihaya. You are the first Water Maiden to meet the Wind Child. And I think that this will change everything. At last the Water Maiden has found the essence of that which she seeks."

Saya looked at the old woman apprehensively. "But I'm so thoughtless. I've failed at everything so far. Even though I was the first to meet Chihaya, do you think there's a chance that I may take my own life again if I fail this time?"

"Are you nervous?" Lady Iwa said with laughter in her voice. As if teasing her, she added, "Are you still afraid of Chihaya?"

"No," Saya said defiantly, but Lady Iwa shook her head.

"No, Saya, that would be a lie. After all, he's the Dragon. It would be false not to fear him, and a big mistake. Yet it's also wrong to fear him completely. For he isn't evil. If you treat him with integrity, you will be rewarded with integrity. He is the Dragon, but in order for him to transcend the Dragon you must fear, and transcend your fear."

chapter six

THE EARTHEN
VESSEL

O winds of heaven, bring up the clouds
and seal the vaulted sky
Lest these heavenly maids should wings possess
and away from us should fly.

—Bishop Henjo

The Earthen Vessel

THE COMMANDERS SAT IN A CIRCLE and watched Lord Akitsu carefully, waiting to see how he would respond to Saya's request. He spoke slowly, as if trying to postpone making a decision. "I understand what you're saying. And I know that Chihaya wasn't to blame. But what can you hope to gain by going off in search of him? He'll never come back to us. After what we did to each other, we'll never be able to look one another in the face again."

"No. We're capable of forgiveness," Saya argued earnestly. "If we can forgive him, he will forgive us. Those who let his immortality blind them already regret it. And besides, everyone now knows that we were deceived and manipulated by Princess Teruhi."

"Do we really need to go to such lengths to regain him as our ally?" Lord Shinado demanded harshly.

"Yes. The Dragon Sword has always been guarded by the people of Darkness. Chihaya is the Dragon Sword. He's our strongest, our greatest power."

"But you yourself said that we had lost him."

Saya flinched at this and replied in a small voice. "Yes. And that's precisely why I myself must go in search of him."

"Do you think you can just wander about looking for him when you don't even have any idea where he is?" Lord Shinado exclaimed. "In the midst of war when the slightest provocation could spark another full-scale battle? The forces of Light have set ambushes everywhere. Such a search is impossible!"

"I'm going with her," Torihiko interjected. He had seemed engrossed in preening his feathers but he looked up and said, "I've sent out my troops and they're already wheeling through the sky looking for him."

Lord Shinado frowned. "Torihiko, you're a military weapon we can't spare. Do you intend to desert your post?"

"All I have to do is fly back here to maintain contact," the crow replied indifferently. "And, in case you've forgotten, it was for Saya's sake that I chose to stay in this world as a bird."

Lord Akitsu gazed at Saya as if wondering what to do. "Can't you wait a little longer, just until things settle down? We can't afford to split up our forces at this time, yet I can't send you out without protection."

"No, it can't wait. Please!" Saya leaned forward, pleading. "Let me go. If Torihiko comes with me, I can protect myself. I must leave now. The longer I wait, the farther away he'll go."

Lord Shinado broke in. "What on earth do you see in Chihaya, that Prince of Light, that monstrous Dragon? Granted, it was you who brought him to us in the first place, but of what use is this devotion which drives you to throw your life away in order to bring him back? You act like some love-struck maid running after her lover, blind to everything else."

This remark was so unexpected that Saya could only gape at him in surprise. At that moment, she heard Lady Iwa's voice. The old woman had been sitting apart in a corner of the room, her eyes closed, listening. For the first time, she opened her eyes and looked at them. "That's right," she said. "Saya is the Priestess of the Sword, and that's what it means to be priestess. A priestess is someone who can wed a god despite being of mortal frame."

The blood rushed to Lord Shinado's face and there was anger in his voice. "Are you saying that the god Saya serves is Chihaya? I'll never accept that! Especially not such a—"

"I didn't say he was the god she serves," Lady Iwa interrupted swiftly. "But you must recognize that with the Sword between them, Chihaya and Saya form the opposing poles of one axis. They are like opposite sides of the same body. Whether they choose to give or to take, they seek in the other what they lack within themselves. Just as a god cannot exist without a priestess, so a priestess cannot exist without a god."

Lord Shinado did not utter another word.

Granted just seven days, Saya was given a horse and provisions on the condition that Torihiko fly back daily to report. After they left the meeting, Torihiko flew over and perched on her shoulder. "That must have been quite a blow to Lord Shinado," he said. "It looks to me like he's the love-struck one—although I can sympathize with his unrequited feelings."

Saya gave a small sigh. "Well, I won't pretend that I don't understand what you're talking about. But it's no use, though I feel badly for him."

"What do you think about what Lady Iwa said?"

"It never occurred to me before," she said hesitantly, her eyes downcast. "If Lady Iwa says so, then I suppose it must be true, but it's hard for me to believe. After all, I hardly understand Chihaya myself. I have yet to guess correctly what he'll do next."

She fell silent, but after they had walked a little farther, she suddenly added, "But at the same time, I think that probably no one else understands him better than I do."

The crow shrugged his wings. "Either way, it doesn't really matter to me, so long as you're happy."

"Either way?" Saya asked.

"Whether you're lover or priestess. Either way, it isn't the business of a bird."

* * *

IVY LEAVES REDDER THAN FLAME and clusters of red berries on the bare branches of the shrubs vied for attention. A biting wind blew in gusts along the ground, and the trees shed their colorful leaves with each blast. The fallen leaves lay thick upon the forest floor, and with each passing day the scraggly branches of the trees were further exposed. Birds left, birds came: migrating throngs at the end of their journey.

Torihiko gazed up at a flock of large white birds crossing the sky high above and said, "Those birds are no help. They won't join our ranks. They feel no attachment, no loyalty to Toyoashihara because they come from across the sea."

"So somewhere across the sea is another land."

From her horse Saya gazed across a wide sandbar out into the distance. The sea was very near. She could feel it even in the breeze. "Let's go over there."

"To the seashore? Is there some reason?"

"Not really. I just wanted to see the ocean again."

Grumbling about the dangers of going where there was no cover just to please a foolish whim, he flew into the air, returning almost immediately.

"I've sent out some scouts. We'll stay here until they report."

They waited for a while in front of a field of swaying reeds until the birds returned. A flock of about twenty greenfinches appeared one after the other, beating their gray-green and yellow wings. As soon as they caught sight of Torihiko perched on Saya's shoulder, the friendly round-eyed birds swooped down in a rush and perched without fear on her arms and fingers, chirping merrily.

"All right, then. Let's go," Torihiko said in human speech, and the flock rose once more into the air. Saya parted with them somewhat reluctantly. She urged her mount forward and rode until they came to the tideland. Only migrating snipe could be seen in this forlorn and desolate landscape, resting their wings and poking their beaks in the mud. They learned nothing from them, and as Torihiko judged open spaces to be too dangerous, Saya was forced to turn back and follow a path through the black pine forest that grew in a belt along the coast. It climbed up from the shore, bringing her to the top of a sheer cliff where, through the branches, she could glimpse white-capped waves crashing against the rocks below.

She slept each night under the open sky and was on her own most of the day. Although Torihiko was extremely cautious, he spent most of his time flying in all directions, searching for Chihaya. When night began to fall, Saya would tether her horse to a tree and gather dry branches to make a small fire. Despite having gone to all the trouble of gathering dry leaves to make a bed and curling up in it, she often found that she could not sleep. More than the cold or loneliness, the fear that she was heading in the wrong direction and traveling farther and farther away from Chihaya tormented her at night.

"You know, a lot of things become clearer when you're on your own," Saya said to Torihiko when he flew down to join her. "It's funny but, although I always thought I was alone, I never really have been, at least, not in the true sense of the word."

"Are you feeling discouraged?"

Saya shook her head. "No, it doesn't make me feel like that. But for some reason I feel like the girl I was before I came to Hashiba."

From the first day she awoke in Hashiba, Saya had hated the frightened little girl in her dreams. She had despised her fear, her wretchedness; had rejected her and scorned her helplessness. She had not wanted to recognize her as part of herself. But she had been wrong. For was she not even now wretched, crushed by fear, pitifully pleading and searching for the warmth of love? She was no different from that little girl who wandered lost in the middle of the night. Now, at last, she realized that she must accept and recognize this part of herself. For without accepting it, she could never transcend her fear, could never move forward.

Perhaps the place that she was searching for and never found was me, Saya thought.

At night the wind carried the faint sounds of battle, and, peering through the trees, she could see torches flickering like foxfires on the distant shore. Although she knew from the reports gathered by Torihiko that the battle was still limited to local skirmishes, it was obviously bloody. Far removed from the tranquil peace of the passing autumn season, the final battle between Light and Darkness, on which hinged the fate of Toyoashihara, was about to begin.

The next morning an unusual number of gulls wheeled over the coast. Diving through the white-winged flock, an excited Torihiko flew toward her like an arrow. "We've found him!"

At his triumphant cry, blood pulsed hotly through Saya's veins and she was surprised to find herself feeling faint.

"Where is he?"

"On the beach at the foot of the cliff on the cape. The stupid plovers mistook him for a drowned man and never said a word."

The cliff protruded like a nose, and it was with great difficulty that Saya clambered down the rocks. At the bottom was a shallow cove covered in coarse sand. When she finally saw Chihaya, she could not blame the plovers for their mistake. He lay across the sand like a beached corpse, half-submerged in the waves that washed the shore. From the fact that he was half-buried in sand, and from the small crabs that scuttled heedlessly over his body, it was obvious that he had not stirred for a considerable time. Seaweed had twined itself around his hands and feet, and his salt-stained clothing was charred and torn. She felt her heart beat wildly with every step she took toward him. Perhaps there was a chance in a thousand, one in a million, that even a Prince of Light could die.

But when she came to a halt, hesitating to touch him, Chihaya opened his eyes and looked up at her.

"Are you awake?" The words that fell from her lips sounded ludicrous.

"I'm so tired," he whispered weakly. "I didn't know that the bottom of the sea was so far away."

"You went there?" Saya and Torihiko exchanged looks of surprise.

"I wished to meet the God of the Sea . . . but I couldn't reach him."

"Can you stand?"

"Yes." Chihaya sat up slowly, but he seemed so weary that she had to help him walk.

"How did you find me? In the end I stopped caring and just let the tide carry me."

"Torihiko found you," Saya replied. "We've been traveling all over for the last six days. And it took another day to get here once we had found you. It will soon be dark. We've used up all seven of the days given us."

A little way along the narrow beach was a small hollow in the bottom of the cliff, enough to serve as a shelter from the weather, and Saya helped him over to it.

"I'll carry the news to Lord Akitsu and the others before night falls," Torihiko said. "If possible, I'll bring some help. It doesn't look as if we'll be able to make it up the cliff with him like this."

After watching the crow fly away, Saya went in search of dry driftwood. When she returned with the kindling, she found Chihaya leaning against a rock as if asleep once more. But when she began rummaging in her bag for a flint he said abruptly, "You brought the Sword. I thought you loathed carrying it around with you."

She looked at the Dragon Sword protruding from her bag and smiled. "I used it as a talisman. I felt that if I had it with me, I would find you."

"Why did you come looking for me?" Chihaya whispered, his voice barely audible.

"Because I wanted to apologize."

"Apologize?"

"For thinking that you killed Natsume."

"But what does it mean, to apologize?"

She looked at him, perplexed, and then realized that he actually did not understand. "It means to say 'I'm sorry.' But don't you know that?"

"I've never heard the word before," he said seriously.

"Well! What a predicament!"

For the first time Saya felt that she understood what the novices had been taught in the Palace of Light; why a priestess who lost favor with the gods was held responsible to the degree that she would take her own life. It was because the gods could not forgive. If one erred, one could not make amends. There was no second chance. For the immortal Children of Light, this was accepted as a matter of course. The words of Princess Teruhi came back to her: " . . . we who may never hope, nay, are not permitted to run away from our mistakes." To them, reflecting on one's mistakes must surely appear to be an aberration. Saya suddenly felt unsure of herself and, with eyes downcast, began hesitantly to explain.

"To apologize is to tell someone that you realize you've made a mistake, that you wish you'd never done it. And then to beg them, in consideration of this feeling, not to punish you, not to be angry with you; to ask them to forget the past and have no bitter feelings. I know it's a very selfish thing to do. But among our people, when we realize that we've done something wrong, the first thing we do is apologize . . ." Saya's voice grew fainter, finally fading away completely.

Chihaya remained silent. Just when she felt sure that he could not understand, he asked abruptly, "Then, if I apologize, do you think Lord Ibuki will forgive me?"

"He already forgave you, even before you could apologize," Saya replied gently.

"Can I see him again?"

"No."

"Then he died?"

Seeing Saya nod slightly, Chihaya said softly, "Then it's the same as not being forgiven."

"No, it isn't!" she said hastily. "That's not true. Before he died, Lord Ibuki said that he hoped to see you once more. In some other guise, he said. After all, we have the saying 'until we meet again.'"

"I don't understand." Chihaya turned his face away and pressed his forehead against his arms, which were folded upon his knees. "Everyone dies. Natsume died right before my eyes. She sought my help, but I could only watch her die. I'm different. I can't be like my brother or my sister, yet I'm shunned by the people of Darkness. I only cause harm to Toyoashihara. Do you think that gods or people can be brought back to life just by apologizing? It can't be done. Because I cannot go to the Land of the Dead to apologize."

"If you think that you're all alone, you're wrong," Saya said. "I'm here."

"But even you, Saya, you'll die, too. You, too, will leave me."

"Yes, that's true. Someday." Then taking a deep breath, she said, "Yes, maybe even tomorrow. And that's why I came to apologize. Even if you can't forgive me—before we're parted, at least I want to do that much."

"Well, if you must apologize," Chihaya muttered, "you'd better find someone who's angry and wants to punish you. I don't know who that might be, but it certainly isn't me. Who on earth could think of you like that?"

"Well then," Saya began, and then suddenly realized that she could say nothing at all. She wanted to laugh or cry but could do neither. Finally she said, "Let's eat. That should make us feel better."

The driftwood was permeated with salt and, as it burned, the flames turned grass-green. Intrigued, Saya kept feeding the fire until it blazed brightly and the hollow in the rock was warm. She divided all the remaining provisions in half: chestnuts, walnuts, and a bamboo flask of sake. When she offered Chihaya chestnut dumplings that she had roasted over the fire, he said with feeling, "It's a long time since I last ate. I had totally forgotten."

"But you always ate normally before, didn't you?" she asked in surprise. "Or did you stop eating, like Princess Teruhi and Prince Tsukishiro?"

"They don't eat because they wish to retain their youth. If they eat too much of the things of the earth, they don't feel right. When I was in the shrine, I was rarely allowed to eat." Then, as though the thought had just occurred to him, he added, "Maybe that's why my sister said that I had changed."

"I don't think that's the only reason . . ." Saya faltered as she looked at Chihaya on the other side of the brightly dancing flames. And no wonder. For he looked just like what she had once imagined the Ground Spiders looked like.

"But then I think perhaps you've grown a bit taller. I noticed that when I was standing beside you earlier."

"Maybe if I continue to eat I'll even grow into an old man."

"Hmm." Imagining it, Saya suddenly burst out laughing. "If you stayed an old man forever, you'd suffer a lot of aches and pains in your bones. The old people in Hashiba were always grumbling."

Chihaya did not laugh but whispered seriously, "The voice of the God of the Sea . . . it was the voice of an old man. A very, very old man."

"Why did you decide to visit him?" Saya asked. She had been longing to ask that question for some time.

"Because he knew me. He knew me much better than I knew myself . . ." Seeing the inquiring look on her face, he continued. "Do you remember the other time we came to the seashore? The time I met the messenger of the Sea God on the beach?"

"You mean the shark? It was midsummer. It seems like so long ago."

"I thought then that he had mistaken me for someone else, and I didn't pay much attention to what he said. After all, old people are often forgetful—like the handmaidens of the shrine. But it wasn't so. The God of the Sea knew I was the Dragon, even though I didn't know it myself. He told me that there were only two paths before me: to slay my father or to be slain by him."

"What?" Saya paled. "What did he mean?"

"That's what I wanted to ask him." Chihaya clasped his hands together. "But it was no use. I traveled along the sea floor until I came to a bottomless fissure, and though I descended into it, I lost consciousness partway down. It was filled with a blackness more relentless than the night, one which the strength of neither Light nor Darkness can ever penetrate."

Imagining what it must have been like, Saya shuddered. "You're lucky you made it back."

"Perhaps I was sent back. When I regained consciousness, I was floating far out at sea. The ancient one said that we were both isolated, alone. Perhaps he meant that I should think for myself." He had been staring into the dancing green flames, but now he raised his eyes and asked, "What do you think, Saya? About killing my father or being killed by him?"

"Did he mean the God of Light?"

"I guess so."

Saya muttered, "I–I don't want to think of such a thing. Such a terrible, frightening thing!"

"But still, if there were only two paths . . . ?"

The flames lit up his eyes as if they were spangled with gold dust. His soiled and tattered clothing, his sand-encrusted hair, made no difference. He was a Prince of Light, and the superiority of his being shone through his outer garments. Saya suddenly realized that no trace of girlishness remained in him. *It's as Lady Iwa said,* she thought. *Chihaya knows who he is.* She knew he had not asked her this question with any intent to follow her instructions.

"If you must choose," she replied earnestly, "then I'll tell you. I don't want you to be killed. If that's the choice, I would rather you killed the God of Light."

Chihaya smiled unexpectedly. It was the first time she had seen him smile in a long time, and it seemed as if the golden light deep within his eyes were strewn all about her. "I feel better now. I will doubt no longer. If there's no way to avoid this fate, I'll go out to meet it with sword in hand rather than standing by with arms folded— even if it means I must fight my own brother and sister. That's the road I must take."

Saya was surprised to catch herself returning his smile. Hearing him voice his decision, she felt as though a ray of clear light had lit up her heart. In that moment she realized that the problem was not hers to judge. The decision was his alone to make and she must leave it in his hands, no matter what might happen.

"Now I can finally return the Sword to you. You have no need of a priestess to still you. For you, yourself, are the Sword that must be wielded, and you must follow your own path. Of that I'm sure because, for the first time, I can see you for what you truly are."

Taking the Sword from her hands, Chihaya hesitated slightly and looked at her. "And what does that look like? My true self?"

"Don't you know?" Saya gave a little laugh. She was tempted to evade the question by leaving it at that, but thought better of it and said seriously, "There was never any time when you looked more like a Prince of Light. Dazzling to our eyes, powerful, pure, absolute—and beautiful. Yet at the same time completely different from Princess Teruhi or Prince Tsukishiro. You know how to grieve for those who have died, and you know enough to hate killing. Although you are immortal, strangely enough you have what we call compassion. You are even capable of forgiveness. And that is why, although you possess a terrible power, I do not fear you. Now I understand why you are the one whom the Water Maiden has sought so long."

Chihaya looked as though he wanted to feel pleased but could not. "I have no right to be described like that. I've already killed countless people, and I don't know what I might do in the future."

Stroking the hilt of the Sword, he hung his head and then continued. "What you said sounds like just another way of saying that I'm different. If it comes to a confrontation with my father or with my brother and sister, then I expect I'll terrify you again."

"No. No matter what happens, I won't lose sight of you a second time. Just watch me," Saya said with conviction. "I'll join you. If they call you 'different,' then I, too, will gladly be different. After all, I'm the only person in the world who has found the Sword's true form."

The burning wood crackled and popped, and the green and gold flames wavered sharply, causing the shadows on the rock wall to dance. Outside the shallow cave it was completely dark, and the sound of the waves on the shore was the only thing reminiscent of the daytime world. The rocks and the sea had merged into the jet-black night. Neither moon nor stars could be seen. Saya was suddenly caught up in the illusion that the shallow cave was the one spot in the ever-changing land of Toyoashihara that remained unchanged, and that the two of them were at its center. The world in constant motion swung like a busy pendulum, dancing through time. Yet before her were the eyes of Chihaya, which continued to hold her gaze, reflecting the light of the flames, rivaling the entire world.

As though a thin silk veil surrounding her had suddenly fallen away, she understood what all lovers feel when they exchange glances, what they all know.

AT DAWN the eastern sky was dyed a deep crimson as if a huge quantity of blood had been spilled along the border between water and sky. Then, the sun rose from the sea, round and full like a ripe fruit, and instantly the waves and clouds turned to gold. The sun, haloed in white, was almost ephemeral in its paleness. Saya, who had gone down to the beach alone to watch the sunrise, wondered if this was an omen. Although uncanny, it was nevertheless beautiful, and the flutter of anxiety that touched her heart was replaced once again by joy.

There's nothing in this world that isn't beautiful, she thought contentedly. Like the water lapping the shore at her feet, waves of happiness welled up inside her, immersing her in a sea of bliss. She was so warm and snug within, she almost felt guilty. The freezing dawn wind that pierced her skin did not bother her at all, and she continued to sit on the windswept beach, wrapping both arms about herself as though hugging the warm glow within her breast.

Even when she had decided to look for Chihaya one last time, she had never imagined she would find such contentment as this. Last night she had suddenly realized how close the place she had been seeking had always been; so close that she had only to reach out her hand to touch it. And she found this amazing.

Change is something we should be thankful for. Saya pondered this thought. She would continue to change—she and Chihaya, both of them, for they had only just learned how to open the door that had been closed. That thought, too, was part of the happiness that enveloped her.

A flock of gleaming white gulls flew across the brightening sky. The sea opened its blue bosom to welcome the new day. Billions of little silver fish dwelt within its generous, surging waters and there, too, resided life and death. Saya realized that she could now accept Princess Sayura without resistance.

By leaving her footprints in the palace, Princess Sayura led me to Chihaya. And the Water Maidens before Princess Sayura showed her the road to take . . . Together, the Water Maidens have followed a single path. But just as today is not a repeat of yesterday, so I am not Sayura. I am Saya. And I found Chihaya . . .

"Saya." Chihaya had come over without her noticing and was standing behind her. Looking up, she saw that his face, bathed in the morning light, was bright and animated.

"Let's leave this beach. You should get back as soon as you can."

"But what about you? Are you all right?"

"I'm fine now. Let's go to the top. Your poor horse—his feedbag is empty."

Saya was startled and then she laughed. She could not recall having mentioned a word about her horse, which she had left tethered at the top of the cliff. "Well! You certainly haven't changed in that respect."

She slung her lightened bag across her back and they left the cave together. Returning to the cliff and looking up, she saw the rugged rock face looming far up into the distance and found it hard to believe that she had actually climbed down it. She had been so impatient yesterday that she had not stopped to consider how she would get back up. There was no easier place, however, so, steeling themselves, they grasped the rock and began the long, grueling climb. Less than halfway up, their breath came in gasps, their clothes were drenched in sweat, and they could not drag themselves any higher.

They paused on a narrow ledge, too narrow to sit upon, and rested where they stood. Saya leaned her head against the rock and caught her breath. Suddenly she was struck by the ludicrousness of their position. Chihaya was watching a bird wheel in the sky but turned to look at her when he heard her laughing whisper.

"What did you say?"

"'No climb is too steep when with you, beloved,'" Saya repeated. Seeing Chihaya's puzzled look, she explained. "It's one of the Kagai songs. It means that no matter how steep the mountain, it doesn't seem so steep when I'm with you. It's a good song don't you think? Everyone used to sing it."

Chihaya smiled vaguely. It was clear that he did not really understand. For the first time it dawned on Saya that there was still one major problem left.

What does Chihaya think about me? she wondered. Not even she could imagine him bearing a betrothal gift and coming to ask for her hand like other men. This realization discouraged her, and Chihaya was left to puzzle over her sudden gloomy silence.

In any case, the most urgent problem was to master the cliff. Refreshed after their rest, they patiently labored upward while the sun slowly climbed the sky behind them, until at last they reached flat ground. It was already close to noon. They stretched out upon the ground for a while, unable even to search for Saya's horse. But at last they rose and turned toward the forest. It was bright among the leafless trees, but no matter where they looked, they saw no trace of living creatures; all was silent and still.

"How strange. He should be here. Perhaps I tethered him carelessly," Saya said, scratching her head.

"Let's look for footprints. I doubt he's gone far."

But just as Saya had begun to scan the ground, Chihaya said in a hard voice, "Run, Saya!"

"What?"

"I said run!"

He grabbed her hand and as she began to run, uncomprehending, armed soldiers stepped out one after another from the shadows of the dry thickets. They wore helmets emblazoned with the copper disks of the army of Light. Pursued, Saya and Chihaya fled toward a gap in their ranks, but through it came a group of horsemen riding abreast, galloping straight at them. They turned back, but there was no avenue of escape. They ran to the edge of the cliff and, there, were surrounded. Confronted by soldiers brandishing their weapons, Chihaya drew the Dragon Sword. Although the soldiers instinctively recoiled before its imposing shower of blue-white sparks, not one of them broke rank. They were standing glaring at one another when suddenly a cool voice rang out.

"If you wish to fight, I'm sure you're perfectly capable of doing so. But you'd best take a good look at our numbers. Saya will most certainly die. Do you still want to go through with this?"

Looking up, they saw among the horsemen with their arrows cocked one lone figure shrouded in white from head to foot. His face was hidden in a fold of cloth, like that of a shrine maiden. But the curve of his cheekbone, only partially revealed, and the tall dapple-gray steed he rode were all too familiar.

Prince Tsukishiro! What's he doing here? Saya wondered.

Chihaya, too, recognized him instantly. The tip of his Sword, tinged with light, drooped a little as if his confidence was waning. Prince Tsukishiro spoke again, his face still concealed. He looked like someone in mourning.

"Why did you come back? I saw you go to the bottom of the sea. Why did you return? Now we'll be forced to kill you."

"There was no other place for me to go. That's all," Chihaya replied in a subdued voice. "But my fate is not to be killed by my brother."

"The time of our divine father's coming will soon be upon us. If your fate is to die, wouldn't you rather it was by my hand than his? In comparison with our father, even Teruhi is more merciful."

A nearby soldier suddenly grabbed Saya's arm and yanked her toward him. Before she could utter a sound, blue light flashed like lightning from the Sword. The soldier released her with a scream and fell with a thud, not cut by the blade but with his hair and body engulfed in flame. Although the soldiers were thrown into confusion, the death of their comrade fanned their fear and rage, and in the next instant they set upon the two of them with a guttural cry. Saya, who had closed her eyes before the sea of blades and spears that rushed toward her, felt someone catch her deftly as she reeled.

"Put down your sword. Do you hear me? Or you'll never see Saya again."

The voice came from right beside her ear. Opening startled eyes, she found herself in Prince Tsukishiro's arms. Moreover, she was seated upon the saddle of his dapple-gray stallion. What could have happened in that one short instant? She was at least fifty paces from where she had been standing. Struggling frantically, she screamed, "Chihaya!"

She saw him turn and glare fiercely at the Prince across a forest of spears. "If you harm Saya, I will kill everyone. You, my father, everyone."

"That sounds like something the Dragon would say," Prince Tsukishiro said with contempt. "But think of the consequences before you speak. You can't have developed such power yet. If we take the time, we can certainly tear you limb from limb. Unfortunately, I have no desire to engage in further combat here and now. I came here only to get Saya. Let's strike a bargain. If you let me take her, I'll let you go. I vow that I won't harm her as long as you retreat from this spot."

"No," Chihaya responded immediately.

"Then you had better bear this in mind: promises made by the Children of Light are eternal, whereas the lives of the people of Toyoashihara are fleeting."

He casually moved one hand to Saya's chin. She tried to twist away, but her arms were pinned and she could not move.

"If I strengthen my hold but a fraction you will lose her. She'll return to her own land, where you can't follow."

"What are you going to do to her?" Chihaya asked in a low voice.

"Nothing in particular. This girl was originally one of my handmaidens. I thought to make her my bride."

"Don't be ridiculous! I'll never become your bride," Saya snapped angrily. "How can you say that when you don't even want to—"

Prince Tsukishiro cut her off with a sudden laugh.

Saya wanted to warn Chihaya to be careful, not to trust him. But she could barely speak. She looked at him in earnest appeal, but he did not notice and stood hesitating. Finally he said, "If you promise . . ."

"Very good. I promise." And as soon as the words had left Prince Tsukishiro's lips, he cast aside his shroud. Before the white cloth had floated to the ground, he had grasped his bow and fitted an arrow to the string. The bowstring twanged and the arrow sank deep into Chihaya's heart.

"You monster!" Saya shrieked. Without a backward glance, Prince Tsukishiro wheeled his horse lightly around and galloped away with her.

"Liar! How can you call yourself a Prince of Light!" Saya screamed at him as she struggled wildly, trying to look back.

"I didn't lie. I merely prevented him from pursuing us," the Prince replied calmly.

"But your soldiers—"

"Alas, they'll have no time to cut him to pieces. For I saw your allies approaching."

CHIHAYA opened his eyes. There was a metallic taste in his mouth.

"He's come to."

Lord Shinado approached at the sound of Torihiko's voice. The soldiers of Light had vanished and Chihaya was now surrounded by soldiers wearing familiar black vests. He himself lay on the yellowed grass at the foot of a pine tree. He sat up quickly but was suddenly overcome by unbearable pain. Looking down, he saw that the wound in his chest still gushed blood, staining his clothes bright red. The other injuries he could bear, but this deep wound was a telling blow. He would have to sleep a long time, but before he allowed himself to sink into the oblivion of renewal there was something he must do.

"Saya—" He broke off and turned his head away, vomiting blood.

The cleft between the brows on Lord Shinado's tanned forehead was deeply etched and as hard as stone. "Saya was taken. She exposed herself to the enemy in order to find you and, just as I feared, she has been captured. We should never have let her undertake such a foolish task."

Chihaya wiped his mouth and stared back at him. "I promise to bring her back."

"You?"

"Yes, me."

Lord Shinado paused and then said in a low voice, "I don't suppose you'd like to hear what I think of you."

"I already know," Chihaya replied as he struggled desperately to rise. "You'd like to carve me into pieces, as the soldiers of Light would have done. But wait. Before my brother took Saya he said that our divine father's advent is near. If that's true . . . and though my brother and sister may deceive, they don't tell outright lies . . . it will mean disaster."

"What?" Doubting his ears, Lord Shinado stooped forward to catch Chihaya's faint voice. "Do you mean the God of Light?"

Chihaya's eyes were starting from his face; his skin bore a ghastly pallor and beads of sweat stood out on his brow. The hand he pressed against his wound was already dyed red with blood.

"We knew that our father would someday descend from heaven. But for a long time even my sister, who reads the omens, did not know when. If our father sets foot upon the earth, the battle is over. The forces of Darkness won't stand a chance. Toyoashihara will belong to him. That's why you've seen no noticeable movement from the army of Light."

Lord Shinado paled and said in a low voice, "If that's true, it's the worst possible news. Are you saying we're finished?"

"There's still time. We've got to penetrate the palace and prevent the ceremony from taking place. I must tell Lord Akitsu. We should forget everything else and attack at once . . ." Chihaya's voice faded and ended in a gasp but, gathering his strength, he continued, "Take me to the camp. It doesn't matter how. I know that you don't trust me, but I can show him a way into the palace."

"You've no need to ask. I'll take you," Lord Shinado told him sullenly. "Because if I don't, Saya's efforts will have been in vain. For her sake, I'd storm the palace right now. Just do something about that wound, would you? You may be immortal, but that's unsightly."

Chihaya, however, gritted his teeth and shook his head. "I have to talk with Lord Akitsu first. Once the healing begins, I won't be able to wake for some time."

Seeing Lord Shinado walking toward him where he perched in the treetops, Torihiko said, "I know. I know. You want me to fly to Lord Akitsu."

Lord Shinado stroked his chin irritably. "Damnation!"

"My sentiments exactly. We were right there with our men, but Saya was whisked away and instead we rescued your hated rival. My wings feel heavy just at the thought of reporting it. But perhaps, having seen what happened to Chihaya, you feel somewhat revenged?"

"That's exactly why I feel so foul." Lord Shinado paced about, his irritation increasing.

"Could it be—you don't mean that you actually feel sorry for him?" The crow looked down at him, his eyes bright with curiosity.

Lord Shinado glared back and then, averting his face abruptly, said, "Is that what they mean by immortality? To bear the agony of death countless times more than mortal men, despite the fact that the pain is no less?"

"It seems so," Torihiko replied, unusually sober. "It makes it look as if it would be much nicer to die."

LORD SHINADO rose when he saw Lord Akitsu push aside the curtain and step outside the tent. "How's Chihaya?"

"I had them take him away. He had exhausted his last ounce of strength. I've told them to let no one touch him." Lord Akitsu looked at him, the severe expression on his face slightly softening. "You've rendered us a great service. It was some feat to bring Chihaya back."

Lord Shinado shook his head and ran his hand over his face as if to dispel an unpleasant memory. "It was like watching over his deathbed the entire journey."

Lord Akitsu smiled faintly. "I know what you mean. I thought I was listening to his dying words. Even though I know he won't die, it's hard to believe."

Lord Shinado's expression remained grim. "In any case, no mortal man could withstand that degree of agony; they could never have the strength or determination. That much I know."

Lord Akitsu nodded and his voice was tinged with awe. "Perhaps that's why he has been endowed with the power to destroy even the God of Light. We appear to have been gravely mistaken. Chihaya is our last hope for saving this land from subjection by the forces of Light."

"Will you raise the army?"

"Yes. It's time for a council of war." Lord Shinado followed him as he began to stride away. "If Chihaya spoke the truth, time is our only ally. And I, for one, plan to believe him. We'll split into four or maybe five troops. We must choose some men to infiltrate the Palace of Light and open the gates from inside, too."

"I'll go," Lord Shinado said, as though it were already decided.

TORIHIKO flew in to report. It was afternoon, the day after Chihaya had returned to the camp of the army of Darkness.

"The forces of Light that were camped upstream have all been recalled to the palace. The palace guard has been tightened and young women are being summoned to the palace from all over the capital. According to the ground thrushes they're being recruited as handmaidens, but have you ever seen them go to such lengths before?"

"I'm guessing that the fire inflicted a heavier blow than we thought," Lord Akitsu murmured. "I wonder . . . The idea that a purification ceremony is scheduled for the end of this month makes me uneasy."

"Do you think the advent of the God of Light may take place at that time?" one of the generals asked with dread.

"It's possible."

"Then there are only ten days left."

This caused a stir within the tent. Lord Shinado stood up impatiently and said, "Speed has always been our forte. We must move immediately. Any further delay will be fatal."

Lord Akitsu cast a sharp glance in his direction. "Very well then, you may proceed. When do you leave?"

"Now."

"With how many men?"

"There are five of us."

"Is that enough?"

"The more we take, the harder it will be to move."

"All right then . . ."

At that moment a voice came from outside the entrance to the tent. "Won't you take one more?"

Chihaya appeared. He was dressed in a new robe and looked calm and collected, as if nothing had happened.

Lord Shinado frowned. "This job isn't for you. You'll be detected as soon as you set foot in the palace."

"There are plenty of ways to disguise myself."

Lord Akitsu asked, "Are you well enough?"

Chihaya nodded. "Let me go."

After some thought, the one-eyed lord responded, "Our fate depends upon whether or not we can open that gate. Those who infiltrate the palace hold the key to victory. They may need you. Go and help Lord Shinado."

The two left the tent together. Once outside, Lord Shinado turned to face Chihaya angrily. "Show me your wound."

"It's better."

"Then show me."

He reached out to grab the front of Chihaya's robe, but Chihaya evaded his grasp.

"Just as I thought!" Lord Shinado exclaimed severely. "What a boldfaced lie! Who do you think you're fooling when your face is still so pale?"

"It's nothing. Just a scratch. It ought to have disappeared by now," Chihaya said defensively.

"It seems that even an immortal Prince of Light has his limits. But this time we can't afford any mistakes."

"I know."

"We can't allow anyone to hinder us," Lord Shinado snapped unsympathetically. "If you're going to get in the way, you can stay here and sleep."

"Never."

Three soldiers of indeterminate age and no distinguishing features approached them. They were members of the infiltration team, and Lord Shinado introduced them to Chihaya.

"This is Yahiro, Tsutsuo, and Shiomitsu. They've distinguished themselves as spies in our service and are highly skilled. They can become trees or rocks."

Chihaya stared at them with eager curiosity. "I have become furred creatures, birds, and fish, but never a tree or a rock."

Lord Shinado was momentarily robbed of speech. "I was speaking metaphorically," he explained. "I meant that they can remain undetected." They were staring at each other in some confusion when Torihiko flew up. Lord Shinado turned and said, "And, the last member of our party is, of course, Torihiko. These are the members who will penetrate the Palace of Light. Torihiko is fine as he is, but the rest of you must disguise yourselves and find your own way into the palace. We'll have more chance of success if we split up."

"Excuse me," the most senior of the three interjected hesitantly. It was hard to tell whether it was Yahiro, Tsutsuo, or Shiomitsu. "It seems to me that this fellow here will attract attention no matter how he disguises himself."

Before Lord Shinado could reply, Chihaya said, "Then I'll disguise myself as someone who attracts attention."

"What are you up to?"

Chihaya smiled impudently at their dubious looks. "I'll infiltrate the palace as a handmaiden. I'm sure I can manage that."

2

"DON'T BE SO ANGRY." Prince Tsukishiro had come to see how Saya was doing, only to find her sitting on the floor, her face to the wall and her food untouched.

"Do you expect me to smile?" she retorted sharply. "When I've been taken captive by my enemies and brought here against my will?"

"Am I your enemy?"

"You seem to have lost your senses," Saya answered hotly and turned to face him. "I can never be your bride. For I love all that lives in Toyoashihara more than I love the Light. You're my enemy against whom I must fight. You may despise me if you like. For if I had had a bow and arrow, I would have shot you when you shot Chihaya."

Prince Tsukishiro had removed his armor and was dressed in a soft shade of blue. Slim and graceful, he in no way resembled a warrior. She could scarcely believe it was the same man who had but a short while ago shot Chihaya. "Let me go," she demanded once again. "Either that or kill me. For I have no desire to live as a captive. Let me go back to Chihaya."

Smiling wryly, the Prince shook his head. "They say that young girls' hearts are fickle, but to think that yours could change so much in such a brief time."

"Have you forgotten? I left the palace of my own accord."

"But you also left with the words that you still loved me."

Saya faltered and fell silent. It was true; moreover, whether she liked it or not, he still struck a chord in her heart as he stood there before her. He had not changed at all since they had first met on the night of the Kagai. No matter how bloodstained his hands, his presence still inspired awe. Yet such immutable purity was beyond her grasp. She murmured, "Sometimes one realizes the truth only later."

"That's absurd." Prince Tsukishiro laughed. "You seem to be taken with Chihaya, but he, too, is a Prince of Light. You claim to fight against the Light, yet you're still drawn to it. That's your nature."

Saya reddened. "Chihaya isn't like you or Princess Teruhi. He learns; he overcomes; he changes. And he intends to protect this land from your hands."

"He always was a useless fool. Whatever Chihaya may do, it's futile. He can't save Toyoashihara."

"Can you be so sure?"

"Yes. For it is Chihaya himself who summons our celestial father." The Prince's voice echoed coldly. "At the time of his birth, the God of Light placed a seal inside him. If it is broken, our father will descend from the heavens. There's nothing Chihaya can do."

"It can't be!" Saya gasped, appalled.

Prince Tsukishiro looked at her sadly. "And you, Saya, you also summon our father. All of this was revealed in Teruhi's reading of the omens. She has been locked up in the shrine for the past few days, reading the future."

Still not fully comprehending, Saya gazed at him, both hands held to her mouth, unable to move. She felt caught, bound by an invisible thread, and seemed to glimpse in her mind a huge spinning wheel, spinning, spinning, oblivious to the desires of men.

Prince Tsukishiro spoke softly. "Teruhi intends to use you as the sacrifice in the purification ceremony. But I brought you here before she could find you. Come back to me. If you'll give me your heart, I will give you the power of renewal, and so save you from being sacrificed. If it is your nature to change your affections, then surely you can do so once again."

Saya stepped back slightly. With her eyes riveted to his face, she slowly shook her head.

"Even though by doing so you could prevent the advent of the God of Light?"

"Yes," Saya replied in a scarcely audible voice. "My heart moves of its own accord. I can't control it with my mind."

Another voice unexpectedly endorsed her statement. "She's right. It's impossible."

Saya and Prince Tsukishiro caught their breath and turned. Leaning one arm against the doorway stood Princess Teruhi. She wore a snow-white robe over white trousers, and her long hair hung loose in disarray as though blown by a fierce wind. Her eyes glowed eerily, making her appear demented.

"It never occurred to me that you of all people would attempt to interfere, Tsukishiro. For what foolish whim do you intend to obstruct the advent of our father?"

Concealing his consternation, Prince Tsukishiro asked casually, "What are you doing here, sister, when you haven't set foot outside the shrine sanctuary for days?"

Princess Teruhi laughed abruptly, her voice shrill. "Don't be a fool. When I sought the omens for Saya's location, didn't they point directly to within this very palace? Well, at least you saved me the trouble of capturing her myself."

Her laughter ceased and she fixed her brother with a murderous glare. "You'd better have a good explanation. Why did you try to steal Saya away? You must have some reason when you know full well she's needed for the sacrifice."

Seeing that the Prince did not answer, she continued, "Don't think that I'll forgive your actions on the basis of your reply. Anyone who tries to thwart me now when my work upon this earth is almost complete is my enemy."

"You still don't understand, do you, sister?" Prince Tsukishiro said softly. "I didn't wish to disillusion you, but as you insist, I'll speak. I did this because I know the true reason for our father's descent. He comes to summon the Goddess of Darkness back to the realms above."

Princess Teruhi's eyebrows shot up. "Nonsense!"

"No. Although you're the omen reader, you've been so enraptured by our father that you ignored this one fact concealed within all the omens. Or rather, you didn't attempt to understand it, despite the fact that, from the very beginning, our father's thoughts have always been centered upon the Goddess."

"Our purpose on this earth was to cleanse it of all things tainted by the Darkness."

"Don't you see? To destroy the power of Darkness is to destroy death. To destroy death is to summon the Goddess before us." Prince Tsukishiro sounded resigned. "Our celestial father intends to restore everything to its original state, to join earth and heaven once more in chaos and begin all over again. To return the Goddess to his side. While we have no control over that decision, for myself, I wish to gaze on Toyoashihara just a little longer, for it's beautiful in itself, just as it is."

An expression of shocked disbelief spread across Princess Teruhi's face. "The God of Light and the Goddess of Darkness are incompatible. It can't be. They despise each other." Walking forward, she stopped directly in front of Prince Tsukishiro and demanded, "Are you saying that all our efforts to purify the earth for so many years have been for the sake of the Goddess of Darkness?"

"It isn't I who say so. It's simply the truth. Think carefully about why Saya should be chosen as the final sacrifice."

For a while, Princess Teruhi did not respond. Then she asked in a strangely quiet voice, "When did you know this?"

"I had an inkling of it some time ago," Prince Tsukishiro replied.

At that she suddenly shrieked, "I've had it with you. Always, always you disappoint me."

"Teruhi."

"How, then, could you continue to fight?"

The Prince whispered, "What else could we do but fight?"

Princess Teruhi gripped one hand in the other and bit down on her fingers in an attempt to control her trembling. "I don't believe it. I won't believe that the war we have fought is meaningless. I won't believe that our father's sacred eyes could be fixed on the filth of Darkness. The God in heaven is pure and stainless. We're here to worship and praise him." Her voice suddenly weakened. She murmured as though to herself, "Surely our celestial father must love us."

Her eyes were hidden in the shadow of her tousled hair. Prince Tsukishiro reached out his hand and gently brushed a lock from her face as though soothing a child. "Of course he does. We're his children."

Without raising her face, Princess Teruhi said, "You always speak so lightly."

"I just can't bear to see you grieve."

After a brief pause, she recovered and gave her head a shake. "There's still much to be done. The war isn't over yet, and the ceremony is long overdue. The main hall must still be rebuilt, and changes must be made in the purification rite."

She looked at Saya and then at Prince Tsukishiro and said, "There'll be no change in the sacrificial offering. And you wouldn't have been able to give her immortality in any case because she's too useful as bait. You can be sure that Chihaya will come after her."

3

THE ROOM in which Saya was imprisoned was at the top of the high wooden tower that stood between Prince Tsukishiro's and Princess Teruhi's halls. No doubt the view would have been splendid, but the only windows were small skylights located near the ceiling. Enclosed by four bare walls, she felt suffocated, and like a small bird beating its wings against a cage, she paced unceasingly about the room in search of an opening. Her search was futile, however, and she only succeeded in bruising her fingers. Although she wept occasionally, she did not abandon herself to despair. For, in parting, Princess Teruhi had declared that Chihaya would come. Her predictions inspired a fear that seemed beyond hope, yet Saya still longed to meet Chihaya once more. Regardless of what happened, no matter what the future might bring, it could not stop her from hoping that they would meet again, nor quell her yearning to see his smiling face one last time.

The temperature dropped each night, and piercing cold permeated the unheated room. The guard, pitying her plight, gave her a fur to wrap herself in, but even huddled within it she was frozen. Several days passed in which only the color of the sky glimpsed through the skylight told her of the changing of day to night. Then one particularly cold morning, as she sat huddled in a corner, her feet and hands tucked as close to her body as possible, she heard the sound of the latch opening. Thinking it was the guard coming to collect her dishes, she thought that he would do well to notice the film of ice on the water in the pitcher. But to her surprise, the person who entered the room was none other than Princess Teruhi. The cold air turned her breath frosty white, but she wore only a single robe of thin white cloth, which made Saya shiver just to look at. Princess Teruhi, however, seemed totally unconcerned, and her fair skin had the healthy glow of a peach.

In a clear, sweet voice, she said, "So, we were about to turn the Water Maiden into an ice maiden. I'd forgotten that you need the warmth of charcoal. Never mind. It snowed."

Saya was well aware that the sleet of the previous day had turned to snow in the night as some of it had actually blown through the skylight. Wondering what the Princess had come to tell her, she stared back at her warily, waiting for her to speak.

"It's unusual to see so much snow in the first snowfall. Come, let's go and look at it together." The sight of her speaking so gaily reminded Saya of the little girl Fawn, and she was taken aback. Somehow this naiveté strangely suited her, and Saya found her heart drawn to her unwillingly as she followed her out of the room. Climbing gingerly down the steep stairs on numb legs, they came to a floor that consisted of an open-walled colonnade from which the scenery could be viewed in all directions. The storm clouds had gone, and beneath the bright silver sky everything was white as though wearing a new coat of paint. The snow was not deep, but it covered every inch of the ground, every crack and cranny. The black thatched roofs and red-lacquered columns of the buildings were accentuated by the white snow's damp embrace. The ancient green pine trees brooded silently. Even the blackened remnants of the main hall's columns burned in the summer fire appeared beautiful in the snow. Sounds were muted as though absorbed by silk floss, and in the bright silent morning Mahoroba seemed a different world.

"I love snow, even more than flowers," Princess Teruhi said light-heartedly as she leaned out over the balustrade. "How white the snow that falls from heaven! I love its coldness, a manifestation of purity. It soothes all troubles away."

"Children love snow, too. They romp about in it heedless of frostbite," Saya said.

"Do you like it, too?"

"Yes. But I like flowers, as well. And summer, and autumn, and everything."

Princess Teruhi smiled faintly and looked at Saya. "You wish to tell me that you love Toyoashihara. But you know, in my own way, I have also been working for the good of this land." The Princess continued as though talking to herself. "While I'm a child of the God of Light, this is the only land I know. I often used to imagine when I saw snow fall that this place must be like the palace in the heavens. But most likely I love this view simply because it is all I know."

She turned once again to gaze at the view, and Saya stared at her back. She lacked her usual arrogance and appeared instead to be deep in thought. "There's still time," Saya said frankly. "Won't you stop the coming of the God of Light?"

"I can't," Princess Teruhi responded in a low voice. "No one can bend the will of the God. I am only his child, a demigod."

"But you understand, don't you, that his intention to destroy Toyoashihara is wrong? For it is only in cherishing this land, in nurturing it, that he is truly our divine father."

Princess Teruhi thought for a while but then, instead of replying, she asked Saya a question. "What is the Goddess of Darkness like? Is she beautiful? No, I can't believe that one who receives all the defilement of the earth can be beautiful or pure. After all, our father was so seized with dread at the sight of her in the underworld that he sealed the opening with a stone. But why, then, does he summon her?"

Saya hesitated and shook her head. "I don't know. Only those who reside in the Land of the Dead know what she looks like."

SHE was returned to her room, but the guard brought her a brazier.

Princess Teruhi. She killed my parents; she killed Natsume and the child she bore; she has snuffed out countless innocent lives. And she'll try to kill me, and Chihaya as well, without any compunction, Saya told herself. She had more than enough reason to despise the Princess, yet she could only pity her. Like a naughty child, she destroyed whatever she laid her hands on without knowing what she had done. Perhaps she would only realize it with surprise after she had lost everything.

But then it will be too late. I can't just let her kill me. If only I had the power to win back my life. As these thoughts were running through her mind, she caught the faint sound of wings. She raised her head but without much hope, for she had heard this sound so often in her mind. Just then, however, a glossy black beak and head peered through the bars of the window. Folding his wings and squeezing through, the crow dropped down to the floor.

"Here I am," he said.

A lump rose in Saya's throat so that she could not respond immediately. "I—I knew you would come. But oh, I'm so glad!"

"Actually, I would have been here much sooner, but I've become so well known that there are mist nets hung all around this place. It was hard work making a hole in them."

"Is anyone else with you?"

"Lord Shinado, Chihaya, and three others. They're all concealed within the palace in disguise: Lord Shinado as a musician, of course; the three others as servants or soldiers; and, best of all, Chihaya as one of Princess Teruhi's own handmaidens. We'll open the gate tomorrow at sunset, and the army of Darkness will invade the palace."

"What about the purification ceremony?"

"It's scheduled for the day after. I have no intention of allowing you to be sacrificed. That's the most disgusting ceremony I've ever seen."

"Please stop them. I don't want to be the one who summons the God of Light."

Suddenly she began to tremble. It was a strange time to feel afraid, but the hope of imminent rescue seemed to have multiplied her fear.

"Do you think Chihaya will be all right? A handmaiden of all things! He mustn't underestimate Princess Teruhi."

"Don't worry. He disguised himself well. You wouldn't recognize him," Torihiko replied, cheerfully spreading his wings. "He isn't stupid. Although there are times when he seems so."

"That's true." Saya tried to smile only to realize that her cheeks had become stiff over the last few days.

"My job is to mobilize all my underlings and get you out of here. A pretty good role, don't you think? It's going to be spectacular. I have such an army of birds it would take you your whole life to count them. Together we'll lower you to the ground."

"Can you really do it?" Saya's eyes were wide with astonishment.

"Just wait and see." And with a flap of his wings he flew up to the window.

"I'm so excited!" Saya cried.

"That's the spirit. The woodpeckers will come as soon as I leave. It'll be a bit noisy but be patient."

Now that her spirits were raised, Saya desperately wished there was something she could do. To simply sit and wait to be rescued seemed the least attractive role to play. "Wait!" she called out impulsively, longing to contribute in some way. She removed the Water Maiden's magatama from around her neck and held it out to Torihiko. "Give this to Chihaya for me. Tell him to keep it until we meet again."

The crow flew down and grasped the blue stone in his beak. "Right. I'll take it to him."

Once he had left, a flock of woodpeckers came, just as he had said. They clung to the window frame and began patiently pecking at it with their beaks.

THE NEXT DAY was also cold and snow still covered the ground. Chihaya knelt on the verandah, pretending to gaze at the garden, while Lord Shinado, having checked to make sure the coast was clear, passed by casually.

"A performance is to be held at noon," Lord Shinado whispered rapidly.

"But this is the period of abstinence!"

"Teruhi knows nothing about it. It's Prince Tsukishiro's plan."

Chihaya thought a moment before replying. "This will make it easier for us to act."

"Inform the other three. I plan to stay in my place until the last moment."

Without changing his expression, Lord Shinado proceeded along the passageway. Chihaya rose after waiting a little longer and stole into Prince Tsukishiro's palace. People hurried up and down the connecting passages. The palace had always been short staffed, but its elegance had gradually declined since the fire. The complaint of the elderly that this was a degenerate age was not necessarily an idle one. Although the capital surrounding it still retained an air of grandeur, within the Palace of Light something had been broken and irretrievably lost. Certainly the fact that the two immortals no longer paid attention played a major role in its decline. Princess Teruhi had not returned to her quarters for a long time, remaining closeted in the reconstructed shrine. Because of this, Chihaya had been able to pass himself off as a novice without being challenged, but it was not pleasant to see how lax discipline had become in the handmaidens' quarters.

Even without being attacked by the army of Darkness, this place would fall into ruin. It would have been better that way, Chihaya thought as he stopped in a corner of the passageway and watched the people passing by.

"Excuse me. If you have a moment, perhaps you could help me?"

A handmaiden he had never seen before suddenly spoke to him. She was just an innocent young girl; probably a novice such as he was pretending to be. "I didn't know that there was to be a recital today and I have no idea what I'm to do."

Red-faced, she was on the verge of tears. "No one here cares about anyone else. I've only just entered service in the palace, yet they tell me I must dance. I don't even know which fan I'm supposed to use. And then they tell me that anyone who makes a mistake will be executed on the spot."

"In that case, fear no more," Chihaya reassured her. "I will teach you."

The girl's face shone. "How kind of you! Are you one of the dancers, too?"

"No."

The girl looked up at him a little bashfully. "But how strange. You would make a much better dancer than I. You're so tall and beautiful."

"I'm one of Princess Teruhi's handmaidens," Chihaya explained.

The girl covered her mouth in consternation. "Oh! I'm sorry. I shouldn't have asked such a thing of you."

Chihaya grinned and said, "But only you and I need ever know."

AT NOON the sun, a silver disk bereft of warmth, peered through the clouded sky. It remained cold, and the frozen landscape spread out in all directions. The sound of string and wind instruments hung in the frosty air, echoing mysteriously. Prince Tsukishiro had had cushions placed around the veranda on the south side of the hall. Here he sat with the assembled guests, watching the dancers perform in the inner courtyard while the musicians played on a platform set up alongside a connecting passageway. The Prince himself, however, did not appear to be enjoying the music. Rather, he seemed deep in thought, his arm laid along the armrest as he stared at the performers. The musicians were infected by his mood and, despite the gay costumes of the dancers, the music assumed a melancholy air.

This is indeed farewell, thought Lord Shinado as he played his reed pipes. *Win or lose, this is the last performance for the forces of Light and Darkness.*

"You there!" Prince Tsukishiro spoke without bothering to look at the musicians. "You're flat. Didn't you know that I'm musician enough to tell?"

Before anyone had had time to even grasp his meaning, armored guards leaped out and surrounded the musicians' platform. Some musicians dropped their instruments in surprise, the music came to a sudden standstill, and the dancers stood trembling.

The soldiers stood over the musicians, their spears held ready, but, perplexed about which musician the Prince had indicated, one of them asked, "Which one has offended you?"

"He knows who I mean," Prince Tsukishiro replied. The commander queried the musicians, but no one responded.

"It doesn't matter," Prince Tsukishiro said listlessly. "Behead them all, starting at the end."

A soldier grasped the collar of an elderly flute player, who had turned deathly pale, and hauled him from his place. As he drew his sword and held it aloft, Lord Shinado rose.

"It was I."

Before the soldiers could turn around, Lord Shinado jumped from the platform. The soldier who had been about to lop off the old man's head turned and swung his sword, but Lord Shinado swiftly parried the blow with his pipes. The hoop binding them together was severed, and the bamboo reeds flew apart with a loud noise. Momentarily distracted, the soldier found himself pummeled with fists and feet, and dropped his sword. Grasping the fallen blade, Lord Shinado desperately attacked the milling soldiers. Some fell back under the vigor of his assault.

"My bow," commanded Prince Tsukishiro calmly. Taking the proffered weapon, he shrugged one arm out of his sleeve and grasped an arrow. No matter how agile Lord Shinado might have been, the Prince could not miss at that range. By the time Lord Shinado was aware of him, it was too late. With a shrill noise the arrow was loosed. But at that moment someone threw a fan. The arrow pierced its handle and, swerving slightly from its path, struck the column beside Lord

Shinado. Everyone turned in disbelief to see that one of the five dancers was empty-handed.

Prince Tsukishiro said in astonishment, "So there you are."

Chihaya leaped lightly over the heads of the crowd, his jade-green and crimson hem billowing, and landed right beside Lord Shinado, as if scorning their incredulity.

"You fool!" Lord Shinado said angrily. "We agreed that anyone who was discovered would be left behind."

"As an extra member, I never agreed to anything," Chihaya replied. "Besides, I'm in your debt."

"You're every inch a fool, my brother," Prince Tsukishiro said with deep disappointment. "To come here, to this place, playing into our hands. Don't you realize that I'm holding this performance for Saya's sake?"

Chihaya looked at his older brother in surprise.

"Teruhi won't use Saya for the sacrifice. If I know her, she won't let her live that long."

THE FLOCK of woodpeckers now numbered twenty or thirty, and they continued to chip away at the wood like carpenters. They had already begun to remove the second panel of wainscoting, and it looked as if Saya would be able to squeeze through. Suddenly, however, the birds became tense and silent. As they flew hastily away, Saya heard the sound of light footsteps. The latch drew back. Saya stood up hurriedly and tried to conceal any evidence of the woodpeckers' handiwork with her body. Before her stood Princess Teruhi. Her expression was calm and peaceful.

"Saya," the Princess addressed her in a quiet tone. "Do you wish to preserve Toyoashihara no matter what the cost?"

"Yes," Saya replied.

"Well, I've been thinking. I can't help feeling that it would be too heartless to return this land to chaos."

Saya's eyes widened. "If both sides think this way, then the war is no longer necessary. Will you stop the coming of the God of Light?"

"As long as the Goddess remains in the Land of the Dead, Toyoashihara will be preserved even if the God of Light descends upon the earth," Princess Teruhi said. "It's the meeting of the two divinities that must be prevented. Regardless of what our divine father wishes, the Goddess must not be summoned before him. I have decided to ignore this one point only. The purification ceremony will be conducted without you—because you, along with our celestial father, would surely summon forth the Goddess. I don't wish to see our father's eyes turned toward anything other than us at his arrival. I can't bear that that should be the end of all our efforts."

But just as a bright ray of hope was lit in Saya's breast, Princess Teruhi calmly drew a long-bladed sword from the scabbard at her waist. The winter sun lent the naked blade a cold light. Staring at the cruel steel before her eyes, Saya paled and fell back, only to bump into the wall.

"Why?" she whispered almost inaudibly.

"You asked me to stop the coming of my father. But to me it is the Goddess of Darkness that stands in the way. I don't want her to return. But I cannot disobey my father's command. No one can go against his will, no one except the Goddess of Darkness herself." Princess Teruhi continued to speak calmly. "That's why I wish you to return to the Goddess before the purification ceremony. Tell her to refuse our divine father's summons. I can trust you to do this, can't I? Because, in return, Toyoashihara will be saved."

"Do you mean to kill me here?" Saya's lips trembled. The icy blade filled her with terror, death in tangible form, and her entire youthful being rejected it with all its strength. She could not possibly die now. Not in this narrow room, so unprepared, without even seeing Chihaya . . .

Princess Teruhi's pale bare feet stepped closer. "If I could, I would go myself to meet the Goddess. But that path can be trodden only by the people of Darkness."

"No!" Saya screamed as she watched the Princess raise the sword. In that small room there was no escape, but still she tried to flee, groping along the wall, dodging aside. Seeking help, she called out for Chihaya, for Torihiko. But—

The tip of the sword described a graceful arc as it descended. It was a deft, a masterful stroke. For an instant Saya glimpsed the window and saw the white and distant sky. Then she saw Princess Teruhi's serene and beautiful face. *Even when she kills, she still looks pure,* Saya thought, recalling the shrine maiden in Hashiba so far away. And then she thought no more.

Like a priestess, Princess Teruhi knelt beside Saya's body where it lay upon the floor, watching as the last warmth fled from the dead girl's body. She almost looked as if she were praying. Into the still and silent room, however, a richly colored apparition suddenly floated and immediately became solid. It was Chihaya, still in dancer's robes but now holding the Sword. Gold ornaments swayed on his costume, but his feet were bare, his hair was in disarray, and he was gasping for breath.

"So you've finally learned how to travel between time," Princess Teruhi murmured without surprise. But Chihaya did not reply. He gazed only at Saya, at the girl who lay like a broken-stemmed flower.

"It seems that you are a moment too late. Saya has already left for another land."

"I will never forgive you," Chihaya whispered.

Princess Teruhi laughed. "Unfortunately, those are my lines. As long as you remain a threat to our father, we cannot let you stand before him alive. I'm sure, however, that you've come prepared for this, haven't you?"

Her hair stirred as though a wind had suddenly sprung up.

"The people of this land have no inkling of what would happen should the Children of Light loose all their power. You may be more terrible than thunder and lightning, but we are your older sister and brother. We are the sun and the moon. Now you'll see what happens when the powers of the sun and the moon are unleashed together." Looking at Chihaya with a grim smile, she turned on her heel and slipped between time. Without a moment's hesitation, Chihaya raced after her.

Although the intervals between time are indescribable, they are not composed of nothingness. Rather, the shadows of many things hang suspended. Princess Teruhi, slipping between these like a speeding arrow, looked like a golden shadow that left a long trail behind it. After a while Chihaya became aware of a gleaming silver shadow approaching from another direction and knew it must be Prince Tsukishiro. The two shadows, silver and gold, drew closer and closer until they became one. At that moment a light burst forth as though the world between time had exploded. The light, whose heat and strength transcended that of incandescence, turned black, piercing, shattering, burning, and melting all in its path.

WITHOUT WARNING the sun darkened. Despite the fact that it was midday, darkness arose from all four corners of the land and covered the sky, turning the day to an inky blackness. The palace was thrown into confusion, and the soldiers rushed about, unable to remain at their posts. It was little different among the invading soldiers of the army of Darkness. The horses panicked and reared, and the soldiers broke rank, cowering in terror. As if this were not enough, violent earthquakes rocked the land. Landslides buried villages at the foot of the mountains, and a great tidal wave washed away fishing villages along the shore. People lay prostrate on the ground, unable even to stand. They could only pray with heart and soul that this convulsion of the world would prove but a passing phenomenon.

* * *

HAS CHIHAYA BEEN DESTROYED?
  Not yet.
  What could be protecting him? Our father?
  No. That's impossible.
  At any rate, we can't withstand this much longer.
Princess Teruhi and Prince Tsukishiro slipped between several intervals of time and continued to run. Whenever they reappeared on the earth they could hear the rumble of Chihaya's thunder beneath the dark sky. At last they came to a place at the end of the world where there were only rocks and snow. The air was surprisingly thin,

and it was well below freezing. Snow crystals, driven by the wind, were reluctant to fall to the ground. Hot steam rose from a rock wall nearby, the only spot bereft of snow, exposing fantastic formations in the black rock around the fissure.

"Where are we?" Princess Teruhi asked.

"At the mouth of Mount Fuji," Prince Tsukishiro replied, looking at the smoke. "It seems to have come to life with that last earthquake."

"Let's go. I don't want to stay in a place like this."

Prince Tsukishiro said teasingly, "Why not rest? This is the closest place to heaven."

"You've got to be kidding. The stench of the underworld is so foul that I can barely breathe."

Receiving such an irritable response, Prince Tsukishiro rose and slipped into another interval of time. "Then let's go somewhere more pleasant."

Princess Teruhi attempted to follow him but was suddenly flung back. Losing her footing on the slope from the shock of the impact, she almost slipped inside the mouth of the volcano. The sight of the glowing red lava bubbling and belching smoke in the depths below was enough to make even the Princess turn pale.

A voice spoke quietly. "Not even you, dear sister, could possibly survive if you fell in there, could you?"

Princess Teruhi started and looked around. Prince Tsukishiro was nowhere to be seen. He was on another side of time, ignorant of her plight. Chihaya's shadow, blurred by the smoke, appeared before her. In his hand was the shining blue Sword. The Princess was unarmed, for there was no need of swords when battling between time. She cursed herself for her carelessness. Chihaya now stood immediately over her. The Princess looked up at him from where she lay at the edge of the volcano.

"You! So you can follow me even here?" A hint of wonder tinged her voice.

"I told you that I would never forgive you," Chihaya replied, and his sister smiled faintly.

"How gallant. I like that."

As he turned the Sword toward her, she asked without any trace of regret, "I have just one question. What's protecting you?"

"Nothing."

"You didn't fall even under the combined forces of Tsukishiro and myself. I can't believe you could do that alone."

"There's nothing," Chihaya began but then fell silent. Placing a hand on his breast, he felt Saya's magatama through his clothes.

As Chihaya remained silent, Princess Teruhi sighed. "Won't you hurry up and get it over with. It's rude to keep your victim waiting."

"I've changed my mind," he said abruptly.

Princess Teruhi's eyes widened in surprise. "Are you mad?"

The expression on Chihaya's face as he gazed down upon his sister was one which, as a child of Light, she could neither believe nor comprehend.

"Even if I kill you, it won't bring Saya back to life."

Sheathing the Sword, he turned his back on her and vanished between time.

BY THE TIME Chihaya reached the open palace gate it was already late at night. Although the place was still filled with confusion, the battle was over and the palace was in the hands of the army of Darkness. Torihiko found him walking in the torchlight and flew up to him.

"The army of Light has been routed. Without their leaders, their troops have scattered. We've won!" Torihiko said in a rush, then seeing Chihaya's face, he faltered. "Where have you been, Chihaya? The main hall collapsed in the fire, but the birds managed to carry Saya out."

When Chihaya still did not reply, Torihiko furled his wings wretchedly and said, "Go and see Saya, will you? They're holding a ceremony for her over there."

Inside the fenced enclosure where she lay, grown men wept unashamedly, moved by the sight of Saya's small, pale form lying pathetically upon its bier, bereft of flowers in the midwinter season. Chihaya gazed at her steadily but knew that he would never find her here. She had already left, racing to a place where he could never join her, leaving him with her magatama, which she had given him until they should meet again.

Opening his closed fist, he stared at the pale blue stone and whispered, "How can I return this?"

At that moment someone moved at the foot of Saya's bier. She was so small that he had not realized anyone was there, but when he saw the white-haired head turn toward him, he recognized Lady Iwa. Opening her wrinkled eyelids, she looked at him.

"That belongs to the Water Maiden. Without it she will come to grief."

Chihaya nodded with great effort. "Saya protected me, even though I couldn't save her, even though I let her die all alone. Before, I thought that I was always alone. For as long as I can remember there was never anyone else. Why didn't I realize that she had come to me? And not once, but many times, again and again, even after she died. Now I know. Without Saya I'm incomplete."

His voice broke off, and Lady Iwa looked at him curiously and said, "Oh, so you claim that you now understand? You know you need Saya?"

"Until I met her I was nothing," Chihaya whispered. "She called me forth. She taught me about Toyoashihara, and about myself. She helped me realize what I must do. But there are still so many things that I must learn. Without her I'll remain a blind Dragon."

"But you must go on alone. Saya has already returned to the Goddess," Lady Iwa said bluntly. Chihaya remained silent, but a spark of light, a faint stirring of anger, kindled in his previously vacant black eyes.

"And why can't I follow her? Whether to the Land of the Dead or not, is it really impossible for me to follow where Saya has gone? Even my father once went to see the Goddess in the underworld. So why shouldn't I? Saya always came looking for me. Now it's my turn to find her."

"How?" snorted Lady Iwa.

Suddenly at a loss, Chihaya looked down at the tiny old woman. "Isn't there some way?" he asked.

Lady Iwa turned away indignantly, tossing her white head. "Supposing I did know . . ."

Realization dawned on him and he knelt hurriedly upon the floor. Laying the Sword aside, he prostrated himself meekly before her. "Please. Tell me. No matter what it takes, I wish to go to the Land of the Dead," he pleaded. "If I could return Saya to life, I would begrudge nothing."

"Do you speak from your heart?"

"Yes."

"Then you should have said so from the beginning," Lady Iwa said, brightening, as she turned to face him. "I don't know of any trick that will take an immortal to the underworld. But Saya gave you the magatama. If the bond between you is strong enough, there may be a way."

"What is it?" Chihaya leaned forward eagerly.

"I can't promise anything," Lady Iwa warned him sternly. "You may find Saya, and then again you may not. You may be able to return again, or you may not. The path of Darkness is shadowed and fraught with danger."

Chihaya answered emphatically, "It doesn't matter, so long as there is hope."

"In that case, swallow the magatama you hold in your hand. It's part of Saya. No matter how far the distance, it will be drawn toward her soul. Whether you reach her or not, how far you travel along the road to Darkness depends upon you."

The next morning, Chihaya was found lying cold and lifeless at the foot of Saya's bier. His breathing had stopped; there was no heartbeat, and no sign of renewal. Lord Shinado, who had just returned from pursuing the remnants of the army of Light, exclaimed, "But the children of Light can't die. Surely he'll come back to life again."

Lord Akitsu said in a low voice, "Yet I can understand his desire to follow Saya. Let's lay them side by side on the bier. Then Saya will be less lonely."

4

SAYA WAS STANDING near an open marsh. The summer grasses grew tall, and the bulrushes along the shore showed their brown heads. Pale blue dragonflies flitted lightly above the surface, their figures reflected in the water. The red glow of sunset lingered in the sky, while a soft twilight drifted across the land. She heard a gentle voice that filled her with warmth.

"Where have you been, Saya? It's time to come home. Supper's ready."

That's my mother, Saya thought.

Turning around, she saw a path leading through a meadow dotted with evening primroses just beginning to open, and in the distance she could see houses, thin trails of smoke rising from their hearths. If she ran home, she would find the familiar hearthside, the bowl her father had made for her, the soft, comforting lap of her mother there to greet her.

But she could not move. Instead she burst into tears.

"Why do you weep when you've come home at last? What makes you so sad? What is it that you wish?"

Still weeping, Saya pleaded, "I want to go back."

"Poor little thing. And just where do you want to go back to, when this is your home?"

Finally realizing where she was, Saya looked about her, trying to find the speaker. But she was the only person on the edge of the marsh. Wiping her tears, she whispered, "You're the Goddess of Darkness, aren't you?" Then she added hesitantly, "I died, didn't I?"

"Yes. This is the Land of the Dead. But when my children first return to this world, their wounds are so deep that it's hard to sleep peacefully. First I must ease their pain in this way."

"Won't you show yourself to me?" Saya asked, and a breeze like a sigh blew across the marsh grasses.

"I am everything that you see around you. Think of all the things you have never stopped loving as my arms, my lap. I have no body. I discarded it long ago, when that one rejected me. Now I live in many forms at once."

"O merciful Goddess, the God of Light wishes to summon you to the world above, to bring you back to life," Saya said. Not knowing where to direct her words, she gazed at her own shadow on the water as she spoke. "The God in heaven gives no thought to we who live in Toyoashihara. He intends to destroy the land and return the world to chaos. But you are the loving Goddess. Surely you will have compassion for the world above?"

"There's no need to ask," the Goddess responded emphatically. "I gave birth to all that is in Toyoashihara. Where is the mother who does not love her children? I love Toyoashihara more than you do."

Saya finally smiled. "Thank you. Now I can be at peace."

"Then follow the path. Your long-forgotten mother awaits you." Urged along, Saya began to walk, but after a few steps she stopped.

"Something still troubles you, doesn't it?" the Goddess of Darkness said indulgently. "Go ahead. Tell me what you want, and I'll fulfill your desire."

Saya hesitated at first but then, gathering her courage, said, "I wish to see the field of wild roses once more. Will you show it to me?"

The summer scenery seemed to blur for a moment and then the marsh became a meadow and the season turned to autumn. A cool highland breeze caressed her cheeks and clouds swept across the sky. A mass of pale purple flowers swayed in the wind, just as she remembered them. The beauty of the flowers filling the hollow was breathtaking, perhaps even more breathtaking than reality, but it was true to the memory she had treasured in her heart.

What a fool I am! The beauty of the flowers pierced her like a knife, and she instantly regretted her request. What use was it to recall this meadow when Chihaya was not here? It was like rubbing salt into a wound. Saya stood filled with misery, too wretched to cry.

The autumn breeze swayed through the flowers, through her hair, like a tender caress. When the burning agony of her loss had passed and died to a smoldering ember, a feeling of resignation began to grow within her, seeping through her. For the swaying purple flowers, in their silence, spoke to her, telling her that this was a peaceful place, a place of rest, that there was no point in suffering.

This pain is just an illusion. I should be ashamed of myself. It's pointless to grieve. Chihaya and I have been separated by a distance so absolute that we can never reach each other again. All I can do is accept this fact, she thought listlessly. She could feel the Goddess coaxing her, soothing her. How sweet it would be to let herself be carried away by oblivion and sink into the depths of slumber. But still she clung stubbornly to her pain.

If only I could see Chihaya one more time, just once more, then I could forget him.

A figure appeared suddenly at the edge of the hollow.

It came down the slope, disappearing and reappearing in the tall grasses. The shock was so great that she stood numb, unable to move. No matter how merciful the Goddess might be, Saya had never dreamed that she would go to such lengths as this. Chihaya appeared, looking about him doubtfully. He seemed like a traveler in a foreign land. She stared at him, speechless. But when he caught sight of her standing in the midst of the flowers he broke into a run and raced toward her.

A few seconds before he reached her, she suddenly found that she could move and, leaping into his embrace, she collided violently with his chest. Just to be able to touch him seemed to her a miracle. Feeling that anything was permissible, she kissed him. Regardless of whether or not it was an illusion, if it was this satisfying, she did not care.

"I came looking for you," Chihaya murmured in her ear, his arms still wrapped around her. "As long as I'm with you, it doesn't matter if I never return to the earth again."

Saya thought, *That's just what I wanted him to say. Now there's nothing else I desire.* She smiled.

"Did Torihiko give you the magatama?" she asked. "Keep it always—even if you forget me."

"It was thanks to the magatama that I came here," Chihaya replied.

"Lady Iwa told me. She said that this stone was part of you, that it would find its way back to you. I'm amazed that I actually made it."

It finally began to dawn on Saya that something was odd. This was not something that Chihaya would say if he were truly an illusion. She let go of him and stared into his face, her eyes wide. "You don't mean—you can't possibly have really come? You're not just a dream that the Goddess of Darkness is showing me?"

"Yes, I've really come, to the Land of the Dead."

"How?"

Chihaya stared back at her blankly. "But I just told you."

At that moment a strong gust of wind hit them, taking their breath away, ripping the flowers from their stalks, hurling the dead grasses into the air. Pummeled by leaves, they shielded themselves, looking up when the wind had passed to see the sky filled by dark black clouds twisting slowly like a tornado.

"I sense the presence of one who has no right to be here. Someone, who, like oil in water, doesn't belong. Who are you? And why have you come uninvited?" The Goddess's voice shook the air, no longer gentle but filled instead with a menacing rage.

Chihaya, oblivious to the sudden change, answered unhesitatingly, "I am Chihaya. My father is the God of Light. I came here to meet Saya and if possible to take her back—"

Saya hastily jabbed him with her elbow and interrupted. "It was my fault, O divine Mother. Because I gave him my magatama, he has come with it in search of me."

"What have you done?" the Goddess demanded harshly. "I gave you that magatama as a sign of the Water Maiden. It should have been returned to me. Yet you have given it to a Prince of Light and so exposed the path that I have taken such pains to conceal."

Saya turned pale with shock. "I beg your forgiveness. I didn't mean—"

"As for the God of Light, I intended to forgive him; though he feared and shunned me, turned his face from me and fled; though he sealed the entrance to the path with stone and severed relations with me. He mercilessly kills my children who live upon the earth and causes me to suffer. Yet this, too, I could forgive. But now he invades my very home. Even my mercy has its limits!" The deadly menace in her voice made their blood run cold and filled them with a dread far surpassing the terror inspired by her children, the raging gods of the earth. Although she was trembling like a leaf, Saya managed to speak.

"Chihaya is not an instrument of the God of Light. He fought on our side."

"Don't waste your breath," Chihaya said from beside her. "She won't listen."

They turned on their heels and fled, with the surging black cloud in pursuit. Jet-black tentacles of darkness as dense as mud were just reaching out to grab them when suddenly a voice called out.

"Hurry! Take Morning Star!"

Morning Star, the white mark on his forehead shining, waited, his hooves pawing the ground. And holding him in check was Lord Ibuki. "Flee while I distract the Goddess."

Without wasting time on words, they leaped astride Morning Star, who raced across the dark sky as though he had wings. The vault of the underworld was bejeweled with unblinking stars. Some were as large as walnuts and they cast a faintly colored light. The black stallion ran longer than they could tell, finally landing on a bare rock ledge. It was very dark, with no other light than that of the stars. Lord Ibuki was already waiting for them.

"I didn't expect to meet you again so soon. You seem to be creating havoc even in the underworld," he said frankly.

"I longed to see you again," Chihaya began in a choked voice. "There's so much I wanted to say—"

"I know, so there's no need to say anything. This isn't the time or place. You've angered the Goddess of this land. There's nowhere you can hide. Even here you're safe only for a moment." Wheeling about, Lord Ibuki asked Saya, "Where's your magatama? Of all times, now is the time you most need your power to still the gods. If you become the object of her wrath, your suffering will be eternal. In this world, death will not be the end of it."

Saya said hurriedly to Chihaya, "He's talking about the blue stone. You have it, don't you?"

"I brought it with me, yes, but . . ." He looked troubled and faltered, pointing to his stomach. "It's in here. I forgot to think of a way of returning it."

Saya and Lord Ibuki gaped at him in astonishment. Then Saya asked in a small voice, "What should we do now?"

Lord Ibuki groaned. "Don't ask me! After all, I'm just a dead man."

To their left the stars began to go out one by one. A blackness so total that it seemed to crush the very sky gathered above their heads.

"Let's get out of here," Saya said, grabbing Chihaya's arm.

"It makes no difference whether we run or not if in the end there's no escape," Chihaya said, gazing at the stars disappearing from sight. "Let's go meet her instead. For it's only right that we should seek proper judgment."

"No!"

But Chihaya ignored her. Kicking his feet lightly against the rock ledge, he leaped effortlessly into the sky.

"Lord Ibuki," Saya turned and asked desperately, "do you think that I can fly, too?"

"It's up to you. After all, this isn't the land of the living," Lord Ibuki replied.

ONCE he was as close as he thought necessary, Chihaya addressed the black shadow.

"O great Goddess, Ruler of the netherworld, please hear me. Though I am the child of my father, I love you, and have always yearned for the Darkness." Slender tendrils of darkness, like snakes, reached out and wrapped themselves around his neck, arms, and legs, and he felt them slowly tightening. Ignoring them, he continued, "Since the day I was born I have searched for a path to you. It was Saya who showed me a way, yet even without that, I so desired to meet you that—" The fingers of darkness squeezed him with a sudden bone-crushing force that prevented him from speaking any further.

"How dare you tell such falsehoods? Why would one with the power of renewal be attracted to that which is destined to rot and decay? Even I didn't come here of my own accord."

Chihaya tried to free himself, but it was futile. Although he knew he must not use the power of the Dragon, being unjustly accused had kindled his anger. Just as he thought he was about to explode he felt the touch of a small, light hand. It was Saya.

"O merciful Goddess. Please quell your anger," she said boldly. For Saya, this was her last and most daring attempt to appease. "And if it doesn't please you, then accuse me also. For though I'm a child of Darkness, I love the Light and served at the Palace of Light. Though Light and Darkness are incompatible, even we, who can't live without you, love the Light. For it's one of the purest, most beautiful things on the earth.

"I met Chihaya in the Palace of Light. At first he was the keeper of the Dragon Sword—the Sword with which the God of Light slew the fire god when you left for the Land of the Dead. When we learned that Chihaya was not one who stills the Sword, like me, but rather the Sword itself, we feared him. But this was wrong. For Chihaya, more than myself or anyone else, remained true to you. Perhaps because he's the child of the Sword, the son of the Sword that the God of Light wielded in his grief for you."

The air absorbed her voice, swallowing up any lingering vibrations. A silence like sleep filled the space between them. Then the Goddess of Darkness spoke quietly.

"Perhaps he grieved for me. But when he saw me in the underworld he turned away and deserted me. Since then he has cursed, shunned, and hated me."

"No, that isn't true. For if he really despised you, he wouldn't even contemplate leaving his palace in heaven to meet you," Saya said, leaning forward. "Even now the God of Light still longs for you—so much so that he is willing to sacrifice all of Toyoashihara."

"Is that why you gave this youth your magatama?" the Goddess asked.

"No," Saya replied, somewhat dampened. "I didn't think. I just couldn't bear to be parted from Chihaya. I gave it neither as priestess nor as the Water Maiden. I just did it."

Realizing that he could now speak, Chihaya said, "I was commanded by my father to seek the Goddess of Darkness and to bring her back to the earth."

Saya looked up at him in shock. "Chihaya!"

"This was sealed from me until I met you. I always wondered why I was given this body, but now I remember. I am my father's messenger."

"But what will happen to Toyoashihara?" Saya whispered. Chihaya turned to the Goddess of Darkness and continued.

"However, I was a dangerous messenger. For by giving me the power to reach the Land of Darkness, he gave me the potential to destroy him. If I hadn't reached you I would most likely have turned on him, and we would have fought until one of us was slain. But I came. Saya helped me to transcend the wall of hate between the Darkness and the Light. Is my father's desire now clear to you?"

The Goddess whispered in a voice like wind through the trees. "O Child of the Sword, you are so like him. You came all alone, fearless and undaunted. Yet you are different, too. For the Water Maiden's magatama is now part of you." She paused and then continued quietly, "You have stilled my anger. Looking at the two of you I can believe that he does indeed wish to meet me. I have received your message, Child of the Sword. But I don't intend to clothe myself once more in the body I discarded in order to go to him. Therefore, Prince of Light, you must return to your father."

"Are you saying that I must go back alone, empty-handed?" Chihaya protested.

"Your father did just that."

"Then I would rather stay here."

"You can't do that. For you weren't made to live in the Land of the Dead."

"I'll never go back without Saya. Never." Chihaya grasped Saya's hand and said brusquely, "It's not enough to take back the magatama, I must take Saya, too."

"But you can't. I really died," Saya protested. Just then, however, she heard someone else speak.

"It's all right. Go on back to Toyoashihara."

Saya looked about in surprise. "That voice . . ."

"Renewal requires a sacrifice. I will be that sacrifice. I've already lived too long. Surely it's no crime to seek a rest. Besides, there's something you must do. Go back with Chihaya."

It was Lady Iwa. Her voice sounded strange and fragile, yet, to one familiar with it, it was warmer than any other. Saya turned to question her, but Chihaya pulled her away.

"Saya, let's go home."

WHEN SHE CAME TO HER SENSES her feet and hands were numb with cold. Opening her eyes and wondering what the prison guard had done with her fur wrap, she found herself not in the palace but surrounded by the people of Darkness. Lord Akitsu and Lord Shinado were there, and Torihiko, too. With them, looking as if nothing had happened, was Chihaya.

"You're late. Where were you dawdling?" he said smiling.

"The Goddess of Darkness . . ." Saya whispered. Her throat felt strange and she couldn't speak.

With deep emotion, Lord Akitsu said, "It's just as Lady Iwa told us. She said that both of you would return."

"We met Lady Iwa. Lord Ibuki, too." As she spoke, Saya was hit by the realization that she had come back from the dead. Although it should not have been possible, she was actually breathing. Blood pulsed through her veins. Sensation had returned. She could speak. Suddenly she burst into tears and felt hot teardrops scalding her frozen cheeks. Chihaya gently slipped his arm about her as though she would break and raised her to a sitting position. She thought regretfully that if only there were not so many people here, she could have rested in his embrace and cried to her heart's content.

Lady Iwa's tiny corpse was laid out in the same hut, wizened and frail. The spirit which had made her seem so intimidating when she was alive had vanished.

"She was so old no one knew her age. Perhaps it was her time to die," Lord Akitsu said quietly. But Saya shook her head.

"No. She took my place in the Land of the Dead for my sake. She told me there was something I must do."

"What was that?" Torihiko asked.

"The Goddess of Darkness stopped me as I was about to return and said—"

But before she could finish speaking, a shower of gold and silver dust fell glittering through the cracks of the roughly thatched roof. Or rather, so it appeared. It was in fact light of such blinding intensity that it seemed to pierce the roof like a white shaft. Before their startled eyes, the inside of the hut grew brighter than the seashore on a midsummer's day. The outlines of walls and people became indistinct. Terrified, they looked at one another.

"Is it the coming of the God of Light?"

"It can't be! The two immortals have not yet reappeared."

"Is this the end of Toyoashihara?"

"But I thought we won."

Pushing aside the people who were shouting in confusion, Chihaya rushed outside. The door opened on an incredible flood of light. The sky had turned pearl-white, robbing everything else of color. The mountains of Mahoroba looked like ghosts, and several rainbows clung to the mountaintops. The ground glittered like shattered crystal, so that it was impossible to discern its contours. And not a single shadow could be seen. Chihaya raised one leg to see if he could find his shadow but it was so bright he could barely see his foot. Shielding his eyes, he raised his head slowly. Over the eastern row of mountains, he could just make out the upper half of a towering golden form framed by the rainbows on the mountain ridges. He felt Saya come running after him.

"Don't look!" he ordered her sharply. "Anyone who looks at my father will be blinded. Don't open your eyes until I tell you."

Startled, Saya clapped both hands over her eyes, but she could still feel light burning gold and black against her eyelids. It had been a near thing.

From above them flowed a voice that moved the heart like the strum of a bass string.

"Dragon Child, did you fulfill your task and summon the Goddess of the netherworld?"

"No," Chihaya answered weakly. "She wouldn't come."

"I saw you descend into the Land of the Dead." The God's voice was tinged with displeasure. "For what purpose, then, did you go? And why have you returned alone?"

Saya suddenly stepped forward, and with both eyes still covered addressed the God of Light.

"O my beloved."

Chihaya had put a hand on her shoulder to restrain her but withdrew it hastily. Saya's body was as rigid as stone, and she spoke in a trance. Moreover, the words she uttered were not her own.

"The girl who stands before you is unique—she has returned from the Land of the Dead. For your sake I have twice broken the sacred rules of the netherworld: once when I allowed your son to enter the Land of the Dead, and once when I allowed my daughter to return to the Land of the Living. In this way I have permitted myself the smallest measure of selfishness—to borrow this girl's body and allow myself to meet you for a fleeting moment."

"O my beloved wife." His voice trembled slightly. "A fleeting moment cannot suffice. I have come now like this to take your hand once more. Show yourself in your willowy form, with your long black hair flowing."

The Goddess of Darkness replied sadly, "Do you still not understand? My body has long since crumbled into dust, as fate decreed. It was destined to be thus when earth and heaven were sundered."

"And that's precisely why we must turn back time. Let's return earth and heaven to the original sea of chaos and, side by side, go back to that time. I need you."

The Goddess sighed faintly. "You sent me the Sword. Why did you attempt such a dangerous thing?"

"I've never once forgotten you. Though I knew that you despised me."

The Goddess exclaimed in surprise, "But it was you who despised me! After you cut yourself off from me, you hated even my children who lived upon the earth."

"Because you preferred to remain within that dark pit rather than be by my side."

"My beloved husband," the Goddess said, deeply touched, "Toyoashihara moves with the seasons. She needs a mother—someone to give birth, to nurture and love her. I can't turn back or stop time. All of my children would die."

"Do you love Toyoashihara more than you love me?"

"O beloved." Her gentle tone softly but firmly restrained his simmering rage. "I have received the Sword. Now I know your fierce longing, a longing so great that you would destroy even your own tempestuous self. I can therefore forgive everything you've done, and doubtlessly I'll continue to do so in future. How great was our longing for each other. We were not so far apart as we had thought. The children of Toyoashihara realized this before we did. Behold your son and my daughter, who stand here before us. Is not the union of these two the same as if we had taken each other by the hand?"

As the God of Light remained silent, she continued, "Cherish Toyoashihara. I may have lost my body, but my hand is in every corner of this land. I am reaching out to you with love. People make bowls by kneading water and clay and baking them in the fire. Just as water and fire, which are incompatible, are thus united, so, too, can we be joined as one."

The God whispered in a low voice, "An earthen vessel? It sounds like Toyoashihara—so easily broken, yet kneaded and fired again and again. And you're telling me not to take this task away from them?"

"Yes. If you let your anger rule you, if you destroy this land in rage, the efforts of these two will have been in vain. Rather let them be a sign. Let them be a memento of us, you and me."

"I understand," the God of Light said suddenly. Yet his voice was filled with sorrow. "But do you understand my loneliness as I sit alone in our great palace in heaven with no one at my side? You don't know the coldness of that high and empty void."

The Goddess replied with sympathy, "But you have such wonderful children."

Chihaya, his eyes adjusting at last to the light shed by the God, finally noticed his brother and sister at the top of the hill. They stood on a slight rise in front of their father, like two shimmering pillars. Princess Teruhi's eyes were downcast, and her cheeks were pure white and translucent. Standing before her father, with whom she was at last united, she looked like a modest and reverent maiden. Prince Tsukishiro appeared to be looking toward Chihaya, but it was still too bright for him to tell.

The God of Light regarded his twin children for a while.

"O my children who have served me upon the earth," he said softly. "What do you wish in recompense for your services? Ask of me anything. Teruhi, what of you?"

Princess Teruhi raised her face. In a serene, bright voice she replied, "I desire nothing. I only wish to accompany you, Father, to your palace in heaven."

"And you, Tsukishiro?"

"I, too," Prince Tsukishiro replied.

"Then so be it. You shall both accompany me."

Finally the God of Light turned to Chihaya. Under his gaze, Chihaya felt himself blinded once again as everything about him was bathed in light.

"And you, my youngest. What do you desire, Son of the Sword?"

Chihaya was somewhat surprised but answered frankly, "I wish to be granted mortality. If it's possible, let me live like the people of Toyoashihara, let me grow old as they do; let me die and seek rest with the Goddess."

The God of Light paused before replying. But at last he spoke. "It is granted."

Seeing the joy that lit up Chihaya's face, he added in an amused tone, "I never imagined that you would fulfill your mission in this way—that you would ask for death from your own father. But if that is truly what you wish, so be it."

Chihaya heard Princess Teruhi, who stood far away on the hill, whispering in his ear. Perhaps she spoke through an interval in time.

"My foolish little brother, you choose a different path right to the end. But then, that is your nature. Deep in my heart I have always liked you. I could not be your mother, but my feeling for you was like that of a mother for her child."

A host of memories raced through his mind, but Chihaya could not voice his thoughts. In parting he could only whisper, "For always, without change."

He heard Prince Tsukishiro's voice also from a distance. "If the Goddess of Darkness ever resumed her physical form, I think that she would look just like Saya. Although I'm not my father, that's what I believe."

Chihaya looked at Saya, but she still stood with both eyes covered. He was tempted to speak to her but thought better of it, for it would be rude if the Goddess were still there.

The light gathered in the east and rose to heaven like a gleaming white pillar, then gradually faded from the rest of the land. The blue returned to the sky, the mountains regained their contours, and the buildings once again cast their shadows. The light suffusing the clouds dyed everything a vivid gold, and in the next instant all had returned to normal. But the ground still glittered white. Snow had fallen while no one noticed.

When Saya finally opened her eyes, she saw only the silent snowy landscape. A flock of sparrows descended on a harvested field now wrapped in white and pecked at fallen grains under the snow. A dog began to bark somewhere but ceased abruptly, daunted by the silence. Nothing had changed. It seemed she must have been dreaming.

"Has the God of Light gone?" she asked Chihaya softly.

"Yes, it's all over. Toyoashihara has been saved. My brother and sister have gone, too," Chihaya replied and then added after a slight hesitation, "My brother watched you until the very end."

"Why didn't you tell me sooner?" Saya demanded. "I'll never see him again. I kept my eyes covered just as you told me to."

"I didn't want to tell you," Chihaya said and burst out laughing.

"That's terrible!"

"Are you mad at me?"

"Of course!"

People began to poke their heads out of the buildings and come outside in groups. They looked about with expressions of wonder. They could hardly believe that nothing had changed, that everything had been restored. Torihiko flew up and shook a tree branch, dumping snow on everyone's head.

"It's over, it's over! No more Darkness, no more Light. No more friends or foes. There's nothing left to do. How about a snowball fight?"

"There's plenty to be done, idiot!" Lord Shinado said, shaking his fist. He had snow down his collar. "We have to build a new country—a country that embraces one ruler."

Lord Akitsu came and stood before Chihaya and Saya. "You are the new rulers of all the people. In place of the God and Goddess, you will be the father and mother of Toyoashihara. If you can live together in harmony, this earthen vessel will never be broken."

Saya was so astounded she could hardly believe her ears, and it seemed that Chihaya was no different. With a puzzled frown, he asked Lord Akitsu, "Just what are you telling us to do?"

Lord Akitsu put his hand to his chin. "Well, first of all, you must have a wedding."

"A wedding?"

"Yes, I believe so."

"But Chihaya hasn't given me a betrothal gift," Saya said.

Chihaya choked for an instant and then said, "I gave you the Sword."

"That doesn't count."

"But I have nothing else."

"That's true." Saya looked up in surprise as though she had just realized it. "Neither of us owns anything. Well, I've never heard of two people with nothing being made rulers."

"We'll build you a palace," Lord Akitsu said. "We'll have a ground-breaking ceremony and bury the cornerstone deep in the earth. We'll raise the main post and build the roof high. Everyone will help. By the time it's built, spring will be here."

Saya whispered privately to Chihaya, "I'll invite my parents to the wedding. And I'll tell them that we'll give them so many grandchildren they won't know what to do with them."

"I heard that," Torihiko said, beating his wings above their heads. He barely managed to dodge the snowball Saya threw at him.

Chihaya laughed but then asked seriously, "By the way, what's a wedding? I've never heard that word before."

Afterword

D RAGON SWORD AND WIND CHILD was my first work. I had never had anything published before and was completely ignorant of both the publishing industry and what it means to be an author. I simply devoted myself entirely to writing.

The editor in charge of this project was a friend from university where we belonged to the same children's literature group. It was through her that the opportunity to write this book arose. The publisher where she worked appointed her to launch their first children's literature series. Not knowing where to begin, she decided that her first step would be to find some new writers, and she contacted me. But neither of us really understood what this job offer meant. Being skilled in languages, my friend devoted most of her energy to finding exceptional works at international book fairs in Bologna and Frankfurt, and introducing them to Japan through good translations. This left me free to write at my own pace with very little pressure.

I, too, am a great fan of foreign literature. At the same time, however, I also love the Japanese language, especially classical Japanese. And my tastes are a bit peculiar. Although I am very fond of British children's literature and mysteries, I am quite content to read them in translation, and I enjoy Japanese medieval literature just as much. This unusual combination gave me an idea: noticing that fantasy writers in England and the United States used Celtic mythology as an important element in their work, I realized that I could use the *Kojiki* in the same way. The absorption of the Celtic gods by Christianity seemed very similar to the way Buddhism superseded the ancient gods of Japan.

At the time I wrote this book, many critics insisted that fantasy would never take root in Japan. Excluding works by a few famous writers such as Kenji Miyazawa, Japanese fantasy was dismissed contemptuously as fairy tales without citizenship, folklore lacking the legitimacy of nationality. My work should have fallen into that same category. After all, unlike the next two books in the series, it was clear in many places in *Dragon Sword and Wind Child* that I was not trying to restrict the setting to Japan or to a specific time period. Having recognized that mythology in the broad sense is always at the basis of fantasy, I did feel that it made sense for me to use an episode from Japanese mythology as the model for my story. But when I conceived the three sibling characters Princess Teruhi, Prince Tsukishiro, and Chihaya, I was not planning to mimic Japanese myths concerning the three Shinto deities Amaterasu, Tsukuyomi, and Susano'o. If those ancient tales had been foremost in my mind when I wrote this story, I doubt that the relationship between Teruhi and Tsukishiro, or the idea that Chihaya and the Dragon Sword were one, would have occurred to me.

The concept of presenting the story predominantly from the perspective of the people of Darkness through Saya, the heroine, was inspired by the *ôharai norito*[1] which I read in the *Engi Shiki*.[2] This prayer is a litany of the various deities that carry away human corruption—a river deity, a sea-current deity, and a wind deity. This corruption is finally passed on to a goddess who wanders aimlessly in her kingdom below the earth. It is a story that must strike a chord with Japanese people like myself, accustomed as we are to the Japanese expression for forgiveness: *mizu ni nagasu*, literally, "to wash away in

---

1   A Shinto prayer for purification used in a governmental capacity to cleanse the nation of offences against the gods and re-ratify the lord's right to rule.
2   A fifty-volume collection of rules and regulations detailing court ceremonies, etiquette, punishments, and religious observations.

water." If this noble deity who deigns to shoulder the impurities of the human race were the Goddess of Darkness, then her only logical counterpart would have to be light, the God of Light. And that is how the story *Dragon Sword and Wind Child* took shape.

The Japanese take the purifying power of swift-flowing water and the ubiquity of murmuring brooks and thundering cascades for granted; I felt that this was an important factor we share at our very core. I doubt that someone born and raised along the banks of the Yellow River, for example, would develop this sentiment, even though we belong to the same human race. The waterfalls I came across in northern Wales, which are reputed to inspire poets, on the other hand, were just like the little waterfalls one finds close by in the hills of Japan.

Dragon Sword and Wind Child was first published in 1988. When the original publisher subsequently shifted away from literature, my friend and I moved to Tokuma Shoten Publishing Company and it was republished under the Tokuma imprint in 1996. I am very grateful that the work has thrived for so long, despite its rather negative beginnings. In 2005, at the beginning of a new century, it was published for the first time in paperback in Japan. I hope that it will be even more accessible now that it is in paperback with the added pleasure of Miho Satake's poetic illustrations.

— NORIKO OGIWARA
July 2005

Glossary

Ground Spiders. *Tsuchigumo* in Japanese. A people in ancient Japan thought to have lived in mountain caves until sometime around the fifth or seventh century. They are semi-mythical and share a name with the spider demons from folktales, who spin powerful illusions to catch their prey. The myth of the tsuchigumo is so popular that it has inspired a Noh play of the same name, and the tsuchigumo have appeared in various anime.

Mahoroba. An ancient Japanese name for an idyllic and faraway country surrounded by mountains, similar to Arcadia or Shangrila. It is mentioned in a poem in the *Kojiki* (*Records of Ancient Matters*), a written account of Shinto history, and the oldest surviving book in Japan.

Palace of Light. The Palace of Light is designed like a Chinese palace compound, arranged in a rectangle with the long edge running north to south, and the short edge running east to west.

Prince Tsukishiro. The first character in his name means "moon." The second character sounds like "white," but the kanji used has a more ambiguous meaning. A Shinto shrine called *Tsukishiro no*

Miya was built in Sashiki Castle on Okinawa in the thirteenth century.

Princess Teruhi. Her name means "shining sun." In medieval Japan, there was a shrine to a male sun god called *Teruhi Gongen* on the island Tsushima.

Togano no shika mo yume no mani mani. An exorcism chant based on a story that appears in one of the *Fudoki* (a series of eighth-century records about the culture and geography of the Japanese provinces), most likely the Hitachi Fudoki. A stag swims across a river to meet a doe and tells her of a dream he had where his back is covered with snow. The doe tells him that it means he will be killed and his meat covered with salt. Soon after, the stag is shot and his dream becomes reality. The chant translates as "even the stag of Togano is at the mercy of a dream," and reminds you that if you take a bad dream seriously, it could become true.

Toyoashihara. Also called *Toyoashihara no Mizuho no Kuni* (Land Where Abundant Rice Shoots Ripen Beautifully), it is another name for Japan. In ancient times, the earth was viewed as an imperfect world where salvation could be found through the protection and blessing of the gods. Such poetic names had a power in themselves to attract the beneficence of the gods.

About the Author

Noriko Ogiwara was inspired to write by the classic Western children's books she read as she was growing up. *Dragon Sword and Wind Child* is her first book, which won the Japan Children's Literature Association's Award for New Writers, and which is part of the award-winning Magatama Trilogy. Her other books include *The Good Witch of the West* and *Fuujin Hisho*. Ms. Ogiwara makes her home in Japan.

About the Translator

Cathy Hirano was born in Canada and has lived in Japan since 1978. When she was growing up, her favorite books were *The Chronicles of Narnia*, *The Wizard of Earthsea* series, and *The Lord of the Rings*. Also available in English are her award-winning translations of *The Friends* by Kazumi Yumoto, which won the Batchelder Award for children's literature in translation, and *Moribito I: Guardian of the Spirit* and *Moribito II: Guardian of the Darkness* by Nahoko Uehashi.

HAIKASORU
THE FUTURE IS JAPANESE

SUMMER, FIREWORKS, AND MY CORPSE BY OTSUICHI

Two short novels by the Shirley Jackson Award–nominated author, including the title story and *Black Fairy Tale*, plus a bonus short story. *Summer* is a simple story of a nine-year-old girl who dies while on summer vacation. While her youthful killers try to hide her body, she tells us the story—from the point of view of her dead body—of the children's attempt to get away with murder. *Black Fairy Tale* is classic J-horror: a young girl loses an eye in an accident, but receives a transplant. Now she can see again, but what she sees out of her new left eye is the experiences and memories of its previous owner. Its previous *deceased* owner.

ROCKET GIRLS BY HOUSUKE NOJIRI

Yukari Morita is a high school girl on a quest to find her missing father. While searching for him in the Solomon Islands, she receives the offer of a lifetime—she'll get the help she needs to find her father, and all she need do in return is become the world's youngest, lightest astronaut. Yukari and her sister Matsuri, both petite, are the perfect crew for the Solomon Space Association's launches, or will be once they complete their rigorous and sometimes dangerous training.

DRAGON SWORD AND WIND CHILD BY NORIKO OGIWARA

The forces of the God of Light and the Goddess of Darkness have waged a ruthless war across the land of Toyoashihara for generations. But for fifteen-year-old Saya, the war is far away and unimportant—until the day she discovers that she is the reincarnation of the Water Maiden and a princess of the Children of the Dark. Raised to love the Light and detest the Dark, Saya must come to terms with her heritage even as she tumbles into the very heart of the conflict that is destroying her country. The armies of the Light and Dark both seek to claim her, for she is the only mortal who can awaken the legendary Dragon Sword, the fearsome weapon destined to bring an end to the war.

THE OUROBOROS WAVE BY JYOUJI HAYASHI

Ninety years from now, a satellite detects a nearby black hole scientists dub Kali for the Hindu goddess of destruction. As human society expands to Mars and beyond, the generations-long project to harness the power of the black hole pits the retrograde humans of Earth against the imminently rational men and women of the Artificial Accretion Disk Development association. While conflicts simmer, a mystery within Kali itself tests the limits of intelligence—that of both human and machine.

WWW.HAIKASORU.COM